5-13
7-20

MW00917494

The Long-Shooters

Daniel C Chamberlain

ALL RIGHTS RESERVED

No part of this book may be reproduced or transmitted in any
form or by any means, electronic or mechanical, including
photocopying, recording, or by any information storage and
retrieval system, without permission in writing from the author,
except in the case of brief quotations embodied in reviews.

Cover design by Ashley Eberts

Photo From – Dreamstime.com

Publisher's note:

This is a work of fiction. All names, characters, places, and
events are the work of the author's imagination. Any
resemblance to real persons, places, or events is coincidental.

Solstice Publishing – www.solsticepublishing.com

Daniel Chamberlain©2011

Dedication

This book is dedicated to my wife, Noreen and our three daughters, Lesley, Ashley and Rachel, who tolerated my monopoly of the family computer for research and endless hours of typing, editing and considerable frustration.

This book is further dedicated to the loving memory of my sister, Jayne, who died tragically as the manuscript was heading to the editor for his final review. She expressed great pride in her "Little Brother" having completed this work and was looking forward to seeing my efforts come to fruition. She will be greatly missed.

Prologue

Ballou
1865

Along a line extending nearly thirty-five miles, running roughly parallel to the remnants of the Norfolk-Petersburg railway and all the way to the banks of the Chickahominy and Appomattox Rivers, battle-worn men with rifles quietly eyed each other across a bleak landscape of man-made destruction. Occasionally engaging in contests of marksmanship, their half-hearted efforts managed to do little harm to one another for, by this point in the campaign, the protective trenches on both sides had become well established. Not luxurious by any stretch, the trenches were comfortable and reasonably safe if a soldier was careful to stay down. Now, in the waning months of the war, these veterans were mostly careful — or lucky. All the careless or unlucky ones were long since gone.

With the bitter recollection of Cold Harbor still fresh in the memories of the blue-coated soldiers, yet again they found themselves firmly stuck against fortified Confederate positions. This time they had Petersburg under siege. Much like a great sailing-ship denied a passage through a barrier reef, the army had grounded. Still, everyone knew a storm— the coming storm of battle — would soon force them in. And, like that sailing ship running before the storm, the soldiers would be at the mercy of forces they couldn't control. There would be no room to maneuver, to seek a safe channel. These men knew they would soon be ordered to risk all, just like that tired and aged sailing-ship, when they were forced into the rocks and shoals that were the Petersburg trenches.

Through the Union lines, choked with many obstacles and the refuse of an army stalled and waiting, a young corporal scurried rat-like in the maze of trenches. Bent at the waist, his movements were awkward. In spite of his haste, the young man fought the urge to stand up and run, knowing that to do so would invite the earnest efforts of a hundred Confederate riflemen along that section of line and a hundred more farther on and still more beyond that. The corporal had long since learned that those shoeless bastards in their tattered remnants of gray uniforms were expert shooters if they were nothing else. Few northern recruits knew their way around a rifle as well as their brothers to the south, so the corporal accepted the strain and discomfort of his ape-like gait in favor of the safety it afforded. Still, an occasional rebel sharpshooter caught a hint of blue and tried his luck. Each time the corporal heard the whip of a passing shot or the nasty whine of a ricocheting Minié ball, he pretended not to notice. Despite his bravado, the sweat on his face was as much from fear as from the physical exertions in the heat of the day.

The corporal stopped for a breather. Sitting down, he leaned his back against the rough ground of the trench. The young soldier's tunic was unbuttoned, for despite the time of year, the heat was oppressive. With the stagnation of movement and purpose, the discipline of the troops in some units had slipped noticeably. Many soldiers no longer wore complete uniforms; some wore no uniforms at all. One of the ironies of this seemingly endless conflict was that the opponents were becoming less remarkable as opposing armies, and more similar in appearance and attitude. That they could still muster the strength, courage and desire to rise up and advance on a line against twenty thousand enemy muskets would amaze anyone otherwise disassociated with the whole tedious and bloody affair.

The corporal closed his eyes against the bright sun, and

let his breath return and the hammering of his heart slow to a more normal pace. His constantly sweating face had become a gathering place for what seemed like pounds of Virginia dust and grime. Water — fresh, clean water — was a scarce commodity amid the trenches. Water fit for drinking was little enough, but for washing there was none. The men on both sides were a dirty lot, and even when it rained, they could not adequately wash, for then they were covered in mud. Out of necessity and pride, the weapons carried by the soldiers of both sides were the only things kept meticulously clean.

After his brief rest, the corporal continued on his way. He was searching desperately for Ballou. He'd seen him earlier, with his back propped against a broken carton, the Stephens rifle cradled like a baby in his arms. No one deliberately went looking for Ballou except on a mission like this. Ballou was mostly left alone. He preferred it, many believed. He didn't make friends; didn't take part in general camp life. He always sat alone with just his rifle and his private thoughts.

The corporal spied Ballou and hesitated. The man had moved some distance from where the corporal had last seen him, evidently following the fleeting bits of shade that never remained long in one place. Where Ballou moved, men made room and he always had shade.

Though Ballou's eyes were closed as the corporal approached, it was doubtful he was asleep. The corporal slid into the trench, raising a small cloud of dust that danced and swirled about despite the lack of a discernible breeze. He heaved a deep breath and, taking off his hat, leaned the back of his sweat-slick head against the dirt wall. Wiping his grimy brow with an equally grimy sleeve, the corporal spoke.

"Sergeant told me to find you, Ballou. He's got a shot for you."

At first Ballou didn't respond and the corporal found

himself studying the fuzzy-faced soldier. Ballou was no older than the corporal, perhaps even a bit younger. His soft blonde hair was wispy and uncontrollable and badly in need of cutting and washing. His face was sunburned and, despite his youth, there were crows-feet deeply etched into the corners of his eyes. The wrinkles may have come from squinting through a gun-sight all the time, the corporal surmised.

After a long moment, Ballou answered softly, without opening his eyes. "What is it?"

The corporal shivered, in spite of the heat. There was a distinctive coldness about Ballou. It was a coldness likened to the slithering skin of a water moccasin. The corporal knew it was only his imagination, but the air always seemed ten degrees cooler in Ballou's presence. He shook his head to clear away his musings.

"It's an officer," the corporal replied. "A damned 'Reb' officer who won't keep his damned head down. He keeps walking the Confederate fortifications and daring us to hit him."

Despite himself, the corporal grinned, exposing stubby, tobacco-stained teeth. "Don't think we ain't tried, neither. Anyway, Sergeant said for you to get your rifle and your ass over to 'B' Battery and he'll show you the shot."

His mission accomplished, the corporal was glad for the opportunity to be away. Without another word, he donned his hat, pushed himself to his feet and hurried off.

* * * *

Ballou opened one eye and watched the corporal running back along the trench line, pondering how easy it would be to kill him with a well-placed shot. There was no malice in the thought. It was a simple professional observation. If there was one thing Ballou had learned in this crazy war, it was that killing was very easy and there

4

was always plenty of it to do.

Watching the corporal scurry away, he contemplated the track, the lack of wind and the distance; everything it would require to launch a projectile on a course that would intercept the running man. Metal would meet flesh; blood would spill. He imagined it as if it were already a reality that needed only a simple physical action. Yes, the corporal would be easy. He smiled to himself.

Ballou lifted his rifle. It was a Jersey-made Stephens' target rifle, one of the most accurate weapons ever produced. The bore measured .45 caliber and it could fire a heavy conical bullet with astonishing accuracy over incredible distances. One of its drawbacks, if the rifle had any at all, was the fact the bore was particularly sensitive to fouling from powder residue and lead. This made accuracy difficult to achieve over long strings of fire without careful maintenance. But this was not a battle rifle per se. It was a shooting instrument. There were few occasions for long strings of fire. Regardless, marksmen were solving the problem of fouling by patching the bullets with a greased paper jacket. It kept the residue from the powder soft, and served to wipe the bore with each loading. The jacket also prevented the lead bullet from touching the bore and lead build-up was nonexistent.

He'd "lifted" this rifle from a Union sniper who'd exposed his head just a smidgen too much outside of that little Pennsylvania town called Gettysburg. The rifle had been fitted with iron sights, but was also topped with a newly manufactured telescopic sight, made by the Malcolm Telescope Company out of New York. Unlike the method used to mount telescopic sights on the current crop of Confederate sniper rifles, which were mounted to the left side of the rifle opposite the lock, Ballou's rifle had the telescope mounted on top directly over the bore, and the mounts were adjustable for elevation and windage. It was a more accurate system, but also more delicate.

5

After a little experimentation, Ballou had amazed his fellows with the rifle's accuracy, and his shooting ability amongst the best marksmen of the Union Army became legendary. Where the Confederate snipers had heretofore owned the battlefields, they were suddenly finding their own numbers falling to shots that came out of nowhere. The sound of the distant shot would arrive at almost the same instant as the bullet, giving the impression it had come from some close vantage point. But that was an illusion. It was upsetting and served to make everyone nervous. It's hard enough to lead men in battle where a thousand rifles spit anonymous lead toward anonymous targets and most of the shots actually miss, but when a man begins to imagine there's a single rifle somewhere out in the distance following his every movement and waiting — well, brave men had been known to come unglued.

It was fortunate the Federal army let Ballou keep the rifle. He'd proven himself invaluable. He no longer had to participate in the headlong attacks that wasted young blood against fortified positions. He was allowed to pick his targets, which were mostly officers or battle-tested sergeants whom he observed effectively leading the enemy soldiers. To kill such men was to demoralize the enemy, or at least the enemy's officers and sergeants.

It was supposed by many that Ballou actually relished killing, but that assumption was completely wrong. He simply didn't care. He killed so easily because he was one of those rare individuals capable of killing without bother or pangs of conscience.

Ballou's blue eyes wandered over the rifle. The wood was oiled and polished and the metal furniture was charcoal-blued and gleaming. Despite having seen many battles, the weapon showed few signs of hard use. It had been well cared for, both before and after it came into Ballou's possession. The pale man admired the craftsmanship of it. It was the finest rifle he'd ever seen and more valuable to him than gold.

He carefully fitted the rifle's heavy barrel with a muzzle protector to prevent unnecessary wear to the bore during the loading process and to more properly align the bullet with the rifling. Taking the ramrod, Ballou carefully wiped the bore with a lightly greased cloth, followed by a dry one, then another dry one. When he was satisfied, he fired two musket caps to clear the flash-channel of any oils his wiping may have forced into the breach. He followed that up with a final dry patch wipe. With a wire pick, he made sure the flash channel contained no debris from the expended caps, which might obstruct the flame from reaching the powder charge.

This done, he measured a careful load of powder and trickled it into the muzzle. Tapping the side of the barrel once with his palm to settle the powder, he seated a felt pad over the powder to protect the base of the bullet from the heat of the explosive fire. Finally, he softly pushed a pre-patched and greased bullet into the muzzle protector, starting it with his thumb and pushing it home with his ramrod. He used only the amount of force necessary to seat the bullet firmly against the felt pad and powder. He didn't want to deform the soft nose of the bullet and thereby adversely affect its flight characteristics.

There was a ritual to it, a calming effect. This teaming of a man and a firearm was the foundation of the marksman's art. Though repeating firearms like the Spencer and Henry were making themselves felt on the battlefield of late, there was no art to using them. There was only volume of fire. Soon, the awesome and terrible beauty of massed volleys by thousands of rifles would be lost to history. Ballou supposed future wars would rely on volume of fire over the rifleman's art. Perhaps this was the last war where the rifleman would engage a visible enemy with volleys followed by careful loading under fire, the cadence of the loading steps drumming through the heads of visibly terrified young soldiers, doing that one repetitive chore might be what prevented most of them from losing their nerve and running away in panic. Load and cap and fire! Load — cap — fire!

Finished with his preparations, Ballou stowed his equipment, picked up his pack and rifle and walked upright to where the men of 'B' Battery were crouched along the breastworks. Many men yelled at him to get down; that he was a fool. Still, Ballou walked erect. He wasn't being foolish. He was a fatalist. He was going perhaps to kill a man, and if God didn't want that man dead, then Ballou would not finish his walk. There was a simple, gallant eloquence to his gesture even if the significance was lost to everyone but Ballou. He never explained himself, and no one ever bothered to ask.

The sergeant looked up as Ballou approached, his amazement plain at the sight of the young man. Ballou recognized the look. He knew he didn't fit in with the rest. Where his fellow soldiers were worn and dirty, Ballou took care with his appearance. Whereas most of the men looked years older than their actual age, Ballou realized he seemed younger than his own. He'd overheard the sergeant one time, telling an officer that this was due in part because he believed Ballou never worried; never felt fear, at least by any normally accepted definition.

"You called for me, Sergeant?"

Ballou was always formal with his fellows. He waited patiently while the sergeant looked him over. Ballou could see the sergeant secretly loathed him, hated what he stood for. The sergeant had often ridiculed that killing without emotion, without effort, without exposing oneself to the trials of modern warfare was somehow…unsavory. But despite the sergeant's stated personal convictions, Ballou knew his superior needed him and used him often. The sergeant nodded and pointed out across the killing field.

"Over there. Look beyond the abatis," the sergeant

commanded. "There's a row of brass guns. Keep watching and you'll see him. He's a cocky bastard and we've been trying to hit him for hours. He laughs at us and doffs his hat when we get close, which isn't often, I might add."

Ballou looked where the sergeant pointed. He saw before him a ground torn from the eruptions of exploding shells and deeply furrowed with the bouncing tracks of solid shot. Out beyond the immediate front lay a field of sharpened sticks, a *chevaux-de-frise*. Past that, a tangled abatis ran and, farther yet, the enemy trenches. The Confederate artillery stood well behind the trenches fully six hundred yards away, their gleaming brass distorted and dancing on the waves of heat rising from the sun-baked ground between the lines.

A bullet struck the wall in front of Ballou. The others flinched but he seemed not to notice. Another struck the ground in front and whined overhead. While the men — including the sergeant — crouched behind the log barricade, Ballou stood motionless and looked across the no-mans-land for the soldier he was supposed to kill.

Then he saw him. Ballou knelt, lifted his rifle, and looked through his telescopic sight, watching the Confederate officer making the rounds of his men and guns. The man walked briskly between positions, brave but not stupid. Ballou admired the man from a distance. He could tell he was a regular officer, probably West Point educated, well dressed and — Ballou supposed — from a good family. This late in the war, the officer was likely dreaming of home as so many were. Ballou didn't want to kill him. Perhaps the man only needed to be taught a lesson.

"May I see your Springfield, Sergeant?" Ballou asked, softly. Placing his rifle gently along the wall, Ballou turned to the sergeant and held out his hand. "Sergeant? Your rifle, please?" There was a quiet insistence that the sergeant could no more resist than if he had been so ordered by a higher command. He gave Ballou his Springfield.

Ballou noticed with irritation that the sergeant's rifle was already capped and ready to fire. He shook his head. How many young soldiers were wounded, maimed or killed from this careless practice, he thought to himself? Why cap a rifle and thereby prime it to fire, when there was no immediate need? It was *unprofessional.*

He went about setting the sight leafs for the estimated distance and placed the sergeant's rifle over the log wall. Cocking the hammer, Ballou followed the distant officer with his sights, measuring the man's stride, timing his movements; waiting. The man stopped for a moment and the rifle in Ballou's hands bellowed an instant later, belching white smoke that hung in front of the wall briefly, before drifting slowly back into the faces of the soldiers crouching next to him.

All along the line, men were watching and waiting in silence. Word had spread magically, "Ballou is going to make a shot." The anticipation was thick. In the distance, through the shimmering heat waves, they saw the rebel officer suddenly duck in alarm and drop from sight. Blue-coated men cheered and tossed caps while there was a scattering of return fire that haste and distance rendered mostly ineffective.

After a moment, the rebel officer reappeared, untouched. He looked at the blue line and pantomimed, applauding the northern marksman. Then removing his hat, he bowed deeply from the waist, before resuming his patrol of the line.

Ballou shook his head and bowed it for a moment. A fly buzzed past his ear and lighted on his cheek. Along with the dead bodies of men and horses that had gathered on the field in recent weeks had come a veritable explosion of devilishly persistent, biting flies. He ignored it; perhaps not consciously realizing it was there, being too intent on his purpose in life to attend to minor distractions that drove other men nearly mad with irritation.

Ballou was disappointed. He'd tried. The man should have realized there was someone new behind the far-off wall; a new hand on the rifle, a new finger on the trigger. The officer should have stayed down.

Ballou grimaced, handing the Springfield back to the sergeant, hefted the Stephens and cocked the hammer. Only then did *he* fit a musket cap on the nipple cone. The rifle was now primed and ready to fire.

Peering through the telescope, he placed the delicate crossed-hairs of the telescopic sight at the top of the officer's head and tracked the man's movements. He wasn't trying for a headshot. Already sighted for four hundred yards, this distance was such that his bullet upon completing its arching trajectory would drop into the area of the officer's midsection. The head merely served as a perfect reference point. Where the head went, the body had to follow.

Ballou watched the officer make his way past entrenched cannons. The gleaming of the artillery pieces was almost uncomfortable to the eyes in the bright sunshine. The officer stopped briefly to speak to a man, and the soldiers of the blue line held their breath and waited for their marksman to shoot. Ballou held his fire and the officer moved suddenly.

Instinctively, Ballou had known the man had not intended to stop for long and had he chosen that moment to shoot, the bullet would have been wasted, striking where the officer had been only moments before. At this range, six-hundred yards, a man with a normal stride could walk almost ten feet before a bullet could traverse the distance.

The officer stopped again and bent down at the waist to speak to a prone soldier behind the wall. Ballou didn't hesitate this time. There was an uncanny certainty to his action; as if he knew in advance what the distant target would do next. Ballou fired while the officer was still bent over. In the moment it took the bullet to cover the distance to the Confederate lines, Ballou saw the officer stand upright once again. Through the telescopic sight, he saw the man laughing at some comment he'd heard; saw him stagger in surprise as the bullet struck him at the belt-line; saw him reach out for the wall to support his body and, finally, saw him sag and fall out of sight.

A cheer erupted once again from the blue line, then they all ducked for cover as the Confederate line blossomed with an angry volley of fire from perhaps as many as three hundred rifles. The weight of lead smacking into the wall was enormous and it rattled and clattered for several seconds while dirt, dust and gravel sifted into the trenches from the vibrations of the log barrier. More Confederate riflemen were converging on the spot and lending their rifle fire to the angry effort. So thick and determined was the fire, it would've been impossible to raise a hat on a ramrod above the wall without the article being struck by at least one Minié ball. Bullets clanged off the muzzles of the artillery pieces or gouged deep furrows in the wooden caissons when a lucky shot passed through the small openings cut for the cannon barrels.

Ballou stayed where he was, exposing an inch or two of his head to see if the officer was carried off the field. By some miracle, Ballou wasn't touched. After several minutes, the firing died down, and Ballou saw people attending the fallen soldier. The shot had been true. The man was belly-shot and those wounds were almost certainly fatal. But some men had survived it and Ballou silently wished the Confederate officer well, not hoping he'd live really, but not hoping he'd die either. What Ballou hoped was that whatever journey the officer must take would be as quick and free of pain as possible. Ballou stood again. Turning to the sergeant he asked:

"Will there be anything else, Sergeant?"

Several bullets 'thwacked' against the barricade, near

him. He showed no concern. The sergeant could only shake his head in silence. Ballou nodded once and turned away. He walked erect at an oblique angle across the field, while distant marksmen tried desperately to hit him. An occasional bullet would throw up a puff of dust at his feet or beyond, but once again, he seemed cloaked by some unseen protection. When he reached his trench, he hardly paused before he began to carefully and almost tenderly clean his rifle.

In the bloody days ahead, Petersburg would fall and soon thereafter the war would be over. Those men who'd survived the human catastrophe that was *their* Civil War would begin whatever journeys they were destined to take for the less-eventful remainder of their lives. Some would go home. Others would try on new lives, no longer quite the same men who'd gone off to war and unable to consider going back to the way life was before the terrible ordeal they'd just endured. The rebel officer Ballou had shot never returned to his home and the man named Ballou disappeared, as if he'd never been.

Shaw
1877

The first, faint traces of a reluctant dawn drew the pallid mountain landscape into clearer focus. With the dawn's light came the hint of beautiful autumn colors the moonlight had suppressed. Touching the higher places first, the morning sun spread its light like a golden syrup languidly seeking out the valleys below and erasing the shadows. As the rays touched the frost-coated treetops, the autumn leaves lost their silver cover in an ever-descending line, and a hazy mist developed over the meadows and valleys.

Near a stream swollen by late-season rains in the high country, Shaw sat where he'd spent a sleepless night wrapped in a blanket with his shoulders hunched up against the chill of the early fall temperatures. Before him, a hint of smoke issued from beneath the powdery mound of gray ashes left over from his fire. He didn't replenish the flame. The morning sun would soon make the fire unnecessary and he had much to do.

It was dawn now; time to move. Even as he thought it, he hesitated. Stiff from the cold and uncomfortable night sitting huddled before a tiny fire, he welcomed the spreading warmth of the morning sun. His joints protested. They did that more with each passing year. Though he wasn't an old man, he'd seen some hard use over the years and the body had a way of reminding a person of all the tracks it'd left and those that had been left *on* it.

Despite the stiffness, when he rose he did so with no apparent effort. Shaw had the fluid grace of one accustomed to foot travel over rough terrain. He stood for a moment, breathing deeply of the mountain air. Business seldom brought him to the high country any more but, during those rare occasions, he always relished the tranquility and the satisfying taste of the air.

Shaw walked to his horse, tethered to a picket-pin. The animal stretched its nose to meet him, searching for the usual chunk of sugar in hand. Shaw had owned him for three years now. During that time, they'd ridden some wild trails that took them from low deserts to high-forested wilderness, from communities ranging in size from simple cow towns to fast-growing places like Denver and San Francisco. He and the horse did well together, the gray acting as though it liked the feel of constant movement and the fresh experience of new places as much as Shaw did.

The day was going to warm up. Shaw removed the blanket from the horse's back and filled a canvas feed bucket with ground corn, placing it on the gravel at the horse's feet. The gray would feed at its leisure, the picket line allowing ample slack for the horse to water and reach the drying autumn grasses that grew at the banks of the stream. It was Shaw's intention to return by evening or the next evening at the latest. The horse would remain behind. Still, if something should happen to him, he knew the horse could eventually pull the picket pin from the ground when there was no more food and it would move on alone. The line was a light one, easy to break in the event it hung up somewhere and the horse needed to get free.

Shaw hefted his pack and rifle. He swung the pack easily to his shoulders and then, rifle in hand, started off into the thick curtain of brush that bordered the high-water mark of the stream. He followed a barely-visible game trail that took a more or less northerly route up the sides of the deeply forested valley.

Earlier, he had scouted the valley and determined this route to be the fastest and safest line of travel to where he wanted to be around noontime. He had several miles to go and they were tough, high-country miles in which he had to deal with stream crossings, navigating slopes of loose rock and avalanche cuts, all while steadily climbing for the tree line. It was not a place to bring his horse. A man on foot could travel faster.

Even now, with summer still a recent memory in the lowlands, Shaw could see a line of snow which had descended to about eleven thousand feet in just the last week. Where he walked, the aspen had gone gold and across the valley spread out below him, the reds and oranges of the mountain hardwoods blended with the mottled brown of the underbrush and the deep green of the thick pines. Up ahead, the softwoods gave way to the bristle-cone and cedar. Still farther on lay the bushy, treeless expanse of mountain tundra. That was the direction he traveled.

A tall man of quiet demeanor, Shaw dressed in good quality clothing that bore the wear of hard but careful use. His sheepskin coat had been skillfully made by a Chinese tailor in Denver. It was heavy and warm and had kept him comfortable in more than one high-plains blizzard. His black hat was of the cavalry design, its front brim pulled low to shade his hazel eyes from the sun he so often faced, either setting or rising on some new country he was crossing. He wore black canvas denim pants and while he normally wore Mexican tooled riding boots, he'd exchanged them for a hiking variety used mostly by men familiar with the mountains of Europe. They were made for walking over treacherous ground, and laced high to afford support to the ankles. They were a style popular among the lumberjacks in the northern timber operations and he'd purchased these from a timber company store along the Flambeau River in Wisconsin.

By nature, Shaw was distant. While he had an easy way with strangers, he was neither overly friendly nor particularly approachable. He was polite and considerate, but didn't encourage people to either like him or get to know him. He had a house in Denver but seldom stayed there long enough to meet new people, preferring to spend his limited leisure time reading, or seeing a play or concert— most always alone.

People, especially the women he met, considered Shaw mysterious and aloof. He was a man who was careful in his grooming, his clothing, his guns and his relationships with others. Hard lessons had taught him people were sadly, weakly human and they would ultimately − given the chance − fail to live up to his expectations. He was not an easy man to understand in that regard.

There'd been a woman some years before who apparently thought to play him for either a sucker or a fool, neither of which fit. In the end, it took a killing for her to acknowledge Shaw didn't allow the insincere to intrude in his life or his business. The one who was killed had told his friends he was going to fight for honor and love, never knowing that he was a patsy to a trifling young woman. By all accounts, she'd neither cared for him while he lived nor particularly cared when he died. Since then, Shaw had remained uninvolved, preferring the solitude it provided.

The mountain that he was on this morning joined another with a much more pronounced peak a number of forbidding miles to the west. His destination was actually lower than his current elevation, but to get there he had to cross a saddle in between the two mountains, which cut through the rim-rock.

He took a break from climbing around ten o'clock and had a long drink at a trickle that fell from a crack in the rocks. He carried a canteen, but water was plentiful and refreshingly cold as it seeped from the countless mountain cracks and crevasses. A handful of dried elk was his breakfast. The sun had warmed the surrounding air and to ward off possible trouble later on, he carefully wiped the surface metal and bore of his rifle to remove any moisture that may have condensed on the cold steel.

The gun was a heavy-barreled target rifle made by the Remington Company, of the Rolling-Block design. The measurement of its bore was four hundred and fifty-eight one hundredths of an inch — or more simply of .45 caliber— and was chambered for the two and seven-eighths inch straight-walled cartridge. He loaded his own cartridges and he could pack one hundred and ten grains of fine rifle powder under a four hundred grain, paper-patched bullet. Scoped with a telescopic sight, with this combination, he could kill an elk at an easy four hundred yards on a windless day, and buffalo a hundred yards farther. Deer required a closer shot, say two or three hundred yards or thereabouts. He'd often taken turkey at that distance as flocks crossed lowland meadows in their typical single-file fashion. This rifle was made to shoot at things; as the mountain men used to say: *"Over the next mountain top and across the valley beyond."* That was why he carried the weapon today.

With the morning beginning to warm up, Shaw removed his coat and tied it in a tight roll under his pack. With less than two hours to go, he set a brutal pace up the remainder of the mountain and, once he cleared the trees, crossed a large meadow that from a distance looked deceivingly flat with a gentle slope. Up close, it was crossed with deep cuts caused by erosion from snowmelt and, if anything, the slope grew slightly steeper until he reached the point where the mountaintop began to round off.

Reaching the saddle that cut the mountain's spine, he stopped for a brief rest and to cache his pack. He wouldn't need it for the next part of his task and it would be waiting for him when he returned. The altitude left him somewhat breathless and, despite his physical conditioning, there was a slight tremble in his legs. Shaw allowed himself some well-deserved rest. He'd pushed himself hard and, while it was down-hill from here, walking down-hill on uncertain ground with tired and oxygen-starved leg muscles was a recipe for injury — and injury meant disaster in mountains where the nighttime temperatures fell to below freezing.

After he'd rested enough, he started down the other side of the mountain. He took with him only his rifle and ammunition, his canteen, some jerky and a battered pair of binocular-lens telescopic glasses. Far below, in a half-bowl formation scoured out by a long-extinct glacier, he could see a fan of waste dirt from a working mineshaft. He needed to find a place from which he could watch that opening. It took him thirty minutes; but when he was settled, he had a perfect position from which to cover the entire area immediately above and surrounding the mineshaft. Now, he had only to wait.

Somewhere inside the mine, a man worked alone. Shaw had come to find him and, sooner or later, he'd come out. He had to. He couldn't remain in there forever and there were those who wished him gone. That was why Shaw had come here. There were always people who paid men like Shaw to deal with the obstacles in their lives.

Ravens called as they flew across the expanse of thin mountain air between the rocky slopes. At his present altitude, Shaw was actually looking down at them as they skirted the treetops of the valley below. On the opposite slope, goat trails were visible. It would be a good place to hunt some other day when there wasn't work to be done.

Noon had passed and the sun had moved off on its westward slide when three horsemen came into sight from a spot where a fold in the valley obscured his view beyond. They were riding a switched-back trail that would bring them to the mouth of the mine. Shaw frowned. Through his glasses, he studied the riders with care.

One rode a chestnut gelding, with a beautifully groomed mane and tail. This man was tall in the saddle. Even from this distance, Shaw could tell he was the one the others were subordinate to. The other two were hired hands, no doubt. Their horses were fair saddle-stock, but not especially notable for either their coloring or conformation. The chestnut, on the other hand, was quite a horse.

Shaw watched the men descend the trail. Sometimes it became so steep the horses' forelegs stiffened and splayed; talus pushing loose ahead of them formed mini-avalanches and the sound rattled across the valley to Shaw's ears. He wondered if the man in the mine could hear it.

Finally, from the mouth of the mine came a ghosting of a lighter color. Soon it became apparent the miner was just inside the entrance. Shaw looked closely. The man held a rifle — a brass-framed Winchester. Shaw smiled. The Winchester was a good fighting gun, but not a long-range weapon. No, Shaw definitely held the advantage in that department. He continued to wait.

Below, he watched the riders come to a halt on the trail just above the mine. The man inside the entrance moved again, getting closer to the light. Shaw lifted his rifle and inserted a thick cartridge into the chamber and gently lifted the pivoting breechblock into place. Snuggling his cheek against the stock, Shaw looked through the telescopic sight.

He saw the miner come out, rifle in hand. The man was tense, facing three armed men. Shaw didn't worry about that. He concentrated on making the crossed-wires of the sight in the telescope remain steady on his target. Shaw was conscious of the miner levering a cartridge into his rifle in anticipation of a fight but he ignored it. He increased the pressure on his trigger until the heavy weapon bellowed in the mountain stillness.

He didn't reload. There was no need. He'd been paid to make a shot and he'd made it. Through the scope, he watched the man on the chestnut sway in the saddle. The horse danced and swung up-slope so suddenly the rider spilled from his back. Like a rag doll, the man tumbled past the mineshaft and on down the tailings slope, either already dead or soon to be.

The miner didn't waste time. He fired rapidly, left and right, spilling the other two riders from their horses. One rider tried to fight back, but couldn't stop sliding on the loose gravel. He fell from his horse and came to a stop at the feet of the miner, who coolly fired another shot into him, anchoring him for good. In the space of twenty seconds, it was all over.

Shaw moved off quickly. He didn't need to stay and he didn't want to be seen, even by the man he'd helped. He'd been paid and he'd done his job. The miner was safe — for a while. He might make a go of it, or he might not. But for now, one of his obstacles was out of the way. Shaw didn't know much about the man he'd shot, other than his name was Garity and he had a reputation. Garity was known around the Colorado diggings as a man who held questionable title to several claims whose original owners had either deserted or sold just before disappearing themselves. Many silently believed Garity was both a murderer and claim-jumper and few if any would miss him and a few more might even be willing to take his place. For now, the miner would have a reputation as a man who could hold his claim. No one would know that the shot that killed Garity had come from across the valley.

Shaw had a long walk ahead of him and evening came fast in the mountains. He'd camp a mile or two from his previous night's campsite and tonight he'd get some much-needed rest. In the morning, he'd head for the steam cars to Denver. Winter was fast approaching and winter in the high country was an astonishingly beautiful but intensely brutal season. Shaw had no intention of hanging around for it. There were places he'd not yet seen and, of course, there were always things that needed doing.

Roark
1878

Samuel Roark lifted the empty water pail and wiped his brow. Despite wind-chill temperatures outside the stable well below zero, he was sweating heavily. He'd been forking hay to his horses and lugging what seemed like a ton of water to their trough, one bucket at a time. It was actually only one barrel full, but quite a chore with cold hands and an aching back.

After looking around the dim interior to see if there was anything he'd forgotten, he opened the door. A blast of frigid air greeted him and a gusting wind pulled the breath from his lungs. Closing the door securely behind him, he jogged for the cabin and its promise of warmth and comfort. A ghosting of smoke lifting from the chimney, torn apart by the swirling wind, indicated the fire was dying and would soon need more wood. There was plenty of it, chopped, split and stacked for the winter. That wood represented close to a thousand hours of work by him, his wife and son. Winter was long in the high country — and always cold. Thankfully, wood was more than plentiful, much of it deadfall that needed only gathering, cutting and splitting. Despite its plentitude, setting it aside had been terribly hard work with axes and a two-man crosscut saw.

Samuel moved quickly, a strong gust forcing him to grab his hat tightly before the mountain wind ripped it from his head. The wind was deceiving, one minute a dead calm and the next causing near-white-out conditions with blown snow and ice particles that threatened to first freeze and then scour raw any exposed flesh. On the way to the cabin, Samuel dropped the bucket near the well and continued running to the door. He should have placed the bucket so it wouldn't freeze to the ground, but his fingers were already stiff with cold and by the time he'd reached the front door, he was barely able to clumsily manipulate the latch. Once inside, he gratefully accepted the cabin's warmth even though it pained his nose and forehead. He removed his heavy coat and hung it with his hat on a peg beside the door.

A large cast-iron pot of stew bubbled over coals in the fireplace and hot coffee waited in a gallon-sized pot on the small stove. The smell of fresh bread lingered from the morning's baking, and the stove gave off the welcome heat his body needed. Though the cabin was small, it was a wonderful refuge from the long winter. The warmth and smells inside belied the inhospitable conditions outside but, winter or no, a ranch required steady labor and a lot of it. Regardless of the weather or time of year, a person couldn't stay locked up in a cabin. The cold and snow were an inconvenience, but not a limiting factor.

Samuel was not a large man, rather he was a man built more for the exercise of the mind. Though used to physical labor, he'd never developed into the substantial kind of man often seen on the frontier or in the western communities that sprang up haphazardly across the territories. He wasn't a frail man, but no one would ever mistake him for a blacksmith or timber jack.

He had an unruly mop of red hair turning to gray about the temples. His eyes were of a sea-green color, found mostly in the first generation immigrants from the old country, and surrounded by a field of laugh-lines and wrinkles that spoke of his good Irish humor and a willingness to smile. Now, looking at his wife, Samuel grinned.

Near the stove, Sarah peeled potatoes for the stew; elk by the smell of it. There was half of a beef in the side-room along with a couple of elk sides. Hunting had been good this year as the elk migrated from their summer graze to their wintering grounds and they had enough meat set by to easily last till the first thaw.

Sarah was his second wife. His first, a fiery-tempered Irish lass named Claire, had died after bearing him a son. The loss had devastated him, but Stuart was eighteen years old now and a reminder of everything Samuel had loved about the woman who'd borne him — her quick wit and Irish temper and the way she jumped into every problem with both feet and wouldn't rest until it was solved.

Samuel no longer missed Claire the way he had those first years after her death but, from time to time, he found himself looking at his son and wondering how much it bothered the boy not to have known his mother. To her credit, Sarah appeared to have taken to Stuart like a natural mother despite the fact their ages were not that far apart. The youngster had responded in kind. Theirs was an easy relationship, without any strain or hint that Sarah was not part of Stuart's family, or hadn't been from the beginning. Samuel smiled. Family was what really mattered in this world.

* * * *

Sarah paused and looked up at her husband and noticed him watching and smiling. She smiled in return and went back to work. That he was smiling at all was a comfort. Smiles had been rare these last few years since their daughter had passed. She knew he often thought about Rebecca when he looked at her. Gone three years now, Becca had — at only five years — begun to take on the quiet grace and gentle beauty that had so attracted Samuel to Sarah. She and the little girl had the same long, thick strawberry blonde hair. While Sarah fondly recalled that her own mother's flaming-Irish hair had been done up in a bun every day of her life, Sarah and little Becca had liked

24

to let theirs fall loose around their shoulders when they weren't dressed up for a church event or an outing to town.

It was the influenza that took the little girl. Later, Sarah heard it was a terrible epidemic that decimated entire communities. Stories abounded of men who were strong as horses that had lain down with a fever one day and were dead the next. The very old and the very young were struck hardest, and it was nearly impossible to hear of a family that hadn't been touched by the terrible sickness. What little news she got was mainly of funerals; an almost daily occurrence in the neighboring towns and frontier communities. Out on the isolated ranches it took longer for the disease to reach some families, but it eventually hit many of them as well.

Samuel caught it in town and he'd brought it home. While he slid into fever-induced delirium, Becca took to her bed with the same raging fever. The little girl had passed while her father was incoherent. Sarah was kept awake many nights helping Samuel battle the fever and listening to him hold little Becca in his dreams. He'd even been too weak to attend her funeral, and full recovery took months. Sarah knew Samuel blamed himself for bringing the disease to his family. He'd told Sarah that the thought that he'd missed holding Becca and tending to her in those last hours when she'd needed her father most, came within a hair's breadth of driving him totally mad. In a way, while she knew he might have physically recovered, Sarah also knew he was still so emotionally haunted by his loss he occasionally suffered deep bouts of depression that might last for days. When that happened, Sarah feared for him. He would eat little, lose weight and refuse to communicate.

Sarah didn't often speak of the past, though she felt the loss of her little daughter sharply. It was her strength that had saved Samuel from the influenza and that same strength carried him through those dark moods that claimed him, often without warning. But today Samuel was smiling and Sarah knew relief.

"The stew will be ready in an hour and not a minute sooner," she said. "If you stay out of it, I'll let you have pie later."

"Pie?" A voice drifted down from the loft. Stuart could be heard shuffling around in his bedroom. He'd come in an hour ago from chopping water holes for the cattle. The job was enormously brutal and almost never-ending and it began long before dawn when the cattle needed to drink after a night of pawing in deep snow for fodder.

Sarah giggled, girlishly. If she had drawn the word pie on a slate with chalk, Stuart would've no doubt read her mind. "Yes, pie, you goof. Blackberry if I'm not mistaken and you have me to thank for it too. You and your father went hunting for days on end and while you had all the fun, I picked berries until my fingers bled and then I dried them so I could make winter treats like pie for the likes of you!"

"Don't let her kid you, lad," Samuel joked. "I've picked berries with her and she always manages to eat twice as many as make it into her pail." He winked at her.

* * * *

Samuel watched Stuart come down the ladder. He was a tall lad with his father's features, especially the red hair. Strong for his age, most of the ranch work was left to him in the summer months while his father kept a law office in town. Law work was steadier in the summer and Samuel would keep office hours four days a week then. With the coming of winter, Samuel cut down to one or two days a week, to focus on keeping their cattle alive through the heavy snow and arctic freeze. Stuart was his partner in that labor, though Samuel had hopes his son would also consider law as a profession in a few years. He was already tutoring the lad and having him read the right books.

In the summer, lush grass provided excellent forage for

their small herd of beef but the work was still never-ending. Stuart had to keep water holes cleaned out, and mountains of meadow hay had to be cut and stacked for the winter months when the snow became too deep for the cattle to forage. Predator control was a constant problem and protecting young calves from wolves and big cats meant days in the saddle, hunting and trapping during the calving season. Stuart had taken to it, leaving Samuel with the luxury of resuming the practice of law which he'd abandoned before they'd come west. It was Becca's death that lured him back into the mind-steadying routine of law. The thick, leather-bound books he'd saved and dragged across half a continent, as well as others he'd ordered shipped to his new office, had kept him sane through his grief and months of recovery. It gave him something to ponder besides the memories of a beautiful child taken from him so swiftly.

Becca was buried where the morning shade was cast from an old mountain pine, one of the few trees not gnarled and twisted from the torturous winds that brought the cold down from the distant peaks. The pine was visible from the small kitchen window and it was the first thing Samuel looked at when he rose in the morning. He never left the cabin without glancing at *The Tree*. They never referred to Becca's resting-place as anything but The Tree. On Sundays, before church, the family went to The Tree for a few quiet moments, each with their own thoughts and memories.

Samuel caught himself before he got lost in his dark thoughts. Sarah had put the potatoes in the pot and poured Samuel a cup of coffee. He took the cup as much to warm his fingers as to taste the brew. He looked around the cabin, neat and clean. Their life here had changed little with the death of Becca, other than to leave an aching emptiness that remained constant. Three years gone and still memories plagued him. It was as if he saw her ghost in everything.

27

He knew that the emptiness would grow less noticeable with the passing years but, from time to time, he brooded over it. He was a man prone to brooding — it was his Irish birthright. First, his young wife had died and later, as a young soldier in the war, he'd often found the death around him so oppressive he fairly withered and shrank from it like a leaf before a flame. He never fully escaped the nightmarish hell he'd witnessed while following the blue army up and down the eastern countryside. Even now, there were days when normal routine was made imminently harder by those thoughts. He was occasionally troubled by his inability to shake off the bouts of depression unless he was near the comfort of his books and his family. At times, when the dark moods struck, he almost felt himself sway with the weight of his desire to see Becca's face again; to hear her humming a tune while she followed her mother around the cabin.

Samuel glanced out the window. Outside, the sun was almost gone behind the western peaks. With the coming of evening, the wind had died a bit, but the cooling of the cabin reminded him they needed fuel for the night's fire.

"I'm going for wood," he said.

Stuart spoke up. "I'll get it, Pa. You just came in." Stuart grabbed his boots and stuck his feet into the calf-high leather. Rising, he stamped them a couple of times and reached for his coat.

Samuel saw the boy's coat was still soaking wet from chopping ice. "Take mine, son." The boy nodded and shrugged his father's coat on. It was almost a perfect fit. Samuel knew a fierce pride in the boy he'd watched grow into a man. He smiled. "Better take the hat too, lad. One doesn't work without the other."

Stuart grinned and stuffed his father's hat on top of his head. Slipping on a pair of gloves, Stuart went out into the cold, quickly closing the door behind him.

Samuel sipped his coffee and looked out the little

kitchen window for one last glimpse of The Tree before dark.

A wet, smacking sound came from outside a mere instant before a distant boom penetrated the thick walls of the cabin. "Pa!" Stuart cried weakly.

Samuel dropped his cup and dashed for the door. Panic made him forget the rifle that hung on pegs above the doorjamb. He flung the door open and ran carelessly into the ranch-yard. The still form of his son was face down in the snow. Samuel ran to his boy. A large fan of sprayed blood spread out for a dozen feet on the snow around his son's body and terror gripped Samuel like a hand on his throat. Grabbing the coat by the collar, Samuel turned and dragged the boy back up the porch stairs and through the cabin door where Sarah stood, the rifle in her hands.

Once inside, Samuel turned Stuart over and opened the coat. Behind him, he was barely aware of Sarah closing the door and locking it. When he got the heavy leather garment open, Samuel was aghast. Only moments had passed, and already Stuart's face was pale. The chest wound had already stopped bleeding — the strong young heart forever stilled.

Samuel cocked his head in momentary confusion and then, from the depths of his body and soul, there came a hideous, bubbling cry like a roar from some pain-stricken animal. He screamed in protest until his lungs threatened to give out. When he could scream no longer, he gave in to great, racking sobs. Sarah watched in confusion and dread.

Outside the cabin, a sudden gust of wind tore the rancher's hat away from where it fell, rolling it along like a wheel until it bumped against the stable wall and lay upside down, slowly filling with the wind-whipped crystals of icy snow. At last, the purple sun slipped under the horizon and the fading light gave way to sudden darkness.

Inside the cabin, Samuel cradled the bloodied body of his dead son. The rancher rocked back and forth on his knees, pleading forgiveness over and over, as he slowly approached the dark and frightening cliff's edge of total madness — and, at long last, he let himself step off.

Comes the Spring

In the mountain meadows, greenery had begun to sprout despite the slowly melting remnants of huge snow drifts and evening temperatures that still dipped below freezing. Amidst these early signs of spring, Shaw encountered the carcass of a steer dug from a drift and mostly eaten by crows and other predators. He paused to study the scene. The remains were little more than a tattered bag of desiccated hide that held some bones together.

From where Shaw sat, he could see other bodies dotting the meadow and black blots here and there signified crows feeding on them. He'd counted close to twenty dead cattle in less than two hundred acres and he was sure the draws and ravines held more of the same. The past winter had been a fierce thing but, in his estimation, the kill shouldn't have been this severe. These cattle had been left to fend for themselves. On the prairie they might have made a go of it, but this high up, they were no match for the weather and deep snows that would drift them in as effectively as a fence. After that, it was slow starvation until they froze in the snow.

Though the valleys were already greening up nicely, the peaks were still snow-covered and wind-whipped. Shaw had come over the high country through a pass that had only just opened within the last week or so. Now, with the sun full on the meadow and his destination in sight, he took the time to remove the heavy fleece-lined coat he'd needed in the higher elevations, replacing it with a lightweight hunting jacket made of elk hide, handsomely cut and modestly adorned with short fringe.

A half-mile below, a cabin sat nestled at the foot of a

steep, boulder-strewn hummock, safe from avalanche danger. To the west, a grove of aspen spread down into a picturesque valley, in the center of which wound a mountain stream now full to its banks with recent snow-melt. The water would be the clearest and coldest drink on earth. Shaw smiled. He'd drunk from many such streams in his life and relished the taste of melted snow, a by-product of his heritage kept alive by his infrequent but welcomed travels to the mountains.

Shaw started his horse again. The trail was rocky but well used. Perhaps it had once been an elk trail that wound up from the wintering grounds to the shadowed places among the pines where the calves were born. Shaw knew the Arapaho had hunted here years ago, before the last "remove." Now, cattle and little else used the draws and meadows for grazing. Elk and mule deer could still be found, but their numbers had steadily dwindled with the coming of the gold seekers and the meat hunters who had fed them in the early days. Ranchers and their white-faced and mixed-breed cattle supplied the miners now, and the livestock competed for the grasses and browse needed by the elk and deer. Shaw noted with grim satisfaction, the deer and elk would find less competition on this mountain at least, now that spring had come.

Riding up to a tall pine, he paused again. At the base of this majestic tree were two graves; one of them was older and had a stone that bore an inscription; the other was fresh and bare. The inscription on the stone told that a five-year-old girl named Rebecca had died. She was gone three years now. He looked away at the far-off peaks and breathed deeply. Having never been a father, but a man warmly drawn to the sight of small children, he could only imagine the gut-wrenching sorrow of losing a child so small. Shaw was an intruder to this spot. Though the inscription was there for anyone to read, he somehow felt it was private, not meant for his eyes or — at least — the eyes of his like.

He'd noticed the fresher grave had no stone, yet. Shaw had a sudden, chance thought. *Perhaps it never would.*

How many such graves could be found in the high country? Certainly he'd come across more than a few on the trails between what life below offered and the promise of something else, just beyond the next ridge. Would anyone ever know where all the souls rested?

Below the pine, the cabin seemed still. No smoke issued from the chimney. A stable door stood open and a half dozen horses circled the corral, nervously looking up the trail at his mount and testing the wind with flaring nostrils. They were good horses by the look of them, though their winter coats were beginning to fall away, leaving them with a shaggy and poorly cared for appearance. He could tell they were adequately fed but something told him, even from this distance, they were in need of attention.

Shaw sat on his horse for several minutes longer, not moving. The ranch, modest in size, presented a lovely picture in concert with the surrounding hills. It was just such a place as he'd often dreamed of while riding to one destination or another. He wondered sometimes if he'd be able to step away from himself; to quit the lonely trails that had so often led to conflict and dust and death, in favor of a quiet life of hard work and solitude amidst the whispering pines.

It wasn't money that kept him from such a dream for he had money enough for several ranches of this size. He knew the work; could do the myriad chores that were necessary to keep a ranch afloat, but in his heart he doubted the lifestyle of running a ranch could long hold him. His life was one of range wars and mining towns out of control. He never went anywhere without a purpose and that purpose was always tied in some way to acrimony and struggle, and often the dying of men.

Too often, he found himself riding the lonely trails

between the law and the lawless, and now Shaw took stock of his life. He had money, but money mattered little to him; possessions even less. His eyes were almost always touched by melancholy, though they fairly glowed on those rare occasions when he smiled. He dressed well and spoke well, having received an education he hadn't had to work at or pay for.

Born to a wealthy Virginia landowner, he wandered away from his family when the war afforded an opportunity to leave without a care. On the issue of slavery, he was cold. Being the oldest son, he was expected to take over the farm but he didn't share his father's dream, nor did he share his father's love of the family *"ground."* To him, it was forever tainted by the oppressive disgrace of slavery. Having never reconciled himself to his heritage, he joined the Union army and by doing so, insured his family's lasting possessions were forever lost to him. When the war was won, he never went home. He didn't miss it, nor was he missed.

Shaw's only talents were holding the reigns of a horse or cradling the mechanism of a rifle or pistol and facing other men of a similar persuasion. He maintained no illusion that his life or his livelihood had any merit beyond his specialty. He was a mercenary, no more, no less. He'd come to this place by request, having received a letter from the lawyer in Denver who handled such affairs as this for him. Someone apparently needed a hunter; needed his particular brand of hunter. There was a vague trail to follow toward an uncertain conclusion and good money to be made in the bargain.

Of course, the promise of money was merely an excuse. The hunt was the real attraction, but few people would understand that unless they were themselves hunters. Shaw's eyes were again drawn to the unmarked grave. Someone needed his brand of hunter. He looked away again and did not speculate further. He'd know soon enough.

The wind made a whispering sound as he walked his horse carefully down the trail. Recent frost had made the ground uneven, the gravel loose. It would not do to lame his horse this high up so early in the season. Tomorrow could bring temperatures in the sixties, or it might bring three feet of snow. A man had to be careful of his horses, especially at this altitude, and he'd always been a careful man.

Shaw stopped his horse in the ranch-yard and waited. He wondered if someone inside would appear at the door. He didn't call out, for he wished to observe as much as he could before he made any human contact. An axe lay propped against a severely depleted woodpile. The edge of the axe-head had rusted. They should have left the head buried in a log-end to protect the shiny, work-polished metal from moisture and corrosion. The pump handle was down and there was some vague hint of rust on the pump's piston rod. Not a lot, but enough to show it hadn't been cared for lately and had not been greased in quite a while.

He looked to the ranch-yard for sign. There were recent boot-prints leading to the stable made by either a woman or a youth. The woodpile showed evidence someone had removed a few slabs of wood as early as this morning. There was a rime of frost on a lower section of the pile still hidden from the morning sun. Halfway along the section, the frost ended, indicating some logs had been removed after the frost had been laid just before first light. Looking closer at the chimney, he realized that while there was no visible smoke, a minor distortion of light at the top confirmed some heat was escaping.

The stabled horses had fresh hay forked to them. Someone had broken a skim of ice in the water trough and Shaw could see it held enough water to last a few more days at these temperatures. A recent storm had caused some damage to the stable roof. It would require new shingles –

bought or made – to replace those blown off. On closer inspection, he noticed the tracks of a horse being led out of the corral. Whoever rode the horse away from the ranch had done so early and probably just after dawn. An older track of a wagon led away from the stable doors, headed in the same direction the horse had traveled.

Shaw turned his attention back to the cabin. "Hello the house?" he called out. "I'm peaceful."

He waited for a minute and, when no answer came, he dismounted. Leading his horse to the corral, he tied the animal where it could stick its neck through the rails and drink from the water trough. The other horses came forward to tentatively make acquaintance with his mount. Their hoofs were long and needed trimming. Several minutes passed while Shaw enjoyed the spring air and the proximity of the horses. They were good saddle stock, though they shied away from his hand when he tried to pet them.

Shaw walked back to the cabin, stepped onto the porch, and knocked on the door loudly. "Hello?"

Getting no response, he walked back off the porch and looked around. Overhead, a raven glided swiftly by on a stiff breeze that couldn't be felt at the cabin. It was a protected place and would be fairly safe from the north winds and drifting snows. The cabin site had been carefully chosen for protection and comfort. Shaw liked it.

The horses in the corral were making a fuss over his gray. There was considerable nickering and head-shaking going on. He smiled at the antics. He was a man who appreciated horses and dogs. He looked around again, surprised that there wasn't a dog here. Perhaps it was best. Not all dogs liked strangers.

There was nothing left to do but wait. He turned a porch rocking chair to catch the sun, and sat down in the warming spring air. Taking his revolver from its holster, Shaw rotated the cylinder one full turn and checked the loads.

Satisfied, he returned it to the holster and covered it with his jacket. He decided to doze a bit in the sun to pass the time.

It was mid-afternoon when he heard the approach of a wagon. He didn't rise or go to meet it, preferring to wait on the porch. After a few minutes, the wagon came into sight around a hillside, drawn by a team of horses in a double harness. A third horse — a Pinto tied to the wagon's tailgate — trotted spiritedly along behind. Even though the wagon was still some ways off, Shaw could tell a girl or a woman was driving it. He frowned. He'd been told to meet a man.

When the wagon driver noticed there was a man on the porch, she slowed her team and Shaw noticed she glanced at her rifle. She was being careful and Shaw appreciated that. This was a country that demanded care. The condition of the ranch began to take on new meaning. Running a ranch was a hard full-time job, difficult enough for a man with help. For a woman alone, the demands would be too many and some things were bound to suffer. He could tell the deterioration had already begun. If this was the right ranch, there were questions to be answered. He thought again of the unmarked grave.

When the wagon reached the ranch yard, the girl pulled it up to the stable gate, and set the brake. She rose and smoothed her simple gray skirt before climbing down. Once on the ground, she retrieved her rifle and walked across the yard to the cabin.

Shaw rose and politely removed his hat when she reached the steps.

She gave him a measuring look for a moment, before speaking. "This is my house. What can I do for you?" Her tone was easy and confident.

Shaw smiled one of his rare smiles that crinkled the corners of his eyes as he looked at her directly. "Good day, Miss. My name is Shaw."

At the name, the young woman's brow furrowed but there was no apparent recognition. He should have been expected. Someone from this ranch had sent for him through his intermediary in Denver, yet clearly this woman was not familiar with his name.

"I beg your pardon, but does someone else live here? Your husband or father, perhaps?"

She wasn't wearing a wedding band, but in the West, such things weren't uncommon. She was an attractive young woman, with her long hair done in a thick braid down her back. Her blue eyes held his with steadiness.

"My husband..." She hesitated. "My husband is in town on business. What brings you to our ranch, Mr. Shaw?"

"Well, I apologize for surprising you like this. I'm here because I was sent for by someone from this ranch. I was to meet someone named Roark."

She raised her hand to her throat and took half a step back, gripping her rifle tighter. So, his presence meant something to her after all. Shaw recognized the reaction. He'd encountered it before. Men who hunted other men or were known to have killed other men, without the legal protection or the authority afforded by a badge or appointed office, were often considered by some to be outlaws.

Few people populating these lands were actually products of the West. So many had come west from eastern existences where law and order ruled their lives, where policemen saw to their safety and courts upheld their rights. A man who stood in direct conflict with those social parameters couldn't possibly be civilized. Shaw knew the woman who stood before him was even now wondering if it was safe to be alone with him.

He smiled, despite himself. He wasn't offended. He'd long since become accustomed to the vagaries of people who were willing to let others fight for them and were later proud of the fact they'd done no violence themselves. Each little community's social elite often treated even their lawmen with mild contempt. Never mind that the sheriffs and marshals were often all that stood between that which was right and just and that which was ugly and violent, usually for meager pay and little thanks. This woman finally realized who he was and why he'd come and, by her reaction, it was likely she didn't approve. Regardless, she now knew him and she was frightened.

"Ma'am, is this the Roark home place?" Shaw asked, pleasantly.

After a moment's hesitation, she answered. "Yes." She took a deep breath. "My name is Sarah Roark. My husband is Samuel. He's an attorney in town and I'm sorry he's not here, but he's...well, he's been ill. I fear you've made a long ride for nothing." She said it a bit defiantly.

Shaw smiled again. The woman was gathering courage and he was amused. "Mrs. Roark, I never make a long ride for nothing." He saw a quick look of fear come into her eyes and her hands gripped the rifle tightly. Shaw read the uncertainty in her eyes and posture. He knew that this young woman was wondering that if he believed his ride had been for naught, would he try to extract payment in another way? Though he understood, he was now mildly annoyed. He was willing to make allowances for a person's lack of experience and worldliness, but his character and reputation were things he didn't compromise on. His irritation was kept in check only because this woman had no idea of the caliber of man who faced her. He went on, patiently, "Mrs. Roark, I've been retained already. It doesn't really matter whether or not your husband is ill as far as my business with him is concerned. All I need to know are the facts of the matter, what exactly it is you want me to do for you; everything that can be remembered and related to me. Once I have a place to start, I'll leave you alone and be on my way."

"What if...what if we've changed our minds? You

could take your expenses and return the rest to us. Whatever my husband did on the spur of the moment, in the midst of his grief, shouldn't be held against him — against *us*!" Her face took on an angry expression and her voice wavered.

Shaw thought for several seconds. "Mrs. Roark, I hold nothing against you. I have a business arrangement with your husband. If he's changed his mind, I understand and will respect that, but what about you? Regardless what you might think of me or men like me, there is the issue of an injustice. Based on the letter I received, I suspect that a wrong has been done against your family. For whatever reason, I have been sent for. Tell me, Mrs. Roark, if not me, who'll help you?" Shaw paused and smiled. "It's not an issue of satisfaction or revenge. Justice is something people out here place a great deal of emphasis on. Who will help you do what needs to be done?"

"I would doubt that *justice* could be adequately served by a man who's probably very much a killer himself!" she snapped. Her voice betrayed fear and revulsion.

Shaw doubted she'd ever met a man-hunter or even seen one in the flesh, though she'd almost certainly heard stories of such men. They were often the topic of discussion where men and women of the west gathered to gossip.

"Perhaps you're right," Shaw replied softly. He glanced around the yard, considering what to say next. "To you, I must appear horrid. There are a variety of reasons people seek my assistance and often when I've finished they might feel vindicated, or they might be embarrassed, or worse. Normally, they send for me when the law has failed them. It doesn't take away from the fact that they need me to do what they can't do for themselves."

"And that is?" she asked acidly.

Shaw smiled a particularly sad smile. "Why, Mrs. Roark, I find their devil, whatever or whoever it might be, and I deal with the problem."

"By killing it?" she asked, almost spitting the words.

"Not necessarily." Shaw went on patiently, "You're making what I believe are some unfair assumptions. I'm not a bounty hunter or a hired killer. I don't go looking for people who have committed crimes and are fleeing justice. I help people who need my specialty. Sometimes I succeed where the law fails and yes, sometimes I have to kill."

She looked at him doubtfully.

"It's true," he said. "Ask your local marshal or sheriff. Tell them my name and ask them if there is any paper out on me. I assure you, I'm not wanted in any jurisdiction."

"Well, you're not wanted here either!" she stated flatly.

Shaw suddenly chuckled at her unintended joke.

She blushed.

She was looking at him carefully. Even though he probably frightened her, he knew he was not an intimidating figure. He dressed as a westerner, but with obvious care and taste for quality. His clothes were freshly washed and he was carefully groomed. His hair was neatly trimmed and his face freshly shaved. His speech and demeanor was that of a man who was, if not formally educated, certainly well read. He was sure that whatever the Roark woman expected, he didn't fit with any preconceived notions she'd entertained.

Shaw had been making his own inspection as well. Having already determined she was pretty from a distance; up close, he realized she was beautiful. Along with her thick, reddish-blonde hair, she had a dusting of freckles on her nose and a dancing light in her blue-green eyes. If he looked closely into those eyes, he'd see the apprehension that was there. He knew the anxiety went deeper than just her concern over meeting him for the first time. He surmised she'd been worried for weeks. Shaw could see this woman hadn't been sleeping well for quite some time and was on the ragged edge of exhaustion. It showed in the slightly gray look to the skin around her eyes. That was always the first place you noticed it.

Ranch life would never be easy even in the best of times with her husband involved and healthy. Now that she was taking on all the responsibility, it was slowly grinding her down, past the point where she could cope. To see such a lovely woman so worn out by the rigors of keeping up a home and ranch while he carried around no similar burden of responsibility in *his* life gave him a sudden and profound sense of shame.

The Roark's were builders. They and their like were the salt-of-the-earth. Shaw, on the other hand, had built nothing but a reputation as a man to call when something unpleasant needed doing. When the Roark's of this world passed on, they'd leave behind a legacy. The world would be a better place for their having built something. Shaw's legacy would be nothing more permanent than vague and mostly ugly memories in the lives he touched.

He looked around at the ranch yard. There was work that needed doing. His job, the one that had brought him here might wait another day or two. He had no hope he could win this woman's trust, and in truth he honestly didn't care to. But, for once, he could leave behind something or someone a little better off physically than when he arrived.

"Mrs. Roark, I'll ride to see your husband in the morning." She started to say something, and he held up his hand, silencing her. "I'm not without compassion for your predicament. If your husband has changed his mind, I'll refund the money, minus my expenses. Until then, if I could bed down in your stable, I'll not bother you any more. But if you don't mind, I see an axe that needs sharpening and some wood that needs cutting. I'm not very handy, but I can certainly do that, with your permission."

Sarah seemed surprised. She probably hadn't been prepared for his easy acquiescence. Then too, having such a man as he sleeping in her stable undoubtedly conjured up unpleasant thoughts. On the other hand, Shaw had seen the easy way she carried a rifle, so while she might be considering such things, Shaw had no intention of approaching the cabin after dark.

She glanced at the woodpile before making up her mind. "That's a very generous offer. I'll take you up on it. I'll even cook you a supper when you've finished." She paused a few seconds. "And yes, you may bed down in the stable. There's plenty of hay and the horses will keep it comfortably warm." Taking her rifle, Sarah turned and entered the cabin.

Shaw smiled when he heard the door being locked with a latch.

He tended to his horse first, and then unhooked her team and the pinto, and put them all together with the others in the corral. There was plenty of hay and water, so he didn't need to do anything else.

With the horse cared for, Shaw moved to the woodpile. Taking up the axe, he looked at the edge critically. It had not been sharpened for a while. Near the side of the stable was a grinding wheel with a tin cup hung over it. Retrieving the bucket from the well, Shaw dipped it in the horse trough and moved to the wheel. He filled the cup, which began to dribble water, wetting the sharpening surface. Sitting astride the seat, he first turned the wheel with his hand to get it started, then pumped the pedal to keep it going. When the stone was wet and turning quickly, he began to sharpen the axe. The ring of the axe-head on stone was a pleasant sound.

Shaw finished the axe and tested the edge. It wasn't perfect, but it would do. Returning the bucket to the well, he approached the woodpile with gusto. As a boy, he'd loved chopping wood. Endless hours of it had shaped his young body, building muscle in his shoulders and arms, muscle he still carried on a lean frame. Removing his coat, he selected a piece to be split and set it on the chopping block. Gauging the distance, he swung the axe gracefully. It buried itself in the chopping block and two halves fell easily on each side. He quartered that and selected another piece.

The end of about an hour brought a large pile of freshly cut wood to be stacked. Completing that, Shaw buried the axe in the chopping block. Then he moved on to the stable. Inside, he found a can of grease with a brush sticking out. Taking it, he went back to the well. With the grease brush, he dabbed a liberal amount on the pump mechanism and the piston rod. He pumped the handle for several minutes, letting the grease work while filling the trough with fresh water. When he was satisfied, he returned the grease to the stable.

He hoped to find some shingles inside, but there were none. Returning to the woodpile, he selected a piece of aspen and, with careful axe strokes, hewed it square. Taking a club-sized log, he placed the axe head on the squared pine and began shaving off shingles — each one half an inch thick — by pounding the back of the axe with the club. In this manner, he made a dozen shingles for the stable roof.

He found a hammer and some rusty nails and placed a ladder in position. He climbed to the stable roof and easily repaired the wind damage. When he'd replaced all the tools, he went to the stable and looked to the horses one last time. The Roark stock was in need of attention. Their hoofs needed trimming and the shoes needed replacing. He found there were no tools for the job, but wasn't surprised. Few ranchers were experienced farriers. It was better he leave that job to a good smith.

With one last look around, he was satisfied there was nothing left to be done that could be accomplished before dark. The temperature had dropped steadily as the afternoon progressed toward evening and, now that he wasn't working, he noticed the cold. At the pump, he stripped to the waist and washed up, the bone-chilling cold of the water re-vitalizing him. Finished, he put his shirt back on, retrieved his coat and stepped onto the porch and rapped on the door.

His knock was answered immediately. Sarah was in a different dress; this one was a bit more festive than the gray riding garment he'd seen her in earlier. Her hair was no longer in a braid, but was brushed and loose about her shoulders. Shaw was again struck by just how lovely this young woman was as she stood aside and allowed him to enter.

Shaw noticed a well-kept cabin that was clean and comfortable. Not being able to keep up the ranch, it was obvious Sarah hadn't let the house chores slip. Something was bubbling in a Dutch oven on the stove and a delicious aroma filled the place. The table was set with glazed white plates covered with a blue pattern of English design.

There was a rifle; probably the one Sarah had carried with her on the wagon, now hung on pegs over the door. A shotgun leaned in the corner with pegs gently laid in the twin muzzles to keep dust and spiders out. Shaw wasn't sure, but he suspected there might be a pistol near to hand as well. To allay Sarah's fears, he unbuckled his gun-belt and handed it to her to set aside. She seemed surprised but he also detected some visible relief.

Sarah indicated a chair for him and he sat, while she went about ladling a generous portion of meaty stew onto his plate. There were thick slices of bread in a basket with butter and jam as well. Shaw had eaten in restaurants from New York to San Francisco, but he'd long ago decided that home cooking after a long ride and hard work tasted better than the finest meal that could be bought for any price.

"I want to thank you for what you did outside. You've accomplished more in an afternoon than I have in several months." Sarah said. "I've not been able to keep up with the ranch work with my husband's illness and all. Things have slipped…."

"I did what I could. I wish it was more but I'm not that handy myself." Shaw smiled briefly then added, his tone more serious, "You've lost a lot of cattle. Do you know how many you still have?"

Sarah looked down at her plate. "I have no idea. I haven't been able to make a count as the snow only recently melted. That and I've had to go to town almost every day to see to Samuel. It takes the better part of the day just to make that ride and back. I'm afraid if he doesn't get better soon, I'll have to sell what cattle and horses we have and move to town. We own the place, but it will fall apart if we can't keep it up."

"It's none of my business, Mrs. Roark, but what exactly is the nature of Mr. Roark's illness? I mean, is he expected to get better?" He normally wouldn't have broached this subject, but he suspected Sarah needed to talk about it.

After a moment, she responded, "Samuel hasn't been well since Stuart died." Sarah blinked away sudden tears.

"The unmarked grave by the tree?"

Sarah looked up and, after a moment, she nodded.

Shaw's face softened. "Stuart is the reason I'm here then?"

"Yes." Sarah's voice was almost crushed by despair. "After Stuart was killed, Samuel became inconsolable. He blames himself. You have to understand, we also lost a daughter to influenza three years ago, and he'd hardly gotten over that when…" Sarah fought against the tears, her head bowed.

Shaw was impressed by her strength, but he felt himself nearly choked up by the weight of the emotions she was trying so desperately to suppress. There were no words he could offer her, so he simply remained silent and attentive.

After a few minutes, she won the struggle, if barely. She resumed speaking, her voice a little stronger. "Stuart was wearing Samuel's coat and hat when he was shot and because the shot was meant for Samuel, he can't forgive himself. He never leaves his office, and wouldn't even eat if I didn't bring it to him." Sarah sighed.

Shaw was uncomfortable delving into this family's problems, but those problems were precisely the reason he was here. To do his job to help this family, he needed to know every aspect of the situation. He began to probe. "Why would someone want to shoot your husband?"

Sarah gave a rueful smile. "Samuel is a lawyer. In some places, that would be reason enough." Her smile quickly died, and she went on, "About a year ago, a local rancher came to him for help. He had a tenuous claim on some very desirable range and there was another, larger ranch vying for it. Samuel took the case, and won. The rancher who lost out hasn't forgotten it. He's a very powerful man and there was some, well, some harassment. Samuel brought a suit against him and a jury awarded damages. Needless to say, the man is very bitter."

"What was the nature of the harassment?"

"We've had some cattle killed; a few horses as well. Someone desecrated the grave of our daughter by the tree. Samuel was ready to challenge the rancher to a fight but I talked him out of it." Sarah smiled that same rueful smile. "I begged him not to, is more like it.

"Things seemed to quiet down for a while. There was a peace, of sorts. The rancher even offered an apology for the way 'his men' had acted. Of course, Samuel accepted; not that he believed a word of it, but Samuel is too much of a gentleman not to accept a man's apology."

She toyed with her food, but didn't eat. "Now, we suspect the rancher was simply establishing his peaceful intentions in the minds of those in the community. Samuel is convinced the rancher was behind the attempt to murder him, and therefore responsible for Stuart's death. There's no evidence, of course, so the law is no help here. Samuel made inquiries and learned of you. I didn't know he'd contacted you until afterward. I objected, as you can well imagine — considering the welcome I gave you." She smiled faintly. It quickly faded. "I still object! You need to know that. Whatever happens; whatever you decide to do, I object with all my heart to this kind of vengeance," Sarah finished, shakily.

"Mrs. Roark, what kind of vengeance would that be? This killer can likely be caught. Don't you want that?"

"You don't understand, do you? Samuel doesn't care about the killer, at least not in a way you'd consider normal. The killer is a means to an end, but he's not the real reason Samuel contacted you. The rancher is the one Samuel believes is responsible for Stuart's death. He's the one I'm certain Samuel wants you to..." She paused, as if searching for the right words, "wants you to deal with."

Shaw thought for several minutes. Taking a piece of bread, he slathered it with butter and jam. While doing so, he carefully considered what to say. This woman was deeply wounded by the tragic circumstances that had entered her life. Shaw was attuned to this, and it weighed on his mind. Whether she knew it or not, Sarah Roark needed some finality to these events and Shaw might be able to provide it. "Mrs. Roark —"

"Sarah, please," she interrupted, and then blushed.

"All right, Sarah, if you prefer. By the way, my name is Matthew. I don't often go by Matt or Matthew, preferring that people simply call me Shaw."

Sarah thought for a moment. "If you don't object, I'll call you Matt. Shaw is too impersonal, and you've been nothing but a gentleman."

He smiled. "Matt it is, then. What I was starting to say is the killer *is* a means to an end. It will require some investigation. The trail is old and the killer can't be tracked through conventional means, but if I can find him, I might learn all that your husband requires to satisfy the law."

She leaned forward, interested.

"Sarah, you have to understand that on occasion I have killed men in the course of my jobs and I suppose in your eyes that makes me a killer. But there are people the law can't or won't touch. Either the evidence is not legally sufficient, or they're too well connected, politically, financially, or what have you. Then there are those whose entire lives have been spent in lawless pursuits. Often, they simply won't be taken alive and the only way to deal with them is to kill them. So, I have done that and I won't offer apologies for it. Over the years, I've hunted all types of men, but I don't take a job on just anyone's say so. For me, there has to be evidence. There has to be more than just suspicion that someone is responsible for an act. Even if your husband is sure, that wouldn't be enough for me to deal with this rancher in the manner he might require of me."

Sarah looked relieved. "Then you'll tell my husband you can't help him?"

Matt shook his head. "No, I can't do that. If your husband still wants me to, I'll try and find the killer. If I can do that and it leads me back to the one who paid him, then we'll discuss the new information, and the two of you can decide."

Sarah looked resigned. "I suppose there's no reason to continue talking about it then. It doesn't make pleasant dinner conversation. Let's change the subject. Tomorrow is soon enough, don't you agree?"

Shaw smiled. "Yes. I agree."

She seemed relieved. Perhaps she was realizing a feeling of understanding, and compassion. He was a gentleman, well-spoken and with an easy manner about him. Shaw found himself thinking that under other circumstances, or perhaps another time, the evening would have been enjoyable for other reasons. "Well, Sarah, in the morning we'll ride to see Samuel. In the meantime, I've a bed to make in the stable and I've had a very long day. Thanks for the supper. It was delicious."

Unexpectedly, Sarah blurted out, "Please, don't go yet." As if realizing how this might be misconstrued, she continued, "I…we don't get many visitors to the ranch, and when I get to town, I don't have time to visit or seek out friends. Frankly, I'm starved for news and conversation. The horses listen, but they never talk back. Besides, I've made pie."

Shaw smiled. "Pie? I never could refuse pie. It's a curse, I suppose. In any case, I would be pleased to have a piece of pie."

He made the pie last an hour and a pleasant hour it was. Sarah seemed hungry for news and asked a thousand questions. Shaw talked easily and she hung on his every word. Sometime during the evening, he decided that if he spent too much time with this woman, he was certain to fall a little bit in love with her and the thought left him sad. Nothing good could come of it. She was a woman married to a man who needed her. Regardless of what Shaw might feel, or what Sarah might need, he wouldn't allow himself to interfere. After that hour passed, he said goodnight, but sleep didn't come easy for him. He realized it was a little too late. She was already on his mind.

The Broken Man

In the morning, Shaw tended the horses, breaking a skim of ice from the watering trough and forking fresh hay. The dawn had broken clear and cold, but with a bright sun. In the high country, summer was slow in coming and there could be temperature differences of forty degrees or more between the afternoon and early morning. He worked the chill out of his body, drinking in the fresh mountain air.

When he was finished with the horses, Shaw brought an armload of wood to the porch. At his knock, Sarah let him in. This morning she was wearing a nice dress for traveling to town. Her face looked freshly scrubbed and there was a warm color to her cheeks. Shaw was startled to realize once again that this was truly a beautiful woman and he had to caution himself to keep in mind his business arrangement with her husband. It would not do for him to become too comfortable around her, particularly when she was so emotionally vulnerable. Yet, there was no denying her beauty.

Sarah had made a breakfast of pork belly and fried potatoes with fresh biscuits and gravy. Shaw ate it all with gusto. Their conversation was limited and mildly strained compared with the easy dialogue they'd shared the night before.

Shaw believed that Sarah was once again facing the grim reality of why he was here in the first place. Though he hated even to broach the subject, there were things he wanted to learn before he met Samuel. "Can I ask a couple of questions?"

"What kind of questions, Matt?"

"When your step-son was killed," he began, but Sarah interrupted him.

"Stuart." Sarah said quickly. "His name was Stuart. I'd prefer we use his name rather than referring to him as my step-son." Her eyes glistened with sudden tears. She rose and stepped away from the table. She looked out the window — at the tree. She stood silent for several moments, composing herself. Finally, she said, "Stuart wasn't that much younger than I am. I could never think of him as a son; more of a brother I'd guess." She turned to face Shaw. "I loved him like a brother, or even a best friend." She looked down at her hands, folded against her apron.

Shaw saw she was silently crying and he turned back to his breakfast, giving her a moment alone with grief that was still raw and obviously very painful.

After a few minutes, Sarah returned to the table. "I'm sorry I interrupted you. What were you going to ask?" Her face was tight, her eyes red and moist. Shaw hesitated even to start the question again, but since she was still coming to grips with her loss, he decided perhaps talking about it might help her cope.

"When Stuart was killed, to what degree did the local authorities investigate?"

"Oh," Sarah began derisively. "The marshal came out and did a little scouting. He *'discovered'* the killer had hidden above the house, up by our big pine tree, as if we didn't already know that. There was quite a wind gusting the evening Stuart was shot, and an inch of fresh snow that followed that evening had drifted over everything and made any tracking difficult. He didn't find much, just a depression in the snow where the man had lain."

"Nothing concerning a horse?" Shaw prodded gently.

"That's the odd thing. The marshal couldn't find any evidence of a horse. Apparently, the man arrived on foot, which was remarkable considering the depth of some of the snowdrifts he'd had to go through. Also, it was very cold. Anyway, the man used snowshoes, and came up from the valley below. It looked like he'd lain there all day, waiting for his chance."

Shaw thought about what Sarah had just told him. She'd shared something very important even if she didn't realize it. The west was filled with killers for hire. They were a dime a dozen. But a killer who'd subject himself to the extreme rigors of winter travel on foot, and lay in wait in an almost arctic cold was rare indeed.

Whoever the killer was, he was no cheap saddle tramp looking to earn a grubstake with a quick killing. No, this certainly sounded very professional. Professional killers were a breed apart. They were generally expensive and one had to know where to find such people in the first place; the method of contact; arranging a meeting or payment. All these things left a trail if one had the know-how to unravel it.

It also called into question the importance of the job. A cheap killer was one thing, willing to do a nasty job and move on. But the kind of man who would endure what this one had was either a dedicated professional killer or had some personal interest in seeing this killing done. If he was dealing with a professional killer, the odds for identification improved somewhat, but it also made a significant difference in how one would go about hunting him. Professional killers were good hunters as well.

"That tree stands about three hundred yards from the cabin, give or take a couple dozen," he remarked. "That's a very long shot. You say there was a gusting wind that night?" She nodded. "There are not many men can make that kind of shot. Not many would even attempt it. It's a chancy thing when a gusting wind might blow at precisely the wrong time. Or a gust can be blowing where the target is standing and it can be dead calm where the shooter is laying up. Not many killers would take that chance."

"Would you?" Sarah looked at him very deliberately; challengingly. Her eyes were no longer red, but the intensity of her gaze made them shine.

Shaw felt a sudden pang of shame, knowing that she saw him in much the same vein as the killer of Stuart; a hired gun, a *killer* and really nothing more. But then, she was partly right. He'd killed from ambush, when he deemed there was no other way. He decided not to let himself be baited or made angry by someone who simply had no way of understanding the distinction between him and the men he hunted.

"Would I? Probably not," Shaw replied honestly, gently. "It depends on how important it was, I suppose. What would be the consequences of waiting for a more opportune time? Would there be a likelihood of another chance? Would my escape be hindered in any way? Everything must be taken into consideration.

"Making a three hundred yard shot isn't child's play, but it isn't so difficult that I couldn't teach someone such as yourself how to fire the right rifle at that distance and guarantee a lethal hit. In any case, I'll take a look around before we ride to town. I'd like to get a feel for the scene, to see exactly what the killer would have seen."

"Why?" Sarah asked. "What can you learn about something that happened so long ago; months ago, during the winter? Nothing will look the same."

Shaw wondered how much he should tell her. For that matter, how much would she understand? He decided to try.

"Sarah, you'd be surprised what I might learn," he replied. "People seldom move over the earth without leaving a trace of their passing. In many cases, such evidence might actually last through years of changes; seasonal changes, climactic changes, or even human changes where the ground is affected during efforts toward progress. You need to know *what* to look for and then you really need to look. Actually, looking is not enough. You need to be able to *see*. It's what I do for a living."

She looked doubtful, so Shaw continued, "When I rode up into the ranch-yard yesterday, I saw things that told me a story about this place and what had been happening here in the recent past. First of all, there were numerous dead cattle in the meadows above the cabin. Properly cared for, by a rancher who understood the high country and prepared for severe weather, there might have been a dozen lost at most. As it stands, you probably lost fifty and likely twice that number.

"The wood pile hadn't been replenished in weeks, the axe unsharpened and the blade allowed to rust. The pump piston was rusty, the roof of the barn needed repair and the horses in the corral needed tending. All of these things indicated this ranch was no longer being run. Had I ridden up to an empty homestead with all that evidence there to be seen, I would have surmised a rancher had abandoned the place either during or immediately after a severe winter, and I would have been partly right.

"When I met you, you looked tired. Not just a little tired, but *bone* tired, on the ragged edge of exhaustion. Your dress looked like it was cut a size too large, so I could guess you'd lost some weight, either from worry or neglecting yourself for other concerns."

Sarah blushed and made to speak.

Shaw raised a hand; he hadn't quite finished. "You see, there are stories to be found everywhere. The track of a horse can tell you if it was being ridden or bearing a burden. An area of mature growth in the forest unlike its surroundings can tell of a long-ago fire even when there's no visible evidence of any burning. A slash might indicate an avalanche zone. The list is endless. There are things a careful person can see that might escape the notice of someone who isn't looking or doesn't care.

"Of course, none of this means I'll find anything of importance, or an answer to any questions or any useful clues but, then again, I might. The only thing I know for certain is, I won't find a thing if I don't look."

Sarah nodded while she picked at her food. Then she looked into Shaw's eyes and smiled. "I look like I've lost weight? I guess that means we had better finish that pie." She went to the cupboard and retrieved the pie they'd started last night and together they finished it, followed by a couple of cups of good, strong coffee.

After breakfast, Shaw walked slowly up the hill to the tree. No grass grew in the area, it being too rocky along the crest of the hill. The gravel showed the indistinct tracks his horse made but nothing else of immediate importance. Shaw stopped to look at the graves again. Now that he knew who was lying in the unmarked burial place, he felt a little uneasy. Months had gone by and still there was no marker. After meeting Sarah, he couldn't imagine her wanting to see the grave neglected. That meant Samuel, for some reason, was hesitating.

Shaw looked down the slope to the cabin. From this distance, any shot intended to hit a man must be made with a rifle fitted with a Vernier-style target sight or a telescopic one; another vote for a professional hunter. Anything else would have been pure luck, and a lucky man would not have put up with the conditions present the afternoon of the killing. A professional might have, if it was the only sure way to succeed.

Professional shooters weren't unheard of, but there were not so many of them floating around that they could remain anonymous. Even Shaw had a reputation, not necessarily as a long-shooter, but as a man-hunter who could, when necessary, make long shots. Being a shooter just naturally went with the profession. Even so, Shaw doubted he would have risked the shot under the conditions it was made. A miss could spell disaster for a man on foot, bent on getting away in deep snow. If he missed his first shot, he might have to close with the cabin and kill everyone inside to gain the luxury of time. A hit, on the other hand, almost guaranteed he would have time to escape.

While Shaw was looking down at the cabin, he noticed Sarah through the kitchen window. She watched him intently. No doubt with more contempt than curiosity. Perhaps this was one of the reasons he preferred to remain alone in his life. There was a lot less explaining to do. He smiled ruefully and returned to his chore.

Shaw started at the base of the tree and began a meticulous search of the ground, inch by inch. He circled the tree in an ever-widening spiral, eyes scanning for anything out of the ordinary. He didn't hold out any hope that there would be evidence that survived the winter, but this was a good place to start thinking about the man who'd killed young Stuart.

The ground held some interesting mineral deposits. He found slivers of petrified wood; the original larger pieces most likely crushed and ground down by an ancient glacier. There was quite a lot of quartz as well. A lot of gold had been discovered in these mountains, and quartz was very common in the gold fields.

A hint of unusual color caught Shaw's eye. He bent down and picked up a small cup of metal resembling a tiny top hat with four flared edges at ninety-degree angles from the sides of the cup. It was a percussion cap, of the kind used for priming a musket-style weapon loaded from the muzzle.

The copper of the cap had turned mostly a pale green from exposure to the elements and this one was unfired. He'd found similar artifacts in his travels, and immediately knew there was something very odd about this find. The age of muskets was past. Certainly, there were still a few to be found in the hands of dirt farmers or old soldiers, or perhaps some Indian or old hermit who used one to put meat on the table. For the most part, the use of muskets was fairly rare in this day of preloaded rifle cartridges.

This percussion cap appeared too new. The corrosion was not heavy and there were still areas where the copper hadn't begun to tarnish. This cap had not been lying on this trail for years. He'd have to question Sarah about it but he was certain this cap had been dropped in the recent past. Its proximity to the area from which the hidden marksman had fired could be coincidental, but this was a game in which all coincidence was suspect. If the shooter had dropped this cap, it might help identify the man who'd killed Stuart and had intended to kill Samuel.

An hour of further study failed to turn up anything of importance. Shaw scanned the countryside. Instinct confirmed what the marshal had already discovered. The shooter had come up from below. Escape in heavy snow and cold would be easier if one were descending rather than climbing. Less energy would be expended and better time and distance could be made, even though it would make checking one's back trail a bit more difficult.

Shaw wondered about the timing of it all. Just as he had pre-scouted the area of his last work, actually walking the distance and climbing the heights and tentatively deciding on his position, he felt certain this shooter had done so as well. That meant he would have remained in the area for a day at least, maybe even a week. And, as cold as it was, Shaw doubted the man had been without a place to seek shelter and prepare.

Shaw could see that once off the trail the land descended rapidly through an area of heavy forest that had grown up through the millennia over the steep, rocky sides of the mountains. Far below, the forest gave way to lower valleys and rich, fertile ground.

Shaw glanced at the sun. Deciding he had time to spare, he descended into the forest in a gradual, switchback method of covering ground. He was looking for a natural shelter, knowing such a place would provide a much better location from which to observe and plan. It took him a little more than an hour to find it.

At the base of a pine-sheltered outcropping, he located a shallow cave. It was more an overhang than an actual cavern, but it had a narrow opening and went back into the mountain for about twenty feet and then ended abruptly. It offered shelter on three sides, but was high enough to allow a man to stand erect, if he wasn't too tall. A barely discernible track led to it. The trail was old, starting out as a game trail made by a bear perhaps. Later, some ancient Indians had probably used the cave either as a permanent home, or a place to shelter during seasonal migrations.

Now that he knew what to look for, Shaw gazed at the surrounding forest. It was only then that he noted branches on several pine trees displayed cuts to the bough ends. Not near the trunks, but farther out where the branches were supple and the needles softer and thicker. The cuts were made at an angle and on the off sides of the branches so if someone stood at the cave entrance or above it, seeing the cuts would be very difficult. The trees bearing cut boughs were scattered in the forest and no two were standing anywhere near each other. Only if one walked down the hill some distance and looked back, would the whites of the freshly cut branches stand out. This was a careful man. Shaw decided the shooter was also a passable woodsman. It was a thing to remember.

This would have gone undiscovered by a casual passer-by. There were no branches lying about the area, so Shaw was certain they had been used to help shelter the cave opening. Shaw entered the hole and waited for his eyes to adjust to the dim light. When the interior became relatively clear, he noted the ceiling of the cave had traces of soot from long-ago fires, and evidence of more recent ones. Pine would give off thicker soot, particularly if it wasn't adequately dried before burning. The smell of wood smoke was present in the damp interior. Such a smell could survive for months in a cool, moist environment. The cave floor had been carefully brushed out and there were no pine boughs inside. All the evidence pointed to the cut pine boughs having been carefully burned before the person sheltering there had abandoned it.

Shaw frowned. This would have taken considerable time. Would a man who'd just committed a murder calmly remain in the area erasing the evidence of his passing? Certainly, he couldn't have tidied up in advance of his mission, because there would be no certainty that he'd be offered a good target on a specific date and time. This shelter seemed to indicate he'd used it over several days.

A meticulous search of the cave floor turned up nothing of interest. Whoever had used it had been thorough in erasing his sign. After determining there was nothing else that would provide any more useful information, Shaw returned to the cabin.

Sarah opened the door when he stepped up on the porch. "You found something?"

"Yes, as a matter of fact, I did. I located a small cave several hundred yards below the tree, deep in the forest. It showed evidence that someone used it for shelter in the last few months. And then there's something else a little out of the ordinary." He reached into his pocket and removed the percussion cap.

Sarah leaned closer to peer at the object in the palm of his hand.

She was so close Shaw caught a whiff of soap, and noticed how her hair shined by the light coming through the cabin windows. He resisted an almost overpowering impulse to touch it. Shaking it off, he went on, "It's a percussion cap. This type is a musket cap, used to ignite the powder charge in rifles of the type soldiers carried, which were loaded from the muzzle. This one hasn't been fired. Do you know of anyone locally who uses a musket?"

"I'm sorry, but I don't even know what a musket is." She looked confused.

Shaw smiled. She was obviously unschooled in obsolete weaponry. "Most rifles and pistols today hold cartridge casings made of copper or brass in which the primer, powder and bullet are all contained. It wasn't too many years ago when guns were loaded from the muzzle with loose powder and a patched ball or a conical style bullet. Earlier models commonly used by the military were referred to as muskets. Some are still in use today for sporting purposes, but fewer by far than a few years ago. To fire the weapon, one would have to place a cap such as this on a cone located on the breech end, to be struck by the hammer."

"No one that we know uses such a rifle, I'm sure of it. Why would the shooter use such an old gun?"

"Some muzzle-loading rifles, properly loaded and prepared, can be incredibly accurate. They're still used in target competitions around the world. For a sure-thing killer, one shot might be all he needs. But this is a musket cap. Most target rifles are versions of existing hunting rifles. Some might have been modified to take a musket cap for a more certain ignition." Then he remembered something. He smiled and shook his head. "I'd forgotten. During the war, both sides used very accurate European and domestic rifles and muskets for sharp-shooting and long-range killing. If our shooter dropped this cap, it would mean he's certainly a traditionalist. It could mean he's a veteran of the last war. That will narrow our search down a bit. A man with a rifle like that will not go unnoticed out here where people have a tendency to take note of unusual guns and the men who carry them."

"Where would we start to look?" Sarah asked.

"We start with your husband. Everything starts with your husband, Sarah. He holds the key, whether he knows it or not."

* * * *

Eagle Town nestled in a valley with picturesque mountain peaks visible in every direction. It was served from three sides by narrow wagon roads carved from the steep sides of the mountains. The roads switched back and forth in their precipitous journey into the settlement. Here and there on the mountainsides were the sun-bleached boards and wheels of wagons that failed to negotiate a turn and fell off the trail. Shaw knew that if he looked closely enough, he'd find that often mingled with the boards would be the equally bleached bones of the horses or oxen that were dragged down with the wagon and whatever cargo it had carried.

The journey into Eagle Town from the Roark ranch was hardly dangerous. The trail Sarah and Shaw traveled into the valley was a gradual slope of no more than two thousand feet. It followed a long finger-like meadow that had once been the base end of a narrow glacier. The meadow snaked back and forth as it descended but was amazingly flat and gentle to travel on horseback or in a wagon.

While on the trail, Shaw was treated to spectacular vistas that frequently reminded him how much he missed the high country. On any other day, he'd have taken the time to stop and take it all in; maybe camp beside the stream and try his hand at mountain trout. Shaw had learned that life is fleeting enough, that any moment of beauty should not be wasted or taken for granted. But he also knew that promising he'd one day return was often promising to make a liar of himself.

Eagle Town was a mining town, plain and simple. Having originated as a wild and raucous boom town, it had settled down when many of the first mines played out and the more savvy mining engineers and claim holders began buying off the less energetic, get-rich-quick types who were only looking for some dust and a few nuggets to keep themselves in whiskey and other trifles. Now, it was a working town. Four mines were working shifts and a few of the saloons and gaming halls stayed open all night.

Unlike many boomtowns, Eagle Town hadn't died out or shifted to a better location when miners began bringing their families to the region. The streets were cut roughly parallel to each other, with smaller cross streets at sharp angles up steep hills. It was a town that offered healthy exercise for a person on foot going from one neighborhood to the next. Many of the buildings were built of native rock and mortar, or half rock and heavily timbered. They would stand for a long time.

In addition to the mines, half a dozen ranches, located in the many gentle valleys and along the river basins where the graze was rich and the weather less severe, combined with the mining operations to keep Eagle Town a going concern. It wasn't overly wealthy, but there was money here and many nice homes along the streets.

Samuel's law office was located on the main street in a small Spanish-style stone building that boasted two floors. The upper floor, Sarah explained, held a two-room living quarters, where Samuel stayed when in town. He lived there alone now, having all but abandoned the ranch and the memories connected to it. Shaw knew from experience that leaving a place because of the memories it held seldom served to negate the recollections. It only made them emptier. It appeared Samuel had all but forsaken Sarah as well, though she wouldn't speak of such a thing. And, while Shaw might think it, he kept such thoughts to himself. It had been years since he'd met a female who made him take more than a passing notice. Sarah was just such a woman. It made him wonder how a sane man could desert someone like her?

As they drew up, Shaw observed tightness around Sarah's mouth and eyes. Apparently, she didn't relish going inside. Shaw was beginning to understand how taxing it was for her, living as she was. It was easy to see she hadn't wanted to return so soon. Her loyalty to her husband — despite his illness — was emotionally difficult, while trying and failing to adequately keep up the ranch was physically draining. Shaw knew she was getting no relief at all.

Shaw climbed down from the wagon and untied his horse. "You were just here yesterday. Maybe I should meet Samuel alone, while you go up-town and have some coffee." Shaw was being less noble than it might first appear. He wanted to speak to Samuel in private, without any indignation or righteous interference by the young woman who'd made her feelings so plain. He hoped her mental state would make it easier for her to accept his offer and not see through his subterfuge. It was clear she didn't really want to go inside again, so soon.

"If you think it will be all right, I'd rather do that. Samuel hasn't been…well, let's just say he can be difficult to talk to. There's a great deal of anger there, toward everything; toward everyone." Sarah's lower lip quivered as she fought back tears. She dropped her eyes momentarily.

"Don't give it another thought. Not wanting to go in isn't cowardly and it's not disloyal," Shaw said. "There are things happening here to both of you that can't be easily corrected. It might take finding the killer of Stuart to right them." He paused, hesitating to say what was needed. "It might be that nothing ever will. You have to be prepared for that."

Sarah nodded and, without another word, started the wagon up the street toward a small restaurant.

Shaw watched her drive away. That any man could have her love and loyalty yet forsake both of them made him think that Samuel was beyond help. But he wondered if he truly believed this or merely *wanted* to? Whatever justice or even vengeance meant to the grieving man, it might only serve to drive the wedge between Samuel and his wife deeper still. Shaw wasn't sure exactly how he felt about that at this moment. Of course, his role in the matter might make Sarah look upon him as the worse of two evils. He set such thoughts aside, stepped up onto the boardwalk, and knocked on the door.

"Come in." A strong voice called out.

Shaw opened the door and was immediately struck by the darkness and the smell. All the shades were down, leaving the room in a state of permanent dusk. The unpleasant smell was of leather and dust; unwashed clothing — and whiskey. Shaw noticed a man sitting in a far corner of the room. As his eyes adjusted to the lack of light, he noted that while the man was clothed in a suit, it apparently had not been laundered in some time. The shirt was yellow from sweat and the collar grimy. More than likely, it had not been off the man in weeks. And the suit no longer fit well, either. Samuel had obviously lost considerable weight. He appeared gaunt. His eyes were sunk back into the head and there were darkened patches beneath them that almost made it look like he'd taken a beating. Metaphorically speaking, Shaw knew he had taken a drubbing as real as any physical pummeling he could have experienced.

His face and neck bore the whisker growth of a month or more and his hair was uncut and uncombed. He was unwashed and unpleasant to look at. Shaw wondered if the man even cared about his appearance, or if he appreciated the effect it had on others. This was not the man Shaw had expected and he fully understood why Sarah hadn't wanted to come in. He was sure that this man was a total stranger to Sarah. He was not the man she had known, and visits with him could not be pleasant for her.

Yet, for the unpleasant and irrational image portrayed by the man, there was "sanity" in the eyes; he seemed fully aware of the picture he was painting by his physical condition. This man may have been insane from grief, but he was not necessarily out of touch with reality. His manner said that things, which might have been important to him once, no longer mattered to him. Appearance, grooming and hygiene were part of his old life. His new life was one of complete and utter dissipation. A man like that may not commit the physical act of suicide, but he wouldn't lift a finger to go on living either. It was something to ponder.

"My name is Shaw."

Samuel screwed up his eyes, as if in thought, and then recognition came. "Oh yes. Yes, I'd wondered when you might show up — *if* you would show up." He fixed Shaw with a direct stare. "You've met Sarah." It was not a question, but a statement. "I thought I heard the wagon. She wouldn't come in." It was another statement of fact and the very nature of the fact was not lost on either of them. Samuel looked away. "I don't blame her," he said quietly.

He indicated a chair. "Please, sit down, Mr. Shaw."

After he was seated, Shaw said, "You wired my lawyer in Denver. Money was placed in my account, so I'm here to listen to what you have to say. Understand that my appearance here is not an agreement to anything. After I've heard you out, we'll either agree on terms or I'll return to you the money you wired, less my expenses."

Samuel Roark considered Shaw. "Are you a lawyer, Mr. Shaw?" He asked with a faint smile. When Shaw didn't answer, Samuel's smile faded. "Your terms are fair enough. I do understand your caution. My son Stuart was murdered and I believe the killer thought he was shooting at me. There is absolutely no reason to believe it was a random act so the possibilities do not rest well with me, nor does the murder of my only son. I've sent for you because you come well recommended."

Shaw nodded. "May I ask who recommended me?"

"You could, but I would have to refuse. You would understand, of course. I trust you don't release the names of

66

your clients either."

Shaw nodded. "No. You're right, I don't. Have you given much thought to who might have hired the shooter to kill you?"

Samuel's look hardened. "I've had little else to do but give it thought," he responded with some heat. "I've given it plenty of thought and I know perfectly well who contracted the killing. He's a rancher named Mason who has a reason to dislike me intensely."

"The rancher you defeated in a law suit? Your wife told me about that. People have contracted a killing for less, I'm sure, but if he's the one, what exactly do you want from me?"

Samuel had a confused look on his face. "Mr. Shaw, I want the killer of my son found. I want the man who hired him identified, and then I want both of them *dead*!" he ended fiercely.

Shaw pondered that for several seconds. Apparently, Samuel Roark was operating under the assumption that Shaw was a killer for hire. Others had made that mistake but he was disappointed nonetheless.

"Roark, I hunt men, but I don't murder them," Shaw said flatly.

"But you do," Roark responded, calmly. "I know you do. You did that very thing just last fall not fifty miles from here. You helped that miner who hired you to kill a claim jumper who was trying to run him off his mine. I know all about it."

"That's not completely accurate," Shaw said. "I was not hired to *'kill'* a claim jumper. I was hired to help even the odds against a lone miner if there was to be a fight. As it turned out, I learned that a group of men were going to move on the mine on a certain date. Knowing the odds against the miner, I had no other choice."

Samuel snorted disdainfully. "You shot first, from a position of concealment. What would you call it? There's an important distinction to be made here. You could have stood beside the miner in his fight. For me, I have my own definition, and so would the law!"

"Mr. Roark," Shaw explained, "the miner wanted it known that he could hold his claim but he didn't want it known that he had help. He knew they'd be coming. He wasn't afraid to fight them, but he was pragmatic enough to understand he couldn't hope to win alone." Shaw paused. He'd already said too much, but since Samuel already knew the identity of his client, he decided to offer another angle.

"Mr. Roark, when one is faced with a man — three men, in fact — who will kill without hesitation, and they're bent on doing exactly that, and cannot be dissuaded by argument, which party actually fires the first shot is not really an issue. When an army is facing a determined enemy who intends to attack, do they wait to be fired on first before opening their barrage?"

"But the *'enemy'* didn't know you were there!"

"Yes, it happened that I shot first, but the killing itself was preordained. Whether I stood beside the miner or stood off some distance, I was still siding with him in a gunfight. Not taking a hand would mean the miner would now be dead and others would be sitting on a claim that they weren't entitled to."

Samuel snorted. "A mere technical distinction, to say the least. You shot, from a position of concealment, at a man who was not aware of your presence. Regardless of his intentions, you would be hard pressed to make a case for self-defense."

Shaw laughed out loud. "Come on, Mr. Roark. You're an attorney, are you not? Who said anything at all about self-defense? Am I not legally justified as a citizen in defending the life and property of others when I see them threatened? For that matter, if I determine that a violent act against a fellow citizen is imminent, is there some requirement that you are aware of that I first call out or otherwise announce myself before I act?"

After a moment, Samuel nodded and smiled. "You're a careful man, it seems. Yes, one would find it difficult bringing you up on charges of murder for coming to the aid of a threatened citizen." He leaned forward with a look of intensity, and then continued to spar with Shaw. "Of course, your assignment could involve the presumption that you knew in advance that to successfully protect your client's interests, you'd have to do precisely what you did. It *was* an ambush, Mr. Shaw." Samuel concluded, smiling. "But I also see that the law would be forced to accept the fact that you had acted in a technically lawful manner, as long as the court did not *officially* know of the contract you had been fulfilling."

"What contract, Mr. Roark?"

Samuel smiled broadly. "Of course." He nodded. "There was no contract." Then he shook his head gently. "None of that really matters in this case, because I'm not hiring you to murder anyone, or even kill anyone."

Shaw looked at Samuel quizzically. "You told me you want these men found and put to death. I believe those were your words. You didn't say you wanted them brought to trial. That sounds like murder to me."

Samuel laughed abruptly. "Don't be silly, Mr. Shaw, of course it's *murder*. But I don't want *you* to murder anyone. I merely want you to find the men responsible for my son's death. After you've located them," Samuel leaned forward and whispered – his teeth clenched, "I intend to kill them myself. I intend to kill the man who shot my son — and the man who hired him and anyone else you manage to identify who was personally involved."

Motive

"He said what?" Sarah couldn't believe what she'd just heard.

They were sitting together in the restaurant over a cup of coffee and, despite the sensitivity of the topic, Sarah didn't even try to keep her voice down.

"He wants me to find the men involved in the killing of Stuart. Once I have, he intends to kill them himself," Shaw replied, taking a sip of coffee. His calm, matter-of-fact tone exasperated Sarah even more.

"Surely, Matt, you're not considering this foolish idea?" she exclaimed. "Why, the very thought of it goes against everything I've ever known about Samuel. He's a pacifist. My God, he's a lawyer! His experiences in the war left him with a passionate hatred for violence, and for men of violence. That's why I was so disturbed to find he had sent for you in the first place." She shook her head. "You can tell he's not well. He would never consider this under normal circumstances."

"Sarah, it's really not my place to judge what your husband would or wouldn't do under normal circumstances. His son was murdered. He himself was marked for murder and still may be targeted for murder. We have no way of knowing. I hope you'd agree that these are *not* normal circumstances for a man — or for a family. For that matter, I see nothing fundamentally wrong with his request."

She cocked her head. "You don't see anything wrong?" Her voice — just above a whisper — held a barely controlled anger.

"No, I don't. Speaking simply from the standpoint of a *man*, I'd feel compelled to search out the killer of a member of my family and challenge him whether or not society approved. We aren't talking about some trivial slight of honor, but the brutal murder of a young man and the apparent lack of any legal remedies being available to the victim's family. People have been killed for much less.

"Of course it would be my preference to establish evidence that the law and the courts can use and I assure you any investigation I undertake will work toward that goal." Shaw shook his head. "In fact, Sarah, I see nothing fundamentally wrong with Samuel's request, and I can't find a valid reason not to help him."

For several seconds, Sarah was stunned into silence, unable to formulate a response. When she finally gathered her thoughts, she replied with hot anger. "But that's crazy! What about bringing the men to justice? You yourself used that term. Surely you can see the wrong in what you and Samuel are conspiring to do? Why, it would be illegal, would it not?"

"Yes, technically it would be illegal. But I can, to my own satisfaction, reconcile the illegality of it with the morality of it. We'll never get a conviction without evidence. Only a confession or eyewitness testimony would count in a court of law. The man who shot Stuart would never confess and there were no other eyewitnesses. Without either, we have no justice. So, what's left?"

Shaw's eyes roamed the room as if looking for the right words. "In cases such as this, normally law-abiding men might seek a personal justice, if they're willing to accept the consequences for their acts. Besides, we have no way of knowing at this point if Samuel doesn't intend to face the man rather than merely murdering him. Samuel may insist it be a fair fight."

Sarah was dubious and started to interrupt, but Shaw raised his hand and continued: "Man's law does not always fill the voids. Sometimes the law doesn't go far enough. There are men who feel no written law applies to them.

They hurt anyone they want; they take what they want. When men like that are encountered, there isn't always a legal authority available for society's protection. In such cases, good and just citizens often must decide if the presence of personal justice makes up for the absence of society's law. If they decide it does, then they have to accept responsibility for seeing justice done, in whatever form is necessary."

"An eye for an eye?" Sarah asked bitterly.

"It's not as simple as that but, yes, an eye for an eye. That concept was understood long before courts were established to mete out justice under any modern kind of legal system. Good men must confront bad men, for the benefit of all men. This has always been understood."

"What if Stuart wouldn't want justice like that?" Sarah was on the verge of tears.

"Sarah, a person who wouldn't want it doesn't really deserve it. Right now, there's a man who takes money to kill otherwise innocent people. He's free to kill again. You knew Stuart, I didn't. Tell me now so I can pack up and ride away before this goes too far. How would Stuart have reacted if the bullet had struck his father, or you? How hard would he be arguing with me, against hunting down the killer even if it meant the killer had to die? Tell me Sarah, so I don't have to make a fool of myself further."

A single tear fell down her left cheek. She looked straight into Shaw's eyes, still angry, still defiant, but after drawing a shaking breath she whispered, "He'd want to kill them all, no matter whom, no matter how many; no matter how long it took. Stuart would do exactly what Samuel is doing, except perhaps he would not have consulted a *professional*!"

* * * *

Sarah returned to the ranch that afternoon, while Shaw

stayed in town. As he watched her ride away, he was struck with a most overpowering sense of melancholy. Sarah's use of the term "professional" had stung. He knew now that she hated him for what he stood for. He couldn't really blame her. She and people like her were the future of the country. No matter how hard he tried, Shaw could not envision a place for him in that future.

She was right, of course. He had arrived at the moment he knew would ultimately come. While he desperately wanted her understanding, he knew Sarah would never accept that, illogical as it might seem, some circumstances in life demanded amoral responses. While normally he didn't set out to commit a killing, he understood that in many cases a killing would be exactly the right solution to an otherwise irresolvable dilemma — as long as the right people ended up dead.

Why was it that people who would consider the deaths of dozens or hundreds or even thousands of enemy soldiers in conflict as moral and justified, regardless of the cause for which they fought, would shrink from the notion that society's war against the lawless required violent men willing to kill? Shaw might succeed in gathering the evidence necessary to gain a conviction of Stuart's killer and that would still be his primary goal, but it was highly unlikely the shooter would provide the testimony to convict the man who ordered the murder. One without the other wouldn't be justice.

At the same time, Shaw had no reason to believe that the actual killer would be the kind of man who'd give up without a fight, nor did he believe his own talents were necessarily superior to the man they hunted. He had no way of actually knowing this in advance. While he was confident in his own abilities, this endeavor could quite possibly lead to the deaths of Samuel and himself, rather than the man or men they hunted. The difference between the terms "murder" and "killing" were often minor legal distinctions and Shaw believed that some people, by their very actions, deserved killing.

Something inside told him this was the woman he'd always hoped to find yet, without a doubt, she was as lost to him now as if he'd never encountered her. Of course, she was already married to another man, even though Shaw believed that union looked too fragile to survive the events that had overwhelmed it. What most convinced him was that Sarah made no secret that she detested everything he represented.

While he ought just to saddle up and ride away, he couldn't do it. First, there was the case before him reawakening the hunter's instincts and, second, there was Sarah. He'd fallen in love with this woman. He knew that nothing good could come of it, but the truth of it could not be denied and he'd do just about anything to remain near her, even if it meant she'd only hate him more. Another truth, starker and equally undeniable, was that the end of this trail would only bring more heartache for everyone involved.

Shaw turned away and walked up the street to the town marshal's office. Entering, Shaw found it was a two-room affair, consisting of a front office with two small cells in a rear wing. The marshal was in.

He wasn't sure what he'd expected, but he found himself mildly surprised at the man sitting behind the desk. Based on the story Sarah told, he'd pictured the town marshal as lazy, stupid and overweight. Yet this man still evoked the image of a military uniform, proudly worn. The marshal was calmly cleaning his fingernails with a long, slim-bladed "hide-out" knife commonly worn in the boot top. While Shaw might be impressed by the *man*, he knew that this didn't automatically place the marshal firmly on the side of law and order, despite his badge.

The marshal didn't smile, nor did Shaw.

"I'm Marshal Morg Blake. What can I do for you?"

Blake asked evenly. He'd noticed Shaw's dress, his grooming and, of course, his gun. This was not one of those rowdy cow towns where a no-gun policy was needed to stifle whiskey-induced merriment, or the all-too-frequent serious gunplay. This was a mining town, long past its wild and lawless boomtown period and the predictable chaos that seemed to accompany all such settlements in their early stages. In this town, guns were worn freely, or not, depending on the person. Having a gun didn't mark a man one way or another. But some men bore more subtle marks that were as obvious to a lawman as a sign around their necks.

"May I have a seat?" Shaw asked. At the marshal's nod, Shaw took a seat in front of the man's desk. "My name is Shaw. I've been retained by Samuel Roark to look into the murder of his son."

Blake's eyes studied Shaw. "Look into it or avenge it?" he asked matter-of-factly.

Shaw smiled. The question held no malice. It was a simple and honest question. "That hasn't been established yet. For now, I'm looking into the murder. Where that leads, and to what eventuality — well, it's too early to predict."

Blake nodded. Shaw knew he had a reputation that was known by many authorities. Blake had undoubtedly heard of him and knew a little of his character. Shaw had demonstrated that he could be a dangerous man to the right people but what Blake could not be sure of at present was whether or not Shaw posed a danger to him, professionally or personally.

"What do you want from me?" Blake asked as he reached behind him for a well-worn coffee pot. He tested the heat with his hand and, satisfied, poured a cup of coffee for himself. Holding the pot up, he offered a cup to Shaw.

Shaw declined. "I'd like your impressions of the murder. To hear what you did, what you discovered...what you may have surmised. Then I'd like to hear why you didn't go farther with it, if what Sarah Roark says is true." Shaw stated it flatly, knowing Blake would not like it.

There was a slight narrowing of Blake's eyes, but nothing else. It seemed Shaw was right, but while the marshal probably didn't like being confronted in this manner, he didn't overreact either. "Why should I share this information with you? You have no official standing, do you? You're not associated with the law, last I heard." Blake sipped his coffee. "Just the opposite, I'd guess."

"No. I have no official capacity. I'm conducting an inquiry. I'm a simple man who sees things as they are. You, on the other hand, do have an official capacity." Shaw paused for a couple of seconds to let the words sink in. "One that appears to have not been as aggressively utilized as it could have been. So, where does that leave the two of us?"

Blake's face reddened. He stared with a look of intensity that Shaw recognized as part anger and probably a little embarrassment thrown in for good measure. In either case, Shaw wasn't sure how far he could push Blake before things turned ugly.

The marshal finally took a deep breath. "I don't know who killed Stuart. I wish I did — I liked the lad. Everyone did. I do know that no local man made that shot. He was a professional. He burrowed into a snow pile and wrapped himself up for quite a while. I can't understand how he didn't freeze, or how he even managed to aim a rifle. Ten minutes in that weather and I'd have been shivering so bad I wouldn't have been able to hold my weezer to take a piss!" When Shaw didn't respond to the jest, Blake added. "Anyway, by the time I was able to get to the ranch, a couple days had passed. Wind had blown away all the tracks except those down the slope protected by the cedars. I noted the man wore snowshoes and I didn't have any. I followed as long as I could. Anyway, his trail didn't last so we never found where he'd kept his horse, or which direction he left in."

Shaw pondered. So far, Blake had offered nothing he hadn't already established. On the other hand, he'd left out a lot of things that he could have offered. Shaw decided to push him a bit. "The nearest town is a good distance away. That time of year, the passes are no doubt closed. I'd bet the only clear road out of this country goes from Eagle Town toward Soulard to the west. That's the nearest rail line. I'm thinking the killer had to have come through Eagle Town from Soulard. Perhaps he even stayed a while, asking questions; looking at the lay of the land and meeting with his benefactor. A curious town marshal would, to my way of thinking, notice strangers; ask a couple of questions of his own."

"Who said he was a *hired* killer?" Blake asked mildly. "What makes you think he wasn't just some man who had a grudge against Roark?"

"You yourself said you thought he was a professional. Do you have so many professional long-shooters living in Eagle Town that they'd go unnoticed by the law? I don't believe it for a minute. But, I don't have an answer to it either. Rest assured, I will. For now, I'm going to operate on the assumption the killer was brought in by someone local; someone who would benefit by Roark's death, either financially or otherwise."

"Who might that be?" Blake asked.

"I was hoping you'd tell me," Shaw responded with a slight smile.

After a long hesitation, Blake shook his head. "Nope. That doesn't fit with anything I know about. Somewhere, somehow, Roark made an enemy. I couldn't solve the killing, so I sent everything I had to the sheriff in Soulard. Unless something else comes up, I'm no longer looking."

"Maybe you aren't, but know that I am. One word of warning and I will leave you alone."

Blake's eyes narrowed. "I'm not in the habit of taking warnings from strangers in my town, friend."

Shaw's easy smile did not touch his cold eyes. "Nevertheless Blake, understand that since you've neglected to, I've taken on the task of looking into this matter further. A boy's been murdered in your jurisdiction and, while it appears there are some logical leads to follow, for some reason you've decided not to follow them. It makes a person wonder. Certainly the Roark's do and, after hearing their story and talking to you, I have to wonder how you've kept your job."

Blake started to get up. Shaw knew the man's first inclination would be to toss Shaw out onto the street if he could, but evidently better judgment reined him in. He settled back into his chair and took another deep breath. Shaw smiled evenly, unconcerned with any potential action the marshal might be contemplating.

"So now that I've put you on notice, I'll let you know that I'll follow this trail wherever it leads. It's what I do for a living. It's what I've done for a long time and, so far, I've never failed."

For the first time, Shaw noticed something in Blake's eyes. Where man-hunters were concerned, Shaw was one of the best but, all at once, he had a feeling this man found something Shaw had said mildly ironic. Instinctively, he wondered if it might not be time to fold his hand and get out of the game. Shaw stood up and left the office.

He stood on the walk for a few moments, taking in the town, getting a feel for the pace and activity. From this moment on, he had to be very careful. He'd declared himself a player in a most dangerous game. He needed to measure the cadence of life on the street at a time when it was peaceful and presented no threat to him. This would help him recognize any telltale signs that something was amiss later on. The people in mining towns had a way of knowing when the "fuse was lit," so to speak. They had a sixth sense when something was about to blow and Shaw wanted to recognize it when the time came.

Now that word would quickly spread about his presence, and his mission, he'd have a target painted on his back. If the killer was a local man, he'd soon know Shaw was looking for evidence of his crime. If in fact the killer was a professional for hire who had long since departed the area, it could then be assumed the client was a local man and would be interested in keeping the truth deeply buried. In either case, Shaw presented a problem and, because of that, he would now be in constant danger.

Shaw walked across the street to the hotel and restaurant that advertised available rooms. He had much to do and it was not practical returning to the Roarks' ranch on a routine basis. As much as he desired seeing Sarah again, he knew the sooner he put her out of his mind the better. He didn't want to damage her reputation and, frankly, she was a distraction he could no longer afford.

After securing a room, he rode his horse to the stable and placed it in a stall, hanging the saddle and tack on hooks. The hostler appeared from a rear door and strode over to Shaw with a nod. "Full feed and water, two-bits a day," he said with a friendly smile.

Shaw looked the man over. He was older, gray haired and full bearded, and his face bore the lines of a hard-working man, of the type who had probably known a lot of different jobs over time. His face was sun-darkened with age spots and Shaw guessed he was on the other side of fifty, but he moved like a younger man, with an economy of motion. Shaw liked him immediately.

"Two-bits it is then." Shaw counted out his coins. "Here's a week's advance. You take care to mind his tail," Shaw said, smiling. "He flicks it just before he kicks."

The hostler chuckled. "I've been kicked."

Shaw held out his hand. "Name's Shaw."

"Tucker Frey," the hostler replied. They shook.

Shaw noted the hostler was missing his little finger on his right hand. "Looks like you've been bit, too."

The hostler looked at his hand and smiled ruefully. "That? Naw, a Union saber took that off at the 'Crater'. I'd already fired the charge in my '*Mississippi*', and it seems I was just a mite late with my bayonet."

"Better late than never." Shaw then added. "I was there as well."

Frey looked surprised. "Yank?"

"Guilty." Shaw smiled. Surmising he was speaking to a former Confederate soldier, he added, "But I promise I didn't use a saber."

"Aw, I know it wasn't you." The hostler chuckled. "That officer's dead and buried. Got his saber in a trunk back of the stable. I said I was late with my bayonet — but not *that* late." The hostler dipped his head and went about his chores.

Shaw looked around. The stable was a well-kept place. Hostlers were a lot like barbers and bartenders. They worked hard, listened a lot and normally talked little. Small towns held few secrets from such men and much of what they heard they kept to themselves. Not so much out of a sense of propriety, but rather because such people tended to be ignored. You couldn't pass on gossip if you had nobody to talk to. Shaw made a mental note to come back and spend some time with the old soldier.

The afternoon sun was starting to dip behind a distant peak and the temperature would soon fall dramatically. Shaw walked across to the restaurant and ordered dinner. As he ate, he contemplated what he'd learned about Blake. While not openly hostile, the man hadn't been completely forthcoming. There could be several reasons for this. Shaw knew a town marshal had to be cognizant of the local politics. Sometimes they strode a fine line between enforcing the law as it was written, and enforcing the law as town leaders interpreted it. Marshals, being mostly

80

honest men, generally understood that discretion was demanded of them and used it when necessary.

On the other hand, the idea of graft was not out of the question. Marshals didn't receive a large salary. It wasn't uncommon for one to receive gratuities for certain favors rendered. For a few, the line between being a full-time lawman and a part-time outlaw was sometimes a little fuzzy. Shaw took for granted Blake hadn't told him everything he knew. The question was, did he know anything that might help in his search and, if so, what would Shaw have to do to gain his cooperation — if that were even possible?

After dinner, Shaw retired to his room for the night. The saloons and gambling halls held no interest for him. A good night's sleep in a bed rather than a bedroll was all he wanted right now. In the morning, he'd speak with Samuel again.

The hunt was on.

* * * *

After breakfast, Shaw returned to Samuel's law office. He knocked and was immediately called in. The unpleasant odor of the previous afternoon was somewhat diminished by the cooler morning temperatures, but it hadn't disappeared. It was possible Samuel had slept in his chair, as there was no evidence he'd moved at all since Shaw left him yesterday.

Samuel still wore the same clothes, and he had a drink on the table beside him.

Shaw was struck by the incongruity of the scene and what he knew about the man. Samuel Roark was educated, bookish and articulate. Shaw could believe that the old Samuel would have been shocked at the new. Perhaps it could be explained away by grief and a loss of all concern for what others thought, but Shaw was growing suspicious that this might be a staged scene; an act for someone's benefit, but for whose? Was it meant for Shaw or Sarah — or for someone else entirely?

It was a difficult thing to do to degrade oneself publicly; to establish that you're a broken shell of what you once were. Deliberately allowing oneself to become something contemptible in the eyes of others was a hard part to play convincingly or to maintain indefinitely. If this was an act, it was certainly a great one.

"So, where do we begin?" Samuel asked directly after Shaw sat.

"You tell me everything I need to know, and I decide if it's enough to go on."

"How do I know what you need to know?" Samuel asked coyly.

"You've had more time to think about this than anyone. Sarah told me a little about some trouble you've had with a local rancher, but it's possible that has nothing to do with it. Perhaps it goes back further than that. Have you had difficulties with anyone else locally?"

Samuel shook his head. "Not killing trouble," Samuel said. "I'm a small town lawyer and small time rancher. I prepare wills and handle property transfers and register deeds. The only time I actually appeared in court since coming west was over that trouble that Sarah referred to. At first, I didn't think of it as such a major thing."

"Okay, talk to me about that."

"All right, if you want to know, a rancher named Kent moved in a few years ago and claimed a nice high flat piece of grass bordering my property to the north. It's excellent summer graze. Kent has a small outfit just like mine. He and his family run it small, squeezing out just enough profit to make it worth keeping. He has a couple of mining claims located on the property that he works as well. Between the two concerns, ranching and mining, they do all right."

He sipped his drink, licked his lips. "Another rancher

named Mason liked that piece of grass. He claimed Kent sold it to him. He even had a bill of sale. Kent disagreed and we went to court. It wasn't hard showing the bill of sale was fraudulent. The problem was, Mason is a powerful man and his ranch spends a lot of money here in town. It was hard getting a jury to decide against him. Some of them were embarrassed and not just a little intimidated by his power. But they did the right thing because my client promised not to swear out a charge of attempted theft. Even then, those jurors who had stores or businesses in town no longer get any of Mason's money."

"Sounds like a man who might hold a grudge," Shaw offered. "About that bill of sale, how was it fraudulent and how'd Mason explain it away?"

"Ah, that's where it gets interesting." He held up his glass and grinned lopsidedly. "Mason claimed he had his foreman make an offer to Kent. Mason explained he gave his foreman some cash to cover the purchase and the foreman came back with the bill of sale. After that, the foreman disappeared, ostensibly with the money — two thousand dollars. Mason was quite surprised to find the bill was fraudulent. He was not, however, apologetic. In his complete and utter arrogance, he even suggested that the jury award him that parcel of land anyway, as his herd was larger and he needed the ground more than the Kent ranch." Samuel shook his head, ruefully. "I made sure the jury understood that this was outside the limits of their authority. Had I not, I'm sure they would've gone and awarded Mason the land."

"And for this, he'd hold you responsible? The case was full of holes from the beginning. Any lawyer could have won the judgment."

"You doubt my considerable legal talents?" Samuel was smiling and Shaw was surprised at his attempt at humor. It seemed out of character for a man consumed by the tragedies that befell his family and his physical state.

"I managed to make Mason look rather silly on the stand. It wasn't that I did so deliberately, but arrogant men with limited intelligence make for clumsy witnesses." Samuel offered a trace of a smile at the memory. "You see, of the three lawyers in town, I was the only one who would take the case for the Kent's. Without representation, it's possible the Kent claim wouldn't have been believed by the circuit judge."

"Why?"

"Mason presented witnesses that confirmed Kent's signature on the bill was authentic. A couple of them were respected townsfolk. I argued that Kent was illiterate and could not write and had never — in his entire life — signed his name to any legal document. This defense of course could have been a fabrication, but to prove it I retrieved his original claim to the property in question, as well as the mining claims he maintains. These were on file in Soulard. In each case, he made his mark wherever a signature was required. We even produced his wartime pay book, which further demonstrated the history of illiteracy. The attempt to force the authenticity of the bill of sale was infantile; nearly comedic. The jury agreed, albeit with some hesitation." Samuel lifted his glass and took a drink and grimaced at the bite of the whiskey. "Case closed, or so I thought."

"And then?" Shaw prompted, watching with interest as Samuel set down his glass. His hand did not tremble and his physical dexterity was smooth and natural. The man may be drinking, but he wasn't drunk.

"And then there were some minor incidents of harassment which I took in my stride." Samuel had a distant look in his eyes. Anger showed in his expression and Shaw found it genuine.

"Tell me about them."

Samuel re-focused his gaze, settling on Shaw's face, the anger still there. "Some ruffians who work for Mason accosted me in one of the local stores. Nothing serious, but it badly frightened Sarah." He paused, and then offered, "You must understand that it's difficult for a man to see his wife frightened; yet, because of conscience and a belief that violence is fruitless, I did nothing to resist it."

"Who were the men?"

"Well, the one in charge was the heir-apparent to the missing foreman. His name is Parker Lewis. There's a rumor he may be known under other names in other jurisdictions, if you know what I mean. His two companions I can't name. It doesn't matter. They were minor thugs who I could have whipped at any time, had I been so inclined."

Shaw looked closely at Samuel to see if he was making an idle boast. Samuel noticed and smiled.

"Surprised? No, Mr. Shaw, I'm not a gunman and I don't like violence for its own sake, but I am — or, at least, I was — a fairly accomplished amateur boxer. I actually enjoyed fighting in the years before the war." His face bore a hint of a smile touched with sadness. "Anyway, these men were confident they had me buffaloed. I had no reason to show them differently. One doesn't demonstrate one's talents to just any audience. The day may come when I would need to get serious, and I wanted my skills to remain unknown."

Shaw nodded. He'd begun wondering just how legitimate the current persona of Samuel Roark really was. He was sure there'd be another surprise or two along the way. "So, they roughed you up a little in front of Sarah, and went on their way. And then what?"

Samuel took another drink. "Then, there were incidents of a more violent nature. Some cattle were killed when they were run off the edge of a ravine. At first, we thought they may have been running from a predator, but some suspicious tracks made us reconsider. And then there was a horse. Stuart had…" Samuel's voice trailed off. Then,

85

blinking his eyes he continued: "Stuart had to walk in one night after he'd been doing a count of our cattle. He'd picketed his horse while checking a rather treacherous canyon. He heard a shot, and later he found his horse dead." His tone darkened and he ground out between clenched teeth, "Finally, there was the incident of the desecration of our daughter's grave."

Samuel's face suddenly turned to stone. Shaw recognized a different kind of anger present now; a *killing* anger, barely suppressed, but hidden behind a poker-player's expression. Shaw remembered that Samuel had been a soldier, and of course there was the new revelation of his fighting past. Perhaps he was a pacifist according to his own admission and in the opinion of Sarah, but Shaw could see before him a man for whom the idea of violence was not totally foreign. Shaw had originally wondered if Samuel was truly serious about finding the killer or killers of his son and personally seeing to their fate. There was little doubt now this man had finally been presented with a reason to kill.

Samuel went on: "My daughter, little Rebecca, we called her Becca. Her grave stands on a slope overlooking our home place."

"I've seen it."

Samuel leaned forward in his chair and fixed Shaw with a powerfully intense gaze. When he spoke, he did so with a slowly measured pace, each word individually emphasized by the deadliness of his expression. "You can insult a man, Mr. Shaw; you can intimidate him or threaten him or do a hundred things to get his goat and he will either let it pass or he'll fight back. As an educated man, a passive man with a family, I'm inclined to let many things pass. I know that violence is seldom rewarded with feelings of serenity or peacefulness and then there is also a spiritual and emotional cost to doing violence. I believe that the only way for a man to separate himself from his violent past is to completely repudiate violence in all its forms."

Samuel sat back heavily and looked about the room; his gaze falling on a wall containing a shelf filled with leather-bound law books. Then he resumed speaking. "Of course, there is a cost involved there as well. One's reputation or character can be adversely judged by people accustomed to responding to insult with deadly earnestness. If a man has a reputation for being passive, it can mean his courage is in question. Ordinarily I wouldn't worry about such nonsense — *but there comes a limit!*" Samuel ground out those last words and his eyes brimmed with un-shed tears. Now, his voice was tremulous: "I am a peaceful man, Mr. Shaw, but certain things are just not allowed. The grave of a precious little girl must not be trampled by the hoofs of horses and defaced with animal excrement! This goes beyond insult — beyond anything I could bear." His voice broke. "Or at least I thought it was."

Shaw remained silent, listening.

"I was enraged! I'd planned to seek out Mason and challenge him to fight with fists, knives or guns; whatever he chose. Sarah talked me out of it. If there is anyone more passive than me, it's my lovely Sarah."

Samuel smiled, sadly. "Now, in retrospect I wonder if doing something might have prevented what eventually happened..." He pressed a big fist against his forehead. "I think I should just have killed the man. I think that would have saved Stuart's life, even if it condemned mine."

Shaw was developing an understanding of this man that completely belied his present appearance. Despite the man's grief and fragile mental state, Samuel was apparently sane. He was simply driven beyond a normal man's capacity to suffer humiliation and rage and still contain it. There were more than just mental devils at work here. Samuel's mind was clear, but there'd been too many heavy blows to his mortal soul. Perhaps there was nothing he could have done to alter the events as they unfolded, but the uncertainties, the possibilities, were driving him beyond normal reason.

Shaw could tell that little else mattered to Samuel any more; certainly not his own life. How much he thought of Sarah was unknown. Samuel was at the initial stages of something known as a *death run*. Not a physical death per se, but certainly an emotional one. Shaw was certain that if Samuel succeeded in killing those responsible for the death of his son, he wouldn't be emotionally fulfilled. Shaw felt confident that at that point, rather than being healed, Samuel would finally give himself over to his demons.

For several minutes, he pondered what Samuel had told him. He decided it was a good time to alter the direction of their discussion, if for no other reason than to move past these memories and focus on the present task.

"What might be the chances that Stuart was actually the target of the killer?" Shaw asked.

Samuel glanced up, brow furrowed. "None, I would think. Stuart was wearing my hat and coat; it was rapidly getting dark and the killer had only a second or two to decide to shoot. I can't imagine any reason the shot was intended for anyone other than me."

"Well then, tell me about the moments leading up to the killing. Recall your observations as best you can," Shaw prompted gently.

Samuel's glance held a bit of irritation. "As best I can recall? Sir, can't you understand that those moments are indelibly imprinted on my memory like a photograph? I can recall the death of my son as if it were five minutes ago. The pain of it is as strong as if Stuart were lying on the floor of this office right now."

"I'm sorry," Shaw acknowledged. "I understand this is difficult. If you can, please indulge me and my questions for a little while longer."

Samuel took a deep breath, and then sighed. "Fair enough." He leaned back and closed his eyes and rubbed his forehead. "I had seen to the horses. It was late afternoon and the sun was setting. It had been a cold day, blustery and occasionally windy. I don't like the cold and tend to move very quickly while outdoors in the winter." Samuel offered a trace of a wry smile. "I run, actually. It makes Sarah laugh to see me. I don't suppose I'd offered the killer a very good shot during those times when I was visible to him." He shrugged. "I'd neglected to bring in wood for the night and Stuart offered to do it for me. He put on my coat—"

Shaw interrupted, "Why your coat?"

Samuel smiled sadly at the memory. "His was soaked from chopping holes through the ice in the tanks for the cattle. Anyway, he put on my coat and I told him the coat went with the hat and if he was going to take one he had to take the other, or silly words to that effect. He put them both on." Samuel's eyes misted and he blinked back the tears. "I remember being proud of how he filled out the coat; of the man he'd become." His voice cracked and then he hardened his tone and went on: "Anyway, he went outside and it was a moment later, five or ten seconds — the time it takes to walk to the first woodpile — when we heard the shot. I was stunned. At first, I couldn't understand why someone was shooting outside our home and then Stuart called for me. I ran outside and found him face down in the snow. There was — there was quite a lot of blood; way too much blood. You yourself would understand, I'm sure, that when you see that much blood, you instinctively know there is no hope even though you pray for a miracle."

Shaw nodded but didn't speak.

Samuel's voice went soft, almost a whisper. "I didn't think. I just dragged him into the house. Sarah had taken the rifle down and was standing there." Samuel rubbed his eyes and bowed his head. "I didn't know what to do." He whispered, "*I didn't know what to do.* By the time I got

Stuart in the house, he was already dead."

Samuel paused for a lengthy half a minute. When he resumed, Shaw noted the man was silently crying. There were no sobs, just steady tears streaming down his cheeks. "I'm afraid I don't recall much of the rest of the evening — except for Sarah. She doused the lights so no one could fire into the cabin and remained at the door with the rifle in her hands until well after dark." He slumped back in his chair, as if exhausted, and put his hand over his eyes.

"It doesn't sound as if the killer had a great deal of time to make the shot," Shaw observed. "Most likely considering Stuart was dressed in your coat and hat, he thought it was you and when Stuart paused at the wood pile the shooter took that opportunity to fire."

"Those were our thoughts as well."

"So, I guess we can operate on the assumption you were in fact the actual target of the killer. But the motive seems too obvious. Mason would have to know he'd be suspected of the crime."

"Mason is a brute. He's incapable of a sophisticated thought. At the same time, he's totally convinced of his own rightness. Therefore, I wronged him and anything he does to me is justified."

"And you don't think hiring a killing is beneath him?"

"I'm certain he ordered his men to harass me; the killing of my stock; Stuart's horse. All these things were done at his behest, I'm sure. He even came to our home with a large crew, ostensibly to apologize for it." Samuel made a derisive sound. "Who brings an army to offer an apology?"

Shaw pondered this. "You're probably right. But remember he has men who ride for *him*. It's possible one or more of them decided to make your life miserable just because you cut Mason down to size. As long as he's the *cock-o'-the-walk*, they are too. When someone cuts him down, their reputations are diminished as well. I'm not

90

saying it's a fact, only a possibility we should consider."

"I suppose it's possible, but we would then have to consider the cost of hiring a professional killer. I wouldn't think a cowhand could afford it."

"If a killer was actually hired, you mean. Maybe one of the hands did the killing?"

"Would such a thing be possible?" Samuel asked. "Could you make such a shot?"

"In an uncertain wind, at that range in freezing temperatures — I'd hesitate to chance it even under better conditions."

"If one of his hands was that good, surely we'd know about it in town."

"True," Shaw admitted. No, everything points to a professional. I just wanted to explore other options."

"So, what's your next move?"

"I may have to send a couple of telegrams. I can send them off by the stage, or ride to Soulard and send them from there, but that's a day's ride one way."

"What would be the nature of your telegrams?"

"I need to query a couple sources of information. I believe the killer may have used a precision muzzle-loading target rifle, based on a musket cap I discovered on the trail near where the shooter lay." As he said it, he watched Samuel's face carefully.

Samuel's eyes were sharply focused again. "A muzzle-loading rifle? You're certain?"

"Not completely certain. Why, does that mean something to you?"

Samuel's eyes narrowed. "There was a horse — I'm trying to remember exactly, but I recall Stuart calling my attention to a horse that had such a rifle in a scabbard." Samuel cocked his head as if were listening to a far-off sound. "It was tied to a rail here in town. The rifle's stock was beautifully made. The tang was of the style known as a saw handle if I have the terminology correct. I recalled thinking it was odd because it was a percussion target rifle and I'd thought they went out of style a decade ago. It had a heavy octagon barrel by the impression it made in the leather of the scabbard. Also, it bore a telescopic sight. Stuart had never seen one and I'd only seen a couple in my lifetime. I took a moment to explain to him its use. Later, the horse was gone. We never saw the rider."

"When was this?" Shaw asked, with building excitement.

"I don't know," Samuel responded. "I can't recall, exactly. It was the beginning of winter, sometime before Christmas, I'm certain of that. Maybe a month or two before Stuart...." His voice dropped off. Then he looked at Shaw. "Is such a thing possible? A muzzle-loading rifle at that range?"

Shaw nodded. "It's certainly possible, but the timing isn't right. If this was our shooter, did he stay in the area, or was he just scouting? If he stayed, where did he remain hidden for the next couple months in mid-winter?" He shrugged. "It doesn't really matter right now. It's a start. Do you remember where the horse was tied?"

At first, Samuel's eyes were unfocused as if he was lost in thought. Then, all at once, he fixed Shaw with a cold stare. "Yes, I do. The horse was tied to a rail outside the marshal's office."

How the Game is Played

It was late afternoon when Shaw stepped out of Samuel's office and, as was his habit, he scanned the street. Immediately, he noted two men lounging at the entrance to the hotel. It appeared they took notice of him as well. Both men were dressed in range clothing rather than miner's garb and they carried side arms.

Shaw debated his choices. He could return to his room at the hotel but, by doing so, he'd force whatever confrontation might possibly be looming. Another alternative would be to go see Blake and question him about Samuel's revelation of the mysterious target rifle and the unseen rider. Putting off trouble seldom averted it for long and he much preferred to face issues forewarned, so he decided to see what these two cowhands intended. It was always better to meet a difficulty when mentally prepared.

As Shaw stepped off the walk onto the street, he noticed one of the men make a comment to the other and both rose. One of the men was left-handed and seemed to fancy himself a gunman; his holster being slung low with the gun-butt close to hand. This was in contrast to the other man who carried his gun in a sloppy, cross-draw manner with the weapon nestled so deeply into a Mexican loop holster that only the end of the butt showed above the leather. It was a safe method of carry, better suited for handling cattle from horseback or other strenuous activity but it precluded any hope of rapidly accessing the weapon. As Shaw stepped up onto the porch at the hotel, the gun-handy cowboy strode forward and addressed him.

"Are you Shaw?"

"I am. How can I help you?"

"I'm Wes Gordon. Mr. Mason sent me to fetch you. He'd like a word with you." Gordon's tone was not overly respectful, but not necessarily dismissive either. Gordon apparently was used to having people accommodate him.

"And where is Mr. Mason?" Shaw asked.

"He's out at his ranch, the Rocking R. It's about four miles south. He'd like you to be his guest for dinner." Gordon finished with a wry smile.

Shaw didn't relish going to another man's ranch this late in the afternoon. He'd be making the trip as darkness approached and he'd be without an ally and outgunned. Sending two men to pass such a message seemed like overkill when the message could have been left at the hotel or delivered by one man. He was mildly irritated and decided this was a perfect opportunity to put Mason and everyone else on record that he was not a man to be summoned at will, or coerced into a meeting. He had no doubt that if he decided to turn down the invitation, these men were supposed to deliver him to Mason. It was time for Mason, and whomever else might be interested, to receive an education in how to properly deal with him.

"That's a kind offer, Gordon. However, it's late and I'm not in the mood for a ride this evening. Besides, I've grown fond of the food here at the hotel. Perhaps Mr. Mason would care to join me here, say tomorrow evening?"

Gordon's eyes narrowed perceptibly and he chewed his lip. The other cowhand stood a little straighter. Gordon spoke again, forcefully: "Mr. Mason don't come to town much. I think you'd better come to the ranch with us."

Shaw smiled. "Thank you, but no."

He stepped toward the hotel entrance.

Gordon reached out with his right hand and laid the palm flat against Shaw's chest. Shaw hesitated momentarily, and then quickly grasped Gordon's wrist with his right hand and twisted it sharply to the right while stepping back and to the left. Gordon was forced to pivot left to avoid a broken arm, exposing his back to Shaw. When Gordon reached for his gun, it was no longer in its holster. Shaw let his arm go, and stepped back. He held Gordon's Colt revolver casually in his left hand. The other cowboy started to reach for his gun, but stopped abruptly when Shaw leveled a deadly warning look at him.

"It's always advisable never to lay a hand on a stranger," Shaw said, smiling slightly. "You got off lucky. There's another option to that move that would have left you with a broken elbow. You'd have been crippled for life, but I'm feeling generous today."

Gordon's eyes burned with heat. By now, a small but growing number of people were watching what was going on.

"You fancy yourself, don't you?" Shaw said.

Gordon glared.

"I suppose eventually I'll have to give you your gun back." Shaw flipped the Colt and caught it by the barrel and handed it out to the man, butt first. Surprised, Gordon reached for it instinctively but too late realized his mistake. Shaw caught his arm and threw him off the steps and into the street where he stumbled and sprawled on his face.

Turning to the other cowboy, Shaw said, "Here, hold this," and handed him Gordon's pistol. The cowboy reached for the gun as if it were a venomous snake. Shaw smiled and said, "Don't worry, oh, and don't be stupid." Then he turned away from the startled cowboy.

Stepping down off the veranda, Shaw walked up to Gordon, who'd already risen and was waiting, hate burning in his eyes. Shaw spoke evenly. "If I give you your gun back, I believe you'll make me kill you. I'd rather not do that. On the other hand, I don't believe I can expect you to be reasonable, can I?"

"The minute I get my gun back, I'll kill you with it!" Gordon spat out.

Shaw nodded. "I thought as much." His left arm snaked

out, deceptively fast, and his fist met Gordon's chin with a solid blow that made a sound like a stick cracking. Gordon staggered back two steps on rubbery legs and dropped to one knee. Trying to rise, he was unable to gain his balance and settled heavily on his left hip and elbow, shaking his head.

"That's known as a jab." Shaw walked in closely. "If you get up, I'll show you a left hook." He smiled. "I might even follow it up with a right-cross if I think you're a slow learner. By the end of the afternoon, you should be well educated."

"What's going on here?" Blake's voice boomed.

Shaw didn't turn to look, but kept his eyes focused on the gunman who was still trying to shake off the effects of the blow.

"Boxing lessons, Marshal," Shaw said evenly. "I think my friend here would rather give me a shooting lesson, but I much prefer quieter, more gentlemanly sports." Shaw smiled. "Wouldn't you agree?"

Blake wasn't smiling. Turning away from Gordon, Shaw fixed Blake with a hard look. Shaw was ready to continue the fight, whether with Gordon or the marshal, at that moment totally indifferent to the man's authority. Shaw stepped away and walked back to the hotel. Climbing the steps, he stopped, facing the cowboy. "You were smarter than Gordon. Best stay that way." Then he entered the hotel.

He walked into the restaurant portion, and took a deep breath. The brief confrontation had left him with that familiar anxious feeling; his muscles were still tingling in anticipation of a deadly fight that wasn't going to happen, at least not just yet. It would take a bit before he'd settle down and relax.

It was too early for dinner, but he didn't particularly want to go back to his room. He was thinking of how pleasant it would be to have dinner with Sarah, but he pushed the thought from his mind. Taking a table where he was not visible from a window and from which he could watch the door, he asked the waitress to bring two cups of coffee. She glanced at the empty chairs but Shaw graced her with such a warm smile, she returned it before moving off to fulfill his request.

A moment later, Blake came in and, seeing him at the table, walked over. "May I join you?"

Shaw indicated a chair. "Be my guest." Just then, the waitress set down the two cups of coffee.

Blake glanced at the two cups. "You expected company?"

"I made a bet with myself. It would either be you, or Gordon." Shaw smiled. "If it was you, then we'd have coffee together."

Blake wasn't smiling. "You've made a bad enemy. If Gordon came in here, he wouldn't be interested in coffee."

"How did you manage to keep him from coming in here, then?" Shaw took a sip of his coffee. It was good and strong.

"I told him to let me talk to you first. He'll probably be waiting for you when you leave."

Shaw nodded. "His funeral."

Blake looked at Shaw over the rim of his coffee cup. "They say he's pretty good."

There was a long pause while Shaw contemplated that. "I suppose he is," Shaw agreed. "Mostly, I've found what people say about reputations is seldom based on what they actually know. I suppose most of us go through life thinking we're better than the next guy. Sooner or later, we all meet our match, don't we?"

Blake sat back and drank some more coffee, shaking his head. "Well, I don't want you meeting your match tonight here in town, or Gordon for that matter. So after dinner, what say you go to your room and stay there?"

"House arrest?" Shaw said with good humor.

Blake shook his head again, but he wasn't smiling. "No, just a friendly request. Sooner or later, one of you is going to kill the other. I'd prefer it happened somewhere outside of town."

"Fair enough. Join me for dinner? I'd take it as a favor."

Blake agreed and they ordered dinner and sat drinking their coffee and making small talk about the mines and the hard winter. After the food arrived, they dug into it with gusto.

When the meal was done, Blake rolled a smoke and sat back with another cup of coffee.

Shaw asked, "With Gordon, do I have to worry about a shot from the dark?"

Blake shook his head. "I don't think so. But then, you never know. I think he'd face you if he thought he had an edge since he's pretty sure of himself. He killed a man last year. It was a clear case of self-defense — meaning there were witnesses."

"Other Mason men?"

Blake's eyes met Shaw's. "Yes. But I have no reason not to believe their statements."

"Of course."

"There are some good men who ride for Mason, Shaw. I won't call any of them liars."

"I don't suppose. But, what's your gut say?"

Blake hesitated before answering. "My gut tells me Gordon made sure he had witnesses, but the shooting seemed justified. The other man wasn't much; a hard-rock miner who drank up most of his weekly pay. There were some words exchanged in the Golden Nugget and Gordon killed him. The dead man had a gun in his hand when the smoke cleared and nobody refuted what the Mason cowboys said."

Shaw nodded. "Fair enough. So, tell me a little about Mason? What kind of man is he?"

Blake ran his hand across his chin as if irritated. "And just why would you would want to know that?"

"Gordon was inviting me to meet Mason at his ranch. I suppose I may end up having to go eventually. I just wanted to know if it was a good idea or not."

"I wouldn't. If Mason wants you bad enough, he'll come looking for you, eventually. Better to be here than there. Too much can happen to a man on the road to the Mason spread."

"A lot could happen to a man right here in town too," Shaw said. "It might make *your* job easier if I stayed here and waited for Mason to find me."

Blake's eyes narrowed. "What do you mean by that?"

Shaw smiled to take away any offense. "Nothing. It's just that times are changing. Gun fights and killings normally end with a court of law deciding the outcome. Maybe I present a problem for you that might conveniently go away if I were to be involved in gunplay with Gordon, or someone like him. Even if I won, I might end up in jail and out of your hair."

Blake shook his head. "No one likes gunplay. But I doubt you'd go to jail for killing Gordon — Mason either, for that matter, as long as it was a fair fight."

Shaw looked surprised.

"Don't look so shocked. Mason has few friends any more. He was never a friendly man in the past and, since taking that beating by Roark in court, he's positively rancorous now. Of course, anyone who fought him would have to fight a dozen men first. Mason doesn't go anywhere alone. You up for that?"

Shaw smiled. "It's been a while. Normally I try not to take on more than six or seven at once."

Blake took a drink of coffee and looked at Shaw over the rim of his cup. "You were cavalry, weren't you?"

Shaw nodded. "For a time. Is it that obvious?"

Blake smiled a real smile for the first time that Shaw

could recall. "Shows on a man; the way he carries himself. But mostly, the way he wades into trouble. Cavalry have this *Devil-May-Care* attitude; empty their guns and start slashing away with their sabers and the butts of their pistols. You have that look. It was present out there on the street. You see a problem, and you wade into it without thinking."

"Oh, I think," Shaw replied. "I think plenty. I've just never been too good at it."

"I don't buy that either." Blake drained his cup and waited while the waitress refilled it. Shaw declined more coffee. The waitress smiled and walked away.

"I get the feeling you have something to ask me," Blake prompted. "Well, no time like the present."

Shaw wondered if this was just intuition on Blake's part, or if he'd expected further questions. "Okay. Back a month or so before young Stuart was killed, there was a man came into town on a horse that carried a rather specialized rifle. It was a muzzle-loading target rifle, with a telescopic sight. The horse was tied up in front of your office. I'm wondering if you know anything about that."

Blake stared and Shaw continued: "I'm curious about that rifle, and someone who would carry such a gun. Then, I'm wondering why they would be stopping off at the town marshal's office. It gives a man a lot to ponder."

Blake remained silent long enough that Shaw wondered if the marshal was even going to respond to what was a thinly veiled accusation. Finally, the marshal said, "The man with that rifle came by well over a month before Stuart Roark was killed. He was here for one afternoon and then he left. He wasn't seen in town before that day, or after it. I didn't make any connection between him and Stuart's death at the time. I'm not sure I have yet. It could have been a coincidence, all things considered."

"Pardon me, Blake, but that's a bit weak. Somebody comes to town with a very special rifle, and a few weeks later somebody makes a nearly miraculous shot on a poor rancher's kid, and you don't see a connection?"

"Too much time passed," Blake countered. "It was the middle of winter. A man doesn't camp in the hills during that time of year. Where would he have stayed if not in town? Where did he go afterward? The killer was like a ghost and this man was no ghost. I'd have known if he was staying anywhere locally. People would have noticed him."

"What about Mason's place?" Shaw asked.

"Mason wouldn't be that stupid. If he hired someone to kill Roark, he certainly wouldn't have the shooter living at his ranch."

"Okay. Say you're right. Who was the man with the rifle?"

Blake seemed decidedly uncomfortable. He sipped his coffee and began to roll another smoke. When he was finished, he struck a match and fired up the tobacco, waving the match out. Then, in a low voice, he answered Shaw's question: "His name's Ballou. During the war, he was a sharpshooter. Probably the best in the world; at least I never saw any better. That rifle you saw on his horse is legendary. It was made by Stephens in New Jersey. They say it could kill at a mile!"

"You never 'saw' any better?" Shaw asked, pointedly.

Blake nodded. "I was the ranking sergeant in his company at the end of the war. I watched him make a lot of shots no other man I know could have made."

Shaw shook his head disgustedly and recounted what he'd learned, "So, about a month before a long-range rifle expert kills a local rancher's son, just such a shooter happens to come to town and visit you, and you don't make a connection? That would make you a piss-poor law man, wouldn't it?" Shaw fixed Blake with a glare. "Pretty poor by trade, or by intention?"

Blake's eyes flared "I said Mason wasn't too popular. I didn't say he wasn't powerful, or dangerous! He's not a man you want to cross." Blake looked away, as if embarrassed. "That sharpshooter, Ballou, could find a reason to come back and it's considered pretty much a given that he doesn't miss!" Blake paused. "This job doesn't pay much, but I'm not in a hurry to end up unemployed or, for that matter, dead."

Shaw looked at the man with barely concealed contempt. "So, you were the one he came to see. I'd guess that means you were the one who sent for him? Who paid the fee?"

"If I knew what you were talking about, that would make me an accessory to murder, wouldn't it?" Blake responded, poker-faced.

Shaw thought about that. How much could he tell Blake that wouldn't compromise his goal? If his guess was correct and he told Samuel, then it was entirely possible Samuel would want to settle up with Blake. Regardless of Blake's potential culpability, Shaw was not eager to become involved with anything that would result in an attack on a lawman — unless the lawman deserved it.

"I have a pretty good idea that legal charges are not in the near future for anyone involved." Shaw suggested, "I might be able to keep you out of it as long as you didn't know who the shooter was supposed to shoot."

"I didn't, I swear it. But since I was the one who brought Ballou to town in the first place, you can understand my dilemma."

Shaw nodded. "You're caught between a rock and a hard place. Roark doesn't seem like much right now, but he's an angry man."

"So Roark's hired you to settle with whoever was involved?"

Shaw didn't see any reason to share Samuel's actual intentions with this man. "If it can be proven, yes. But then, proof is sometimes a hard thing to come by, if you catch my drift."

Blake nodded. "I can't tell you who paid the fee. I don't officially know."

Shaw's eyes narrowed, but he didn't say anything.

Blake said, "I was asked by a lawyer here in town if I knew of any guns for hire. I asked if he was talking about gun fighters, and he indicated he was thinking more along the lines of a marksman. I told him I knew of a man. I was asked to find him and bring him here and I'd get a nice bonus. Since my job doesn't pay much, I sent a couple telegrams and a month later Ballou showed up at my office. He actually seemed happy to see me again, though I can't see why. We all hated him." He shrugged. "Anyway, I told him to take a room at the hotel, I sent a note to the lawyer, and I washed my hands of the whole affair. I didn't know what the deal was or who it was with. Ballou left town the next day and nothing happened for over a month. When young Roark was killed, at first I didn't put two and two together, until I looked the scene over. I guessed it had to be Ballou, but it didn't make any sense. Where had he gone for thirty days? The sheriff in Soulard hadn't seen him and he hadn't arrived there on the train. One day he was here, and the next he was gone. A little over a month later a boy dies and the shooter disappears into thin air with the passes all closed and only one way out of the valley. It didn't make any sense then, and it still doesn't."

"What's the lawyer's name?" Shaw asked.

Blake looked miserable. Finally, he surrendered the information: "Hardy. Wade Hardy. He's the lawyer Mason uses."

Shaw nodded, finally seeing a trail of evidence he could build on. Despite being the obvious suspect, it didn't appear Mason had done much to hide his tracks. Shaw was not one to jump to conclusions however, so — as far as he was concerned — the suspect list was still wide open. He was beginning to believe that Blake was being honest...finally.

"Okay, one last question. Where do I find Ballou?"

"You don't. You put out the word to the right people and he finds you. That's the only way he works. He receives messages through an intermediary in Dodge City. I have no idea what that man does with the messages; where he forwards the requests to. But if you need Ballou, you do it this way. Then one day, you look up and he's there."

"I need a name."

Blake nodded. "His name is Reinhardt Keys."

Shaw sat back. He was satisfied he now had a direction. Ballou could be tracked and hunted. A man who carried that kind of rifle would be known. It was like a calling-card. He stood up.

"Thanks, Blake. I'll keep this between the two of us. I have to find Ballou and it's not going to be easy if he knows I'm coming. I'm counting on you to honor your end of the agreement. I'll keep your name out of it, and you make sure you *stay* out of it! If you warn Ballou or tell anyone who might do so, all bets are off. You'll be fair game."

Blake nodded, and Shaw walked out of the room.

Gordon

While Shaw had hinted to Blake that he wouldn't venture out while Gordon was looking for blood, he hadn't actually promised. Besides, he was pretty certain Blake was simply doing his official duty as a civil servant and really had no regard for either Gordon's or Shaw's personal well-being. Shaw went up to his room and retrieved a short-barreled twelve-gauge shotgun from his kit. Opening the breech, he slipped two shells into the chambers and closed it with a click. Then he slipped two extra shells into his pocket.

He descended the stairs and, instead of leaving the hotel from the front door which sported a wide veranda onto the main street, he went to the rear of the building and exited into an alley that ran the length of the street in both directions. It was full dark now, and there was no activity in the alley.

Shaw was, by nature, a hunter. He believed a hunter's greatest asset was his sense of hearing. He stood still for all of ten minutes, listening to the night sounds and getting a feel for the activity around him. While he waited, a buggy went by on the street and the rhythmic sound of a steam engine in the distance identified a late-working mine. Two men were talking somewhere on the boardwalk about a card game while a raucous crowd was beginning to gather in one of the saloons down the street. Nothing seemed out of the ordinary.

Eagle Town boasted a number of streets, some of which were laid out in traditional square block style. But due to the steepness of the slopes in and around the town, some of the streets and many of the alleys were steeply inclined and at sharp angles to the main street. Most of the buildings on the main street were interconnected, one built against another, sharing a common wall and, in some cases, doorways. This was the main reason fires were so often devastating to mining towns. A few buildings were stand-alone and had narrow spaces between them.

Shaw walked down the alley for about one hundred yards and turned into the space between the walls of a mercantile and a laundry establishment. He used this narrow space to approach unseen. Stopping at the entrance, he surveyed the street up and down, looking for Gordon. He was nowhere in sight.

A large ore wagon trundled down the street from the west, kicking up dust, while its team and trace chains made considerable noise. Shaw let it pass and as soon as the way was clear he walked calmly across the street, semi-hidden in the dust cloud the wagon had raised. Once across, he entered a tight space between the Eagle Town bank and a barbershop. Standing still and observing for another ten minutes, he convinced himself things appeared normal on this side as well. Walking towards the rear of those establishments, Shaw entered another alley.

He slowly walked in the direction of his hotel and as he neared its immediate vicinity he stopped and listened. Initially, he heard nothing out of the ordinary but, just when he was convinced he was on a fool's errand, he heard the scratching sound of a match being struck. He detected a faint glow in a space between two buildings directly across from the hotel's entrance. Whoever stood there had cupped the match while lighting a smoke and was keeping the glow of the tobacco embers hidden by his body while he watched the front of the hotel.

Shaw smiled grimly. After he'd beaten Gordon in the street, he knew that sooner or later he'd have to face him again. But knowing this and mentally preparing for it never quite had the same effect on a man as being confronted by the possibility of deadly action. Suddenly, it was no longer just a pleasant spring evening — the darkness held real

106

danger. It was not that he hadn't anticipated this, but coming face to face with the moment of truth always carried with it a startling realization of finality. There were never any guarantees as to the outcome of such deadly encounters and this could be the night that he died. He must fight the body's natural urge to tense up in anticipation of combat. He took several deep breaths to relax, all the while watching the spot where he'd seen that sudden flare. His senses were sharp and clear and, finally, he smiled in the darkness. Something told him this was not going to be *his* night to die.

He moved into the shadows along a pole fence and put the bed of a wagon between him and the man he believed was Gordon. When he was in position, he called out in a harsh whisper: "Gordon. Mason told me to come fetch you."

At the sound, the man's head snapped around and Shaw clearly saw the embers of the smoke between Gordon's lips. He took it out with his right hand. "Who's callin'?"

Shaw now knew for sure it was Gordon and he remained silent and waited. He watched as Gordon dropped his smoke in the dirt and ground it out with his boot heel. In the semi-darkness, he saw Gordon draw his pistol with his left hand and cock the hammer. Shaw eared back the right hammer of the shotgun and waited while Gordon made his way to the corner of the alley and looked both ways. Shaw noted the man walked very softly.

"Who called?" This time a little louder, "Damn it, Kohler, is that you?" Gordon almost hollered.

"No, Gordon. It isn't Kohler," Shaw said quietly.

"You're a coward then, Shaw? I didn't think it of you."

There was enough light to see Gordon's pistol was pointed in the general direction of where he'd heard Shaw's voice. He knew Gordon was trying to keep him talking so he could better locate his position in the faint light. He felt certain Gordon wasn't afraid and that marked him as even more dangerous.

"I have you covered with an express gun," Shaw said calmly. "The range is less than ten yards. You don't stand a chance."

Gordon stood quietly for a moment. "So, what's your play? What are you waiting for?"

"I'm hoping you can be reasonable. I don't want to kill you." He'd be happy if this night ended without a shooting.

"Kill me now, or face me later. Whichever, we're gonna fight! It can't end any other way." Gordon dove into the darkness, blasting a shot in Shaw's direction. The bullet struck the side of the stable behind Shaw's head. It was close, but not that close.

Shaw held his fire.

Gordon had rolled under a wagon and disappeared into the darkness.

Shaw could have killed him easily, but his one major flaw was that he hated to take advantage. In some cases, it couldn't be avoided, but Gordon was game and deserved an even break. He backed up and moved along the wall of the building, fading into the darkness when he reached the corner. Moving back, farther away from the main street, he barely heard a conversation from a few people on the main street who loudly discussed where the shot had come from. Normally, a single gunshot didn't arouse too much attention and, if more shooting didn't follow it up, the people would eventually drift away. What they wouldn't do if they were smart would be to investigate the shot in the darkness. That would be asking for trouble.

Further back from the street, the only light came from stars, or an occasional lamp from a cabin window. Still, Shaw detected movement, a shadow detaching from the background and moving low and fast. He realized Gordon was heading toward where he believed Shaw was hidden, not knowing that Shaw had also changed location. Shaw felt a momentary pang of regret because Gordon had missed his one and only opportunity to end the trouble between them. Had Gordon ridden away, Shaw would have let him go, but by deliberately coming back he'd used up all his chances.

Shaw shouldered his shotgun and called sharply, "Gordon!"

The gunman crouched and blasted another shot in the direction of Shaw's voice. He was quick, but this time Shaw triggered his shotgun and the flame stabbed four feet in front of the twin muzzles.

Gordon was caught full on by the gun's charge and dropped like a rag doll on his face. He attempted to rise once but managed only to push his body a few inches before all strength left him.

Shaw turned and ran down the alley until he reached the end of the street. While people were beginning to gather near the corral, Shaw calmly walked across the street and into the alley on the other side. In a minute, he re-entered the hotel by the back door and climbed the stairs to his room. He was certain no one had seen him.

Once in his room, he opened the shotgun and unloaded the unfired barrel and also removed the fired shell casing. Swiftly he ran a couple of water-dampened patches down the fired barrel to clean it of any powder residue. He followed up with a patch soaked in lamp oil which he applied to both barrels, finishing the job with a couple of dry patches. Wiping the breech face and the action with more oil, he removed any indication the weapon had been fired, or for that matter, even recently handled. Wadding everything up, he opened the window and, gauging his distance, tossed the trash up on the roof of the hotel. He knew that the sulfur smell of gun powder lingered in a room so, leaving the window open, he struck a couple of matches to mask the smell and openly placed them in a cup near the table lamp. Then, he sat down to wait for Blake.

Blake showed up within the hour. Shaw had been

watching the street when the knock at the door came. Drawing his gun, he asked: "Who is it?"

"It's Blake and I'm alone."

Shaw opened the door.

Blake glanced at the gun in Shaw's hand and commented, "Expecting trouble?"

Shaw smiled. "You can never be too careful, especially if you've recently made such a dangerous enemy."

Blake studied his face closely. "You don't have to worry about Gordon, if that's who you're talking about. Someone cut him down with a shotgun an hour ago. You must have heard the shooting?"

Shaw didn't feign surprise. His expression did not change. "I heard the shooting." He turned and walked back to his chair. "It sounded like a couple of pistol shots preceded the shotgun blast. What do you make of that?"

Blake offered a hint of a smile. "Yes, well, Gordon's pistol had been fired twice, so it was most likely a case of self defense. Do you happen to have a shotgun?"

Shaw smiled. "Why, yes, I do. Would you like to see it?"

Blake nodded.

Shaw retrieved the shotgun from where it was wrapped in his bedroll. Opening the breech, he handed it to Blake.

Blake took the gun and pointed it at the lamp and looked down the barrels. Then he stuck his finger in the chambers. Last, he sniffed the chambers. "She looks clean and dry. No reason to believe it's been fired recently."

Shaw nodded. "No reason at all. And I'd bet there are a hundred shotguns within a quarter mile of this hotel. It'd be a hard job to check them all."

Blake closed the shotgun and handed it back. Then he turned to leave. At the door, he stopped and looked back. "Gordon's no real loss. Some killings just go unsolved. But some people don't need hard evidence in a shooting to decide who's responsible for it. Some people may just decide to do something about it."

"Mason?" Shaw asked.

"It would be my guess. He'll already know about the trouble you had with Gordon and he'll ask around and eventually put two and two together and then maybe decide you're the only one who adds up to four."

"Are you going to offer me some advice?"

Blake nodded. "Well, I'd suggest you leave town, but I know you won't. Then, I'd suggest you avoid Mason, but I know you can't."

"What's that leave?"

"Watch your back. That's all I can offer." He turned and left.

Before he set the shotgun down, Shaw reloaded it, and placed it close to hand.

* * * *

In the morning, Shaw went down to breakfast. He was surprised to see Sarah in the dining room, apparently waiting for him. The hour was early, so she must have left the ranch long before first light. He walked up to the table and smiled, genuinely happy to see her.

"Have you had breakfast?" he asked. She looked particularly lovely this morning, in a blue gingham dress, but she didn't return his smile.

"No, I haven't eaten. Perhaps we could breakfast together?"

"I'd be delighted." Shaw took a chair and when the waitress came over, he ordered breakfast for the two of them, and requested a pot of coffee. When the waitress left, Shaw said, "You appear upset about something. Care to tell me what's wrong?"

Sarah began, tentatively, "There was a shooting last night — one of Mason's men. The waitress told me about it. She told me you and the dead cowboy had an altercation yesterday afternoon." The unspoken question showed plain on her face.

The waitress brought the coffee. When she had gone, Shaw smiled grimly. "You want to know if I killed the man."

She nodded. "Well, did you?"

"Even if I had, from what the marshal says, the cowboy fired two shots first. Did the waitress tell you that as well?"

Sarah seemed shocked and then she looked down at her lap. "No. She hadn't mentioned that fact. That would make a difference, I suppose, as it could then be concluded the man's death was the result of someone defending himself." Sarah looked up at Shaw's eyes. "You didn't answer my question. Did you kill him?"

"I'm not going to answer you because, frankly, it's none of your business," he responded flatly. "The man's name was Gordon. You could say he and I exchanged *pleasantries* yesterday afternoon and he was left unsatisfied with the outcome. He was looking for a fight and, evidently, he found one."

"But a man's dead! Doesn't that bother you?" she asked, exasperation in her voice.

Shaw took a sip of coffee and shook his head. "No, Sarah, it doesn't bother me, at least not in the same way it bothers you. The man was a troublemaker and a hired gun. His death is no great loss to the community and certainly not to me."

Sarah looked into Shaw's eyes. "Is it so easy, then? Does taking a life become so commonplace an event that one becomes cavalier about it?"

Since Shaw desperately wanted Sarah to understand, he decided to try to explain further. "Sarah, I didn't say I took his life. You're assuming that I did." He sipped his coffee, gestured vaguely with a hand. "Taking a life should never be a commonplace event. It's an extraordinary occurrence and no sane man does it cavalierly. But, under certain circumstances, the taking of a life shouldn't lead one to be overburdened by personal or emotional guilt."

"Guilt?"

He nodded. "So far, you've managed to go through life without making mortal enemies. It's the same for most people, but you should understand that Gordon would be alive today if he hadn't gone looking for trouble. Whoever killed him is not necessarily totally responsible for Gordon's death. Gordon's own actions were largely responsible for it."

Sarah sat quietly for several seconds and eventually nodded. "You're right, of course. But I can't get used to the fact that I feel compelled toward friendliness with someone who is so obviously a man of violence. It goes against my nature."

"I am not necessarily a *man of violence,* to use your words. I am a man who is engaged in a profession of arms, like a marshal or a military officer. Who I am is defined best by whom I work for, or what assignments I take. Search your heart, Sarah. Do I appear to you to be a bad man?"

Sarah's eyes brimmed and she blinked away the tears that threatened. When she answered, she barely whispered. "No. I don't believe you're a bad man. I'm beginning to think you're a very good man. As I see it, that's probably the biggest reason I continue to try and find fault with you."

She gathered her purse and stood up suddenly. Then she looked intently into Shaw's eyes. "You see, I'd rather hate you than accept the fact that I might find myself caring for you."

She turned and left the restaurant and Shaw could only watch her go.

* * * *

Shaw waited a while, giving Sarah time to visit briefly

with Samuel and to see to some weekly shopping needs. After she'd left town, Shaw stopped at Samuel's office.

When he entered, he wasn't surprised to find Samuel sitting in the same chair, in apparently the same clothes, in the same alcoholic condition as the previous day. Shaw had never experienced personal tragedy before, so he had no understanding of how badly a person's emotional health could be affected by it. All the same, he couldn't grasp how Samuel completely rejected the life he'd previously had with Sarah in favor of this poisonous isolation.

Samuel looked mildly amused. "You were busy yesterday."

Shaw didn't respond.

"Gordon was one of the men who accosted me in front of Sarah. I'm not sad he's no longer with us. Do you have any idea who killed him?"

Though Samuel wasn't smiling, Shaw knew he was being played. "Perhaps the marshal will work out the details and the mystery will be solved."

"Ha!" Samuel snorted. "Blake couldn't work out the details of his suspender straps. Perhaps if there was a sign that read *'the killer went that-a-way'* he might make some progress. I'd say you're safe."

Shaw did not confirm or deny Samuel's suspicions. "I suppose Mason will be asking about me. In your opinion, what can I expect from that quarter?"

"You're new here. Therefore, you're fair game. Mason will have his men test you again. Or, perhaps he'll just have them kill you outright since Gordon evidently failed miserably while *'testing'* you. It's hard to say what Mason will do." Samuel pursed his lips, nodded. "You'll have to be careful." Then he lifted a dirty glass that held about half an inch of amber liquid. He tossed it off and wiped his lips with the back of his sleeve. His eyes watered a bit and this time his hand trembled when he set the glass down. "Have you made any progress?" he asked.

"Yes, I believe I have. I know that a lawyer named Wade Hardy was looking for an accomplished rifleman. He apparently discovered a contact in Dodge City named Reinhardt Keyes who put him in touch with a man named Ballou. Evidently, Ballou was quite a long-shooter in the war. That rifle you noticed on the horse in front of Blake's office belonged to Ballou."

Samuel looked surprised, but not overly so. "How'd you find all this out so quickly?"

Shaw shook his head. "I never reveal my sources of information. I take what people tell me, I try to verify it and I use what I can. But I never tell anyone where it came from."

"Not even to the person paying your fee?" Samuel's eyes were dark and cold.

Shaw didn't hesitate. "I'm prepared to refund your money now. Would you like cash, or a bank draft?"

Samuel looked at Shaw for the longest time, before finally smiling thinly. "No, that will not be necessary. I suppose it doesn't matter where the information came from, as long as it's accurate and leads us somewhere. What business did this shooter have with Blake?"

"It appears that he knew Blake from the war, and they were reliving some 'old times.'"

Samuel considered this and then nodded. He picked up a crystal decanter from the table next to his chair and poured another glass of whiskey. "Don't you find it odd that Blake didn't recall the visit, or make the connection after Stuart was killed?"

"Yes, I find it very odd," Shaw replied. "On the other hand, it's obvious that Blake is afraid of Mason, just like many other people in this town. Then, there's also the consideration that the rifleman knows who *Blake* is…and where to find *him*. Perhaps discretion was more important than officiousness?"

Samuel nodded. "Where do we go from here?"

"Well, I must talk with Wade Hardy to see if he'll divulge the name of his client. I'm told he does some work for Mason."

"Yes, he's Mason's lawyer, or at least he's the only one in town who'll work for Mason. That pretty much cements it in my mind. Mason's the man who ordered the assassin."

"I can't fault your logic. It's probably a good bet you're right. I don't suppose Hardy will talk to me in any case, but it's a logical step that I can't ignore." Shaw rose to go. "Where does Hardy work from?"

"He has a store-front office on the same street as the Royale saloon. You can't miss it. But he won't be there."

"Why is that?"

"It's too close to dinner time. He'll be out visiting one of our local eateries, and then he'll stop off at either the Royale or the Golden Nugget for some refreshments. You'll have a better chance of finding him in the evening, but he may not be sober."

Shaw nodded. "I'll find him."

* * * *

Shaw stopped by Wade Hardy's office. True to Samuel's word, the door was locked and the one-room office empty. The Royale saloon was across the street, so Shaw walked over and entered. Coming in from the bright daylight, he had to wait for his eyes to accustom themselves to the dimly lit interior.

There were half a dozen patrons in the place. Four played cards in a corner, and two sat apart from each other at different tables, quietly drinking, one reading a paper. There was no one at the bar. Shaw walked up to it and scanned the room.

The Royale was a "drinking" establishment. The bar was of walnut, beautifully carved and as smooth as glass. Behind it was a full-length mirror set into a hand-carved frame, flanked by two heavy pillars of figured walnut. Around the room were paintings, hung on walls decorated by floral paper. A wide staircase with a gently curving banister led to where Shaw supposed a miner or cowboy could take a room, or indulge in some feminine company.

A door at the end of the bar opened and a man walked in. He spotted Shaw and approached from behind the bar. "Yer pleasure, sir?" His Irish brogue was thick.

"That would be a beer," Shaw replied.

The bartender smiled. "My drink o' choice as well. I'll join ya, and the first one is on the house."

Shaw dipped his head in a bow of thanks. "I like this place already."

The bartender smiled. "Everyone likes the Royale." He poured two crystal mugs of dark beer, handed one to Shaw and hoisted his own. "Successful endeavors." he toasted.

Shaw nodded and they both took a drink. The dark brew was bitter, strong and flavorful.

"You'd be the one they call Shaw?" the bartender asked.

"Guilty."

"Ben McGinnes is the name." He extended a freckled paw. "I own the Royale."

Shaw smiled and took the hand. "It doesn't take long for people to get to know a man's name around here."

McGinnes bobbed his head, and took a couple gulps of beer. "So right you are. But then, it doesn't help matters when ya thrash one o' the baddest gunmen in town, within the first couple day's o' yer arrival." He grinned. "Normally, we suggest newcomers take a little time to get to know the locals before they go to beatin' on 'em with their fists...or guns, as the case may be." McGinnes drained his beer, while Shaw took his second sip.

The Irishman noted Shaw's deliberation and nodded. "Gordon will not be missed."

"It appears that he wasn't."

The bartender thought for a moment and bellowed a harsh laugh. "By golly, yer right. That's grand! I can no' wait to use that one later tonight. That calls for another beer." McGinnes poured another frothy beer. When he had the brew in front of him, he asked, "So, were ya the one to kill him?"

Shaw shook his head. "No. I hit him with a left jab and I distinctly recall he survived the blow. I'm sure there are several witnesses to that effect."

The Irishman chuckled again, but didn't say anything. For several long minutes, the two men just drank their beer in the quiet saloon. One of the solitary drinkers got up and left the establishment. McGinnes walked over to the table and picked up the man's glass and a couple of coins left behind and returned to the bar.

"How long have you owned the Royale?" Shaw asked.

"Not long — a couple o' years. I'm a minin' engineer by trade. I actually own the 'Belle' and we're working two shifts. I'm not getting rich, but I'm makin' her pay for herself with a little left at the end o' the day."

Shaw nodded in admiration. "Looking at this place, I'd say you have two gold mines."

"I do at that, and thank you kindly."

Shaw said, "I want to speak to a lawyer named Hardy. Have you seen him yet today?"

The Irishman thought about it. "Now that you mention it, I haven't. Have you checked his office? It's across the street."

Shaw nodded. "Closed and locked."

"He'll be around sooner or later. Am I to tell him you're looking for him?"

"I'd take it as a favor if you wouldn't — or anyone else for that matter."

McGinnes nodded. "Not a word, then."

Shaw turned to leave and the bartender stopped him.

"Mr. Shaw."

Shaw stopped and looked back.

The Irishman wasn't smiling now. He had a serious look on his face and appeared to be contemplating something. Finally, he made up his mind and spoke quietly. "If the cowboys think you're gunnin' for their boss, they may come in force. You should know that Gordon wasn't the worst of 'em. Mason has a real gun hand that works for him, and I can tell he's a mighty fast man and he doesn't display it. He doesn't swagger, or brag or get drunk and fight. But he'll kill you as sure as he would a rat, with no more emotion. He's always with Mason. His name's Bentley. You watch him, you hear?"

Shaw nodded his thanks, and left the saloon wondering why neither Blake nor Samuel had mentioned Bentley.

* * * *

After Shaw left the Royale, it was beginning to get dark in the late afternoon. He decided to check on his horse, and walked the length of town to the stable.

Tucker Frey forked hay to the animals in the stalls.

Shaw noticed his horse had a bucket of oats inside his stall. The horse stuck his nose out the gate and received a petting for his trouble. The stall was clean and fresh bedding had been laid. The hostler knew his business.

When Frey finished, he walked over to Shaw and nodded. Leaning on his pitchfork, he smiled. "That's a great horse. I think you were lyin' about him being prone to kick."

"Stretching the truth a bit, I'll admit."

"He's almost like a pet." the hostler observed. "If you don't stop and talk to him and scratch his forehead, he sulks and goes to the back of the stall. Worse than a wife in that way."

Shaw laughed. "I've never been married, but that horse does crave attention. That's why I stopped by to get reacquainted." Shaw winked. "You never know when you'll need a fast horse around here."

"Do you want me to keep your tack in the stall?"

Shaw smiled. "No. I was joking. I've never really been one to ride away fast from anything. I like to take my time and meander. So, if and when I leave, it will be after I've taken care of any trouble I'm expecting."

"You expectin' any?"

"You tell me," Shaw countered. "Should I?"

The hostler picked up a piece of straw and placed it between his teeth and chewed on it a bit. "Never know what to expect around here. One of Mason's men got killed. You being new in town and having had trouble with the man, well, Mason might look you up, or have someone else look you up."

"Would you lay a bet either way?"

Frey considered the question then he took a couple of steps away and leaned the fork against a timber. He retrieved a hanging lamp and struck a match. Lighting the lamp, he glanced around. "Mr. Shaw, this town was built on ore. It's quiet now, but there was a time, during its boom, when a killin' a day wasn't uncommon. When the miners came, so did the men with cattle to feed 'em. Mason was one of the first and it's said he faced a few challenges. He started small, but now he's the biggest rancher in these parts. Many of the first ones are gone now. Some of them left in a hurry and sold their stock to Mason, or so he says. I'm not necessarily doubtin' him, but some of them gone now didn't seem like the type to sell out.

"Then, this rancher named Kent refused to sell his land and when Mason pushed it, Kent was able to back it up. Mason got himself a black eye. When Roark defended Kent in court and won, Mason got another. A man who likes it at the top can't stand back and take too many black eyes before people start to laugh at him. Mason ain't the smartest man around, but he ain't the kind to make boasts

120

either. He just goes about his business quietly, and sometimes people leave — sudden like."

"So, with the killing of Gordon, do you figure Mason took another black eye?"

Frey shook his head. "I'd say whoever killed Gordon did worse than blacken an eye, he done broke Mason's nose. Gordon wasn't a simple cowboy; he was one of Mason's guard dogs. Someone exposed a chink in Mason's armor. If Mason wants his power back, someone has to pay dearly for Gordon's killing."

Shaw nodded his agreement. "Tucker, back before young Roark was killed there was a man who came into town for a day. He had a rifle in a scabbard on his horse that would be hard to miss. It was a long-range, precision shooting rifle. This one was a muzzle-loader. Do you recall it?"

Frey bobbed his head. "Oh, hell, yes! That was a fine looking rifle. I could only see it from the lock back, but I've never seen such a beautiful weapon in all my days."

"Do you remember the man who owned it?"

"Why, yes, I do. He was a slight man, about five feet and eleven inches tall. His face was light, like he didn't get much sun. It was a funny thing, but his hair was so fine and light that you could barely make out his eyebrows. Almost like one of them albino people you hear tell about. He came in to buy oats for his horses."

"Horses?" Shaw asked.

"Yup. Had him his saddle horse and two packhorses. He bought a lot of oats and some corn for the three of them. They were loaded down some. I thought it a bit strange, considerin' the time of year; all the passes being snowed in by then. About the only road open led to Soulard."

"Did he talk at all?" Shaw asked, hopefully.

"Come to think of it, he didn't talk much. He always had this kind of smirk on his lips, like he was amused by a person. I remember when he left, I was glad to see him gone. Are you thinking of him for the Roark killin'?"

"I don't know yet. But that rifle seems interesting, to say the least."

"You know, I'm embarrassed to say, but that thought never crossed my mind in all these months."

Shaw remarked with a wry smile, "Don't be embarrassed. I'm hearing that from a lot of people."

The hostler cocked his head in confusion. "It's funny how everyone around here talks about an event like young Roark being killed, and no one even mentioned that pale looking man with the fancy rifle. Then along comes an outsider, who asks a couple of questions, and — *bam* — the pieces start fallin' into place." The hostler shook his head. "Is Roark paying you to find that man?"

Shaw smiled, politely. "Tucker, there are questions I can answer and things I can't talk about. That's something I can't talk about."

The hostler nodded. "Figured as much. But you can't fault me for bein' curious. People talk, you know? Everyone wondered who brought a professional killer into Eagle Town. Everyone had their favorite theory — but not too many people made their thoughts public. If you know what I mean."

"I know what you mean."

"Most people were pretty sorry for young Roark. He seemed like a fine lad. That Mrs. Roark took it hard too, she not bein' much older than the boy. Most folk around here think that Roark's a fool, shutting himself up in that office and drinkin' himself to death." Frey winked. "Heard you had breakfast with the lass. Well, she's a pretty thing and that husband of hers is a worthless coward."

Shaw didn't like the turn the conversation had taken. "Tucker, I'd take it kindly if you'd keep such thoughts to yourself. I know you don't mean any harm, but people talk. I believe Mrs. Roark is a lady and I don't want her reputation damaged by any spurious rumors."

"You're right — you *are* right and I'm sorry. It's just that folks really like that girl and they want to see her go on with her life, and not be wastin' her time on a man who's already dead inside."

Shaw nodded and changed the subject. "How long have you lived in Eagle Town?"

"Oh hell, since a little after it boomed, I'd say. Near to ten years now." Frey frowned. "Had me a little hole in the hills — one that was showing promise, but being new to the game I never filed on it. One day, I found out someone bought the land and I lost out." He shook his head. "But now I got this place and tell you the truth, it's the real gold mine. I don't put in long hours; I don't risk my life with blasting powder and I don't freeze my ass off standing knee deep in mountain streams or break my back behind barrows of slag. Nope, I don't miss the mining life one bit."

"And when did Kent come to the valley?"

Frey gave Shaw a studied gaze. "He's been here about eight years, I'd say. Why?"

"He has a mine on his property, doesn't he? A mine he *filed* on?"

Frey smiled, ruefully. "Why, yes, he does. You don't miss much do you, Mr. Shaw?"

Shaw shrugged. "I try to understand the lay of the land as much as I can, Tucker. Was that your mine?"

"I'd say you're getting warm."

"Do me a favor, Tucker, call me Matt." He smiled and clapped the old hostler on the shoulder. "You keep a nice stable, Tucker. It says a lot about a man. I appreciate your time."

Shaw headed for the door, somewhat chagrined that people in town were already talking about things that were none of their business. Towns were towns and you couldn't stop gossip, but the wrong words could often lead to deadly trouble.

Trouble Comes in Threes

When Shaw left the stable, full darkness had fallen, bringing with it a chill from the mountains that surrounded the town. He decided to try to find Wade Hardy again. Stopping by the lawyer's office, Shaw found it locked and dark. Figuring he'd do a little scouting in hopes of finding Hardy, he walked down the street in the direction of the Golden Nugget. He took extra care to watch the alleys and darkened windows. From the moment he arrived at Eagle Town and began asking questions, he became a marked man and an attack could come from any direction, at any time. There were forces at work in this town that were not healthy for him and any man who'd hire his killing done for him wouldn't be the kind of man to face Shaw directly.

Shaw had known mining towns, logging camps, rail-line shanty-towns, military camps and myriad other gathering places where one might encounter hard-case gunmen or fighters of every persuasion. If one was so inclined, it would be an easy task to find a dozen men in this community alone that — for a price — would start a fight with a tenderfoot or stranger for the sole purpose of killing him. While no one had yet pinned the killing of Gordon on Shaw, most believed he was the man who'd killed Mason's gunfighter. Now that Shaw had established himself as a dangerous man, there might be fewer takers, and the price would go up considerably, but finding someone to take on the job of bushwhacking him wouldn't be impossible.

The Golden Nugget was a much different establishment than the Royale. While the Royale was finely appointed, the Nugget was geared toward a rougher element that didn't care about mirrors and paintings and fancy wood. People went there to drink and, if they could afford it, seek the company of some of the "evening ladies" who kept rooms in the back.

The saloon had a bar and floor planks made of rough-cut pine, the floor being liberally covered with almost-fresh pine sawdust. A hodge-podge of rickety tables and chairs were set about in casual confusion. A few patrons played cards in earnest, while the dozen or so others tossed down glasses of whiskey or mugs of beer, their miners' clothing covered in the grime of their profession and the stains of their sweat. Shaw stood out in stark contrast to them with his laundered black denim trousers and gray shirt.

When Shaw walked into the room, some of the miners glanced his way and appraised him for a second or two before going back to what they were doing. Only a few gave him more than a passing glance and Shaw didn't sense any trouble from the men in the room. He went to the bar and waited till the bartender finished polishing a glass with an almost-clean rag. He ambled over to Shaw and cheerfully offered the whisky glass.

"I'd prefer a beer and one for yourself if you're drinking," Shaw said, tossing a silver coin on the bar. The bartender nodded and poured Shaw's beer. When he was done, he popped the cork from a brown bottle he kept under the bar. As he poured a glass of dark liquid, Shaw caught the sweet scent of sassafras root.

The bartender finished pouring the foamy brew and nodded to Shaw. "Your health, sir." Then he drank a long pull of his root beer. When he was done, he smiled at Shaw. "Make it myself. I've a bit of a sweet tooth."

Shaw nodded. "Wish I'd have known you had it. It's been a while since I had any." Shaw tasted his beer. "You make this too?"

"Lord, no!" The bartender shook his head. "It comes from Denver by train to Soulard. Denver has the best damn brewers this side of 'Saint Louie'. Good German brewers."

Shaw smiled. "It's good beer." Taking another long drink, he glanced around the place. "I'm told I can meet with an attorney here. His name is Hardy."

"Most nights you'd find him here, or at the Royale. I haven't seen him yet." The bartender added, "If you're looking for him for legal work, I have to warn you, he's not very good."

Shaw smiled. "That's good news. It means he'll come cheaper." He swallowed some beer. "What's this Hardy look like?"

The bartender shrugged. "My height, blond hair. He fancies himself, I'd say. Wears a Derby and always dresses in a black coat." The bartender lowered his voice. "Carries a small pistol under the coat, left side — butt forward. Don't know if he's any good with it, but it's a thing to know."

Shaw nodded and finished his beer. "That it is, and thanks."

He turned to leave just as three men entered. The first one through the door was a rugged looking man with a craggy face and walrus mustache. He wore well-aged range clothes and an old gray sweat-stained cavalry hat, and he carried a long-barreled revolver in a military cross-draw holster. At some time, he'd cut the holster flap away, as an unnecessary impediment. Shaw noted the gun was an old Army model of 1860. Though it was antiquated, that didn't mean it didn't shoot, or that the old soldier couldn't make it shoot when he wanted to. He had a knife or saber scar that crossed the bridge of his nose and right cheek. His blue eyes immediately fell on Shaw — and lingered. Shaw recognized him immediately as a fighting man and dangerous.

The second man was the swaggering sort. Like Gordon, it appeared he fancied himself as a gun-hand. He too was dressed in range clothes, but they looked like they didn't quite fit. He apparently worked for a cattle outfit, but it was also obvious he didn't do cowboy work. His was a different specialty.

It was the third man that made the greatest impression on Shaw. He was tastefully attired in a black wool suit and white shirt. His black beaver-felt hat was flat-brimmed and brushed free of dust. He was perfectly groomed and clean-shaven except for a "Burnsides" style mustache of impressive dimensions. Shaw could tell he was armed, but the weapon was under his coat. The man's eyes took in the entire room, pausing momentarily on Shaw, before moving on. Shaw knew this man was the most dangerous of the three. Though he'd been ready to leave, Shaw knew these men were Mason's and were probably looking for him, so he decided to remain at the bar and see how things played out. The three men walked to the bar and settled beside Shaw.

Shaw looked at the old soldier and smiled with honest friendliness. "Sergeant…." He greeted with a nod.

The man looked mildly surprised. "You know me?"

"No, but you're familiar nonetheless. I know your kind," Shaw said without a trace of malice.

The man smiled. "Well, I suppose I'd better call you 'Cap'n', then?"

Shaw chuckled. "I was a captain once," he agreed, smiling. "But I was a sergeant before that. Bartender, please give these three gentlemen whatever they're drinking," Shaw requested. The bartender knew each man and knew what they'd drink. After the men had been served, Shaw turned to the second man and smiled again.

"It's my guess that you'd be Parker Lewis."

The gunman frowned. "How'd you know that?"

"You were described to me."

"By who?"

"You mean by whom," Shaw corrected, smiling. He noticed out of the corner of his eye that the third man appeared mildly amused by Lewis' irritation. Truly competent men had a low tolerance for tinhorns or show-offs and Lewis was a prime example of both.

"Are you making fun of me?" Lewis asked. He looked tense and ready for a fight.

Shaw smiled. "Of course I am. I'd have thought that was obvious." Then he completely turned his back on Lewis and addressed the third man. "I'm Shaw."

The man nodded and extended his hand. It was the gesture of a gentleman and Shaw shook hands with him. Shaw knew Bentley was sizing him up and while most people might mistake Bentley's manner as friendly, Shaw knew he faced someone who could shake hands with a man one minute, and with the right provocation, kill that man seconds later.

"I've heard of you. I'm Ross Bentley." His voice was cultured and soft. "You've a reputation that precedes you, Mr. Shaw. It's a pleasure to finally meet you." He indicated a table. "Shall we sit down over there?"

"Sure."

Shaw and Bentley sat facing each other while the old soldier and Lewis remained at the bar. Bentley tipped back his hat and unbuttoned his coat before tasting his beer. Shaw caught a glimpse of a Smith & Wesson Schofield revolver in a tooled black leather holster. He knew Bentley by reputation as well. A former Pinkerton detective, Bentley had become somewhat of a mercenary in the rapidly expanding west. It was rumored he might work both sides of the fence if the money was worth the risk. He was also considered a fast man with a gun, and a deadly shot.

Bentley said, "You obviously know that I work for a rancher named Mason. He's very interested in knowing what your intentions are regarding him."

"He could simply ask me. After all, it appears I'm an easy man to find."

Bentley smiled. "Finding you is not difficult. Surviving

the encounter is the question. Anyway, it's a small town. People like to talk and you've made quite an impression. However, Mason sent an employee yesterday with an invitation to meet with him. You turned down that invitation rather abruptly, it's said." Bentley pursed his lips briefly. "Now that employee is dead and of course Mason would like to know who killed his man, though it's not the most important thing at the moment."

"What would be the most important thing — at the moment?" Shaw asked.

"You've been retained by Samuel Roark to track down the man who killed his son. Mason is aware that his previous difficulties with Roark would make it seem he's the most likely culprit. Mason wants me to make sure you understand that he had nothing to do with the death of the young Roark boy."

Shaw studied Bentley's face. "You're convinced of that?"

"Not one-hundred percent, no. But it's what he wants me to make you understand. I merely work for the man. Being the messenger boy, I don't have to be convinced."

"Well, as the messenger boy, what do you think?"

"I'm not paid to think," Bentley said. "However, with what I know about Mason so far, a hired killing doesn't seem to fit. But, true or not, there've been rumors."

When Shaw didn't comment, Bentley added, "Mason's acquired a vast range. Of course, the rumor is he didn't come by it all honestly. Frankly, I don't care about that. Then again, if it worked well before, Mason might expect it would work just as well with the Kent spread. It was before my time. From what I've heard, Roark made Mason look pretty bad. In any case, Roark stopped him cold, whether it was a legitimate attempt at purchase or not."

"So why wouldn't Mason hire a killer to take care of Roark?"

Bentley took a drink, and wiped the beer foam from his

mustache. "It's not that Mason would be totally against killing Roark for the right reason, but he's just not that vindictive over a little parcel of land, to my way of thinking. Honor might come into play, but from everything I've learned, Mason is a man who can do his own fighting."

Shaw pondered that. "If he can do his own fighting, why would he first send Gordon and then follow it up with the three of you?"

"Mason doesn't come to town much anymore. He was hoping you'd ride out to see him. I explained why you might hesitate considering what happened with Gordon, and now he *completely* understands your reticence. So, I've been asked to meet with you instead."

"How long have you worked for him?" Shaw asked.

"Not long. I came on board after Stuart Roark was killed. Mason expected — let's say, he anticipated — retaliation. He went to pay his respects and tried to tell Roark that he had nothing to do with Stuart's death, but Roark wasn't interested in hearing it. Roark warned Mason off the property with a shotgun. That wife of his stood at the door with a Winchester! That's some woman." Bentley smiled.

Shaw experienced a stab of irritation at Bentley's comment concerning Sarah, but he could see nothing to be gained by bracing the man because of it. He half wondered if Bentley wasn't deliberately trying to provoke him since, according to Tucker Frey, there was already some speculation in town about Shaw's relationship with her.

"Can you think of anything going on in the valley that would explain someone wanting Roark killed?" Shaw asked.

Bentley shook his head. "Not a thing. It makes no sense. That's why Mason is so interested in gaining your — shall we say — understanding that he's not in any way involved. He thinks you're a hired killer and he doesn't relish having to look behind him every time he hears a noise. He knows that most people probably believe he was involved and there's not a damn thing he can do about that." Bentley took another drink of beer. "I told him from what I knew about you, you'd not act until you had hard evidence and that you're not, by reputation, a hired killer. That seemed to satisfy him. Of course, then someone killed Gordon and now he's not so sure."

"Let's just assume," Shaw said, "for the sake of conversation if for no other reason, that Gordon went looking for trouble and his death was otherwise completely unavoidable. I have no desire to have Mason looking over his shoulder unless he's the one who hired the killer of Stuart Roark. If he is and I can prove it, he would do well to continue looking over his shoulder."

"I'd say that's fair enough." Bentley fixed Shaw with a direct stare. "But you should know, Mason may get tired of looking over his shoulder and want *me* to do something about it." It wasn't a threat. It was a professional warning and Shaw didn't find any hostility in Bentley's words.

Shaw smiled. "You said Mason can fight his own battles."

"I think he knows now that he's not in your league."

"And he feels you're in my league?" Shaw asked.

"He hopes so, considering what he pays me," Bentley said, and then smiled. "Of course, so do I."

"Well, you and I can discuss that if it ever becomes a problem. I'm not worried about you back-shooting me."

Bentley drained the rest of his beer. "Thank you. In case you didn't know, Parker there was pretty good friends with Gordon."

Shaw nodded. "And Parker *there*, feels strongly that Gordon's death is somehow connected with me?"

"You smacked Gordon around quite handily. He wasn't the kind of man who'd turn the other cheek. His ending up dead the same evening is more of a coincidence than Parker is willing to accept."

"So, you're suggesting that I'm going to have to fight Parker?"

Bentley nodded. "I don't see any way to avoid it, and he doesn't fight with fists. The fact is, he's been talking of little else since he heard about Gordon's killing."

"And how would Mason feel if another one of his men braced me?"

"Mason didn't send me to fight you, but he's a pragmatist. You present a problem to him. He said he didn't have anything to do with Stuart Roark's death. Sending someone to kill you would be bad form. But there isn't anyone in town that truly believes you didn't kill Gordon and everyone knows Parker Lewis was Gordon's best friend. If Parker braces you for that and kills you, it doesn't really make Mason look bad and it solves his problem."

"*One* of his problems."

"Of course. But the best way to deal with *problems* is one at a time. Wouldn't you agree?" Bentley asked.

"What if Parker braces me, and loses?"

Bentley thought for a long moment, and then shook his head. "Mason enjoys a reputation here in the valley. It's a sign of weakness to allow one's men to die one by one and not do something about it."

Shaw considered that carefully. "Where does that leave you and my scar-faced sergeant over there?"

Bentley chuckled. "That scar-faced sergeant is named Adams. He's the real deal and he's the ramrod of the outfit. The men respect him more than they do Mason. Parker sometimes thinks he's the boss but Adams *is* the boss, and he wouldn't cry if Parker braced you, regardless of the outcome."

"And you?"

"I've suggested to him that he leave you alone, but he doesn't really take orders from me. I'm more Mason's — assistant, you might say. I don't get involved in the running

132

of the ranch."

"If I have to fight Parker, will you feel an obligation to get involved?"

Bentley looked straight into Shaw's eyes. "I'd be expected to use my discretion."

"What if I didn't give you a chance to mix in?"

"I'd be excused…this time."

Shaw nodded. It was good to deal with professionals. "Tell Mason what I said. If he's not the man who hired the killing of Stuart Roark, he has nothing to fear from me and he can call off his dogs. If, on the other hand he *is* the one responsible for the young boy's death, he might as well kill me the first opportunity he has." He put on his hat and stood up. "I enjoyed talking with you, Bentley." He turned and started for the door.

"Shaw!" Parker Lewis called out.

Chairs scraped and clattered as the patrons scrambled to get out of the way and under cover. Only a couple of men headed for the door, even though it was dangerously stupid to remain in the room with the imminent possibility of flying bullets.

Shaw knew he should keep on walking, but it was never a good idea to leave an enemy behind who had both the means and the determination to kill you. There are moments when a man decides his own fate, or it is decided for him. Shaw stopped, still facing the door, his back to the gunman.

"Shaw, turn around and look at me," Lewis shouted in the otherwise silent room. Bentley hadn't moved from his chair, but the sergeant had taken several steps away from Lewis and moved his arms away from his gun. Shaw noted the movement and knew Adams was signaling he was out of it and wanted everyone in the room to know it. Shaw knew the old soldier wasn't afraid, but this wasn't his fight.

"I said, turn around, dammit!" Lewis' voice was slightly shrill.

Shaw took a deep breath. "Why, Lewis?" Shaw asked quietly. "Are you in such a hurry to die?"

"Turn around, if you're not afraid."

Shaw's face tightened and he shook his head minutely. This emphasis on courage and not showing deference to another man was so futile, but Shaw saw no other path. Walking away would only delay the fight that would eventually come. Lewis would never leave him alone.

The fight was here and now. Shaw turned slowly. When he was facing Lewis, he noted the man's frame was tightly coiled, ready to strike like a rattlesnake. Shaw appeared totally relaxed, supremely calm.

"Did you kill Gordon?" Lewis demanded.

"And if I did?" Shaw asked, his voice soft and low.

"He was a friend of mine."

"So Lewis, tell me, what *is* your point?" Shaw asked the question sharply, suddenly insolent and dismissive of the gunman.

Lewis' eyes narrowed. "If you killed him, I'll kill you."

"I see." Shaw nodded, suddenly smiling. "Do you think it would be that easy, Lewis? Saying you're going to kill me; even wanting to kill me and actually killing me are all decidedly different propositions." Shaw stopped smiling and with dripping sarcasm he concluded, "I'm not a tin can sitting on a fence post."

"Answer...my...question!" Lewis shouted, his voice more shrill than before.

Shaw let several long seconds go by. "What do you think?"

"I think you ambushed him in the dark!" Lewis said. "I think you're a 'sure-thing' killer who can't face a man with a gun in his hand."

"So, if that's what you think, what are you waiting for?"

"I want to hear you say it."

"Okay, Lewis, but you waited too long. If you were

sure, you should have opened the ball. Of course I killed him."

Even though the talk-of-the-town indicated most people had already come to the conclusion Shaw was Gordon's killer, the bar patrons seemed somewhat stunned by the revelation. There were even a few whispers of surprise. At first, it seemed to the onlookers as if Lewis hadn't heard, or had expected Shaw to deny it. The pronouncement didn't seem to immediately register with him.

Shaw continued in the same even manner. "And if you so much as move your hand toward your gun, I'll kill you too."

Lewis stood, his right hand poised over the butt of his Colt, with the man who'd killed his friend only twenty feet away.

Shaw made no attempt to conceal his contempt for Lewis, letting the corner of his mouth curl up into an easy smile.

The gunman uttered a guttural sound and his hand dropped for his pistol.

Shaw's own gun-hand blurred and a shot hammered the room, followed quickly by another.

Lewis was struck in the belly and the center of his chest. Part of the pine bar behind the gunman splintered with the second shot and a fan of blood splattered the wallpaper. One of the shots must have "spined" Lewis because he fell heavily straight down, as if there was no feeling in his lower body, before flopping onto his face.

Lewis had managed to get his gun from his holster and his gun hand was pinned under his body. He struggled to pull his arm from beneath the deadweight of his frame, causing him to take heavy breaths. With each breath, sawdust on the floor filled his nostrils and mouth, bringing on a racking fit of coughing accompanied by a bloody froth around his lips. He tried to roll over and bring his gun to bear, but couldn't.

A muffled blast came from under the stricken man. The shot blew Lewis's left elbow apart, the bullet spending itself in the base of the bar. The gunman lay there, his breath coming in shallow pants for a couple of minutes before he quit breathing, and all the while Shaw stood with his gun in his hand, vaguely covering Bentley.

Bentley's look showed he took no offense over Shaw's way of guaranteeing the gunman remained only an interested observer.

When Lewis was finally still, Shaw spoke quietly to no one in particular. "I think someone should send for the marshal."

"No need," Bentley said. "He heard the shots. He'll be along directly."

* * * *

It was late in the evening and Shaw sat in Blake's office drinking coffee. Blake was contemplating his current problem. In a town that might have a killing every six months or so, he now had two killings in two days, both involving the man who sat opposite. There was no doubt that a strong case could be made for self-defense in both instances, but he was afraid Mason would be out looking for blood and the last thing he needed was a war in the streets of his town.

There was a knock at the door. Blake glanced at a shotgun propped against his desk and said, "It's open." The door swung wide and Ross Bentley came in, glanced at Shaw and nodded. "Mind if I pull up a chair?"

"Be my guest. You've met Shaw, of course. Care for a cup of coffee?"

"I'll get it," Bentley said. He walked to the stove, retrieved a battered porcelain cup from the shelf and poured himself a cup of coffee that had been too long on the heat. It was as black as dirt and smelled way too strong, but it was coffee and the night was chilly.

"What can I do for you, Bentley?" Blake asked.

"I expect there's something I can do for you. I sent Adams back to the ranch to talk to Mason. I'm pretty sure he'll expect an inquest, but I don't believe he'll come to town looking for war."

"Why would he be so reasonable all of a sudden?" Blake said. "It's not in keeping with his character."

Bentley looked at Shaw. "Perhaps it's in everyone's best interest that this matter quietly goes away. A couple of rambunctious cowboys get on the wrong side of a stranger and the stranger turns out to be a little more than they bargained for. It's not unheard of. It happens all the time. There's no need to make a state case out of it or, for that matter, a war."

The marshal shook his head. "People in town are expecting Mason to ride in with an army. He has a reputation to uphold. I don't see how he can back down from this without losing face. He's strong because no one is foolish enough to buck him. I think Mason has to do something, or lose any respect he has."

Shaw spoke up. "I think Bentley is beginning to suspect that Mason can't afford to turn this into a war. The last thing he wants is an official investigator coming in and turning over rocks. For that matter, I'd think that's the last thing you'd want, considering the Roark killing is still unsolved."

Blake was still uncomfortable. "So that's it? Mason does have something to hide?"

"It's possible," Bentley said. "But look at it this way. Even if Mason wasn't involved in the Roark killing, there's still the question of how he amassed such a huge range when many of the ranches he *bought out* were filed on by their previous owners. Maybe he'd rather not have to explain all those acquisitions in minute detail."

Blake thought that Shaw was a lightning rod and, right

now, Blake needed to restore order in a town buzzing with excitement. Excitement had a tendency to breed more excitement and he didn't need any more would-be gunmen coming around looking to earn a reputation.

At the same time, Shaw had, in his brief investigation, turned over enough rocks to glean more information than he had, and he was the town's marshal. People might begin to notice that. He might arrest Shaw and hold him over for trial, but then it might look like he was concerned where Shaw's line of inquiry might lead. It would be easy for Shaw to cause problems even from a jail cell. What Blake needed, what the town needed, was for Shaw to either die or leave. It didn't look like he was going to die very easily, so the next best thing would be for him to leave.

"Shaw. I want you to get out of town. You've caused enough trouble. You have all the information you're going to get here, so move on and do whatever it is you need to do, but I want you to do it somewhere else!"

Shaw shook his head. "I still have some people I'd like to talk to."

"Like who — I mean, like *whom*?" Bentley asked with a trace of a smile.

Shaw looked at Bentley and frowned. "I'm sorry, but I'd rather not say." After a few seconds, he turned to Blake. "You're probably right, Blake. In the morning, I'll leave. I have a trail to follow and it's time I earned my pay." He stood up. "Gentlemen, it's been a pleasure."

As Shaw walked to the door, Bentley stopped him: "Shaw."

Shaw stopped and turned.

Bentley said, "If I was a betting man, I'd have wagered Lewis would have come out a little better than he did against you. He was a better man with a gun than Gordon. That said, it seems to me you gave Lewis and Gordon more than ample opportunities to rethink their positions. As far as I'm concerned, you earned a pass on this and I'll try and convince Mason of that."

"I appreciate that, Bentley," Shaw said.

"One word of advice, however," Bentley added.

"What's that?"

"If you and I ever face each other, don't give me the same opportunity you gave Lewis — or Gordon, for that matter. It won't help you, and I wouldn't do it for you."

"I'll remember that. You might tell Mason that I'm not done yet. I can't be scared off and I can't be bought off. I'll follow this through, no matter where it leads."

"I'll tell him. He may listen to me, or he may decide to step on you like a bug."

Shaw looked at Bentley for several seconds. "Bentley, if he decides to come, I hope you're not riding with him."

"Why shouldn't I be?"

"Because, then I'd have to kill you first." Shaw smiled, turned and walked out into the night.

When the door closed, Bentley took a sip of his coffee, still watching the door, a contemplative look on his face. "There goes a most dangerous man," he said quietly.

Blake nodded. "But is he dangerous enough?"

"I'm thinking he's as formidable as he needs to be. But a man who can kill from three hundred yards in a gusty wind will not be an easy man to take. A man like that is hard to track, and damned hard to sneak up on. I won't wager a bet either way."

"I hope he don't come back here," Blake said.

"Then you better hope he gets killed because I believe, when all is said and done, the trail he's following will likely end up right back here."

"Shit!"

"Yes." Bentley frowned. "It is indeed."

* * * *

Sarah was up and feeding the horses when she spied

Shaw coming up the trail from Eagle Town. The sight of his horse gave her a sudden and disconcerting thrill. She had every reason to distance herself from this man but, more and more, she was coming to look forward to spending time with him. Life with Samuel had been difficult, almost beyond endurance after the death of their daughter. His depression and black moods, made worse by his drinking, were unbearable. He was never physically abusive, but the isolation she'd often felt was as agonizing as a physical beating.

Stuart had been the one bright spot in her life. He had remained positive and carefree and did the work of three men holding the ranch together while his father seemed unable to recover any vitality. Then, there was a long period when Samuel immersed himself in his reading and finally started discussing his law practice again. Just when it seemed Samuel might come around and rejoin the living, Stuart was taken from him. The damage to his emotional health from that moment on seemed irreparable.

Then Shaw came along. In one afternoon, he'd eradicated months of neglect around the ranch yard and despite her initial fear and mistrust, he'd erased months of her worry as well. She had fantasized about what might happen between her and Shaw after all this was behind them. She knew her life with Samuel was no longer an option. Anything she'd ever felt for him was long dead. He appeared to feel the same. She detested the burden of having to even ride to town and see him. He reminded her of everything that they'd lost and his physical condition was deplorable.

Sarah hurried though her chores and rushed to the house to freshen up her face and run a brush though her hair. There wasn't time to do much else. As she finished, she heard Shaw's horse in the ranch yard.

"Halloo the house." Shaw called out.

She smiled brightly when she opened the door. "Please,

come in. There's coffee, still hot. Have you eaten?" she asked slightly breathlessly.

"Coffee sounds good and, no, I haven't eaten." Shaw smiled.

"Come in and sit. I'll gather some breakfast for you. I have fresh biscuits and jam. I might even be able to find a slab of ham and a couple of potatoes too."

Shaw dismounted and tied his horse. He entered the house and went to the basin to wash his hands. Behind him, Sarah hurried about, making a breakfast and setting a couple of places at the table. She was pouring a couple cups of coffee when he finished washing, but she didn't look at him. After placing the cups on the table, she started looking about for anything she might have forgotten, the coffee pot still in her hands.

"Sarah —" Shaw began.

"I'm glad you came out to the ranch. The trip to town takes so much time and I've been terribly busy here."

"Sarah —"

"I hope I have enough here. I seem to eat so little when I'm cooking for just myself…"

"Sarah, we need to talk." For a moment, he stood looking at her and she noticed and stopped moving. Setting the coffee pot on the table, she wiped her hands on her apron while looking at the floor. When she looked up, she had tears in her eyes.

He took a step toward her.

She came to him slowly and he took her in his arms. The embrace lasted for several minutes, while Sarah cried, her face buried in his chest.

After she composed herself, she looked up into the eyes of a man she hardly knew, but a man so different from the one she was married to. Though her moment of sadness was past, she didn't move away from his embrace. Without speaking, she turned her face up to Shaw's and they kissed, gently at first, but with growing urgency. In that instant, passions were released that neither of them could have predicted or controlled, even if they had wanted to.

It was quite a bit later when they finally got around to eating breakfast. They barely nibbled at their food, or even looked at each other. It was as if both of them were astonished by what had just occurred between them and the frenzied urgency of it.

"Sarah, I'm sorry —"

"No! Please don't say that. Don't be sorry. I don't think I could bear it if you were sorry." She looked at him. "Because I'm not sorry. I could never be sorry any more. I'm no longer Samuel's wife in my heart... He made it impossible for me to care for him."

Shaw looked uncertain and Sarah's heart broke. "Matt, I had no life left with Samuel. Leaving was not an alternative as I have no place left to go and I feel responsible for his care. But, from the moment I first saw you, I wished, despite myself; despite anything I might have said to you, I wished it was you I shared this home with."

He seemed stunned. "Sarah, you have to understand, I have to finish what I started. Your husband hired me to find the man who killed Stuart — and to find the ones responsible. I can't walk away from that."

"But why?" she asked, surprised. "What good will it do? Samuel won't benefit from it, nor will I. Samuel isn't well. You have no idea the depths of his depression. If you help him kill the men responsible for Stuart's death, you won't be doing him a favor. You'll be causing his total destruction. Besides..." she paused, a worried look on her face, "... you could be killed!" Then she added, almost whispering, "I don't think I could bear that."

Shaw reached out and took her hand. "My personal danger can't be the deciding factor between going ahead with this job or walking away from it. Nor, for that matter, will I allow my feelings for you to interfere with my responsibility to find the killer of Stuart. The killer needs to be found and I may be the only man who can do it. You have to understand that, or there can be no future for us."

She shook her head, angrily. "Fine! Go ahead and get yourself killed, but you'll probably get Samuel and me killed as well — because we've decided we're going with you."

* * * *

Later that afternoon, Shaw stabled his horse with the others and tended to their feed and water. Having Samuel along would be bad enough. Having Sarah accompany them would severely limit their mobility and speed of travel, and his ability to act decisively.

There was also the real danger that Ballou would come to know someone was on his trail and want to do something about that. Shaw could move almost invisibly across the country, but three people moving in concert would always attract attention. Nothing good could come of this, but he had no idea how to dissuade Sarah from coming.

Sarah had hitched up the wagon and headed to town. She'd spend the night there and return with Samuel in the morning. It would be quicker to ride directly over the pass to Soulard from the ranch and in that way they could make it in one day's travel. From there, they would ride the train to Dodge City to look up Reinhardt Keyes.

Since he had the rest of the day to waste, Shaw decided to further investigate Ballou's route into and out of the basin. He grabbed his Winchester and a canteen and started up the hill to the little family burial plot.

He paused at the graves to contemplate what he now knew about the souls who rested there. Little Rebecca, barely five years old, had died of influenza. Not an uncommon occurrence, but made more personal now that Shaw had fallen in love with the little girl's mother. Having never had children, Shaw could barely imagine the ache that accompanied the loss of any child. He'd seen a photograph of Rebecca on the mantel of the cabin, taken when she would have been three or so. Light of hair, with sharp eyes and an impertinent little nose, Shaw knew that a cruel fate had taken a lovely little girl away from a couple who had loved her dearly. He had a slightly better understanding of the emotional forces that might actually drive a man mad with grief.

The unmarked grave of Stuart stood in mocking contrast to little Becca's. He could only wonder why Stuart's grave wasn't completed. No stone, no marker or adornment. There was only a bare mound of gravelly earth. Shaw contemplated the possible meanings of this. Samuel was almost certainly beyond usefulness, judging by the way the ranch had fallen into disrepair, but Shaw could not understand Sarah not wanting to somehow memorialize the spot where Stuart rested. Why had no one tended to the grave?

Shaw looked toward the pass through which he'd entered the basin only a few days ago. He felt that he'd been here for years, but he knew that feeling simply sprung from a long intimacy with wild places and all the unusual activity that had taken place in such a short period.

He examined the surrounding countryside. The basin was carved from granite by glacial action in times past. Perhaps one day again, huge flows of ice would begin in the high country and scour the very ground on which he now stood and any surface objects, such as the home or burial plot, would be ground into dust and disappear.

Looking around, this seemed the perfect place for a wanderer to stop and rest, and maybe remain; to build a shelter, to hunt for game, to raise a family and graze stock. Had the Roarks been the first to use this ground? He could imagine some Indian family in this spot long ago, before the first whites settled the country, perhaps even before the last great ice flow. Was he standing on what were unrecognizable fragments, evidence of some past inhabitation? Had their graves simply been erased as well?

Shaw was a contemplative man. He knew the bones of countless men and women littered the countryside unburied and unknown, and in time nothing would remain to tell of a life lost and a story abruptly ended. He'd ridden past the skeletal remains of more than one human being in his travels, both white and Indian. Though he had initially considered burying them, he hadn't done so. It somehow seemed fitting to him that time would scatter the earthly evidence of a past life and wear the bones down in the way of the earth. Shaw felt certain that he'd prefer to be left to lie, his bones covered in the winter by snow and in the summer by sweet grasses and wild flowers; the gentle breezes of spring could pass over his bones and the rains occasionally wash them clean.

Why people needed to commemorate a life by preserving the final resting place had always seemed a bit odd. He'd heard about the Vikings, who took the departed and put them in a boat filled with wood and trinkets and other items, and set it adrift on the tide after lighting a fire onboard. That had always seemed a fitting way to dispose of a corpse, and to commemorate a life. He smiled. There weren't too many places he could launch a boat here in the mountains.

He took a deep breath. There was a taste to the mountain air in the springtime. It was almost like drinking from a glacial stream. In Denver, you might be constantly assailed by the smoke of wood or coke fires, or the smells of stable waste, or of drinking or eating establishments. In the mountains in summer, there was only freshness and the scent of wildflowers or pine.

With one last look around, Shaw headed into the forest off the trail, descending the heavily wooded slope, working his way around random granite outcroppings. He retraced his route to the entrance of the cave he'd explored a few days ago. On this occasion, he took the time to really search the area surrounding the cave.

After an hour of fruitless examination, he descended farther down the slope. It was steep, but it would have been manageable to a man equipped with snowshoes in the winter. He knew the snow would have been very deep in this area, protected as it was from the wind. It wouldn't be unusual for snow to reach depths of ten feet or more. A man walking through this area in mid-winter would be walking among the branches of the pines in some places. It could be negotiated, but certainly not with a horse, or horses, even with a man breaking trail on snow shoes in advance of the animals.

Shaw had traveled close to four miles, meandering through the trees, following an ever-descending depression; a natural trail made by water erosion. He had no idea if he was retracing the steps of the shooter, but knew anyone walking this mountain slope would have found this way the easiest to navigate.

Occasionally, he broke out into small meadows with new-growth mountain grasses that would draw and hold the elk when they returned from their winter graze in the valleys. He encountered a couple of fresh avalanche cuts where the pines had been broken off, leaving stumps about six feet tall jutting out of the mountain slope. After crossing these open areas, he re-entered the thick pines.

A couple hours of indirect travel passed. Shaw heard a mountain stream just ahead, running with a fairly healthy volume of snowmelt. Underfoot, the ground cover was becoming sparse and the earth increasingly rocky. As he approached the sound of the stream, he came to a tiny clearing off to one side of which was a small log shelter. To the south of the clearing was the stream bed and immediately beyond that, the mountain took a steep up-turn. Beyond the cabin, the stream led down the valley in the direction of Eagle Town, several miles to the southwest. There appeared to be a natural trail, or maybe a game trail leading in that direction.

Shaw examined the cabin for several minutes without making an approach. It appeared deserted. There was no sign of fresh activity; no smoke curling from the tin chimney that sprouted from the rough-cut shingle roof. A small pile of cut firewood lay stacked next to the front door. The wood had been cut with an axe rather than a saw and none of the log ends appeared fresh, yet none had the weathered look of having been there for more than a couple of winter seasons. The ground around the pile suggested it had been considerably larger than it was now. Scattered about the pile were pieces of moldering bark that had begun to rot and had fallen free of the quartered firewood.

Behind the cabin and connected to it was a lean-to shelter for stock. Shaw quietly levered a cartridge into his Winchester and approached the cabin cautiously. There was only one window, covered by a single shutter that swung on a nicely crafted wooden hinge. The man who fashioned that shutter was handy with tools. Shaw slid his fingers under the shutter and attempted to open it. But it was firmly secured from within. He didn't immediately approach the door, preferring to walk around the back and inspect the lean-to.

Fairly recently, horses were stabled here. He estimated the shelter held stock a month or two previously and no more than three months for certain. A rusty shovel stood in the corner, no doubt used to muck out the stable floor to keep it clean of horse droppings. Two canvas tarpaulins were rolled and tied up under the lean-to's open ends. Shaw noted that they could be untied and would unfurl and provide protection from the wind. In such a small shelter, the animals would generate enough heat to survive in even the coldest weather in this little valley.

He noticed a circular depression made by a bucket or

feed bag, and next to it a handful of oats had spilled. The oats had been eaten by rodents; but enough of the husks remained to identify the grain. Some kernels of corn had been ground into the mud by a hoof and were still identifiable. Oats and corn made good feed for horses in the winter.

He walked the rest of the way around the building and carefully opened the door. Nobody was in the cabin. A wooden bunk made from sawn timbers supported a leather strap mesh, making a decently comfortable bed. A small three-legged rough-cut table with a matching stool stood to the side under the window. On the table was a miner's lamp. In the corner, a small pot-bellied stove. The lamp still held kerosene and the chimney glass was clean. Oddly, the wick had been neatly trimmed as well. The freshly trimmed cloth had no charring; indicating whoever had done the work had no longer needed light. It was what a careful man would do when tidying up.

The floor had been swept before the cabin was abandoned. Some canned goods were stacked on a shelf. The cabin had been occupied recently enough that there was not a covering of dust on anything, but already spiders had created a network of fresh webs and funnels.

Shaw opened the stove door. Inside was a small pile of ash and nothing else. Some of the ash appeared to have come from burned paper and the ashes hadn't been stirred. He poked through the ashes to see if any paper remained unburned. There was none.

He stepped out of the cabin. By the lack of tracks in the yard, Shaw knew no one had been in the cabin in several weeks. They'd probably left when snow still covered the ground. He began a search of the immediate vicinity, looking for a dump. He found it almost immediately. Whoever had occupied the cabin had disposed of waste in a natural depression on the other side of the stock shelter. In the depression, Shaw discovered dozens of discarded cans and other refuse, including large elk bones.

As he turned away, something caught his eye. Turning back to the dump site, Shaw kneeled at the edge and from the dirt he picked up a small metal object. It was a flattened and exploded musket percussion cap. He shook his head in astonishment. Stuart had been killed several months ago and if this cap had come from the killer's rifle, it could be surmised he'd coolly spent many of those winter months hiding out within four land miles of the scene of the killing and hardly more than a mile as the crow flew.

Shaw commended the sheer nerve of such a man, waiting patiently for the snow to melt enough to make the roads out of the territory passable and take his horses out of the valley.

The cave now made more sense. A marksman couldn't lay in wait in the winter elements for long. He probably outfitted that cave to allow himself to occasionally warm up and take nourishment. In this manner, he could spend several hours or even a couple of days in close proximity to the ranch, observing and waiting for an opportunity to make his shot. The relative closeness to the cabin would allow him to periodically return there to feed his horses and rest up, or replenish his supplies at the cave. Perhaps he even waited for a day when fresh snow was either falling or threatening to fall. This would guarantee his escape trail was obliterated.

Shaw was faced with a real dilemma. Should he share this information with anyone, or keep it to himself? This cabin was much older than the Roarks' holdings. It had been here for decades. More than likely, it was an old prospector's base. Because of its age, Shaw had trouble believing Samuel had not known of its existence. At the same time, Shaw admitted that if Samuel deferred most of the ranching to his son, it was highly likely he hadn't personally ever seen the place. It was entirely possible that if Stuart knew of it and had mentioned it to Samuel in passing, the rancher could have forgotten all about it. Old and abandoned prospector's cabins were not rare in this country. Some of them were even periodically fixed up and used by ranchers as line shacks. This one appeared to have been well maintained. Who had been responsible for that? Samuel or Stuart?

While everyone was wondering what happened to the killer, knowing about the existence of the cabin and sharing that information with Blake would have been crucial. The killer would have been a sitting duck for the law as no one could have gotten out of that small valley in the winter, except on foot. In essence, he'd been trapped here until springtime temperatures allowed him to ride out with his animals.

On the other hand, the brazenness of the act was so appalling, it was doubtful anyone would have suspected it as a possibility. From above, the depth of the snow and the location of the cabin rendered it invisible, unless chimney smoke was spotted. It offered an interesting insight into the kind of man who'd take such a chance, or even consider it.

Another interesting question remained. How did the killer learn of the cabin's existence? He'd arrived in early winter, too late in the season to scout around and discover the place by chance. He must have had prior knowledge of its location. It was just too complicated a plan to be mere happenstance. Did Mason or one of his riders know of the cabin and provide that information? That was certainly a possibility, since cowmen often traveled long distances looking for strays or tracking cattle that had been pushed off their range by rustlers or Indians. It was common to traverse another rancher's property in search of strays. If it wasn't Mason, then who else might have wanted Samuel dead?

Motive was everything. Crimes such as these were based on simple motives. Greed was a big motive for this kind of killing. So was revenge. Mason seemed to fit the bill on the first two. A powerful rancher always looked on his neighbors' land with envy. He might be large enough and he might be rich enough, but a rancher bent on wealth and power always needed more grass.

As to revenge, there was no doubt the townsfolk felt Mason was angry enough about his loss to Roark in court to lend credence to rumors that he was behind the hired killer's presence in the territory. But after speaking with Bentley, Shaw found Mason's apparent ambivalence about the killings of two of his men troubling. Would a man who hired a killer to avenge an embarrassing loss in court sit back and let Shaw walk away from killing two of his riders? He might, if he feared an outside investigation by state authorities.

A third and often overlooked motive for killing was passion. There was no doubt that Sarah Roark was a beautiful woman. In the west, affairs of the heart were not unheard of, as he could now personally attest to, but discretion was imperative. A man infatuated with Sarah might consider removing an impediment to his desire. Such a man would probably try to get closer to the widow through acts of kindness that outwardly appeared innocent.

Shaw reminded himself to broach these questions with both Samuel and Sarah at the appropriate time. First, he needed to know about the ranch and Samuel's claim to it. Some immediate questions that came to mind centered on his title. For instance, had he purchased the range from someone or simply filed on it? Had he ever been involved in a dispute over the ground or had there been any persistent attempts to buy it from him? Was he aware of any mineral deposits that might have value if they were developed?

Questioning Sarah about potential suitors would have to be a bit more delicately approached, particularly since their relationship had taken such a dramatic and intimately complicated turn. Shaw shook his head in disgust. How had he let this happen? More importantly, what did he plan to do about it?

He walked back to the cabin and closed the door to keep out any four-footed visitors. Looking up at the surrounding mountainside, he couldn't help but have the feeling — considering how recently this cabin had been occupied — that he could be in the rifle sights of a hidden marksman. Despite his over-active imagination, Shaw judged that the shooter was long gone, but the feeling lingered. Shaw had believed the trail of the killer was cold, but it was suddenly a lot warmer than he'd thought.

As the afternoon sun began to tuck itself behind the western peaks, Shaw started his long climb out of the deep valley, leaving the little cabin nestled quietly in the gathering shadows, just as he'd found it.

A Trail to Follow Toward an Uncertain Conclusion

It was a few minutes before noon when Samuel and Sarah arrived from town. Shaw was almost shocked to discover how thrilled he was to see her again. He watched as the wagon pulled into the ranch-yard and stopped at the stable, Sarah looping the reigns around the brake handle and nimbly climbing out of the wagon seat. Samuel dismounted gingerly, as if unused to any physical activity.

Shaw was taken aback when he saw how much different Samuel looked in daylight as opposed to the dim light of his office. If anything, his appearance was worse, almost deathly. It wasn't simply a matter of his having no color as much as it was the grayish tone of his skin, particularly around the eyes and mouth. Samuel seemed a very unhealthy man and in a severely depleted state. It troubled Shaw a great deal, not for the man's personal well being, but because he wondered how Samuel was going to make a difficult journey that involved rigorous travel. He was afraid Samuel might slow them down.

Sarah walked around to the back of the wagon and retrieved a travel bag and rifle and, without waiting for Samuel, walked on ahead to the cabin. As she got closer, Shaw realized her face was pale and her expression distraught. She managed a weak smile as she passed him and walked into the house. Shaw remained on the porch.

As Samuel walked across the ranch-yard, Shaw watched him look around. When he stepped up onto the porch he nodded to Shaw. "You've done some work around the place. I appreciate it."

Shaw looked closely at Samuel as the rancher spoke,

trying to read his expression. He was in the grip of an intense feeling of guilt for what he and Sarah had begun, while at the same time possessing an attitude bordering on contempt for the man they were in essence betraying. Shaw couldn't understand how a man could forsake so much in his life because of some emotional weakness. But too, Shaw recognized the fact that he'd never suffered a similar loss as Samuel. Shaw admitted that Sarah had suffered a huge loss as well, but she seemed to have reconciled the circumstances with the need to remain steadfast and look to the future. It was an example of two people reacting in totally different ways to exactly the same events.

It wasn't cowardice that Samuel exhibited, for Shaw understood fear. He'd known soldiers who ran in the face of death and he didn't blame them. He'd known other men who'd fought bravely for several campaigns. Eventually, the war took its toll, and there came a day when they could no longer face the prospect of continued fighting, killing, and death. These men couldn't muster the strength to get to their feet and it shamed them. Shaw understood them as well. He saw in their eyes the personal humiliation they felt and the sadness at having let down their brothers-in-arms; they just could no longer summon the necessary will.

Samuel, on the other hand, appeared to be a man totally consumed by his own personal sense of loss and outrage, yet he seemed thoroughly ambivalent to the feelings of another who'd lived through the same awful events and intimately shared the experiences with him. Shaw knew Sarah mourned the deaths of Becca and Stuart as strongly as Samuel did. The difference was Sarah still cared, if not about Samuel, then for the memories and life they'd shared. Samuel, though, no longer appeared to care about anything but his own loss and thoughts of personal revenge. Sarah could cope through strength, while Samuel relied on hate and self-pity.

For an instant, Shaw fought the urge to tell Samuel that

he was taking Sarah away from him. He managed to suppress the impulse, but it took more effort than Shaw would have believed. Instead, he looked around the ranch and remarked: "The place needs a lot of work. Sarah's done what she can, but she can't do it alone. You've lost cattle. I have no idea how many, but the survivors are scattered about. You're going to lose the rest if you don't make an effort."

Samuel's stare seemed to border on incredulity. Samuel shook his head. "Mr. Shaw, please understand that I no longer care about the cattle. I don't care about the ranch. I don't imagine I will come back here to live after our... our little *mission* is over." Samuel looked away, his gaze falling on the distant tree and the graves at its base. Now, his whisper was barely audible, "Once I leave here tomorrow, I don't care to ever see the place again!"

Shaw was momentarily stunned. Then he asked: "What about Sarah? Do you think she's going to want to leave?"

Samuel stared into Shaw's eyes with a look that Shaw didn't like. The man's eyes were glassy, as though he was in the grip of an intense fever. Samuel continued this gaze for a moment and then turned and walked over to one of the rocking chairs on the porch. He sat down heavily. He looked out over the ranch-yard with his hands on his lap. He swallowed, then spoke: "Sarah will have the money from the sale of the ranch, if she so desires. I don't want any of it. I've drawn up the papers and everything is now in her name. After that, she can go where she wants." He looked up at Shaw. "We have nothing left of our past. I still love her, Mr. Shaw, but we have nothing left and she'd be a constant reminder of everything I want to put behind me."

Shaw shook his head and looked away. He had no recollection of ever meeting anyone quite so self-possessed, and it only added to the scorn he felt for Roark. It also relieved him of much of the guilt he'd felt. It was easier now to imagine a future with Sarah after this unpleasant task was completed. It gave him greater freedom to express his feelings toward her. Thinking back to Sarah's expression when she'd walked past him, he wondered if Samuel had already explained his plans to her on the ride up from town. "What if Sarah doesn't want to leave? She can't run this place by herself, but it is her home. What is *she* to do?"

Samuel removed his hat and wiped the sweat from his forehead. The day was not hot and Shaw wasn't sweating; further evidence the rancher wasn't physically well. He spoke softly, "She can do whatever she wishes. She can keep the ranch or sell it. Perhaps she can hire a hand. It's not unheard of that a woman should run a ranch. It's been done. There may be enough cattle left to make a go of it. There's nothing owed on the property so it will be hers free and clear."

"You've told Sarah that?"

Samuel looked at Shaw briefly and then returned to gazing into the ranch-yard. "We spoke of it. She didn't argue strenuously. These past months have been difficult for her as well. I'm not oblivious to that and I'm sure she is relieved in her own way."

Sarah came to the door. "I'll have a meal on the table in a few minutes."

Samuel didn't look at her. "Thank you, Sarah, but I'm not hungry," he said with an odd detachment, as if he were speaking to a stranger.

She looked as if Samuel had slapped her. Her eyes were wide and she appeared close to tears. Without a word, she turned and disappeared back into the cabin.

Samuel didn't move.

Shaw wanted to shake the man for his callousness and disregard. Instead, he tried another tack. "Samuel, if you're going to go with me, you must eat. Right now, you're weak as a kitten and I can't carry you and I won't baby you. If you can't keep up, I'll go on alone."

Samuel's head snapped around and there was a flash of anger in his eyes. The feverish look of heat returned. "I hired you. You agreed to my terms."

Shaw smiled wickedly. When he spoke, his voice was harsh. "You can't dictate terms to me. I thought I made that clear. I'll hunt your killer for you and I'll even let you deal with him in your own way, but I will not let you get me killed because you can't hold up your end of the bargain. If you become a liability in that regard, I'll cut you lose." Shaw let that sink in a moment. "So, when we have a meal, I'll expect you to eat it!" As an afterthought, he added, "And, there'll be no whiskey on our journey."

Samuel face was livid and his hands gripped the armrests of the rocking chair with white knuckles.

Shaw knew any man would resent being talked to in such a manner and it had been Shaw's intention all along to dissuade Samuel and Sarah from joining in the search for Ballou. Setting these conditions was one way of putting Samuel on notice that he was not in charge when it came to Shaw's profession.

After a moment, Samuel began to visibly relax. "You have nothing to fear, Mr. Shaw," Samuel said softly. "I'll keep up. And, I did not bring any whiskey."

"Fine. Now let's go in and eat — and you can apologize to Sarah."

* * * *

The meal was strained. No one spoke for almost half an hour. Samuel ate a small amount, mostly picking at his food. The whole time he kept his gaze on his plate. Occasionally Shaw and Sarah made eye contact and she'd look quickly away.

Finally, Samuel broke the quiet, without looking up. "Oh, by the way, they found Wade Hardy dead yesterday." He broke off a piece of bread and took a bite.

157

Sarah stared at Shaw, a look of suspicion in her eyes. Shaw smiled. "No, Sarah, I didn't kill him."

"Well, then, he's the only dead person in Eagle Town that you didn't personally kill in the last three days!" Sarah retorted.

"I suppose it must seem that way." He looked at Samuel. "How did Hardy die?"

"Knife to the heart. He was found in an alley behind his office. The marshal asked around and was led to believe you'd been making inquiries about Hardy. That seemed to stick in some people's minds and they were only too willing to report it. The marshal stopped by to see me yesterday afternoon. He feels fairly certain you didn't kill Hardy. He didn't think a knife was your style. Obviously, the person who hired Ballou is interested in closing any doors that might be left open."

"Well, Hardy could have led us to the guilty party in Eagle Town, but killing him can't stop us from looking for Ballou. So, the door is only half closed," Shaw said.

Sarah spoke up. "What *are* our plans for finding Ballou?"

"First, we take the train to Dodge City and look up Reinhardt Keys," Shaw answered. "Then I'll ask him how he communicates with Ballou. More than likely, it's by telegram, though it's entirely possible that Dodge City is Ballou's home territory. For that reason, we must proceed with caution."

"And you expect that Keys will just tell you what you want to know?" Sarah asked. "I'd think it would be in his best interests to deny even knowing Ballou."

"Of course it is. I'll have to convince him that it's in his interests to a much greater degree to tell us what we need," Shaw said with earnest, yet deadly, humor.

"Why can't we pretend that we have a job for this man, Ballou?" Sarah asked.

Shaw shook his head. "The marshal indicated that

Ballou operates on his own timetable. He may be on a job somewhere and we don't have the luxury of sitting around and waiting for him. Besides, I want to find *him*. I don't want him trying to find *me*."

She was persistent: "But what's to stop this Mr. Keys from alerting Ballou after you've *convinced* him to give up the information?"

For the first time, Samuel looked up. He fixed Shaw with a stare.

Shaw sipped from his coffee cup and replaced it on the table. "Two things, actually. First, once he tells us what we want to know, he'll have to realize Ballou would likely consider him a liability. After all, Keys probably knows who Ballou's clients were, if not his targets. After we talk, it will be to Key's personal advantage that we succeed in our search. Certainly, his lucrative dealings with Ballou will be over, but it's far better losing a valuable client than it is being hunted by someone of Ballou's caliber."

"Makes sense, I suppose," Samuel said.

"Second," Shaw continued, "I'll remind him of something Ben Franklin once said: 'Three men can keep a secret — if two of them are dead.'"

"You can't be serious!" Sarah exclaimed. "You'd threaten to kill him?"

Samuel didn't look at Sarah, but rather at Shaw. "No Sarah," he said. "I believe Mr. Shaw will explain to Keys that I'll be the one'll extract vengeance on him if he divulges our intentions. After all, I lost a family member through him. It would be expected that if he were to fear anyone besides Ballou, it should be me. I suppose in some way or another, I will be required to reinforce that belief."

Shaw didn't respond. Sarah looked back and forth between the two. When neither man spoke, Sarah's anger exploded. "Do you actually mean to torture the man if he doesn't cooperate?"

Samuel shrugged and Shaw studied his coffee cup.

159

Picking it up, he finished the last swallow. Sarah made good coffee, he'd decided. Coffee he could get used to. Perhaps he shouldn't become too accustomed to it. After a moment, he looked up with a particular coldness in his tone. "When we arrive in Dodge, we'll get hotel rooms. Then Samuel and I will see Keys. It may be that everything will be fine, or it may be we'll have to leave quickly." He paused and looked directly at Sarah. "So I'll have to ask you to stay close to your room so we know where we can locate you."

* * * *

Later that evening, Shaw was in the stable preparing for sleep. He was just about to extinguish the lantern when his horse's head raised and his ears perked up. Shaw took his revolver, moved into the shadows, and waited. He heard the stable door open and shut and saw Sarah come into the lantern's small circle of light. She carried a blanket. He holstered his pistol and came back into the light.

"Oh, there you are. I brought you another blanket. It's going to be cold tonight. Possibly even another frost."

Shaw noted she'd brushed out her hair and it flowed over her shoulders. In the lamplight, it shone red-gold. He knew he'd never be able to look at another woman as long as he lived without comparing her to Sarah. He took the blanket and his hand brushed against hers.

"Thanks. That was thoughtful," he mumbled. Neither of them spoke for a long and lingering minute; neither of them moved. Shaw felt his heart thudding in his chest and his mouth was dry. Standing before him was an answer to a question he'd never honestly allowed himself to ask. She was only three feet away and yet the distance might have been a thousand miles.

"We can't," she whispered.

"I know," he answered. "But knowing it doesn't make

160

it any easier." In his heart, he knew that she'd come to him if he asked, but with Samuel up in the cabin and their journey yet to begin, Shaw was not going to ask that of her.

A tear ran down Sarah's cheek and she turned and rushed to the stable door and into the night.

Shaw stood there for a long time, looking at the open door and listening to the night sounds. There was a brisk wind coming from the northwest and it made the stable boards creak. His horse stamped his foreleg and shook his mane.

Finally, he walked over to the door and pulled it shut. He slid the bar across to secure it and went back to his bedroll. He extinguished the lamp and lay in the darkness for a long time before falling into a deep and dreamless sleep.

* * * *

The first leg of the journey to Soulard had taken them on horseback through a mountain pass to pick up the road from Eagle Town. Before they'd left, Shaw had tied the corral gate open so the remaining horses could come and go as they pleased. There was graze and water for them on the ranch and it was doubtful they'd run off. More than likely, they'd stay close to the ranch.

At Soulard, they stabled their horses and boarded a three-car feeder line train bound for Holly. There, they planned to board the Atchison, Topeka and Santa Fe Railroad to Dodge City, Kansas. The run from Soulard to Holly took nine hours, for in addition to stopping at every camp and community along the way, the train was forced to take on water every fifteen to twenty miles.

Shaw disliked train travel. It was noisy, smelly and not particularly comfortable. The benches were hardwood and narrow; not built for comfort, coupled with a ride that was erratic and bumpy. Finding a place to close his eyes and get some rest was near impossible.

He had to admit that, bad as it was, train travel was still much better than stage travel. At least onboard a train he could get up and stretch his legs. Depending on the direction of travel and the prevailing winds, he might even be able to get some fresh air on the platform between the cars. If there wasn't any wind, it was best to stay inside the car. To do otherwise subjected a person to clouds of acrid smoke that billowed back from the engine's stack.

By late evening, the train stopped to take on water at Sargent, Kansas. Samuel remained onboard, while Shaw and Sarah decided to stretch their legs and get some fresh air. Sargent was little more than a collection of cattle pens, mostly empty this time of year. In a couple of months, the pens would be full of cattle awaiting shipment east. With the cattle would come the cowboys, closely followed by itinerant businesses housed in tents or temporary shacks that catered to the rougher elements. Now, the settlement was quiet.

Shaw and Sarah stopped by a split-rail corral and stood silently together. After a while, she said, "How long will it take to get to Dodge?"

"We'll be there tomorrow afternoon. All told, about thirty hours travel from Holly."

There was a hissing roar that caused her to jump as the engineer bled a little steam from the locomotive in preparation for taking on water. "Why does he do that? It scares me every time." she said.

Shaw looked back at the locomotive and chuckled. He was fascinated by the machinery and how the power of steam could be harnessed to pull rail cars behind an engine. "They're taking on water. At the same time, they're stoking the fires to help heat the new water coming in. The engineer's adjusting the steam pressure levels. We'll be underway in a few minutes."

"Well, it still startles me, even if I do know the reason

for it."

"I've seen Indians so startled by the steam cars that they tried to shoot them; figured they were some form of monster. People who saw it, laughed at it, but I never found it funny. Looking at it from a primitive viewpoint, I can see the resemblance to a monster and not a good one either, to their way of thinking."

"There's nothing monstrous or bad about a locomotive," she said. "It's just a machine, another form of transportation."

"Maybe to you and me. To an Indian, it's a monster. It's a monster they can't kill and each one that comes down the rails is filled to the brim with more white people. Every time they hear the whistle of an approaching locomotive, they hear the sound of their own displacement." Shaw shook his head. "The far-thinking ones among them see the steam cars as something evil and threatening; another white man's magic trick and eventually it will be bad for their people."

"So, do you think it's bad?"

Shaw pondered her question. "No, I don't suppose I do. I don't think like an Indian. But at the same time, I understand their viewpoint. The Indian way of life is doomed. I see the train as just another reminder that all civilizations have to change with the times. But the Indian won't adapt on his own, so the trains will force him to and the sooner he does the better it'll be for his people."

"I think it's a shame that they have to change at all," Sarah said. "The world is big enough for everyone. Why can't they keep a little bit of it for themselves?"

Shaw smiled a sad smile. "Sarah, if someone was to tell you to plant a garden or you'd starve in the winter; you'd go ahead and plant a garden. An Indian wouldn't. He'd look at the buffalo and the elk and the wild roots and berries and think, 'why should I plant? There's plenty for me.' Then the white man comes along and the buffalo herds and game start to dwindle. The Indian has to travel much greater distances to find game to feed the village. He covers a lot of ground, a fraction of which he'd have used to feed his village if he just planted crops.

"The Eastern Indians have been planting for centuries, but the Western Indian sees the white man planting corn and wheat and oats and he laughs. But in the winter, his children cry because of hunger and he blames the white man for the lack of buffalo, or chasing the elk over the mountains, never thinking that corn and wheat and oats would help to keep his children from starving."

"But it's the white man's way and it's the white man's fault." Sarah said. "It was the Indians' land before we came. Why should they change?"

Shaw understood her argument, sympathized with the feelings that prompted her thoughts. But he was a pragmatist. "Sarah, there were planting Indians here in the west as well. But they're gone, likely chased out by the very Indians we have now; the ones who don't plant. But to answer your question, they should change, because they have to. If they don't learn to plant, their children will starve. If they don't learn to tend cattle, their people will disappear. When you look at the coming winter, you don't say, *'I'm not going to plant crops because I shouldn't have to. I was here first.'* You know you have to, so you do it. They haven't learned that yet. It's too bad. A lot of little children are going to starve before they accept the future."

"I think it's an ugly future. I can't imagine the freedom they had only to have it all taken from them."

"This is why the locomotive is a bad omen to the Indian. When Custer died a while back, the nation woke up to the problems with the Indian in a big way. You see, the outside world is coming to Indian country and it won't stop and it won't make allowances for tribal differences and it won't take the time or make the effort to accommodate their traditions and lifestyle. In twenty years, they'll all be

164

planting and tending stock — or they'll be gone. It's not right, but it's the way it is."

The whistle sounded and Shaw turned back toward the train cars. He stopped when he realized Sarah was still looking into the night. Without turning her head, she spoke in almost a whisper.

"Everything is so cut and dried with you, isn't it?" Shaw wasn't sure what she meant, but before he could speak, she told the darkness, "You have an honesty about you that bespeaks a fierce resistance to compromise, yet you counsel compromise. But not everyone is as strong as you, Matthew Shaw. Most people have failings they cannot bury. I wonder what you think of people who can never live up to the standards you set for yourself. And when this is all over, I wonder how you'll feel about me."

"I can't imagine my feeling for you will ever change, Sarah."

She turned to face him. He noticed her sadness. "You can't?" She touched his hand. "I hope you're right. With all my heart, I hope so."

Gathering her shawl around her shoulders, Sarah walked on ahead of Shaw to the train car. As she walked away, Shaw thought about her words. He suspected she was probably worried about the strength of his feelings toward her. After all, she was a woman who had allowed herself to become intimately involved with him while she was still married. Such an involvement was not readily accepted and could severely damage any woman's reputation. But, if her life had not been so untenable in the first place, Shaw would never have allowed himself to think of her as anything but another man's wife. She'd come to him only because he allowed it. As far as he was concerned, she bore no guilt. He loved her now and, he was certain, he always would. Yet, in the back of his mind was a hint of doubt that he couldn't shake. There were so many things about this situation that didn't make sense. No matter how hard he tried, he couldn't shake the feeling that he might be making some fatal mistakes, and that loving Sarah might be the biggest of them.

He followed her to the train car and boarded. A minute passed and then the engine chuffed great bellows of steam and the heavy iron wheels began to turn. Nineteen hours later, they were in Dodge City.

* * * *

They'd taken individual rooms at the Great Western Hotel and Sarah had retreated to hers to freshen up after their exhausting journey. Samuel and Shaw went out onto the veranda of the hotel to look the town over. There was a cosmopolitan air to Dodge City. This could be seen on the signs and storefronts advertising fine wines, brandies and cigars. It was as if a small part of Saint Louis had migrated to the frontier.

The open carrying of firearms was prohibited in Dodge north of the railroad tracks and enforced by the local constabulary. It was not uncommon, however, or unexpected, for firearms to be carried concealed in Dodge City proper and Shaw had a revolver under his coat. Samuel, on the other hand, carried no sidearm.

South of the tracks was an environment where anything went. Prostitutes and pimps, scam artists, opium and gambling dens and thieves of every sort were the order of the day south of the "Dead Line." Nearly everyone went openly armed in that part of Dodge and the lawmen didn't often bother them.

The town had an early history of lawlessness and since those rough and tumble beginnings, a progression of frontier lawmen had been killed by gunfire during service to the community. Shaw knew the current marshal, a good man by the name of James Masterson. Masterson's brothers Ed and Bat had both served as Dodge City lawmen at one

166

time or another.

Ed had been killed last year while attempting to disarm a man named Wagner at one of the local drinking establishments. It was a killing that many still talked about in Dodge, and it was said that Ed had been a well-respected lawman in addition to being a fair and honorable man. Some voiced the opinion he was too fair or too easy going. While Ed and Wagner had struggled for control of a pistol, another fellow tried to come to Wagner's aid. He stuck his gun in Ed's face and pulled the trigger, but his pistol misfired. Before he could try another shot, Bat rushed into the fray and killed Ed's attacker with three shots.

Wagner managed to free his gun hand and blasted Ed at contact distance, setting Ed's coat on fire from the gunpowder. As Ed fell back, Bat put a bullet in Wagner's head and he fell next to Ed. The whole incident had taken about thirty seconds and snuffed out the lives of three men.

Shaw couldn't see where city ordinances banning the carrying of firearms really played a part in lessening the incidences of gunplay. He figured half the men on the street at any given moment carried a gun under their coats, while the other half probably carried two. It was common knowledge there were killers and thieves about at all times of the year and Shaw felt Samuel and Sarah would have to be suitably armed.

"You're going to have to acquire a couple of good weapons," Shaw told Samuel. "You have one rifle and one shotgun between the two of you, and no side arms. You'll need another rifle minimum; one that hopefully carries a little farther than your improved Henry. I'd recommend getting a couple of side-arms as well."

Samuel smiled. "I wouldn't be able to use a pistol if I had one. I never quite got the hang of them."

"You can learn!" Shaw said sharply. "Samuel, we're tracking a killer. If you don't understand that by now, you need to go back home! We have no idea where we're going to be a week from now and I need to know both you and Sarah are prepared to defend yourselves and, if it comes to that, maybe me. Once Ballou knows he's being tracked, he'll become even more dangerous. More than likely, after he learns we're on his trail, he'll try and kill me first. Having done that, he'd expect that you'd probably give up and go home."

"I don't believe he'd just let us go." Samuel declared.

"Sure he would." Shaw said. "There's no profit in killing you. Ballou will kill for money, or he'll kill to defend himself. But if there's no money in it, and if he's no longer in danger, then further killing doesn't make any sense. It attracts attention and men like Ballou don't want attention. If you pull out and ride away, he'll let you go."

"Are you suggesting that if something happens to you, that's what Sarah and I should do?"

"It's your choice, Samuel. But in truth you wouldn't last an hour if Ballou wanted you dead. If he gets me, your life won't be worth a tinker's damn. I doubt he'd hurt Sarah, but you never know. So, I'd counsel you to ride away."

Samuel appeared to consider Shaw's words. Across the street a wagon pulled by oxen and filled with buffalo skulls and a jumble of assorted bones, rumbled across the tracks, raising a cloud of dust that slowly drifted away. "So, I guess Sarah and I must acquire new guns," Samuel said. "Where do you recommend we get them?"

"Zimmermann's is just down the street." Shaw indicated the direction with a nod of his head. "He used to outfit the buffalo hunters. His business has tapered off a bit since the glory days but he'll have everything we need." Together they started out.

The sign over the door read *Dry goods, Hardware and Gun-Smithing*. During the heyday of the buffalo hunt, Zimmermann's store had racks of rifles at incredibly inflated prices. Well-used Sharps brought two hundred dollars and fifty dollars more was necessary for a new one with accessories. The rifle racks were still there, but no longer completely filled with the big single shots so popular with the hide hunters. There were still a goodly number of Sharps, Remington, Ballard and Springfield rifles to be had at prices a mere shadow of what they'd been only three or four years before, but now the store contained a good stock of repeating arms. Depending on cost, he might outfit himself with an old Spencer or a Henry, or any number of Winchester arms, including the new model of seventy-six. It was that model Shaw asked to see.

It was a heavy rifle with the same basic action as all the other Winchester offerings, but larger in scale and much stronger. It came chambered for the new .45-.75 cartridge, which boasted much of the range and power of the large single shot buffalo rifles, but in a repeating platform. The simplicity of the action allowed for a butter-smooth cycling of the lever. "This is what I recommend," he told Samuel. "It will shoot a lot farther than your .44 rim-fire. I have one just like it, so we can share ammunition."

Samuel held his hand out and Shaw gave him the rifle. It bore lovely case colors on the receiver and the oil finished walnut stock had a wonderful luster. Samuel smiled and nodded. "We will buy this rifle." He handed it back to the clerk. "What do you have in the way of side-arms?"

The clerk set the Winchester aside and walked to a cabinet that held pistols of various sizes and makes. The two most common pistols displayed were Colt's revolvers, as well as Smith & Wesson offerings. "Do you have a preference?" the clerk asked.

Samuel turned to Shaw. "Any recommendations?"

"Do you have any experience with one-hand guns?"

"I've shot a few, mostly the Colt's that took loose powder and ball. I was not very proficient."

169

Shaw asked the clerk for a Smith & Wesson Schofield, in .45 caliber. When it was handed to him, Shaw inspected it closely, demonstrating to Samuel the method by which the weapon was opened for loading and unloading. "You thumb this latch back and tilt the barrel down. It opens all six chambers for inspection and loading. Then you simply close the action and you're ready to go. It's the fastest pistol invented for loading and unloading. When you want to unload it, you merely open the action and it automatically ejects the expended cartridge cases. Plus, it has a reputation for exceptional accuracy and, if necessary, I can use the cartridges in my Colt if I have to. You won't be able to use my cartridges in your gun, however."

"Does that present a problem?" Samuel asked.

"I wouldn't think so. I'm just pointing it out so you won't be confused or surprised."

"It's rather large. Do you think Sarah would have difficulty with it?"

Shaw thought that Sarah demonstrated a familiarity with her rifle and handled it with ease. He doubted she'd have a problem learning to handle and shoot such a pistol. "I think it will be fine."

Samuel purchased two Schofield revolvers and the Winchester rifle, adding one hundred cartridges for each weapon: all that ammunition was needed as Shaw wanted them to familiarize themselves with the weapons at the first opportunity, so a little practice would be in order.

Shaw had the guns wrapped up for the trip back to the hotel. No sense in antagonizing the local law unnecessarily. Once there, he unwrapped the weapons and, together with Sarah and Samuel, again went over the fundamentals of loading, unloading and handling.

When they were finished, it was time for dinner and the three of them decided to take their meal in the hotel's dining room. Knowing what was available in Eagle Town, Shaw felt certain neither Sarah or Samuel had eaten in a dining room with papered walls nor a fancy pressed tin ceiling. The tables were clothed in linen and the silver, brightly polished. Once they had ordered, Sarah made a request.

"I know you're planning to find this man Keyes, but do you think we could hold off one day?"

Samuel's face showed surprise and his tone was a little irritated. "Why?"

Sarah looked down at the table top and Shaw experienced a flare of anger at Samuel's insensitivity, and there was an edge to his voice when he interrupted, "I think Sarah's found the trip to be tiring. It would help if we were all rested. At the same time, Dodge City is a bit more exciting than Eagle Town. If you have never been here, it might be nice to take in some of the sights."

Samuel's expression gave Shaw the impression he was not interested in any distractions, but Shaw continued regardless: "Life is short, Samuel. You of all people should know this to be true. You're here now. Try and take a little pleasure from the unpleasantness of our journey."

Sarah looked hopeful and finally Samuel relented. "Of course, you're right. I have no interest in seeing Dodge City myself, but I should not be selfish. Mr. Shaw, if Sarah wishes to take in the sights, would you be kind enough to escort her? I'd feel better by far if I knew she was protected from the rougher elements to be found here."

Shaw looked closely at Samuel's face. His request was not unusual, given what Shaw knew of the man's nature, but it was quite possible Samuel was beginning to suspect that Shaw's interest in Sarah might be more than professional. Shaw didn't see any signs of duplicity in the man's expression. Rather, Samuel appeared simply to have no interest in life, or living it. Death was all that was on his mind.

Sarah glanced at Shaw. "Would you? I just want to walk a bit and look into the store windows. I know it's silly but it's been so long."

"I'd be honored," Shaw said.

She smiled brightly for the first time in many days. When she did, Shaw felt a sensation not unlike a physical blow to the chest. This woman had the power literally to take his breath away.

When dinner was done, Samuel returned to his room while Sarah and Shaw strolled along Front Street on the north side of the tracks. Sarah commented on the buildings, noting they were all lit up and appeared to be thriving. "Are most of the saloons on that side of the tracks?" she asked.

Shaw felt embarrassed. "That's literally the wrong side of the tracks, Sarah. There are things and places in Dodge City that respectable people avoid — and they're all located in that direction. A *lady* has no business venturing over there; nor does a gentleman."

"Oh." She seemed equally embarrassed. They continued on.

As they walked, Shaw told Sarah a bit about the history of Dodge. "Dodge is a cattle center now, where only a couple years ago it was one of the leading collection centers for the sale of green buffalo hides for shipment east." He paused and pointed out several vacant lots. "There, all along Front Street, great piles of hides were stacked as high as the rooftops, waiting for transportation. In the winter, it wasn't too bad, but in the summer, given an errant wind, the smell of rot was beyond description and the only thing worse than the smell of the hides might have been the smell of the skinners who brought them in."

She laughed. "I can believe it."

His heart hammered and he wanted to see and hear her laugh again.

"Tell me more," she insisted.

"Now there's a lucrative market in the bones that still litter the territory. It's a hunt to find them because they're mostly hidden from view by the tall prairie grasses, which

172

are no longer held in check by the grazing buffalo. Come summer, there'll be dozens of enormous piles of bones and skulls being purchased by dealers for as much as eight dollars to the ton."

"Why do they want the bones?"

"They're destined for the fertilizer plants and china makers in the east and in Europe."

"Oh, I see. Bone china."

He nodded. "Aye. Still, it's cattle that Dodge relies on now. By the end of summer, the pens outside of town will be filled to capacity with bawling cattle. With the cows will come the Texas cowboys. On an evening when the cowboys are in town, it's not safe to be on the street."

They passed several storefronts and Sarah's eyes were drawn to the window of a dry-goods shop in particular. Her gaze lingered on a mannequin dressed in a lovely blue dress and a tag proclaimed it was the current fashion straight from Paris. Sarah touched her own dress and smoothed it with her hands. Shaw noticed everything and it tugged at him.

"Sarah, you'd look wonderful in that dress…but that's not to say you don't look wonderful regardless."

She smiled. "You're sweet for saying so. I've forgotten what it feels like to dress up for some special occasion. You know, I haven't worn a dress like that or danced in years. The last ball I attended was when I was sixteen and my father was entertaining some army officers. I'm sure he was hoping I'd marry one of them and I'm equally certain he didn't care which one." She looked sad. "That was the last time I danced."

He felt a sharp tug of emotions. In his mind's eye, he saw Sarah in such a fine dress, holding his arm as they entered a ballroom, while the eyes of the other gentlemen turned and watched, mostly with envy at his good fortune.

"Sarah, when this is over, I'll dance with you."

She looked into his eyes while hers welled with tears.

"I'd like nothing better than to dance with you, Matt. I mean that."

She squeezed his arm and, after a moment, indicated she was ready to move on. They walked the full length of Front Street and back, taking their time, letting the dusk settle in and the coolness of the evening freshen the air.

There were others on the street enjoying the early evening and when a gentleman passed he touched the brim of his hat in deference to Sarah. Some of the men were rough-hewn cattle drovers, but they were respectful.

As they approached the Great Western, a staccato burst of shots were fired on the south side and Shaw grabbed Sarah, pulling her behind his body. None of the shots sent bullets anywhere near.

"Rowdy cowboys," Shaw said quietly. "Just letting off steam. It's a bit early in the season but a herd came in today."

"How can you tell it wasn't a gunfight?"

"Doesn't feel like it. The shots didn't have that sense of *urgency* to them. It sounded like they were fired up in the air. It gets so you can tell. Instinct, I'd guess."

All the while they talked, neither Shaw nor Sarah realized that he had pulled her close for protection and that they were still so close they could have been embracing. When Shaw suddenly comprehended, he looked down into Sarah's upturned face and could barely fight the urge to kiss her. He saw that she was ready for it, wanting it. After a long moment, he shook his head minutely.

Sarah stepped back and collected herself. "I'd better go in," she said, with a trace of stiffness in her voice. She turned and entered the hotel.

Shaw watched her walk across the lobby and disappear up the stairs. The fatigue of the last few days washed over him. After a few moments, listening to the faint sounds of music coming from the saloons across the tracks, and catching the smell of dust from the street, on the breeze, he went to his room and washed up, in preparation for bed.

He laid out his gun and clothes and was about to extinguish the lamp when he heard a soft knock at his door. Withdrawing his revolver, he opened the door.

Sarah stood in the passage. Shaw stepped back and she entered, closing the door behind her. She turned the lock, walked over to the dresser, where she cupped her hand over the lamp's chimney glass and —without a word —blew out the light. Shaw heard her dress fall to the floor and a moment later, they slipped into bed together, Sarah's cool skin against Shaw's somehow made the Kansas night seem a lot warmer than it was.

Closing In

Sarah left quietly during the night, but Shaw was not sleeping when she slipped out of the room. He lay thinking about the complicated relationship he'd allowed himself to become a part of. He was starting to believe the best thing to do would be to refund Samuel his fee and simply ride away with Sarah. He knew he wouldn't do it but, while they had not discussed the future, he was sure now that she'd go with him if he asked her.

Shaw had never quit a job he'd accepted, which was one of the reasons why he was so careful about accepting one. At first, it had seemed straightforward. Find the killer of a young boy and help the family find justice. But the situation had changed in a major way. The physical and mental condition of Samuel hadn't been anticipated and, despite himself, Shaw was still slightly suspicious of the man's bizarre behavior. Certainly he had all the expected motivations for finding the killer or killers of his son, but something about the man still didn't ring true.

Then there was Sarah. Every move Shaw now made, he did so only after first considering the effect it would have on the woman he'd fallen in love with; a woman married to the man who employed him. Yet, everything about this agreement with Samuel offended her. She was upset that Samuel wished to hunt down and kill the men responsible for his son's death. She was also hurt by the fact that Shaw was willing to facilitate what she felt was Samuel's immoral quest. And finally, she was horrified that Shaw had recently killed two men, even though it was self defense and they'd worked for the man both she and Samuel suspected was behind Stuart's murder. Shaw wondered if it would it be possible to see this thing through to the finish and still have Sarah's affection. It was beginning to look less likely.

For that matter, he cautiously wondered if he really had Sarah's true affection. There was no denying their attraction and the intimacy borne of it, but there was a definite aloofness to her, even after she succumbed to her passion. Was she truly in love with him, or was he merely a lifeline for her at a time when there appeared to be no hope? He could understand her reaching out to someone who seemed to understand her emotional and physical needs but, being a man who trusted his instincts, Shaw knew there was something else that came into play which he couldn't yet identify.

All he could do was see this thing through and hope that when everything played out, the conclusion would justify the effort.

When Shaw went down for breakfast he saw Samuel was already at a table drinking coffee and reading a newspaper. Shaw felt a stab of apprehension brought on by the sense of guilt he couldn't shake. Despite knowing Samuel's true feelings toward Sarah, Shaw knew he would never again be comfortable around the man until everything was in the open.

Shaw took a seat and ordered a large breakfast and coffee.

Samuel looked up, smiling. "Imagine this, a newspaper from Saint Louis that's only two days old! I've forgotten how much I missed this."

"The railroad has its advantages, I guess," Shaw responded. A waitress brought him his coffee and he tasted it. "I'd prefer no news at all if it meant I didn't have to listen to train whistles at all hours."

"That's the sound of progress, Mr. Shaw. Surely you enjoy the hustle and excitement of your home in Denver, do you not?" Samuel's tone was almost jovial. It was the first time Shaw had seen the man looking animated and interested. He hadn't noticed before, but it appeared Samuel had bathed and was wearing freshly laundered clothing. His color was better as well and he'd trimmed his beard.

"I reside in Denver, but I seldom stay there long. I prefer the quiet places. That, and my work normally keeps me away from the city."

Samuel glanced up from his paper and smiled. "It's nice to be steadily employed. I don't suppose your services will ever go out of style." Samuel's tone bore a faint hint of condescension.

Shaw smiled back, however thinly. "I suppose there are always going to be people who need men like me; those who cannot do for themselves."

Samuel's head snapped up. "You trade in human misery, sir! It's not an enviable profession."

"Human misery?" Shaw laughed sarcastically. "Mr. Roark, the sun's first rays illuminate *human misery* every day, in many forms and in many different locations. I don't create personal tragedy and I had absolutely nothing to do with yours, yet it happened and now you need me. I'm willing to help you deal with your situation when others are not, but I'd prefer not to have to tolerate your sneers. You must ask yourself why you need my services in the first place. It's why the blacksmith's profession is more respected on the frontier than the banker's — or, yes, the lawyer's. Anyone can count money or read the law, but it's a rare man who can forge iron. The blacksmith is treated with respect because people know they're going to need his services one day. The blacksmith is always busy and if you've offended him, he doesn't need your business. So either you treat the blacksmith with respect or you learn to shoe your own horses!"

Samuel appeared to think about that for a while. "I'm sorry. I don't believe I purposely meant to offend you, Mr. Shaw. Perhaps it's my way of dealing with my own fears

178

and inadequacies. But think about it. You won't always be able to do the work. It seems like a young man's job. Age is creeping up on you. Have you plans for the future?"

"I have more than enough money set away to buy a nice ranch and be comfortable. Maybe I'll raise horses."

"You should. You should marry and settle down before you grow too fond of solitude. Solitude can become a seductive mistress who shares all your secrets. It becomes too simple a life to merely consider one's own counsel; to trust one's own instincts over those of others. A man's mind is diminished when the only thoughts he has to ponder come from his own head."

"You say this Samuel, yet you're leaving behind the very things you've counseled me to attain. How do you reconcile that?"

Samuel looked directly at Shaw. "I have changed, Mr. Shaw. The world has changed my personal outlook on life. But it hasn't diminished my ability to realize a fresh perspective. I know what I'm speaking about. For the last several months, I had withdrawn. Now, while I'm not back to one hundred percent, I've started on the road to recovery, and I have *you* to thank for it."

Shaw was genuinely surprised. "Me? And just how have I helped you join the living once again?"

"We have communicated," Samuel said simply. "Or, perhaps more accurately, I have pondered aloud, and you have asked the difficult questions and listened to me and challenged me to consider things that I would have preferred not to consider. I only now realize how much I missed that. Stuart and I used to have long and interesting conversations."

"Perhaps if you'd have tried to talk with Sarah —"

"We had nothing to talk about." Samuel interrupted. Then his voice softened. "Mr. Shaw, Sarah is an intelligent woman, but she doesn't have a pondering mind. Her curiosities are more grounded to reality and less to the philosophical or theoretical. She does not wonder if Homer's *Iliad* is evidence of a true historical adventure or merely artful fiction. Without knowing for certain, I'm willing to bet you could debate it with me. Stuart could as well. My son was my only true friend and his death depressed me more than I could have admitted to anyone. When I needed understanding and compassion, all Sarah could offer was a reminder that the ranch was languishing; that things needed my attention."

Shaw barely concealed the contempt in his voice. "I would think you would understand that Stuart's death was not your loss alone."

Samuel's eyes flashed in sudden anger. "I had lost more! She could have seen that."

Shaw shook his head. "Perhaps there are things you *both* could have seen. In any event, people handle loss in different ways. Some attempt to stay busy and to continue on with life while others brood and wallow in self-pity!"

Samuel's eyes shone with a sunburst of anger and for just an instant his teeth bared in a snarl.

For a moment, Shaw wondered if he'd finally brought the man to the brink of a physical confrontation, one that Shaw would welcome if only to help him deal with his own sense of guilt which had been building.

Samuel took a long, deep breath. Finally, he folded the newspaper and set it aside. "I would expect you to defend her. You're a gentleman. All you know of me is the man you first met in the darkened prison of his office. I'm certain I disgusted you. I know, for I disgusted myself. But I assure you, there's more to me than the man you know to date. There's more to me than even Sarah knows. It would be to your benefit not to lose sight of that."

"I have no doubt," Shaw responded. "I suppose it's time we looked up Reinhardt Keyes."

Samuel appeared smug. "There is no need. It is done."

Shaw's eyes narrowed. "And when did this happen?"

"It happened last night, when you and Sarah were walking after dinner. I located Keyes and we had our talk." Samuel smiled.

Shaw was stunned. Inwardly, he was livid that, without consulting him, Samuel would so casually change the plan they'd devised. Outwardly, Shaw appeared calm, but without knowing what dangers the man's brazen and foolish act had placed them in, he could only wait to hear the details. "What do you mean, 'had your talk'?" Shaw asked with barely concealed anger.

"I started thinking about what we had told Sarah. Since I was going to be the man to *impress* upon Keyes the imperative to remain silent about our visit, why shouldn't I approach him alone?"

"Go on."

"Actually, it worked rather well. Keyes was dumbfounded I'd tracked him down. He's not a courageous man. It was relatively easy to convince him that his continued relationship with Ballou was unhealthy, particularly since it had brought so much misery to the family of a man who would return and exact certain revenge if he didn't, first, cooperate and, second, remain silent about it afterwards." Samuel was positively beaming.

Shaw suspected the action had been emotionally liberating for Samuel and he could actually understand its psychological benefits. He started mentally ticking off the possibilities, both good and bad, that could result from this latest revelation.

Samuel continued: "The man we're looking for makes his home in George's Town, in the mountains west of Denver. At first, I was surprised you hadn't known this, believing that people in your circle would at least have a working knowledge of others in the same line of work — more or less. But, it appears he no longer goes by the name Ballou."

Samuel paused long enough that Shaw realized his

employer was waiting for him to ask the obvious. Shaw refused to. He was not a man who asked the obvious or allowed others to bait him into raising foolish questions. He'd just experienced one of the greatest challenges of dealing with nonprofessionals. You couldn't trust them to follow through with a plan and the danger Samuel's actions could cause the three of them was at present incalculable, so he waited for Samuel to finish his account. There was no use in asking questions until he knew how bad the situation had become.

Samuel shrugged. "He now uses the name Pollard."

Shaw remained expressionless.

"Do you know him?"

Shaw took a drink of his coffee. When he answered, he was calm but still angry. "I know of him," Shaw admitted. "We've never met."

"What do you know of him?"

"Well, I didn't know he was a marksman by specialty. I'd heard that there was a man in Georgetown that could be paid to kill, and that he had clients as far away as San Francisco. I heard also that he was selective."

"In what way? Certainly a killer for hire cannot be very principled."

"I didn't say principled. I said selective. On the other hand, the term principled might apply as well."

"You're joking, certainly." Samuel laughed. "He shoots down people from hiding! Tell me where the principles are in that?"

"To your way of thinking, there aren't any. Keep in mind, this man obviously doesn't think like you or me; however, I suppose I might have a little better insight into the way he thinks, according to you. I said I'd heard he 'was' selective. It was believed that he normally took on clients who were morally wronged."

"Well, apparently, he has changed his ways. I wronged no one, *and* the courts agreed with me."

"Maybe. Or, perhaps you don't know you wronged someone. You shouldn't discount the fact that there's a different code of honor out here than where you came from. It's possible that you offended someone and have no recollection of it. I won't begin to speculate. But, if someone hired Pollard to kill you, then that person certainly wanted you dead. Rightly, or wrongly, someone evidently hated you enough. I don't suppose it would be impossible to convince a man like Pollard that you had it coming."

"Well, principled or not, he made an error and an innocent man died. How would he reconcile that?" Samuel asked.

"It's possible he didn't know he made a mistake. He may still not know."

"I can't believe that. Wouldn't his client inform him he made a mistake and demand he correct it?"

"It depends on what happened as a result. From all outward appearances, you were devastated; your life ruined. It's possible the client was satisfied with the outcome." Shaw gestured vaguely at Samuel. "We then have to assume Pollard was either not made aware of his mistake, or told that it no longer mattered."

"Why?"

"Because, you're still alive. If Pollard was aware of his error, he'd have corrected it as a matter of professional pride, and you have to admit you wouldn't have presented a particularly difficult target in the aftermath of your son's death."

Samuel was quiet.

Shaw finally asked the question that had been troubling him since this conversation began. "What about Keyes? He told you quite a bit, and Sarah and I were not gone that long. Tell me how you managed to achieve that."

"Mr. Keyes is unharmed; if that's what you want to know," Samuel said. "Well, perhaps that is an oversimplification." He smiled. "When I left him, he was unharmed, but if someone does not find him eventually, he will undoubtedly die." Samuel sat back with a satisfied look.

Shaw was cautious. "Find him, where?"

"In his office. I left him tied to a desk chair, unable to move or make any noise." Samuel chuckled. "He's a rather rotund man, so I'm certain he's pretty uncomfortable by now, that is, if no one has found him."

Shaw swore quietly.

"Try not to fret. I made it quite clear that I'd return and finish the job if he alerted Pollard that I was coming. I made no reference to either you or Sarah. If he does alert Pollard, only I will be expected."

Shaw pondered everything he'd just learned. If what Samuel said was true, it would mean that Pollard, if alerted, would only know that one man — Samuel — was tracking him. This did suggest an advantage that Shaw hadn't considered initially.

He nodded. "All right. I'm not happy that you did this without consulting me, but it appears we have the information we came for. Get Sarah packed and purchase tickets for Denver on the next available train. I'm going to send a telegram to an associate in Denver. By the time we get there, he'll have had time to gather some information that we may find useful."

Samuel smiled. "Mr. Shaw, try not to worry too much. I told you that there was more to me than either you or Sarah knew. I'm not a complete tenderfoot. I believe Keyes will keep quiet and if he doesn't, well, you already know my thoughts on the matter. I think it's a good development."

"You may be right. Now get going. We have a long train ride ahead of us. There may be people who will remember our arriving together, but let's board the train separately just in case Keyes observes your departure."

Samuel walked to the stairs while Shaw remained seated, thinking. When Samuel was out of sight, Shaw headed for the door. During their stroll the previous evening, Sarah and he had passed the office of Reinhardt Keyes. Both had noticed and remarked about it. Shaw hadn't recalled seeing a light or any sign that the office was occupied at the time. Shaw quickly crossed the street to the Depot where the telegraph office was located. He had no intention of sending a telegram, but wanted to give the appearance that was his destination.

Once inside the depot, he quickly exited the rear door and re-crossed the street to the law office of Reinhardt Keyes. He tried the front door; it was locked. Walking down an alley, he went to a rear entrance. Turning the knob, he found the door unlocked. He looked about and determined no one had noticed his presence, and slipped in.

Reinhardt Keyes was strapped to a chair, bound by rope and gagged, just as Samuel described. He was also quite dead. Shaw noted a knife wound to the man's chest and an abundance of blood that had spilled down his front and pooled on the floor around him. Shaw believed his heart had been penetrated. He briefly examined the shirtfront and noted that Keyes was killed with a thin blade. Shaw didn't stay and conduct a search. He opened the door a crack and looked left and right. When he was sure no one was present, he slipped out and closed the door.

Slowly, to attract no attention, he returned the same way he'd come and went to his room. As he stuffed his clothes into his traveling bag, he contemplated what had transpired. First, Wade Hardy was killed with a knife, and now Reinhardt Keyes. Well, he shouldn't be surprised. Samuel had told him that there was more to him than met the eye. For that matter, Shaw should not feel terribly upset that Samuel was waging revenge on the people involved in the death of his son. Shaw understood that to Samuel's way of thinking, everyone involved in the plan was equally guilty and should pay the price since the law couldn't or wouldn't do it. But it added a dimension to Samuel's personality that Shaw hadn't expected. It also added an element of danger to him and Sarah that he hadn't considered either. A man who'd so quickly kill for a reason like revenge might also quickly kill for another reason, like adultery.

Shaw finished packing and left the room. By twelve-thirty, they were all on the train to Denver, a trip that would take twenty-five hours. Shaw had much to think about to pass the time.

* * * *

When they arrived at Union Station, it was mid-afternoon. Shaw hailed a carriage and they loaded their bags. It would have been possible to take a streetcar almost to Shaw's doorstep, but the trip had been long and arduous and he wanted to spare his guests the inconvenience. A twenty-minute carriage ride brought them to a two-story home on Nineteenth Street, near its intersection with Wazee. The exterior of the house was fronted completely with red stone blocks unique to the region.

"What a lovely house!" Sarah exclaimed. The home had a large porch that took in the entire front of the structure and wrapped around to the right side. On the left side, the house featured a half-octagonal bay that extended the full height of the building. All the windows were tall and of the same dimensions and capped at the top with rose-colored granite lintels and had sills of the same stone. Above the front porch was a doorway that allowed access to the roof of the porch featuring a rail of ornate cast iron pickets.

Shaw climbed down and began unloading the bags. "This is my home. There's plenty of room for us all. We'll stay here a few days to rest up for the next leg of our journey." When Shaw was done unloading, he paid the driver and watched as he started his team, back toward the station. "It's liable to smell a bit musty. It's been closed up for almost a month."

Once inside, Shaw and Samuel deposited the bags at the foot of the staircase, while Sarah wandered about the downstairs. The house was expensively furnished with many pieces that had been brought west. Shaw noticed Sarah's interest.

"I bought the house as you see it. The owner came west for his health. After he died, his widow sold it to me before departing back to Vermont. She left everything. I kept the furnishings, books and artwork and gave the clothing to the local churches."

Shaw indicated the stairs. "There are five bedrooms upstairs. You may take your choice." Then to Sarah he said, "After you've selected your room, I'll bring your bags up. By the way, this house boasts a bathing room. It's located at the rear. I'll show you later, but there's a large copper tub with a hot water line that comes in from an external boiler room. Once I start the fire, in an hour there'll be enough hot water for everyone to enjoy a good, hot bath." He added with a hint of humor, "With fresh bath water for each of us."

Sarah seemed delighted to hear this after their long trip, but Samuel merely nodded. Samuel looked haggard and his face was unusually pale. Shaw believed the journey had left him physically exhausted. Without comment, Samuel retrieved his bags and ascended the stairs alone.

Sarah remained behind for a moment. Tilting her head toward the stairs, she had an impish smile. "Perhaps you should tell me which room is yours so I don't make a mistake in selecting."

Shaw smiled. "You can't make a mistake. My room's located on the first floor, at the rear of the house."

Sarah nodded. "Oh, I see."

"But you may be interested to know the stairs don't squeak."

Sarah blushed slightly. Checking to make sure Samuel was safely out of earshot, she asked, her voice just above a whisper, "What are we doing, Matt?"

He turned serious. "I don't really know. I was hoping you did."

Neither spoke for a moment. Samuel could be heard walking about his room.

"We can't erase the past few days and I wouldn't want to, believe me." Her voice was soft. "I must ask Samuel for a divorce. He'll give it to me, I know. He's made it quite clear that...well, he considers our marriage over."

"Yes. He has mentioned that he intends to return to the east alone when this is finished. I was wondering what you intended to do."

Sarah thought for a moment. "The ranch is my home. I'm not sure I could leave it."

"Perhaps you don't have to. Samuel indicated that it would be yours to do with as you desire. With attention, it could be a valuable ranch."

She smiled with the tired look he recalled seeing when he first met her. He realized now that it wasn't merely a physical tiredness, but an emotional tiredness that went much deeper.

"I didn't mean to suggest that you'd have to do it alone," he said, carefully probing.

She looked into his eyes. "Could you...I mean...it's been so sad there, could you be comfortable in that house?"

"It hasn't been sad for me, Sarah. You're the one who'd be constantly reminded of the past."

She nodded. "Still, I miss it. I miss it terribly."

"Go select your room. I might suggest the second one on the left. It was furnished with a woman's touch."

* * * *

After carrying Sarah's bags to the room, Shaw walked

to a neighboring house. A matronly woman pruning some roses in the last rays of the afternoon sun watched him approach. Mrs. Bell was Shaw's housekeeper when he was in residence.

"Ah, Mr. Shaw, you've returned home! Did you have a pleasant trip?"

"Mrs. Bell, I did indeed, thank you. I have two guests staying for a couple days and then we will be taking another trip. I wonder if you could see to their needs."

"Of course. Two guests, you say? I'll plan for them. Regular meal times?"

Shaw nodded. "If there are any changes, I'll let you know. Tonight we plan to dine in town."

"Very well, Mr. Shaw. It's good to have you home...even if it's only for a couple of days."

Shaw smiled and walked back to his house. The downstairs was empty so he headed for his study. It was a nicely furnished room with a heavy walnut desk. On the wall opposite the desk was a built-in bookshelf from floor to ceiling filled with a wide variety of works, mostly leather-bound, and reflecting the taste and status of the previous owner. Shaw was slowly working his way though the titles and always carried a couple of books with him on his travels. Taking them from his bag, he replaced them on the shelf.

Shaw struck a match and ignited a gas light sconce behind the desk and an oil lamp on the desk. He opened a stiff leather gun-case on the desk. The case was of sturdy cowhide, stained nearly black and bearing the wear of countless horseback miles exposed to harsh sunlight and many rainstorms. It wasn't a work of art; its only task was to protect the two long guns secured inside. Shaw undid the leather straps and opened the flap.

Inside the case was the new model Winchester that had only recently become available. In a separate compartment was Shaw's Colt shotgun. He inspected both weapons briefly and set them in a long rack of guns on the wall behind the desk. The rack held a number of fine rifles and half a dozen different pistols. Though he had recommended that Samuel purchase the Smith & Wesson revolvers, he personally didn't own one, preferring the older and simpler design of the Colt's pistol.

Shaw removed his suit coat, revealing a Colt tucked into a leather holster, which held the pistol inside his waistband for better concealment. He took one of the revolvers from the rack and, after a brief inspection, inserted cartridges into the weapon, then set it on his desk. He sat at the desk, removed the holstered Colt and unloaded it. Working carefully, he stripped the weapon and meticulously cleaned it. When he was done, he placed the cleaned weapon on the rack and holstered the other.

Putting his suit coat back on, Shaw blew out the oil lamp and turned down the gas light to barely a flicker and left the study. He found Sarah sitting in the living room in the gathering darkness. Without speaking, he struck a match and ignited gas lights on each side of a large stone fireplace. Shaw went around the room and lit the wicks on two more oil lamps and the room took on a warm glow.

"I'm impressed! Gas lamps in houses are common in the East, but out here…" Sarah sighed. "I noticed the street lights, but I was surprised to see the gas lamps in my bedroom."

"Not only that, but there is the beginning of a telephone service as well."

"I've heard of that. How does it work?"

Shaw smiled. "I can tell you what makes a rifle shoot or a steam engine run, but I have no earthly idea how one's voice can travel through wires."

"It's roughly the same principal as the telegraph," Samuel interjected from the room's entrance.

Both Sarah and Shaw looked at him expectantly.

"With telegraphy, a continuous current of electricity is

interrupted by a series of key strokes which spell out a code," Samuel explained. "A man named Alex Bell discovered a way to reduce the tones of the human voice in a similar manner and a receiver horn at the other end can actually discern it. Beyond that, I have no idea how it works but it is truly miraculous. Now hotels can be linked with theaters, restaurants or the local constabulary. There'll be no need to send messengers across town. Such messages can be transferred instantly. I suppose the possibilities are endless. The day will come in the not-too-distant future when every home in a city will have a telephonic instrument in it."

"It's hard to imagine," Sarah said. She had a wistful look in her eyes. Shaw felt a pang. Sarah was a woman who loved the simplicity of her home on the mountain, but she also appreciated the finer things that life in a city such as Denver could afford her. This thought brought him back to the reality that Sarah's husband cared greatly for the conveniences of eastern life, but had not a thought of sharing it with her. It was a curious thing.

"Well, you're in Denver now, a truly miraculous city! So, I suggest we dress for dinner and I'll show you the sights. There are a number of fine restaurants to choose from…and some not so fine, but with great food. We have restaurants that feature chefs from all over the world. I recommend the Bavarian House."

"That sounds wonderful!" Sarah exclaimed. "Doesn't it, Samuel?"

Samuel displayed no enthusiasm. "I'm exhausted from almost four days on a train. All I really want to do is rest. You two go on and enjoy dinner. I'll see you at breakfast." He turned and climbed the stairs back to his room.

Sarah and Shaw watched him until he was out of sight.

"I've quit asking myself why," Sarah said softly. "He was never hurtful before, but now I know he wants to push me away. Well, he's succeeded. He's become a stranger to me."

Sarah gathered herself and stood up. "I'll change and then we can go." Without another word or look, she climbed the staircase to her room.

* * * *

Shaw helped Sarah into an open carriage for a leisurely ride to the Bavarian House where they dined on schnitzel and boiled potatoes. For dessert, there were crepes and vanilla sauce. By the end of the evening, Shaw was beginning to feel the effects of four days of constant travel. He could only imagine how tired Sarah felt. After paying the bill, Shaw asked that a carriage be summoned.

The evening was cool and the ride in the carriage helped revive Shaw a bit. Then, from a block away, he noticed the light was still burning in Samuel's room but he made no mention of it to Sarah and had no idea whether she'd noticed. Either Samuel had fallen asleep with his lights burning, or he wasn't as weary as he'd claimed.

Once back at the house, Sarah said goodnight and ascended the stairs. When she was in her room, Shaw stood in the darkness, listening. He heard Samuel stirring upstairs. Since Samuel had demonstrated a proclivity for late-night activities, Shaw decided to invest a little time in quiet observation. He locked the front door and quietly went out the back. Finding a position from which he could watch his house, he began to wait. Roughly an hour later, the light in Samuel's room was extinguished. Ten minutes after, the front door opened quietly and Samuel exited. Shaw shook his head in disgust. He'd hoped his suspicions were wrong, but he could no longer ignore the fact that Samuel was involved in some clandestine affair he had no intention of sharing.

In the darkness, Samuel stood motionless for a couple of minutes. Soon, Shaw picked up the sound of approaching footsteps. A man stopped two houses down and remained in the shadows. Samuel descended the front steps and walked over to where the man waited. Shaw couldn't see the man's face. The two of them spoke quietly for several minutes, their voices too low for Shaw to overhear. Before they parted, Samuel handed something to the man, who then turned and walked quickly down the street. Samuel returned to the house and entered. Shaw heard the bolt turning in the front door as Samuel relocked it.

He sighed. He'd really hoped to get a good night's sleep, but he knew that it wasn't to be. Keeping to the shadows, he followed the man who was still in sight in the distance.

The man turned the corner at Larimer Street and stood waiting under a street lamp. It was too far away to make out his face, so Shaw bided his time. In a few minutes, a horse-drawn trolley approached from the north and slowed as it approached the waiting man. It didn't completely stop, but its speed slacked enough for the man to grasp the rail and step up into the car.

There was no way Shaw could keep up with the trolley and remain in the shadows but, knowing the route of the slow-moving conveyance, he was able to cross several lots and sprint a block to Lawrence Street. He was standing there, trying to control his breathing, when the trolley came into sight. The man Shaw followed was still on the car. Pulling his hat low, Shaw awaited the car's arrival and, as it slowed, he stepped up into it and took a seat at the rear.

The man glanced at Shaw but didn't seem to take any undue interest.

When he was sure he wasn't being observed, Shaw studied the man carefully. He was young, well dressed and groomed, wearing a wool suit and derby hat. The man took a folded paper out of his coat and scanned the contents. Shaw noticed that it appeared to be the same paper Samuel had been reading in Dodge City. There were some notations scribbled in a margin of the page; the man's brow furrowed slightly as he read these. After a moment, he returned the paper to an inside pocket.

When the young man sat up straight and began looking ahead, Shaw took notice. Believing the man's stop was coming up, Shaw took a gamble and stood, asking the driver to let him off at the next intersection, which he did. Shaw faded into the shadows and watched the departing streetcar. When he'd given it enough space, he hurriedly walked after it. At the end of the next block, the car stopped at Fifteenth Street and the young man got off, not even looking in Shaw's direction.

Shaw watched him cross the street and enter a stairwell.

From the shadows, Shaw waited until he saw a light come on in an upstairs apartment. Crossing the street, he noted the address of the building and quietly ascended the stairs to the second level, stopping outside the door he was certain belonged to the apartment the young man had entered. The door bore no number or name.

Cautiously, Shaw descended the stairs and walked in the direction of his home. After a few minutes, a streetcar came into view and he rode it back to within two blocks of his house.

Walking the rest of the way in the darkness, Shaw considered what he had learned.

Samuel had more than one agenda. His stated goal was to find and kill the man who'd shot his son and also the man responsible for the act. Shaw had believed he'd been enlisted to facilitate only that task. But it was obvious that Samuel was involved in a more complicated game of intrigue that he had no intention of sharing with anyone.

The biggest question was why? What could Samuel hope to gain by keeping Shaw in the dark? It made no sense. In any event, there was nothing he could do about it tonight. In the morning, he would begin to get some answers.

Shaw re-entered his house from the rear door and quietly made his way to his room. Without lighting a lamp, he stripped himself down to the waist in the darkness and began washing at the basin. When he was finished, he toweled dry and turned to the bed and stopped cold.

"I wasn't sure I'd be able to stay awake until you got back," Sarah whispered.

Shaw was beyond caring about Samuel, but he hesitated. "I believe you're taking too much of a chance here."

"Maybe. But I'm not sure it matters any more, or that I care. Do you want me to leave?"

Shaw didn't say anything. He wanted this woman more than any he'd ever met, but he could not get over the nagging doubt in the back of his mind that the circumstances he was involved in were not entirely what they appeared. Obviously, Samuel was playing some kind of game. It made Shaw wonder if Sarah was not somehow playing one of her own.

When Shaw didn't respond, Sarah peeled back the covers. In the dim light coming from the window, Shaw could see only Sarah's naked legs, looking almost like white porcelain in the moonlight. "Why don't you come to bed and you can tell me where you've been," she whispered. "Or, maybe you can tell me in a little while."

* * * *

An hour later, Sarah left Shaw's room. They'd never gotten around to discussing what Shaw had been doing while she waited in his bed. Shaw couldn't decide if Sarah's lack of interest in his late-night activities was indicative of true ambivalence, or full knowledge. Though Shaw had much to think about, he fell quickly asleep and slept the rest of the night like a dead man.

Despite the late night and lack of sleep, Shaw didn't stay in bed beyond seven in the morning. Old habits couldn't be broken, even by fatigue. Knowing his housekeeper would see to the needs of his guests, Shaw enjoyed a leisurely walk to a restaurant for breakfast, after which he went to see a colleague.

Shaw found Duggan Hammer in his office, sitting behind his desk and enjoying a cigar with the morning paper. Hammer looked up when Shaw entered and smiled.

"Matthew, me boy, what a pleasant surprise ye give me so early in th'mornin'. Sit down and have a cup o' coffee with me."

"Sounds good. I'll pour." Shaw grabbed a cup and filled it. The smell was wonderful. He topped off Duggan's cup, returned the pot to the stovetop, and took a chair opposite his friend.

Duggan Hammer was a short man, deep of chest and made up mostly of tightly packed muscle. Shaw knew Duggan's apparent stoutness was deceiving. Some might mistake him for fat, but nothing could be further from the truth. Duggan usually dressed in broadcloth suits with freshly laundered white shirts and ribbon bow ties. In fact, the only time he might be found without a suit coat was when he was sitting behind his desk, as he was now. Duggan set aside his paper and took a sip of coffee. "What trouble have ye brought t' me this fine mornin'?"

Shaw smiled. "Duggan. I know you're Irish, but I also know your people have been here since the day after the Pilgrims landed. So if you'd be so kind as to drop the phony brogue so we can have an intelligent conversation, I'd appreciate it."

"Bah! What do you know of it? The brogue is an Irish birthright. It's instilled with our mother's milk. It's as natural as your English pig-headedness." He smiled, and continued in an accent-free manner. "But if it will make things easier on you, then please, tell me what brings you

196

here this fine day."

"Oh, just a bit of detective work, if you're up to it."

"Detective work? Tell me, friend, when you walked in the door, did it say 'Detective' on the glass? I'm only asking because it could have a consequence on whether or not I'll help you or what price I'll have to charge."

"Well," Shaw deadpanned, "the window glass alluded to the fact that a detective operated out of this office, but after looking around, I don't see him. Any idea when he'll return?"

"Bah!" Duggan shouted. "You wouldn't know a true detective unless he was puttin' the shackles on your wrists."

Shaw laughed. "I've come to the right place, then. Can you find out who resides in the front apartment above Louis Bartel's grocery, over on Fifteenth Street?"

Duggan waited. Shaw added nothing further. Duggan asked: "That's it? That's all you want me to do? Why lad, you can do that with no help from me."

Shaw nodded. "Yes, but I don't want anyone knowing that I'm interested."

Duggan smiled. "All right. I'll do it this morning. Expect a boy this afternoon with the name."

Shaw drained his coffee and stood to leave. "Thanks, Duggan. I owe you one."

"Bah!" Duggan shouted again. "You owe me more than you can ever repay." The lines around his eyes softened. "Of course, the reverse is true as well." Duggan's manner brightened. "We need to take in a show sometime, you and I."

"That would be nice. I'll have to schedule the time when I'm not otherwise engaged. Right now, I have a client."

"Does he know you're next to worthless?" Duggan chuckled.

"So far I haven't demonstrated my usual brilliance, so

it's probably only a matter of time," Shaw replied. "Duggan, I have another question for you. What can you tell me about a man named Pollard, from Georgetown?"

Duggan's eyes narrowed. "Sit back down, lad." Shaw complied and Duggan went on: "What have you gotten involved in this time? Pollard's a strange one, a sure-thing killer. He's a one-shot man with a rifle and his price is steep. Tell me you're not interested in his services."

Shaw smiled. He knew that Duggan understood exactly how Shaw operated. "No. I'm involved with a client who appears to have been a victim of Pollard's."

"Victim? You've a client who's a ghost then?" Duggan shook his head. "Pollard is not known to miss."

"It seems his intended target and the one he actually hit were somehow confused," Shaw said.

"It seems?"

"My client's son was killed wearing his father's coat and hat. The shot was from a considerable distance and spur of the moment."

Duggan frowned. "That's a blow. It could happen, I suppose, but Pollard isn't known for making *spur-of-the-moment* shots or, for that matter, making mistakes. When and if he would, I'd be thinking he'd correct any mistake he made out of a professional's pride, at no extra cost."

"I've considered that as well," Shaw added. "It does make one think. If he shot the wrong man, why didn't he bide his time and complete the task? Certainly he wouldn't be overcome with guilt."

"Not Pollard. He suffers no guilt feelings." Duggan took a sip of coffee. "So, are you looking to take him in, or take him on?"

"It's out of my hands. I'm supposed to find him and then it's up to my client."

Duggan looked disbelieving. "You're guiding a hunting expedition? Bah! I hope your sport is good. Pollard won't allow a second chance."

"That worries me as well. Anyway, it's pretty much ironclad that Pollard is our man. I'd prefer to just kick in his door and take him back to face a judge but the evidence is next to nonexistent. Anyway, I took the job and I'll see it through. I don't blame the client really. He loved his son dearly, lost a wife years ago, and another child to illness recently as well. He's just about used up. In any case, first we have to determine if Mr. Pollard is in the territory, or off somewhere."

"I can make an inquiry," Duggan offered.

"Only if you're sure it will be kept in confidence."

"I can promise that."

"Good. Rather than send a boy over, why don't you stop by this evening for supper?" Shaw smiled.

"You still have Mrs. Bell cooking for you?"

"Of course."

"Why then, I'd be proud to stop by."

"Good. Seven o'clock. And come hungry." Shaw stood up to leave and Duggan stopped him again.

"There was some news recently out of Soulard. I was talking to the Chief of Police about an inquiry and he mentioned a rumor that one of Denver's more notorious citizens had been into a little mischief in the gold fields down south. Seems he caused a ruckus and a local rancher lost a couple paid gun-hands. Know anything about that?"

Shaw put on his hat. "Did you learn a name, by chance?"

Duggan nodded with a smile. "I did. The Chief seemed to think it was a name that would mean something to me. I have to admit, it sounded vaguely familiar."

Shaw frowned. "Well if you heard the news, do you suppose Pollard's heard it as well?"

"I'd consider it likely," Duggan replied. "I'd think he'd wonder if your being at Eagle Town had anything to do with him visiting there as well, the two visits being so close together as they were. Professionally speaking, he has to

199

know your name. It would be a curiosity he might want to investigate."

Shaw nodded. "That's the trouble with names, Duggan. Maybe I should change mine as well?"

"You'd still be ugly and that would give you away," Duggan said. "You be careful, Matthew."

Shaw smiled. "Seven o'clock. Oh, and don't mention anything we've talked about with my guests. Follow my lead and don't embellish."

A fine brogue overlaid Duggan's speech. "Bah, me word is th' Lord's own citadel of truth!"

Shaw laughed lightly and left the office.

The morning had warmed and he headed back to his home. Along the way, he considered the developments, and what was happening between him and Sarah. The risks inherent with the kind of relationship they had were enormous. Though she and Samuel were no longer tied to each other emotionally, they were still legally husband and wife. Laws were being broken. More than that, men had been killed over affairs of the heart. What would Samuel do if he was confronted with the fact Sarah was no longer faithful to him, despite their obvious estrangement?

Shaw was still troubled about Sarah's behavior as well, but after the pleasant moments they'd spent together last night, he was less suspicious of her motivations than he was concerned about her lack of discretion. He intended to speak to Sarah about this as soon as time permitted. Meanwhile, there were matters of greater importance that needed attending to.

When he arrived home, he found Samuel sitting in the parlor reading a book.

He looked up at Shaw and smiled. "You have a treasure trove of literature here!" Samuel was actually excited. "Did you collect them?"

"No, I'm afraid not. They came with the home. I try to read as much as I can. When I travel, I may slip a book or two in my bags. What are you reading?"

"*Le Miserable*, by Hugo. Have you read it?"

"More than once. You may keep it if you like."

Samuel seemed astonished. "Thank you very much, Matthew." He seemed genuinely touched by the gesture. "Few gifts mean as much to me as a book. It's one gift you can enjoy the rest of your life."

"Then, by all means, it's yours." Shaw hesitated, and then said, "I've made an inquiry about Pollard. A friend will be stopping by this evening for supper. We'll know more then."

"Good," Samuel said. "I look forward to meeting him. Do you and he share the same occupation?"

Samuel's face betrayed an indifference to the news. It was easy to see that Samuel was just making idle conversation. It struck Shaw that he was being played like a marionette and that Samuel appeared to be several steps ahead in the information department. Rather than confront Samuel, he decided to play along.

"No. Duggan is a detective, though he's done a bit of bounty hunting. Mostly, he conducts inquiries. He occasionally helps the Denver police gather information from an element in town they cannot easily approach. I've known him since the war."

"Known whom?" Sarah asked, coming down the stair. Both Samuel and Shaw turned to look at her, and Shaw felt a very strong and disconcerting wave of emotion come over him. He was looking upon the woman he loved, and who evidently loved him, yet there could be no hint of that expressed. Shaw knew that anyone looking at him would see nothing to betray his true feelings but, watching this woman descend the stairs, he was struck by the thought that any man who saw her couldn't help but want her. Any man that is, except Samuel.

Shaw answered, "A friend of mine. His name is Duggan Hammer and he'll be joining us for dinner this evening."

"Is he a dangerous gunman too?" She had a mischievous look in her eyes.

"No. I'm afraid he's more of a fisticuffs sort. He can use a gun for sure, but he's too much of a gentleman to resort to gunplay when the pugilistic arts would suffice."

"I'm sorry I slept so late. The last few days caught up with me, I guess. Now I'm famished."

"Mrs. Bell was here earlier," Samuel said. "She left some items for you in the kitchen. I'll start some water for tea."

"Don't bother," Sarah said. "I'll do it. You two go back to your discussion and I'll find some breakfast." She glanced at the clock. "Oh Lord! It's practically lunchtime. Matthew, you must have comfortable beds in this house. I slept too soundly."

Shaw wasn't certain but thought he may have actually blushed slightly at her remark. When Sarah went into the kitchen in search of food, he turned back to Samuel.

"If you don't mind, I'll be in my study. I have some correspondence to catch up on."

"Not at all," Samuel said. "I'll sit and read. Don't be surprised if you come out and find me asleep right here in this comfortable chair."

Shaw left him there and entered his study where he sat in a chair and recounted all the facts he knew to this point, and pondered many possibilities that he hadn't yet considered. At that moment, the things he did not have answers to compiled a much longer and much more sinister list than those he did.

* * * *

Duggan Hammer was punctual and, after introductions, everyone was seated in the spacious dining room. Mrs. Bell had prepared a sumptuous meal of roasted shoulder of elk with fresh wild greens and boiled potatoes with a heavy gravy. An apple pie sat on the sideboard for dessert. After setting out the meal, she left them to enjoy her efforts and enjoy them they did. Even Samuel was overcome by the aromas and flavorful course. For the first time Shaw could remember, Samuel did more than just pick at his food. He devoured his first plateful, and took more.

Conversation remained casual and Sarah asked Duggan a number of questions about Denver's places of interest, history and entertainment. Duggan, for his part, ate it up. Having a lovely lady asking intelligent questions and actually being interested in what he had to say in response made for an unusually animated Duggan Hammer and Shaw was both amused and pleased with the friendly atmosphere of the meal. Samuel chose to remain politely silent, offering an appropriate, if not totally sincere, chuckle when Duggan's occasional wit surfaced.

With the meal over, they retired to the sitting room and Shaw offered coffee or an after dinner drink if it was desired. Duggan and Samuel requested brandy, while Sarah and Shaw sipped chocolate coffee. Duggan lit a cigar and drew on it critically, while Samuel looked on with what Shaw surmised to be irritation. With Samuel apparently waiting to get down to business, Shaw knew Duggan's actions were probably annoying Samuel even more with every passing minute.

When Duggan at long last appeared happy with the way his tobacco was drawing, Sarah spoke: "So how did you and Matthew become such good friends?"

Duggan frowned. "It has been my extreme misfortune, on more than one occasion, to have been forced to save his miserable hide...or some such other trivial matter."

Shaw was amused to note that Duggan's thick Irish brogue had disappeared. Shaw knew that Duggan was an exceptionally intelligent man and reverted to the brogue more as an affectation around his friends. He was an educated man whose family arrived in New York in time for his father to have joined in the Black Hawk war. Duggan in his own time was part of the Irish Brigade during the last war and while he and Shaw had only barely known each other then, their paths had crossed a number of times professionally afterward. They found a mutual respect for each other and had even teamed up on a couple of jobs.

Sarah seemed to be enjoying the evening, which delighted Shaw. Her life had been so difficult in recent months that watching her appear so happy made him glad he'd invited Duggan for dinner. Samuel, on the other hand, must have decided it was time to move the conversation into a less enjoyable direction. "Matthew tells us he asked you to gather some information. Were you able to accommodate him?" Samuel asked.

Duggan looked mildly irritated at Samuel's interruption. "I'm sorry, Mr. Roark, and please don't take this the wrong way, but the information Matt asked me to gather was as a favor to *him*. I'm sure he will share everything of importance with you," Duggan said with a disarming smile. While Shaw hadn't totally explained to Duggan the arrangement he had with Samuel, Shaw knew that Samuel's superior attitude would only rankle Duggan. Shaw hoped the detective would be able to maintain his Irish temper.

Samuel didn't conceal his displeasure with Duggan's response. He countered stiffly, "Matthew is working for *me* on this matter. I've engaged his services and anything you have to report to him can be shared with me."

Duggan took a long, silent moment to carve his ash in an ashtray next to his chair. Shaw knew the gesture was an outright dismissal of Samuel's contention. When Duggan was satisfied with the shape of the ash he drew on the cigar and puffed a cloud of tobacco smoke toward the ceiling. Only then did he smile and address Samuel. "Mr. Roark,

Matthew is often engaged in performing various services for people who need such kindnesses but, in my experience, he never works '*for*' anyone." Duggan smiled. "That said, while you might be of the opinion that he works for you, please forgive me for pointing out that *I* do *not*."

Shaw could only imagine how furious this made Samuel. At the same time, the lawyer was out of his element here and Shaw knew that while his client might debate Duggan on any number of topics and hold his own, in this matter he was an interloper while Duggan was a professional. Samuel seemed to understand this as well and managed a weak smile. "Of course. Please excuse my presumptions." He turned to Shaw. "Have you learned anything that will help us in our search for Pollard?"

"Duggan provided me with a report when he arrived, but I haven't had an opportunity to glance at it. Duggan, you can speak freely in front of my guests."

Duggan glanced toward Sarah and Shaw caught his look. "You may speak freely in front of Sarah. Don't be surprised if she asks a question or two as well."

"Very well." Duggan shrugged. "Pollard lives alone in George's Town. The locals have taken to calling it Georgetown now though as George, I believe, has moved on. Anyway, Pollard has a large house on a ridge facing the west and overlooking Sixth Street. According to my sources —"

"Who are?" Samuel interrupted.

Duggan directed his look at Samuel. "*My* sources." Duggan paused. Shaw knew Duggan was not a man to be interrupted, or for that matter, intimidated.

"I beg your pardon," Samuel replied. His words were contrite, but his tone expressed irritation. "Please, continue."

"According to my sources, Pollard seldom leaves his house and never has guests that anyone can recall seeing. He orders his supplies through a messenger and they're delivered to his door. He's an almost total recluse. Most people don't know when he's home or when he's gone. They seldom see a light in the house, even after dark."

"How odd," Sarah remarked.

Duggan agreed. "Yes, isn't it? He's been seen occasionally in town, once when buying a horse and another occasion when he met an unidentified man for dinner at one of the restaurants. He periodically receives telegraph communications from Denver and Dodge City, however none in recent weeks."

Shaw watched Samuel. Duggan's report was short and didn't have much of any substance, yet Samuel appeared satisfied. That implied Samuel already knew everything Duggan had just stated. Of course, they already knew who he might have received telegraph communications from in Dodge, but a logical question would be who he received telegraphs from in Denver. That Samuel didn't ask further implied he probably had that information already at his disposal. Keyes must have divulged things that Samuel was not intending to share. Of course, Duggan hadn't mentioned everything that was in the report he'd handed Shaw either. Shaw knew Duggan was wise enough to understand that there was an element of intrigue involved with the relationship between Shaw and Samuel. Duggan's loyalties were with Shaw and Samuel could go to hell.

"It's getting late," Duggan said. "Time for me to make my way home." He rose and turned to Sarah. "I was particularly delighted to make your acquaintance, Mrs. Roark."

"Please, call me Sarah," she suggested.

"I will." Hammer turned to Samuel. "Mr. Roark, good evening."

Shaw rose. "I'll see you out." He followed Duggan to the front entrance and to his horse.

"Thanks for everything, Duggan."

"Don't mention it." Duggan turned to his horse and

prepared to mount. He hesitated. "You watch yourself, Matthew. I don't like the way this is shaping up."

Shaw shook his hand. "Thanks, Duggan. I shall."

Duggan mounted. "If you need help on this, don't hesitate to ask."

Shaw smiled and nodded. Duggan turned the horse and rode down the street. Shaw looked around one last time, before returning to the house. Sarah had already cleared the table while Samuel sat reading his book.

"An interesting man, that Mr. Hammer," Samuel observed. "Can you trust him?"

Shaw decided it was time to plant a little seed of doubt in Samuel's mind. "I've concluded over time that he is one of the few people I *can* trust," Shaw said without smiling. "Now, if you'll excuse me, I am going to retire."

Shaw said goodnight to Sarah and went to his room. When he was inside, he locked the door and doused the light. After hearing Samuel and Sarah ascend the stairs, he used the adjoining door to his study and entered. He didn't turn on a gas light, preferring to light an oil lamp on the desk. Opening the envelope Duggan had provided, he sat down to read.

The gist of the report was that the individual Samuel had met the first night in town was a young attorney, named Elijah Barrett, who worked for a larger firm in Denver known to Duggan as having some clients of questionable reputations. The morning after Duggan met with Barrett, the young man sent a telegram to another attorney in Georgetown named Felix Gerdes. The telegram, which didn't mention Pollard's name or Samuel's, requested a meeting between himself and Barrett as soon as one could be arranged.

Shaw frowned. This information cemented the fact that Samuel intended to circumvent Shaw in his hunt. What he didn't understand was why he felt he even needed Shaw any more. He knew the identity of the killer of his son. He had a direct path to the killer through his intermediaries and he was cleaning up that path as he went along. Shaw could only assume that Samuel intended for Barrett to arrange a meeting with Gerdes in which Samuel would attend as well. Shaw could only imagine what would happen then but felt certain that, once the meeting was concluded, some creative knife work would undoubtedly follow.

How far was he willing to allow Samuel to go in his vendetta. Leaving dead attorneys across half the west wasn't part of the plan. He was going to have to confront Samuel and reestablish the rules or terminate the relationship. He didn't know how Samuel would react to that, but Shaw knew it was the only way to continue that offered any hope of his own survival. Samuel was playing a game where the stakes were death. Shaw didn't want to be among the dead when the game was over. It might mean he'd have to go to the law with what he knew to date. Tipping the law that Samuel might be responsible for a murder in Dodge City could offer the best way to solve this entire dilemma. Samuel would be arrested and charged with murder and Sarah would have an excuse to divorce him.

Shaw knew he wouldn't do it, however. There was still the thought of justice in the killing of Stuart, but he was going to have to stop Samuel's one-man murder spree and get the wagon back on course. Shaw blew out the light and reentered his bedroom. He left the door locked as he didn't want any visitors tonight. Finally, he had the first decent night's sleep in weeks.

* * * *

In the morning, Shaw entered the kitchen to find Sarah alone, drinking coffee and putting together a meal of bacon, biscuits and fresh eggs Mrs. Bell had brought in. Sarah looked lovely as always, but this morning she appeared more cheerful, probably owing to the pleasant dinner they'd all shared the night before. Shaw said good morning and poured himself a cup of coffee.

"Have you seen Samuel this morning?" he asked.

Sarah shook her head. "No. There's been not a peep from his room. He was still up reading when I went to bed. I would expect he'll sleep late."

Shaw sat at the table and took a plate Sarah offered. Breakfast had always been his favorite meal and he never tired of bacon and eggs, and Mrs. Bell made the best biscuits he'd ever eaten.

"I think it's time I went on alone from here," Shaw said. He waited while Sarah digested his words.

"Samuel won't hear of it," she said. "But then, you already know that."

"I was hoping you might help me convince him that having the three of us trying to take on Pollard is insanely dangerous. He's a killer of the kind even I have never dealt with."

She shook her head. "Samuel doesn't listen to me. Not any more. He certainly won't listen to me concerning this."

"Sarah, Samuel has already gone too far. I didn't want to mention this, but he killed Reinhardt Keyes in Dodge. After he'd extracted whatever information he could get, he stabbed Keyes in the heart while he was tied to a chair."

Sarah's face displayed profound shock. It took several moments before she could speak. She barely whispered, "I don't believe he could be capable of that. How do you know?"

"In the morning, after Samuel told me he'd spoken with Keyes behind my back, I went to investigate. I found his body exactly as I've described." Shaw shook his head. "When Samuel related to me his conversation with Keyes, he was so confident, so matter-of-fact. It stunned me that he could commit so brutal an act and show nothing outwardly. He must have killed Wade Hardy as well." He looked toward the door to make certain no one was within earshot.

"There's something else that I didn't tell you. I followed Samuel two nights ago. He met with a young attorney right outside this house. The man's name is Elijah Barrett. The next day, Barrett sent a telegram to another attorney in Georgetown named Felix Gerdes, requesting an immediate meeting." Shaw paused to let it all sink in.

Sarah's face reflected total confusion.

Shaw went on. "Samuel is keeping important secrets from us. I don't know why, but I do know that it will undoubtedly backfire. Pollard won't allow an amateur to meddle in his affairs. The possibility of Samuel catching this man unawares is nonexistent. If he won't work with me, I'll have to end this immediately by going to the authorities with my concerns about Samuel's connections to the deaths of both Hardy and Keyes."

"You can't!" Sarah clutched Shaw's arm, desperation in her face. "Oh, Matthew, you can't. Please, I know he doesn't love me any more; I know our life together is over, but I couldn't bear the thought of him being jailed after he's lost so much. He's obviously insane."

"I'm not sure I have any options, Sarah."

"Please don't. I fear it would kill him, or if it didn't, it would be worse than death. Besides, it may be he's doing this to protect me. It's entirely possible he's acting on his own so that there's no trail leading back to me — or to you, for that matter. If Pollard thinks he's being pursued by Samuel alone, he may ignore you and me."

"That's a possibility. He actually suggested that very thing when we spoke about his interrogating Keyes on his own, but I didn't place a lot of stock in it. It made some sense then, but at the time, I didn't know he'd already killed Keyes. With Keyes out of the way, Pollard couldn't know someone is trailing him. The killing rendered your theory invalid. Sarah, he's already gone too far. You and I can't be connected to Keyes' death, legally, but I can't ignore it either. If Samuel won't include us in his plans, we have to stop right now. What else am I to do?"

She thought for a moment and her face brightened. "Take charge! Disrupt his plans by jumping ahead of him. He won't know that you've discovered his subterfuge and he'll have no choice but to go along."

Initially, Shaw was doubtful, but after some consideration, he started to see a possible solution. "It might work," he agreed. "I hope you're right. I'm not in the habit of concealing crimes and prefer not being dragged down by a homicidal maniac, even one who lost his only son and is on the trail of the murderer. The law might condone the killing of Pollard, but surely not the killings of Hardy and Keyes. Those were cold-blooded and inexcusable. The only way we have a chance of completing this venture and surviving is if Samuel no longer acts as a lone wolf."

"Don't let him!" Sarah said. "So far, you've been reacting to Samuel's manipulations. Change directions on him and take the initiative away."

She made sense from the standpoint that he could outmaneuver Samuel now that he knew the steps the man had taken, but he wasn't certain he could totally disrupt Samuel's plans when he had no real idea what they involved. Pollard lived in Georgetown. Georgetown was a half-day's travel by train from Denver. Why would it be necessary to bring two more attorneys into the investigation, unless Samuel planned to deal with them in the same manner he'd dealt with Hardy and Keyes? It appeared Samuel wanted to make it a clean sweep and kill everyone who had any hand in the death of Stuart, even if they were merely intermediaries to the relationship between Pollard and whoever paid him. It was too much. Shaw needed to do something that would upset Samuel's plans and it had to appear natural and unwitting. Not only that, but it had to be soon.

* * * *

Samuel slept nearly to noon. At first, Shaw didn't think anything of it, but after a while, he began to wonder if Samuel hadn't gone on a midnight excursion to meet with young Barrett again. Shaw dismissed the thought, as there was nothing he could do about it now.

When Samuel joined them for a noon meal, he seemed well rested and his color was good. Whatever else Samuel was up to, this trip had refreshed him and he certainly looked healthier than the man Shaw had first met in Eagle Town.

"I think it's time we head up to Georgetown," Shaw remarked casually, eating a slice of beef.

Sarah looked on, but didn't comment.

Samuel's face didn't betray anything. "Do you think it's wise? Do we know enough to enter this phase of our plan?"

"I think so," Shaw said. "We know where Pollard lives. We can take rooms in a hotel there and begin our reconnaissance. If Pollard's in residence and not off somewhere, we should be able to take him."

"And how do you plan to do that?" Samuel asked, lowering his knife and fork. "You've built this man's reputation to the point I wouldn't think that it would be so easy. Do you intend to arrest him and turn him over to the authorities? That wasn't the outcome I'd hoped for."

"I haven't forgotten what I promised you," Shaw replied. "Georgetown is a popular destination for travelers from Denver so we wouldn't draw attention to ourselves. It would be easier formulating a plan from Georgetown than it would be sitting here and guessing.

"We can proceed in a number of different ways. Let's look at where we are at this moment. You've interrogated Keyes alone, so if Keyes did communicate with Pollard, he's already aware someone — a lone man — is tracking him." He watched Samuel's eyes carefully to see if they betrayed anything. They didn't. Neither Samuel nor Sarah interjected, so Shaw went on. "If that's still the situation, Pollard should pay no particular attention to three people traveling together. If Keyes didn't communicate with Pollard, then he should be unaware he's being hunted. If that is the case, we should be able to take up residence in Georgetown and look over the landscape and develop our next plan of action." Shaw paused, slicing into another slice of beef, and eyed Samuel. "Can you think of any reason Pollard might be ready for us?"

"No... I can't imagine why we shouldn't proceed to our next step." Then, as if an afterthought, he added, "I guess, when faced with the prospect of finally achieving my goal, the suddenness of it is somewhat disconcerting. I'm not used to this, you see. It's going to take me a little time to adjust to the thought of action again."

Shaw nodded. "Well, we've come this far. We should finish it. But I want you to reconsider your intent. I think we could have Pollard arrested and maybe even gain a conviction."

Samuel shook his head. "No. Both you and I know it would be next to impossible to convict anyone based on the say-so of a hired killer, even if we could persuade him to give up the name of the man who hired him."

Shaw looked over at Sarah. "I want you to reconsider going with us. You can stay here and the Bells will make you perfectly comfortable until we return. There is great danger where we're headed. It would be easier for us if you allowed Samuel and me to deal with Pollard without having to think about your safety on top of everything else."

Sarah's expression hardened. "I will *not* consider staying behind after coming this far. Stuart was my family as well. I don't agree with what Samuel intends, but I feel he deserves my support now that we're under way."

It was the answer Shaw anticipated. He did, however, note that Samuel seemed somewhat taken aback. Apparently, he'd never considered that Sarah would accept their mission as her own, rather expecting she'd continue to argue against it. He looked genuinely pleased.

"It's decided then," Shaw said, lowering his knife and fork. "I'll telegraph ahead to reserve rooms for us at a hotel and we'll take a train in the morning. The run to Georgetown is a lovely one that follows Clear Creek Canyon. In good weather, it's delightful. We should be there before supper." He stood, wiping his mouth with a napkin. "By the way, I've arranged for Mr. Bell to take the two of you on a carriage ride around Denver for the rest of the afternoon. It's a fascinating city and well worth the ride."

"That's not necessary," Samuel protested.

"I insist." Shaw smiled. He wanted to make sure Samuel couldn't do anything to interfere with his plans. Mr. Bell would keep them both busy and out of the way. "You need to get out and this way the two of you can enjoy our late spring weather under the most pleasant of circumstances." He looked at Samuel innocently. "Besides, if you remain idle, you'll just end up getting into mischief."

Samuel smiled thinly. "Of course, you're right. We'd enjoy a ride around town."

"Fine. It's settled then. I'll see you for supper later." Shaw nodded and left them alone in the kitchen.

* * * *

Sarah watched Shaw leave the room out of the corner of her eye. She was almost shocked to feel as though he took the very air with him. It was hard to believe how much her feelings for him had changed from the unconcealed hostility of their first meeting. Her reverie was broken when Samuel spoke. "He's a take-charge sort, isn't he?"

"Yes. I think it best that we let him do so, don't you? After all, it's what he does *and* what you hired him for, is it not?"

Samuel hesitated and then offered a smile. "Of course. It's what I paid him to do. I just never expected he'd be so difficult to deal with. I can exert no control over him. It's as if he doesn't really care about the money or the particulars of the job, for that matter. It's a mystery why he decided to take it."

Sarah wondered if Samuel was growing suspicious and if his questioning was a way of probing her feelings on the matter. Samuel was a complex man with a tendency toward deep thinking. Over the years, she'd realized that her lack of interest in certain matters had led him to believe she wasn't an intellectually curious person who shared his pondering nature. True, she was more pragmatic and grounded, but Samuel had never appreciated the fact that she had ideas and dreams of her own. Her attempts to engage him in intellectual conversations had largely been ignored. "Samuel, I believe he's driven more by a personal code than by the particulars of a job."

"What do you mean?"

"He told me that people out here have a sense of justice and fair play; a willingness to deal with obstacles themselves, or to see them dealt with, even if it means going outside the conventions one might find back East. Or at least that was the gist of what he said. I think that the particulars of our tragedy aren't as important to him as dealing with the people who feel that they can orchestrate circumstances for their own personal gain, with so little thought given to the other people whose lives are affected."

Samuel looked unconvinced. "Why would he risk his life, if not for gain?"

"Look around you, Samuel. Look at this house. He has everything anyone could want. Money isn't what drives him. He's surrounded by material things that seem to matter little to him. This is a place where he rests, not a place where he lives. I'm beginning to think that he doesn't start to really live, unless he's doing something like this."

"So, you ascribe some Quixotic notion to his actions? The search for justice in an unjust world is no different than tilting at windmills."

Samuel smiled, but Sarah saw the old sadness in the smile and it made her heart ache. "Is idealism so ridiculous? Choosing sides between right and wrong isn't a matter of first determining which side has the better chance of winning. We're on the side of right, aren't we, even if we don't win in the end?"

Samuel rose. "I should get my coat and hat before Mr. Bell arrives." He turned to leave the room, hesitated, and looked back. "You're right, of course. I want you to know that. Also, I want to thank you, Sarah. I know you don't agree and that this isn't easy for you. But thank you for supporting me."

"Why wouldn't I? After all, you're my husband."

Samuel's eyes held a vague look. "I haven't been a husband to you for quite some time, Sarah. I know that, and I'm truly sorry. You know that, regardless, I still love you and what we once shared, even if that part of our life is gone."

He turned and ascended the stairs to his room, while Sarah watched him go. She realized there *was* something left of the man she'd married; it was just deeply buried under a mountain of anguish and despair. A single tear tracked down her cheek and she closed her eyes to hide her sadness, and her shame.

* * * *

The ride up Clear Creek Canyon was an odd mixture of stunning vistas and the refuse miners and engineers left, ravaging the hillsides for ore and building a rail line into the mountains. Gold was being dug out of the mountainsides and all along the line, the rocky slopes were penetrated by countless tunnels, below which the waste dirt and slag made ugly mounds. Much of the slag washed into the creek and corrupted the once-crystal-clear water. All the left over material was not wasted, however, as it did allow for plenty of material to serve as a railroad bed.

Clear Creek served as a source of mechanical energy for the miners and the sluicing operation on its banks. The running water turned large pieces of machinery or separated the gold from the dirt and gravel. But, amid all the ugliness, Shaw could look up and see the western mountains at their finest, snowcapped and colorful. Just before the train arrived in Georgetown, they spotted a group of bighorn sheep, the first Sarah had ever seen, watching the train's slow progress up the grade.

The Georgetown depot was a bustling affair and it took several minutes to secure a carriage to take them to the Hotel de Paris. After an accidental mine explosion, the hotel had been opened by a miner named Dupuy who, even though badly injured in the blast, had still managed to save some of his fellow miners. The grateful town rewarded him with a financial stake, which he used to open the hotel and restaurant.

Originally the Delmonico Bakery, Shaw explained that the Hotel's first floor was now the restaurant and kitchen with the hotel rooms being located on the second floor. When they walked into the building, Sarah appeared surprised to see such a lavish establishment up in the mining camps. She remarked on it and Shaw explained, "The owner was once a chef in Europe. He's turned this place into a premier eating establishment. It's the equal of anything you'll find in Denver as far as cuisine is concerned. He offers imported wines from places like France and Italy and the tables are always set with the finest silver and linens. Jay Gould often comes here just to

217

dine." Shaw grinned. "Personally, it's one of my favorite places to dine as well. I don't get here often, but I've never been disappointed."

The interior was a veritable palate of color, from the bright green walls to the hand-painted frescoes on the ceiling. The hardwood floors were an eye-catching pattern of alternating maple and walnut boards, waxed to a fine luster. Along the walls were alternating paintings and photographs with mirrors in hand carved frames. An elaborate copper fountain — also imported — was situated in the center of the room with a continuous murmur of water streaming from the mouth of a goose in the grasp of a cherub.

The rooms of the hotel were located on the second floor and were at a premium. Shaw was able to secure only two for their party. He and Samuel would share a large room in the front, while Sarah had a smaller room near the back. Shaw wasn't disappointed in the sleeping arrangements. He'd better be able to monitor Samuel's actions, and he wouldn't have to worry about Sarah distracting him with late-night visitations in this critical phase. As much as Shaw wanted her company, he was entering into the part of their trek that required absolute attention to detail. He must push Sarah out of his mind as much as possible. The first one to make a mistake where Pollard was concerned would be the first one to die.

After they'd unpacked their bags, they met in the restaurant for dinner. Once they were seated, the waitress recommended a house specialty, Civet de Lièvre, consisting of rabbit, marinated in brandy, red wine, and olive oil and simmered in a sauce of cooked bacon, onions and garlic. The meal was absolutely delicious. It amused Samuel to see men enter the dining room in rough miner's garb and actually order a meal from the French menu in perfect French. Shaw explained that the gold fields brought men and women from every corner of the earth to seek wealth. "If you listen carefully, you'll hear several different languages spoken during the evening."

After dinner, Samuel excused himself to retire early. While he looked better and appeared to be regaining his health every day, it was obvious he was tired. Shaw knew the altitude here was difficult to adjust to, particularly for one whose physical reserves had been so depleted. Sarah remained at the table with Shaw, but his thoughts were elsewhere and not on making conversation so, after she finished her coffee, she too excused herself.

As she walked out of the room, Shaw noted her pass a lean man who was speaking with the waitress. The waitress pointed to Shaw's table. The man smiled and thanked her and walked across the room. Shaw moved imperceptibly in his chair to more easily access the pistol hidden beneath his coat.

The man seemed younger than Shaw and nicely dressed. His face was pale and he had a thin blonde mustache that almost disappeared against his pale flesh. His blue eyes were pale as well, and gave his expression an unpleasantly cold appearance. When he arrived at the table, he spoke softly. "Good evening, Mr. Shaw. Forgive me the intrusion, but I wonder if I might have a word with you?"

Shaw was calm and expressionless, but at the same time, he was poised to react to any change in the situation. He smiled. "Please, sit down," he offered. "May I pour you coffee, Mr. Pollard?"

Pollard seemed surprised, but only mildly so. He took a seat and declined coffee. "I waited until your friends left. I felt we should talk frankly and didn't see any way we could do so with them present. I even came unarmed."

Shaw nodded. "I'm impressed that you knew we were here." He sipped his coffee. "But why tip your hand? If you knew we were coming, you could easily have waited and simply dealt with us when the moment was right."

"I was hoping we could come to an understanding,

while there is still time," Pollard said. "Nothing good can come of this, you know. I won't allow myself to be taken by you or goaded into a gunfight and I won't divulge the names of any of my clients. There's really nothing anyone can do to me..." Pollard hesitated a moment before continuing, "... except perhaps to simply kill me outright, and I've been led to believe that's not your style."

"What style is that?"

"You've hunted bounties, but have been discriminating in that regard. Besides, there's no bounty on me. You're mostly a soldier of fortune rather than a hired gun. I've been told you fight those fights that will allow you to remain mostly on the side of the law. You evidently can't be bought off." Pollard smiled for the first time. "I don't relish having you on my trail, and I don't want to kill you. At the same time, while I wouldn't hesitate to kill you if I needed to, I promise you I don't kill women."

"But you kill boys?" Shaw goaded gently.

Pollard didn't rise to the bait. "What *is* a boy out here, Mr. Shaw? The lad was older by far than many of the soldiers you and I served with. He was as much a man — or more so, perhaps — as his father."

"Regardless," Shaw countered, "his father was the target and you made a mistake. It may not be my style, but the father wishes his son's death avenged. While you might try to defend your actions to me, you certainly cannot defend them to the Roarks. You took money to kill one of theirs. To their way of thinking, you'll have to pay for it."

Pollard's face was expressionless. His eyes gave nothing away. Shaw had known killers in his life, but never had he so casually spoken with one who appeared as coldly efficient and emotionless as Pollard.

"Nevertheless, it's done," Pollard said. "I have no desire to kill Mr. Roark, and certainly no wish to harm Mrs. Roark or yourself. But I won't continue to look behind me for the rest of my life."

"But doesn't your business remain unfinished? Samuel Roark still lives. He's right upstairs as we speak. I could give you the room number."

Pollard offered a thin smile. "I already know the room number."

"In any case, don't you want to finally fulfill your contract?"

Pollard shook his head. "Some jobs go according to the plan. Sometimes, they go awry. While this is lamentable, in the end this particular result satisfied my client." Pollard added, "If my client is satisfied, my assignment is complete."

Shaw remembered something he'd been told about Pollard. The man was a killer, but supposedly had a reputation for not killing innocent people. Of course, Shaw supposed innocent was a relative term to a killer. It appeared Pollard could look at a job and decide how best to complete the assignment and didn't care greatly if the killing was justified or not, or if the victim was innocent or not. Maybe he had changed over the years; his standards had relaxed somewhat.

"Well, *your* client might be satisfied, but you may conclude from my presence here that mine is not," Shaw observed, mildly. "Of course, I have to go on record as having asked you to surrender yourself and testify against your client."

Pollard smiled again with his typical thin-lipped smirk. "That's of course out of the question."

"I knew it would be and that leaves only one eventuality."

Fleetingly, Pollard seemed concerned, as if uncertain whether Shaw would act this very minute. "I've already told you, I'm unarmed."

"Oh, you're safe for the time being. That's a professional courtesy I owe you for the one you provided me. But once you walk out that door, we're on a course that can only end one way."

Pollard frowned slightly. Then he seemed to reach a conclusion. "All right. I can accept that, with sincere regret."

Shaw decided to change the subject. "I found an unfired cap to your rifle by the large tree overlooking the ranch-yard. I assume you dropped it unintentionally, but why do you use a muzzle-loading rifle when there are better rifles suited to your task?"

Pollard nodded and his eyes took on a spark of life for the first time that evening. He brushed his mustache back with his thumb. "It's a Stephens," he said, as if that was all the answer Shaw would need. When Shaw didn't react, Pollard added, "It's probably the finest specimen of a long-range rifle I've ever seen. I acquired it from a dead Union sharpshooter who'd been felled by a lucky shot, probably part of a massed volley into his position. Unfortunate for his life, but you might say it changed mine."

He smiled briefly and raised his head, gazing down his nose at Shaw. "I was always a good shot in the command. When I found that rifle and took the time to practice with it, I astounded my fellows. The sergeant asked me to make some difficult shots that were actually fairly easy with that rifle."

"The weapon may be good, but you have to have the eye and the talent."

"True, Mr. Shaw. In time, my reputation grew. The corps commander asked for marksmen to be utilized to the fullest when the campaign finally settled down to the trenches around Petersburg. I had lots of work."

Pollard's face took on a serious expression. "Mr. Shaw, there is no finer rifle anywhere and, I suspect, no finer marksman alive."

Not modest about his ability, Shaw mused. Was that a weakness?

Waving a dismissive hand at Shaw, Pollard said, "I

know you favor the long shot and I've been told you use a Remington and it's a good arm, but with it, you will run out of range and I'll still be shooting. I can range you by another three hundred yards, easily. You should remember that. If it comes down to a duel of rifles, you'll need to get much closer to me than I will to you."

Shaw nodded in appreciation. "Thanks. I'll try to remember that. By the way, how is it you knew we were coming, from Barrett or Gerdes?"

"I use them both, but haven't been in contact with either in weeks." Pollard seemed sincere and Shaw found himself believing the man. This called into question the purpose of Samuel's requested meeting. He'd have to look into that later.

"And Reinhardt Keyes?"

"Even longer." Pollard offered, and then he smiled. "I see you've managed to unravel *some* of my lines of communication."

"What about Wade Hardy? What do you know about him?" Shaw asked.

Pollard hesitated with a slight frown. "I know almost nothing about Mr. Hardy, except that he's dead and you were heard asking about him. But I also know you are not a knife man, so that doesn't carry much weight with me. You may have to answer some questions about Mr. Hardy if you ever go back to Eagle Town." He checked a gold watch and closed it up. "I have to leave. It's been pleasant speaking with you. Let me make you a promise that you can pass on to your clients. I won't hurt anyone unless they continue to chase me and, no matter what, I won't harm Mrs. Roark unless she takes up arms against me. Please make her understand that she has nothing to fear from me."

"She's not the violent type," Shaw said.

"No?" Pollard asked. "I doubt that. You should know that I watched her through my telescope when the Roark boy was lying dead in the ranch-yard. She stood at the door with a Winchester in her hands. I have no doubt she'd have used it, given the chance." Pollard paused in thought, and then added, "I watched her, Mr. Shaw. Given the right reason, she would kill. In any event, I hope I won't see you again. Please pass that on." Pollard rose and left the dining room.

Shaw sat and thought about the conversation he'd just had, particularly with regards to Pollard's observations about Sarah. He recalled her reaction to him sitting on her porch the first time they met. Before approaching him, she reached for her rifle, even before she knew who he was. Perhaps Pollard was right. Even a mouse will attempt to bite the nose of the cat that kills it. Sarah could probably kill if it were important enough.

Something else about what Pollard said struck a chord and it made him wonder if everything about this job was based on some serious miscalculations. He knew Wade Hardy was dead. That meant he'd remained interested in the happenings at Eagle Town. Also, since it appeared Pollard didn't yet know about the death of Keyes in Dodge City, whoever contacted Pollard could do so directly, without going through the series of intermediaries.

There was something else that Pollard had indirectly made him aware of, probably by accident, or possibly with deliberation. Shaw thought back to the moment he was standing at the tree and looking down at the ranch-yard and trying to picture exactly what the killer would be seeing at the moment preceding his shot. He'd seen Sarah standing at the little window in the kitchen. Later, he'd listened to Samuel recounting how he watched as Stuart dressed to go outside. Now, Pollard casually told him how he watched Sarah at the door with a rifle in her hands. The telescope on the rifle would have allowed for perfect visibility of the ranch-yard and house. Samuel said he'd been standing at the window as Stuart went outside. Obviously, Pollard would have seen Samuel at the window.

There could have been no mistake. Pollard hadn't intended to kill Samuel at all. Stuart had always been the target!

* * * *

In the morning, Shaw took a table in the restaurant and ordered breakfast while he went over the events of the night before. He wondered how much he should share with Samuel and Sarah. Stuart had been the target all along. What exactly could that mean with regards to the identity of the person who ordered the killing? Would Mason kill Samuel's son just to get back at the man for beating him in a court case? It didn't seem reasonable. But what other explanation was there?

At the same time, there was the pressing matter of Pollard. He was here and Samuel would certainly want to deal with him, even if it meant not learning the identity of the person who hired Stuart's killer.

While he considered this, Louis Dupuy approached his table with a slight limp. He smiled and bowed slightly. When he spoke, his French accent was heavy. "Monsieur Shaw, a boy brought zis envelope for you zis morning. He left it with me to give to you."

Shaw smiled and took the envelope and thanked Dupuy and the owner bowed again and walked back to the front desk.

He opened the envelope and found a single sheet of stationery with a short note in flowery script: *I've gone hunting in the hills around Geneva City. If you care to, you can find me there. While the hunting is usually very good, I do hope you find game elsewhere and leave this area to me. Warmest regards, Ballou.*

Shaw read the note one more time before carefully slipping it back into the envelope. He placed the envelope in his coat pocket.

By sending the note, Pollard was giving him three things. First, he was letting Shaw know that, out of professional courtesy, he was willing to give Shaw the chance to come for him on an equal footing. Second, he was letting Shaw know that there was an out that he could take and Pollard would consider their business concluded. Third, by signing his real name, he was telling Shaw that he faced someone who considered what he was doing as a just cause. In war, Ballou had killed without remorse or recrimination. There was nothing personal about it. If Shaw came after him, Pollard wanted Shaw to know that there was nothing personal involved. At the same time, there would be no quarter given. A marksman doesn't give the enemy a chance to surrender. He marks his target, makes his calculations and makes the long shot.

There was a brief surge of a very familiar emotion that passed through Shaw. He was at a crossroad he'd encountered before.

There were three paths he could take. Only one would be totally safe; one might lead to success and the last would most assuredly lead to misfortune. So far, he'd trusted his instincts and had never gone down the last path. This time, he felt an oppressive sense that this decision was already out of his control. Fate would decide the path. Was he ready?

The Hand You Are Dealt

"Where is Geneva City?" Sarah asked, after Shaw told them about Pollard's visit and subsequent note. Samuel remained silent, but was visibly angry that this had transpired without his knowledge. Shaw was totally indifferent to Samuel's feelings by this time, considering the secrets Samuel had kept. Samuel's anger was the least of his worries now that the initiative had been retaken by Pollard.

"Geneva City is a small mining town in a valley some twelve miles south of here as the crow flies. By road, it's easily five times that distance. Half the distance will be a nearly steady climb on a switchback wagon road used to carry ore to Georgetown. The other half will be a steady descent over much the same kind of terrain. The entire way, we'd be open to ambush and there's not a single thing we could do about it."

"You're saying that Pollard, with this invitation, is setting a trap for us?" Samuel asked.

"No, I'm not. I'm pointing out the obvious. Actually, I don't believe he is, at least not between here and Geneva City."

"What makes you say that?" Sarah asked.

Shaw hesitated. Once again, he found himself trying to explain something that lacked certain definition to people who had no frame of reference from which to trust his judgment. He might very well be wrong, but instinct told him he was correct.

"Pollard is telling us, or rather he's telling me, that he'll meet me in the mountains around Geneva City if I choose to go. He won't stop between here and there and wait for us. He is supremely confident that he really faces no danger

227

from any of us. If we come, he'll deal with us there. If we don't, he'll be satisfied and, after an interval and careful scouting, he'll return home."

"What's to stop us from simply waiting here for him to return?" Samuel asked.

"For one, he's certain to have spies here who would get word to him that we haven't followed. The road between here and Geneva City is well traveled every day by wagons coming and going. Getting a message to him wouldn't be difficult. If we were to wait, we'd have to leave Georgetown and wait elsewhere. If that's what you feel we should do, I can see a bit of logic to it."

"But you don't recommend it?" Samuel said.

"No. No actually, I don't."

"What do you suggest then?" Samuel asked.

"I cannot get either of you to reconsider what you've begun?" he asked. When he saw the determination in their eyes, he shook his head and continued. "When Pollard found out we were here, however this occurred, he took the initiative from us. I never planned to duel this man on his own turf. Now it appears unavoidable. I see no other course but to start for Geneva City. It's my intention to camp for the night in the high country near the summit of the mountain we'll have to cross. It will be cold near the tree line and even this late, there's snow in places at that elevation. During the night, we break camp and rather than head for Geneva City, we head off cross-country. I'm certain Pollard will have a vantage point from which he can watch the road descending into the mining camp. While he's waiting to see if we show up, I want to get to the high ground overlooking Geneva Basin. Pollard will head to the high ground as well when he realizes we've left the road."

"But," Sarah said, "why–?"

"I'd like to have a spot near the summit from which I can watch and observe. Maybe we'll get lucky and he'll tip his hand."

"It sounds like a lot of supposition," Samuel said.

"It is!" Shaw said irritably. "It's all we have to go on now. I'd bet Pollard will wait an appropriate amount of time for us to come into the mining camp. He'll be waiting to see us arrive; waiting to see us reconnoiter and decide on a plan of action. When, after a few days we don't arrive, he'll start to wonder. He'll have to move, either to return to Georgetown, or maybe even go down to the camp and speak to his sources. If we're in the right place, we stand a decent chance of seeing him first. But, you have to know, the odds are against us."

"Why is that?" Sarah asked.

"There's a lot of country surrounding Geneva Basin. From the camp it looks like a pretty alpine vista, like a large amphitheater with a little mining community nestled in the center. In truth, that pretty amphitheater is as rugged a piece of land as can be found anywhere in the mountains. Much of it is near vertical, lined with goat trails and avalanche cuts. There's even a small glacier on the south side. What looks like a thousand feet to the rim, is closer to a mile, and what looks like a mile across the bowl is closer to four." Shaw paused to let that sink in.

"After seeing the way Pollard waited in the snow to make the shot at your ranch, I'm certain he's not going to move because he gets chilly or bored or restless. For that matter, when we don't show up at the camp, he's not about to make any careless moves. He's simply not the careless type. He won't move until he's done a lot of careful scouting. If he decides we're not coming, he'll come back to Georgetown, but he'll come cross-country and not by road. There is simply no way we can set a trap for him."

"You're certain of this?" Samuel asked.

Shaw's anger flared. "Of course I'm not certain!" he said fiercely, nearly losing his temper for the first time since beginning the job. "Everything I've just said could be entirely wrong. Pollard could shadow us the entire trip out of Georgetown and we'd not know it. He could know at once when we leave the road and every move we make could be observed. It's possible he could cut us down the minute we leave the safety of this community."

"Oh, my God…" Sarah breathed.

Shaw leveled his gaze on both of them. "Please understand, that all my choices are bad ones — primarily because I have to bring you two along. There's only one thing that's certain about this endeavor and that is if we make a mistake, we're dead. That's why I'm begging you to let me do this alone. I have a slim chance against this man alone, but together, I just don't see how we can succeed."

"I can discharge you now," Samuel offered. "You've brought me to the man who killed my son. I can try to take him at some later date, now that I know where he lives."

"As attractive as that offer sounds, I can't take it," Shaw said. "You'd stand no chance against Pollard alone. Now, after sitting with him and talking with him, I know that he needs to be stopped. This is one of those rare circumstances I've spoken about, where decent men have to step up where the law cannot or will not." Shaw sighed and shook his head. "You could discharge me. But I'd still go after him now that I've seen him up close and spoken with him." He decided to tell a little lie. "He didn't care that he'd killed your son by mistake. As long as his client was happy, he was satisfied he'd done well. A man like that needs to be defeated and you simply cannot accomplish that. He'd play with you like a cat playing with a mouse."

Shaw watched Samuel closely when sharing the revelation about Pollard not caring that he'd killed Stuart by mistake. If the information affected Samuel at all, he did a masterful job of concealing it.

With a stony expression, Samuel asked, "So, when do we leave?"

* * * *

They leased mountain-bred horses for the journey and
Shaw and Samuel also led a packhorse each, while Sarah
rode a lone sorrel. The first few miles out of Georgetown
were relatively easy, with occasional steep grades that
leveled off, following a mountain stream heavily used by
placer operations and sluice box crews. The hillsides were
honeycombed with tunnels; each perched at the apex of a
fan of gray-green or rusty-red waste slag. There wasn't
much vegetation and few trees remained, the rest having
been felled for the meager lumber they'd provide for
shoring timbers or cook-fires.

In addition to the ore wagons that constantly used the
rutted track, lumber wagons with cut timbers headed
toward the mines, while wagons bearing rough-cut logs
headed the other direction en route to the sawmill located
along Clear Creek at Georgetown. It was a fairly busy road.

Shortly, the easy valley they'd been following came to
an abrupt end and the road began its zigzag course that
served to eat up elevation and allow the horse-drawn
wagons to navigate the steep slopes out of the valley. While
it allowed wagons and animals to climb the steep
mountains, it also added considerable distance and time for
any traveler trying to get to the divide.

Here and there, they passed small one-man mining
operations where someone had staked a claim in hopes of
finding the vein that would guarantee wealth to the end of
his days. Not one in ten thousand would ever strike it rich,
yet they dug and toiled over the rock and what they
couldn't chip with a pick, they blasted with powder.
Occasionally, a muted *Kah-rump* could be heard deep
underground, signaling that a charge had been set off.

Despite the early start, the day was quickly warming
now that the sun had risen above the mountaintops to the
east. Once they'd left the shade offered by the steep walls

of the valley, their progress was under the full effects of the sun, made all that much stronger due to the elevation. It would only get worse as they climbed.

Once they rose above the immediate vicinity of Georgetown, the mines grew fewer in number and occasionally they passed small groves of cedars that were too twisted to be of any use for shoring timbers. These trees often played host to raucous groups of magpies or the occasional acrobatics of a red squirrel.

Where they were headed, the weather would be mild during the daylight hours, but after dark the temperatures would fall to near or below freezing, and a dusting of snow or even a full-blown snow storm wasn't out of the question considering the fact that summer wasn't yet upon them. Shaw had seen whiteout blizzards in these mountains in July. Better to haul some extra food and equipment than to venture into the mountains unprepared.

There wasn't much in the way of conversation until noon approached. Shaw was keeping an eye out for a likely place to rest and water the horses while they took a meal. It wasn't long before he spotted a suitable level meadow bordering a pond the beaver had created with the help of a trickle of snowmelt from the high country. The dam was pretty impressive considering the lack of really good timber. It was mostly mud and sticks and about five feet high. The shallow pond was easily five acres in area. If it hadn't been for the dangers of flash floods, this would be a lovely spot for a campsite. But they had several hours of travel ahead of them before they could start thinking about a camp.

Once Shaw had pointed out the spot, they dismounted and he gathered up the horses and led them to the edge of the pond where they would water and enjoy the lush grass that circled the pond. Sarah had gathered some deadfall and it took Shaw a minute to get a good blaze going for a pot of coffee. While he was busy with the fire, Sarah took a sack

232

of bread and smoked meats and began to make sandwiches.

Shaw was tired. Not from the trip, but from the mental effort of being completely vigilant for any sign that Pollard might try to make a liar out of him. He didn't really expect to be ambushed along this road, even when dealing with a killer who gave the appearance of being a man who stood by his word, Shaw could never be totally certain. The price of such vigilance was extreme mental fatigue.

Even now, while resting from the morning's travel, Shaw didn't relax. He scanned the hillsides looking for movement or colors out of place; a glint of light on glass or metal. In a way, the topography made his job easier. The hillsides to their east were mostly rocky and very steep and although they offered the best view of his party for an observer, anyone trying to make a shot from that side wouldn't find suitable cover until they were well out of rifle range.

To the north and west, the slope was more gradual and there were plenty of stands of pine in which to hide and even an occasional stand of aspen that hadn't yet seen the edge of the woodchopper's axe. Shaw knew the aspen wouldn't survive long since the mines were slowly making their way up the mountainsides as the newcomers sought out fresh slopes to sink shafts into.

"How far have we come?" Sarah asked.

Shaw looked down the valley, gauging the interval. Though Georgetown was now well out of sight behind the hills they'd entered, it wasn't difficult to approximate the distance. "Eight or ten miles, I'd say. We made good time the first hour, but these switchbacks are slow going. We spent the better part of an hour earlier just climbing half a mile. There are two more stretches like that up ahead, but the rest of the trip to the divide will be faster. By late afternoon, we'll have made near to twenty miles and by then the horses will be done. We'll rest there for several hours, then before first light we'll leave the trail and wait for daylight to head overland."

"How far will we need to go after that?" Samuel asked.

Shaw saw the tiredness in the man's eyes. He simply wasn't ready for an arduous trip up the mountain and down the other side and the thin air didn't help his recovery. Shaw had counted on Samuel's condition being a limiting factor in his search, but it also worked into his plan. "By late tomorrow afternoon, I think we'll be in a place where I can put you two up for a day, while I scout around. I need to travel like an Indian up there. You won't be able to go with me." Samuel began to object and Shaw put up his hand. "Listen, I promise I won't try to take him alone. But I have to find him first. The only way to do that is to get above him and hope he makes a mistake so I can see where he's holed up. I can do that alone, but the three of us can't. Either you do this my way, or I turn around and you're on your own."

Samuel's expression told Shaw he didn't like the thought of being left behind. Sarah remained silent.

It took a moment, but finally Samuel nodded. "All right. I'll have to trust you," Samuel said. "You're the expert in these matters."

"No, I'm not. *Pollard* is the expert in these matters. Keep that firmly in mind because you can bet I am."

They finished the rest of their meal and allowed a full hour for the horses to rest before they mounted up and continued their journey.

* * * *

By late afternoon, the elevation had robbed them of the warmth of the daytime sun. The temperature was dropping quickly and an incessant wind swirled with the contours of the broken land that made the chilled air even more uncomfortable. They stopped long enough to don warmer clothing, then continued until the land began to level off, signaling that they neared the top of the mountain's divide. There, they stopped again so Shaw could consider their location in relation to his memory of the basin where Geneva City was located.

They were close to the tree line and, while this mountaintop wasn't high enough to guarantee year-round snow, some peaks to the west were still snow-covered. To the east, there was a vast plain that looked flat as a dinner table and nearly devoid of anything but grass. Shaw knew that was an illusion. The distance across the plain to a rugged spine of rock face hardly looked to be more than a mile, but was closer to five. With no trees to measure against, distances were unbelievably difficult to estimate in the mountain tundra. What looked like a grassy plain was more like an almost impenetrable barrier of waist-high or shoulder-high brush, fractured by occasional water-cut ravines. Despite the desolation, the beauty of the landscape struck Shaw and, evidently, he wasn't the only one.

"This is lovely!" Sarah remarked.

Samuel, who had pulled his coat collar up around his face snorted in reply. "It is *not* lovely. It's cold and lifeless. This damnable wind would drive me crazy."

"You never did like the cold," Sarah chided. "I can live with it. It's exhilarating."

Shaw smiled and shook his head. "No, Sarah, I have to agree with Samuel. It's cold. And it's going to get colder. We need to head west from here across the side of this mountain and find a place where we can be protected from the wind. The horses will need it as much as we do."

Shaw reined his horse off the track and began to descend, taking them on a course that would cut across the side of the mountain they'd just climbed. He hoped to find shelter in the thicker line of trees about a thousand feet below that would also allow them to have a fire which wouldn't be observed.

It took the better part of an hour and, with darkness

approaching, Shaw found a perfect spot. The site nestled in a jumble of cabin-sized boulders with an easy entrance from only one direction. Mountain pines completely hid the nest from above and a natural depression would allow them to have three walls of granite to reflect the heat of the fire. A hidden marksman wouldn't be able to fire into the depression from any distance at all. There was even a small trickle of a stream just outside that came from a mountain spring on the hillside above. During the day, the water flowed freely, but at night, it would freeze at the edges. Still, close to the source, the water would not completely freeze this time of year. It was a near-perfect spot.

With the temperatures approaching freezing, Shaw worked swiftly to gather the makings of a fire and place it where the heat would reflect into their sheltered spot. Sarah and Samuel began unburdening the packhorses and saddle stock. While Sarah gathered up the necessary items they'd need for camp, Samuel took the horses to the stream for water.

After a good fire was built, Shaw went out to gather a night's supply of wood while the last minutes of daylight remained. When he had a good pile set aside, he took two small lodge poles he'd cut from a couple of young pines and braced them so he could take a canvas ground cloth and make a partial lean-to and wind break on the side of their shelter that was open. The fire and the heat from the horses would guarantee their reasonable comfort, but the temperature would never be much higher than forty degrees inside.

With the horses watered and picketed outside for an hour to graze, they shared a quiet meal of stew made from more smoked meat and water boiled with a handful of parched corn and a little flour for body. The hot stew and coffee helped warm them up and the overall mood was fairly cheerful, considering the seriousness of their business.

"My, this is cozy." Samuel joked with chattering teeth. "In truth, it's better than I expected."

Shaw was quiet. He'd been considering all the possibilities that came to mind and the dangerous nature of the man they hunted, and he wasn't happy. Though he felt fairly confident they had managed to reach this place undetected, he had chosen it more for its defensive capabilities than any physical comforts it offered. If he'd been alone, he would have made cold camp. As it was, he was restricted to finding places that could support his party, if not in relative comfort, by at least offering an element of relief from the cold.

"In the morning," Shaw began, "the cold will take a long time to leave, but by noon it should be fairly warm. We're still several miles from where I'd like to start my hunt, so we can't stay here. Chances are, we won't find anything nearly as nice ahead." Shaw paused to let that sink in. "I'd like to suggest you two stay here and let me go on ahead for a day or maybe two."

"I'd like to be closer to where you expect to find Pollard," Samuel said.

"I expect to find Pollard anywhere! Hell, man, he could have watched us make camp for all I know. Every step we take from this moment on must be taken with the consideration that we may already be in his sights. We simply cannot travel as a group and accomplish that."

"Yes, we can," Samuel argued. "You go on ahead and locate a likely spot that will put us in the right area and come back to get us. We'll travel after dark and be set by the time the sun comes up. If we do it carefully, he'll never know we've invaded his territory." Samuel looked satisfied.

Shaw shook his head angrily. "Samuel, I'm guessing. That's all I'm doing here. With Pollard, there are no absolutes. While we shiver through the night, he may already be back in Georgetown dining on prime beef, laughing at the joke he played on us."

Blood drained from Sarah's face. "Surely, he wouldn't…"

"He might." Shaw shrugged. "Once I leave here in the morning, I must have the luxury of moving like a cat and if that means I have to sit in a crack on a mountainside all night, I want to be able to do that without worrying about you two."

"A little closer, Matt." Samuel's voice softened. "That's all I ask."

Sarah looked at Shaw expectantly, but remained silent. Shaw knew she trusted he'd do what was best for all concerned, given the nearly impossible circumstances Samuel had already put on him.

He dropped his head and pondered Samuel's request. Everything in his mind screamed out that this was as close as he could put Sarah to the danger zone and still feel reasonably sure they were as of yet unobserved.

At the same time, he knew that this sheltered spot wasn't really all that exclusive to the terrain he was going to navigate in the morning. It was likely there were a dozen similar sites within easy reach of the area where he intended to begin his hunt for Pollard. But they would also be easier for Pollard to detect through careful observation.

The mountain formed a continuous ridge line shaped like a teardrop with its base pointing to the southwest and its apex broken by a very narrow valley that widened into the large amphitheater called Geneva Basin. The bottom of the basin was four thousand feet below the ridge line at its highest point. Shaw expected to find Pollard overlooking Geneva City somewhere on the opposite side of the mountain from where they now camped. From the vantage point of an eagle, that was a mere two or three miles. The distance was double that on foot.

It would be easier for Pollard to find a spot on the other side of the basin, but Shaw knew he was looking for the hardest terrain he could find. It would offer the most difficult approach for someone hunting him. Pollard and Shaw were now both hunter and prey. Every move or decision they made had to be done with the thought that either one of them could have the momentary advantage. Pollard was testing himself at the same time that he tested Shaw. He'd indicated that it was nothing personal, but Shaw disagreed. There was nothing quite as personal as a deadly test between two men.

Shaw thought he knew where Pollard would be; well, at least the general area. But that area included three or four miles of rocky crags and occasional stands of mountain pine located in small areas of alpine meadowland. That was a lot of area to cover. He intended to do so from the heights, so he could survey as much ground as possible before he moved through it.

Finally, he acquiesced. "Okay. One more move and only one. If you're not satisfied with the next site, I take Sarah back to safety and you're on your own!"

Samuel simply nodded and smiled. "Thank you." He didn't look like a man who had won a battle of wills. He merely had an expression of satisfaction one expected to see on the face of a man who was approaching some long sought-after goal. Shaw knew Samuel only wanted to be closer to the man who'd killed his son. That's all he'd asked. This created a conflict with Shaw. While he wanted Sarah safe, he also wanted Samuel close enough to act if Shaw needed to create a diversion. It wouldn't do to have Samuel outside the zone of action.

"You find him and if you can, put me within striking distance," Samuel said. "That will satisfy me."

"What if I can find him, but putting you in that position will be impossible?"

Samuel fixed Shaw with a hard look. "If the only way we can win this is by your hand, I'll accept that. I won't like it, but I'll accept it. If I can look upon his dead carcass and know that Stuart is avenged, I'll be satisfied. But you have to promise me you'll give me a chance if there is any possibility of success."

Shaw nodded reluctantly. "I promise I will try. But that's as much of a guarantee I can give."

Then Samuel did the most unexpected thing. He extended his hand. Surprised, Shaw took it. It was the first friendly gesture either of them had shared in the entire time they'd known each other.

Out of the corner of his eye, Shaw noted Sarah's expression. It seemed profoundly sad; as if Samuel's gesture and kindness reminded her of what she and Samuel had once shared, now lost forever. Of course, there could be another reason for her sadness, but none that Shaw could know for certain. In any case, he was too preoccupied to dwell on it.

* * * *

In the morning, it took Shaw a couple of hours to locate a good spot to put Samuel and Sarah. He'd instructed them to be ready to move upon his return and, as soon as he made it back, he led them by a safe route to the new campsite. It was actually similar to the site they'd just left, but it was smaller and more confined. There was a good view of the valley below, but their visibility toward the ridge line was obscured by large rocks. There was ample graze outside the enclosure and a seep of fresh water from a crack in the rocks. It would only fill a gallon canteen in half an hour, but would provide enough water for both horses and people during the course of the day. It would freeze up at night, so they needed to get their water while it was running.

Shaw began his instructions. "This is it. It's not perfect. On the plus side, you'll have the first light of morning to warm you. On the negative side, you'll lose the sun a bit earlier than where we were before. That makes a difference because now you can't have a fire. It's too risky this close."

Samuel objected. "The rocks will hide any light from above."

"The rocks will not contain the smoke," Shaw said. "The wind will carry the smoke into the valley after dark, but while there's still light, it will carry it up, over the crest and along the ridge line for miles. Then there's the wood-smoke smell, as well. Better to avoid the whole issue. The horses will generate as much heat as a small fire. Get close to them and huddle up. You'll be fine."

"All right. I'll top up the canteen." Samuel left them and moved to the water cascade.

"How do we cook?" Sarah asked.

"I'm sorry, Sarah. This has to be a cold camp. You wanted to be close and that brings with it a whole new set of rules. You're in the hunter's lair now. You're close. Too close, actually. You'll have to make do with cold meats and bread and you've got plenty of both."

"What will you do now?" she asked.

"I'm going ahead on foot. You won't see me again until I find Pollard — *if* I can find him. If I haven't returned in three days, you need to pack up and return to Georgetown. Follow the same route we used coming in and move quickly. Once you make Georgetown, you'll be relatively safe, but don't stay there. Make it back to Denver and on to Eagle Town. If I'm not back in that time, it's over. Pollard won and you have to get to safety."

Sarah started to speak and Shaw stopped her. Samuel was out of earshot, but he kept his voice low anyway. "Sarah, listen to me. Frankly, I don't care what happens to Samuel, but I want to make certain you're safe. He can do whatever he wants after that, but you have to promise me you will leave. Pollard already promised me he wouldn't hurt you."

Sarah's expression told Shaw she didn't like it. But he

could also tell that she was beginning to finally understand the danger they were all in this close to the killer. He added, quietly, "If Pollard wins here, there's no reason to remain. Samuel won't leave and that means he'll kill himself with his foolish thoughts of revenge overriding any common sense. If I don't return, you have to promise you will leave."

Samuel returned with his canteen, while Shaw continued his instructions: "Like I said, no fire. If you're discovered, hunker down and fire your weapons. I'll hear them. Stay under cover and protect yourselves as best you can and I'll get back here as quickly as possible, but it might take some time. I won't rush headlong into trouble, so it could take quite a while for me to sort out the situation and make a safe approach. Just stay under cover."

Sarah wrung her hands together, her eyes teary.

"Also," Shaw went on, "if you hear shooting, give me a day after you hear the last shot and then pack up and leave. If I'm not back in a day, I'm not coming back. That means you two are in imminent danger. Samuel, I don't care what you do, but promise me you will see to Sarah's safety first."

Samuel considered this. "Won't our moving out put us in danger?"

Shaw shook his head. "No, not if you're leaving the area. Pollard won't harm you if he thinks you've given up. Keep heading down and you'll be safe. He'll let you go." Shaw paused, decided on a final warning. "That doesn't apply if he discovers you here waiting. Here, you're fair game because you're part of the hunt. On the move, if you're retreating, I believe you will be relatively safe."

Shaw stuffed enough food for three days of meager rations into his daypack. He had his coat, a ground cloth, a heavy wool blanket and a gallon canteen. With his rifle and sidearm, he was weighed down; but he'd carried more than this before in these mountains.

Despite the danger, he was surprisingly positive. He was a hunter and once again he was entering the hunter's environment. Alone with just his equipment and his wits, he knew his capabilities and he believed he understood Pollard's. There was nothing left to do but do it.

"Remember what I said." Shaw smiled and left the little enclosure.

* * * *

They lost sight of him quickly. Sarah wondered if she'd seen him for the last time. The thought almost caused her to lose control. Stifling an urge to run after him and beg him to come back and quit this stupid endeavor, she put her hand to her throat and tried not to look worried.

"He'll be all right, Sarah," Samuel said in a comforting tone. Looking somewhat sad himself, he added, "He'll come back to you."

She was momentarily shocked, but before she could speak or object, Samuel said, "It doesn't matter. I mean it! You have every right to be happy and all I've done is make you miserable." He looked at her intently, but with understanding in his eyes. "What's done is done. You've come this far and I appreciate it, I really do. You've shown me the kind of support I should have shown you, but I denied you."

Samuel looked away, into the distant valley. "Don't feel bad, please don't. I'm still a lost soul and I'll never come back from that. When this is done, you will have the ranch and you'll never see me again."

Sarah couldn't contain her emotions any longer. The sadness she'd held in since the death of Stuart finally released and she cried like a little girl, her body racked by huge sobs. For the first time in half a year, Samuel took her into his embrace and held her against his chest while she wept. It was the gesture of a caring friend, or at most a brother. She felt neither of them had a shred of the love that had bound them together for so long. That was surely lost, but they were still bonded by the emotions that came from having once loved, and their memories of Rebecca and Stuart.

* * * *

When Shaw left the hidden camp, he entered a dangerous environment where the smallest move required a methodical study of all the visible terrain. It might take an hour of careful observation, scouring the ground with a glass, searching for anything that might signal danger, just to make a movement that would only gain fifty yards. There were no shortcuts to be taken. He either did it right or he died.

He wasn't new to this game, having played versions of it in the past while soldiering or avoiding hostile Indians on his many treks across the territories of the west. Despite the influx of miners to these mountains, there were still small bands of Kiowa and Arapaho who traveled through and occasionally made trouble for the miners in the lonely and far-flung camps. But Shaw wasn't worried about Indians. He was worried about an unseen marksman who might even now be looking at his sweating face through a telescope.

Despite the dangers, Shaw was comfortable doing what he was doing. He and Pollard were equals here. Pollard may be the better marksman but Shaw felt he could compete with that, based on his ability to blend in and move carefully.

After several hours of cautiously searching and moving, he'd come to the rim rock and, below him, he could see Geneva City. It had grown some since he'd passed through this area a couple years ago. There was a large log building that appeared to be a stable and he counted a dozen horses in the corral. Ten decent sized cabins and at least fifteen half-buried dugout shelters fronted with logs lined the hills. Several of the cabins had thin tendrils of smoke curling from their stacks. Some appeared to be abandoned. Miners came and tried their luck; some stayed and some gave it up. Soon, a new hand would try his luck and an abandoned shelter would be reopened and swept out. The population of such a mining camp changed continuously.

Shaw was in a good spot. From his vantage point, he could make a long and studied observation of the valley below. He was concealed from view from below and if anyone moved within half a mile, he'd see them before they saw him. He decided he'd stay here the rest of the day, sweeping the terrain with his glass, hoping Pollard would make a mistake. While he watched and waited, he'd take the time to select a number of potential vantage points he could navigate to in the dark, should he later decide to move. In the back of his mind there was a vague uneasiness that he'd made a mistake, but he recognized that as a typical emotion. He realized that no one could consider all the possibilities or cover all the options. There wasn't anything he could do about it now except refuse to allow his doubts and fears to get the better of his common sense. He had to trust the plan and Sarah's good judgment.

* * * *

Darkness began to creep into the little sheltered spot Sarah and Samuel shared. It was still vividly daylight across the valley but, where they were huddled, the shadows were deep and with the growing shadows came the chill that would only increase as darkness descended. The horses were taken out for an hour of grazing and then being brought back in for their own safety and the heat they'd provide.

Sarah knew that cold, more than anything else, sapped a

person's power to resist doubt and depression. She was cold, but Samuel seemed literally assaulted by the chill. It happened to people who were at one time in their life near to freezing. After an experience such as that, cold took on an almost profound and insidious threat. It was almost akin to not being able to properly breathe. Samuel had nearly frozen to death as a young boy and was quick to take a chill when the weather turned harsh. It affected him deeply, both physically and emotionally.

Now, he sat next to her, a blanket wrapped around his head with only his eyes and mouth exposed. Even so, his frame was racked by intense bouts of shivering. Sarah was sure it was made worse by his dismal physical condition. The cold was certainly a discomfort, but she was able to glean enough warmth from her blankets and the proximity of the horses to remain cheerful.

She tried to engage him in conversation to take his mind off the cold. He responded, but she knew his efforts were only halfhearted. He mumbled his responses and didn't add anything to keep the conversation alive. She decided shared warmth would help him better cope and gathered her blankets around his to nestle in and give him what warmth her body had to offer. After a while, she drifted off to sleep.

She wasn't sure how much time had passed when she found herself being slowly dragged out of the depths of sleep by a persistent crackling that sounded a little like a light rain against the wall of their cabin. She lay drowsily, trying to avoid coming fully awake, but the insistent snapping and crackling finally made her open her eyes. It took a moment to realize that their little enclosure was brighter, made so by the dancing flames of a tiny fire. Samuel huddled beside it, carefully feeding small sticks to keep it alive.

"My God, Samuel, Matt insisted we not have a fire!" She was shocked and fully awake. She hadn't realized how badly Samuel had been affected by the cold, that he'd take such a risk for what little warmth this small fire offered.

"It's late at night," Samuel mumbled through cold-stiffened lips. "Shaw said the cold would carry the smoke down the mountain. I waited until it was safe. I'll douse it before the wind changes and I'll catch up on my sleep when the sun warms our enclosure."

Sarah knew there was no arguing with him. He was beyond reason now. The cold scared him more than anything else and he was incapable of fighting it in the darkness. She looked at the little fire and she, too, found comfort in it but fearfully watched the smoke curl up until it reached the top of the little fortress of rocks they were nestled within. When the wind caught it, it was carried away, apparently down the valley, opposite the direction Shaw had indicated was dangerous to them.

Maybe Shaw had been overly cautious. If they killed the fire before daylight brought the warm air up from the valley, they could stay warmer throughout most of the night. It would certainly help. Sarah moved closer to the fire too, and together they soaked up the added comfort the tiny flames provided. Sometime later, they both fell into a deep sleep and the fire died.

* * * *

Sunlight made its way over the lip of the depression where Shaw huddled. The light made it to his eyelids and they fluttered open. For a moment, he didn't move, as was his habit. He lay there, silently listening. Had it been the sunlight that roused him or something else, some sound or vibration? He couldn't be sure, so he remained completely motionless and continued to listen.

From across the rim came the unmistakable sound of a pistol shot, muted by distance and terrain. Another shot followed in close succession and yet another. Shaw experienced the most unyielding sense of fear, followed by shame. He'd made a terrible mistake bringing Sarah into these mountains, despite her insistence. Too, he'd either overestimated his ability to control events, or underestimated Pollard's cunning and grasp of the situation.

There was no further shooting. Shaw didn't know whether that was a good sign or a bad one. It didn't matter. He was nearly a mile from the campsite and because it was necessary to take the exact same precautions today that he'd observed yesterday, covering that distance safely would mean using the better part of the entire day to get there and even that was risking exposure. He hoped he wouldn't be too late. Whatever had happened and whatever was yet to happen in the immediate future was out of his control for at least the next several hours. He had to put everything else out of his mind and proceed with the same caution and deliberation he would call upon had nothing been amiss. He could only hope that the pistol shots meant that either Samuel or Sarah hadn't been surprised and had made a defense of their little perimeter.

Shaw quickly stowed his blanket in the daypack and began his careful scouting of the ground he had to cover. It was maddening, having to take the time to do this. When, after half an hour, he was convinced it was safe, Shaw scrambled two hundred yards to a new position. From there, he started all over and — always — fear and anguish hid just beneath the surface of his demeanor. Panic, however, was not.

* * * *

Sarah had awakened to the sound of Samuel leading the horses from the little compound. He was taking them out for an hour's graze. Looking about, she noticed that the hour of first light was almost upon them. They'd overslept, the heat from the little fire giving the extra comfort to allow them to get some much-needed rest.

"Samuel, you can't graze the horses after daylight," she called out. "It's not safe."

"I'll keep them really close to the rocks. They won't be visible from above," he insisted. He smiled and held the horses close. Sarah couldn't believe how much better he looked this morning. She had to admit the fire had given her a lift, but it had positively boosted his spirits. She was glad. Looking about her, she started to fold the blankets in preparation for breakfast.

The boom of a heavy gun in the distance caught her by surprise and, for a moment, she was certain Shaw had fired it. Yet, something about the sound seemed uneasily familiar. Standing up, she looked around. Shock and disbelief struck her like a blow. Samuel was down on his knees with a look of embarrassment on his face. He hugged his midsection where a growing red stain already soaked the arms of his coat and the legs of his pants.

Sarah started forward and Samuel stopped her with a weak shout. "Stay there! Get a gun and get under cover."

"I'm coming to bring you back in!" she shouted. She started forward and Samuel shook his head angrily.

"No! Stay there. I don't think he can see me here. I'm down lower now. Stay there. I'll come in myself after I've caught my breath."

Sarah watched in horror. Samuel seemed to have grown weaker in just the minute since he'd been shot. Indecision gripped her, until she saw the butt of the Smith & Wesson revolver sticking out of the pack where she'd set it the night before.

She grabbed it and darted outside the rocks to Samuel's side. With the gun in one hand and taking Samuel's arm, she started dragging him toward the rocks. She wildly fired three shots up toward the rim rock, not intending to hit anything, but hoping to distract the hidden marksman and maybe alert Matthew.

Before she could make the safety of the rocks, she lost her footing and fell heavily, letting go of Samuel's arm. He was still conscious, but his face was pasty and white. It didn't seem like his eyes were focusing on anything and his breath was coming in shallow puffs. She dropped the pistol and used both her hands to drag Samuel the rest of the way to the safety of the rocks. Along the gravel, over which she'd dragged her stricken husband, a large smear of dark blood gave evidence to his terrible injuries. The heavy musket bullet had plowed through his body, leaving a bloody hole in the back of his coat as well.

Once inside the rocks she stopped and lay there, exhausted. She gauged whether she could safely retrieve the gun she'd dropped and then remembered that there was another pistol and two loaded rifles inside the compound. She didn't need to take the risk.

When she had the strength, she rolled Samuel over and looked at his face. His eyes were fixed on some distant spot and he had an almost amused expression on his face.

"Samuel, can you hear me?" Tears streamed down her face.

His eyes flickered and finally focused on her face. "It's hot," he whispered hoarsely. "I'm hot, finally. The fire was a good idea, Sarah. Don't let it go out."

"I won't. I'll keep it burning," Sarah promised. "You rest now. You get some rest now." Wiping tears from her face, she pulled him up so his head rested on her legs. Grabbing her pack, she started tearing a shirt into strips to try to plug Samuel's wounds but, before she could attend to them, she heard gravel rolling down the hill. Gently lowering Samuel's head to the ground, she grabbed one of the rifles and took up a position behind a boulder. The sound didn't repeat itself; she sat, straining to hear anything.

"Is he dead?" A calm voice asked from just outside the

rocks. Sarah was shocked he'd been able to get so close.

"You bastard!" she screamed. "Go away and leave him alone!" She levered a cartridge into the chamber of her rifle to emphasize she was prepared to fight. She heard a mild chuckle from above.

"You're game. I told Shaw you'd fight, given the chance. It was never my intention to hurt you, so here's the deal. You go away. I'll let Shaw come back in and you leave with him. If you go, I won't stop you. But that's the last of it. Your husband is dead or he's going to be. He shouldn't have come. I truly wish he hadn't. Now that's the end of it, you hear? Go away and leave me alone. That's the deal."

He didn't speak again. Sarah listened intently, but didn't hear him depart. She grew certain the sound of gravel when he approached had been deliberate. It had been a way of announcing his presence. After several minutes, she was sure he was gone. She turned back to Samuel and used the strips of cloth to plug the wounds to his front and back. There was little else she could do. Once done, she sagged against a rock, put her head back against the cold granite and looked at the clouds floating by, all the while keeping the rifle cradled on her lap.

Roughly an hour later, Samuel smiled and called out to Stuart. He mumbled something about cutting wood for the fire and then was silent, save for his rattling breath. Within ten minutes, he passed away without another word. Sarah finally closed her eyes and fell into a deep and needed sleep.

About an hour before the sun finally set, Shaw entered the shelter and woke Sarah. She climbed stiffly to her feet and rushed into his arms. While they held each other, Sarah cried harder than she'd ever cried before; as though she'd never cry again as long as she lived.

To Finish What He Started

Shaw wrapped Samuel in a blanket and carried him to a shadowed place outside their shelter where the sun wouldn't touch him. He piled a few rocks in place to protect the body from scavengers. It would have to do for now. When he finished, Sarah told him what Pollard said.

"It's the best course," Shaw said finally. "I'll get you to safety and then I'll figure out how to deal with Pollard later. There's no real hurry now."

Sarah seemed to consider, then shook her head. "No," she said. "I want to finish what we started. He's out there now, watching to see what we do. I say we stay. I could never ride away from here knowing he killed Stuart and Samuel and believed we'd just give up. No!" She added with ferocity, "I want him dead. I don't just want him dead, Matt...I want the ravens to peck his dead eyes out!"

Shaw wasn't surprised, but he also knew it wasn't a particularly smart course of action. As much as he too wanted to see Pollard dead, the job had finally become exactly the nightmare he'd feared all along. "Sarah, this man's better than good. He's a freak; a phenomenon. Frankly, I'm no longer convinced that I have what it takes to beat him, at least not out here on the ground of his choosing. I might stand a better chance waiting for another opportunity. Not only that, but to stay up here and hunt him, I'd have to leave you alone again and I'm not going to do that."

"I'll leave then," she said. She looked at Shaw with a feverish light in her eyes and spoke with finality. "I'll ride out alone. I know the way home from here. You said yourself, he'll leave me be. But I have to know you'll stay and finish this. Samuel thought he could do it and he was wrong. This man has taken my family from me and I could never go on, I could never again be happy knowing that he was still alive, hurting other people for money."

Her eyes softened. "When I first met you, I hated everything you stood for. I refused to accept that any man who willingly set out to meet violence with violence was anything but an inherently bad man. Even when I was starting to fall in love with you, despite myself, I still hated what you represented." She looked down at her feet. "Now, God help me, I'm willing to send you out to kill a man, and to risk your life because of my weakness, because of my *fear*."

Shaw nodded. "I'll go with you to the wagon road and start you down. Then I'll come back and finish it."

"No!" she objected. "That will just put you in greater danger. Don't worry about me. You have to take every advantage there is. Start now, tonight while it's dark. He's going to be somewhere near, waiting to see what we do. Use the darkness to your advantage," she pleaded. "He knows we're here. I'll make a fire and talk quietly and in the morning, I'll ride out. By the time he sees that I'm alone, you should be somewhere where you can spot him."

As much as he hated the thought of leaving her behind, Shaw recognized the logic of her suggestion. But he didn't truly trust Pollard's word. After considering the situation for several minutes, he said, "All right. You ride out in the morning and don't try to hide or be cute. Sit up straight and head down the mountain so he knows you're out of it and he'll probably leave you alone." She nodded and Shaw added, "Keep your rifle in your hands. Cover anyone you see with it until you know their intentions and don't hesitate to shoot first. I've told you what Pollard looks like, but that doesn't mean he doesn't have help nearby."

"I will."

"You shouldn't be riding this country alone anyway. Keep a watch out," Shaw warned. "There are bad men about."

Sarah managed a tired, weak smile. "I think we've already established that."

Shaw smiled and took her in his arms and held her close for several minutes. There was no passion to the embrace. It was an emotional grasp, each of them soaking up what strength and courage they could from the other. It was a clasp of purely spiritual support. At the moment, their closeness was more important than all the happenings of the past or their dreams for the future.

When they finally broke apart, Shaw refilled his canteen and replenished his rations. He inspected his weapons and carefully examined his cartridges. He didn't know how long he'd have to play cat and mouse with Pollard, but he was going to prepare for several days.

"You take the horses and ride out. If everything works out, you and I can come back for Samuel's body together. If it doesn't..." he hesitated a second, "... if it doesn't, you may as well leave him here. It's a good place to be. There's a good view of the valley from here." Shaw looked off toward the distant peaks. "I wouldn't mind resting here myself."

"Don't talk like that, Matthew. Now you listen to me," she said fiercely, "the only bones I want to know are up in these rocks are Pollard's!"

Shaw nodded. He understood perfectly what she was feeling. She'd closed the door to her old way of thinking. She'd never look at life in the same manner. The illusion of society's safety and security that so many people rely on had been destroyed. She was through being a victim of circumstances. She'd finally embraced his world, rather than insisting he accept hers.

It seemed a long time since he'd last kissed her. So much had happened and he wasn't sure how appropriate it would seem, given the circumstances.

As if she were reading his mind, Sarah smiled and came

to him with her face uplifted. The kiss was soft and hot. When she stepped back, she smiled again.

"Remember how that felt," she said. "You don't get another one like it until I see you again in Georgetown."

Shaw looked down the valley. "I'm sure I could get another one like it down in Geneva City," he joked mildly.

Her eyes became a little wet with tears when she replied, "No. Not one like that. You'll never find one with as much love as that anywhere in the world."

He looked at her for what seemed like an eternity, memorizing her every feature as if it might have to last him a lifetime. "You're right, Sarah. Until I met you, I'd never had one like it and now I can't imagine ever finding another."

"You come back to me!" Sarah commanded. "I feel like I'm sending you away where you could get killed and it's going to be my fault. You have to beat this man, and then you have to come back to me!"

Shaw touched her face with his fingertips, and silently left the rocks.

* * * *

It was an hour after daylight when Shaw watched Sarah lead the horses down the mountain. From where he hid, he estimated she was nearly a mile away down the slope and crossing a meadow. He quit watching her. Instead, he scanned the side of the mountain for any sign of Pollard, wondering if he'd seen her too. Instinctively, he knew Pollard would already be aware that the game was back on.

Shaw took off his hat and rubbed his eyes. Glancing at the sun, he gauged the time and took a bite of bread. The chill was leaving him, finally, but he gave personal comfort little thought. Pollard was as good as any man he'd ever faced, probably better than he could hope to beat. He'd snookered Shaw the night before and it was Shaw's intention that the man should receive no more breaks from now on. Shaw's advantage was that now he didn't have to worry about anyone's safety but his own. He and Pollard were finally on equal footing in that regard.

After four hours of careful observation and seeing nothing unusual or threatening, Shaw decided to shift positions a bit. He thought a small shelf of granite about fifty yards above would give him a better vantage point to scan this side of the mountain.

He started low and moved like a mountain lion, with the kind of fluid grace only an experienced climber can achieve. He slipped between rocks and slithered over them like a liquid human shadow. Unless someone was looking directly at him, they'd miss his movement completely.

A raven glided across the face of the mountainside barely ten feet above the ground; floating on the thermal waves of the warming air coming off the rocks. Shaw was studying the terrain when the bird made an almost imperceptible correction in its flight. Ravens have eyesight second to none.

From the distance, Shaw saw the bird turn its head and look back briefly. He trained his rifle on the spot where the Raven seemed to be looking. Through his telescopic sight, he detected a patch of brown that didn't match the pale shade of gray in the surrounding rocks. It might be a coat or a pack, but was too indistinct to identify perfectly. It didn't matter. Whoever won this match might do so by shooting at a glimpse of color and shadow or a fractional movement. It might be the only target offered. If he waited, he might lose the chance, knowing how the jumble of mountain boulders could hide movement into and out of a position of concealment. He centered the patch in the sight and fired.

The shot was close to two hundred yards and he was certain his bullet struck the brown patch. Through his telescope, he noticed that the color was no longer there. Shaw started to wonder if the difference in color shade had merely been a trick of light when the rock in front of his face exploded in fragments that blasted against his cheeks and threw small particles into his eyes. He rolled down and out of sight, furiously rubbing his eyes to get them tearing up in an effort to wash the grit away. After a few seconds, he could see again.

The shot came from another location, at about an angle of thirty degrees from where he'd believed Pollard to be. He realized that his shot at Pollard had either missed completely, or only slightly wounded him. Regardless, Pollard had been able to move from that location unseen and apparently unhampered by injuries. Shaw knew that the mountain offered a maze of rocks and depressions that couldn't be detected from ground level. Well, two could play that game. Shaw slid between two large rocks and managed to drop into a natural trough that allowed him to move away from the firing zone. Then the agonizingly slow contest started all over.

* * * *

Pollard wrapped a cloth around his left forearm. Shaw's bullet created a shallow furrow; more than a cut, but not a hole. It was three inches long, ragged and exceedingly painful, but it was more messy than debilitating. Pollard was somewhat shocked. In all his time as a soldier, he'd never actually been wounded. Shaw had missed killing him by inches. Pollard had turned to watch the raven and the slight shift of his body had caused Shaw's bullet to pass his chest by mere inches. *Inches.* Some might have thought it nothing but random luck. Pollard knew it was God's will. He was being reminded to keep his pride in check.

He had no idea where Shaw had crawled off. Pollard knew his shot hadn't scored, seeing it crash into the granite a few inches lower than he anticipated. It would have been a miraculous shot in any case, but Pollard knew there would be another opportunity. He merely needed to be patient.

* * * *

Shaw took up a position where he could scan several hundred yards of terrain. He liked the spot. He felt certain Pollard was located somewhere within this span of rocks. Pollard's shot had been off by several inches and Shaw knew his opponent had shifted position again after making it. Shaw's own spot commanded enough ground that he was positive the man could not slip away during daylight. Pollard might remain unseen, but he would have to wait until nightfall to extricate himself from the area. That is, *if* Pollard wanted to leave.

He had to do something to help narrow the potential ground he'd have to search. Having pre-selected a position that offered good cover and a means of escape, Shaw darted to it, offering a brief target and expecting Pollard to try his luck. There was no shot. Shaw rested, catching his breath and resumed his patient study of the terrain.

As he watched, out of the corner of his eye he caught a puff of smoke. He reacted instantly and ducked, but not fast enough. The bullet tore through an inch of flesh on the top of his left shoulder between the neck and collarbone. The boom of the rifle arrived a fraction of a second later.

Shaw didn't fall as much as he sat back suddenly. The pain or shock of the bullet passing though the top of his muscle hadn't been heavy enough to knock him down, but it numbed his shoulder and arm. He knew that he was now out of Pollard's sight and in fact could retreat to another pre-selected position without being observed. He needed some space to attend to his wound and formulate another plan of action.

He crouched and gathered his pack and rifle. Working his way out of his sheltered spot, he gained the new position without being seen. Pollard would be looking at the spot where he'd fired but he couldn't approach it without Shaw having a good shot at him. Pollard must feel fairly certain his shot had been good, but would he believe Shaw was dead? Probably, but Shaw was confident a man of Pollard's caliber wouldn't simply rush up to look for a body. He was too much the professional for that.

Shaw took a moment to look at his wound. It was bloody and ugly, but shallow and not very serious. An inch lower and his collarbone would have been badly fractured. It had been a terribly close thing. Taking a bit of cloth, Shaw was able to stuff it into the hole and staunch the blood flow, but doing so wasn't meant for entertainment. Though there was considerable pain at the site of the wound, the arm was beginning to tingle and throb with the returning sensation. The pain was going to be bad, but nothing greater than he'd endured before. He was able to overcome it and put it aside while he planned. How long would Pollard wait? Shaw peered through an inch wide gap and watched.

* * * *

Pollard sat and considered his predicament. Shaw had shown himself only briefly, but that was enough. Instinctively, he'd managed to adjust his aim and through the telescopic sight saw Shaw drop heavily. Pollard was fairly sure his bullet hit Shaw in the upper chest; a lung gone, maybe. If he gave the man an hour, it would be enough. Even so, he'd approach from another direction. If he felt the need, he'd wait for nightfall.

He took care to reload, following the same meticulous process he'd done a thousand times. As usual, he found the practice soothing and calming. He took no joy in killing Roark — or Shaw, for that matter — but he found great satisfaction in once again proving that he was better than anyone he'd ever faced. He only had one friend he could talk to about his life and then only occasionally, when they got together to share a meal. But, a man only needed one true friend in his life. He'd certainly have a story to tell the next time.

Picking up his pack and rifle, Pollard moved backward behind a line of rocks that would shield his movements from Shaw. He was able to move diagonally across the face of the mountainside in a fold of earth that could not be seen from Shaw's position, but would allow him to close the distance by half before it ran out. After that, he'd set up and see if he couldn't detect where Shaw was lying. If he could see a body, he'd fire into it again, just to be sure.

Once he reached the end of the fold, he removed his hat and, ever so carefully, raised his head above a line of rocks. Scanning the ground below, he waited for movement.

A bullet whipped past his right ear so close it sounded like a slap and was actually painful. The snap of the bullet's passing was so loud he didn't even hear the boom of Shaw's rifle. He let himself go limp and twisted his body between two rocks, instinctively cradling his rifle so the delicate sighting equipment wouldn't get damaged. He had to move before he became trapped. Crawling on his belly, he managed to slither a dozen feet to an outcropping that allowed him to drop out of sight once again.

Pollard was shocked. He put his hand to his ear and found that in fact the bullet had cut the skin, so close had been the projectile's passing. The quickness of the shot could only mean Shaw had anticipated his move, or somehow he'd been tipped off by a sound or a changing color or shadow. Shaw had to have been watching exactly the spot Pollard selected to make an observation. It was uncanny.

Twice he'd managed to cheat death by inches. Admiration for Shaw's ability swelled in Pollard. Because his opponent was so good, it elevated Pollard's status in his own mind. Strangely, while most men would be considering the two close calls as evidence of their own mortality, Pollard looked at it as simply another warning not to get too cocky. He couldn't conceive of Shaw eventually besting him. He smiled. Checking the lenses of his telescopic sight, Pollard made another move.

When he had a position from which to scan the rocks, he spent several long moments letting his eyes play over the landscape. After a while, he noted a change in color. A minute patch of brown had shifted to expose the blue-gray granite behind. Pollard gently pushed the Stephens rifle forward and looked through the telescope. The patch of brown moved again.

There was Shaw, looking in another direction. Pollard smiled. He could see Shaw's coat was bloody but he couldn't see the man's whole body. From here, it was impossible to tell how badly injured the man was; however, even from the distance, he could tell Shaw was still alive by the almost imperceptible movement of the man's clothing.

It didn't matter. This was an easy shot. Pollard cocked the hammer of his rifle and carefully capped it, now that he was ready to shoot, as was his habit. A touch of his finger on the trigger and the rifle bellowed. For a second the smoke obscured his view of the sight below. When he was able to re-acquire the position in his sight the brown patch of clothing was gone, but in its place was a bright smear of fresh new blood on the rocks.

The game was nearly over.

* * * *

Shaw rolled on the ground in agony. The second bullet had plowed into his side at the left breast and pushed on under his armpit and exited from his back. His chest felt like it was being squeezed in a vice and he had trouble breathing. He knew he had to move. He was too weak to pick up his pack and could barely hold on to his rifle. Moving crabwise over the rocks, he scrambled further down, trying to remain out of sight as he sought distance and cover.

He had no doubt that he was badly injured. How badly he couldn't tell without a closer examination, but he couldn't take the necessary time to check his wounds. His exertions caused him to breathe deeply and every breath brought a tearing agony to his chest.

The shot had come from a typically unexpected direction. It was obvious that Pollard had pre-scouted a number of positions from which he could fire and move without being observed. Shaw hadn't had as much opportunity to do so and, because of that, he was now running for his life.

While sliding over a rock, Shaw lost his balance and fell heavily into a crack between two large boulders and lost hold of his rifle. It clattered across one of the boulders and out of sight, falling several feet before landing in the rocks below. From his position, he could neither see it nor take a chance of retrieving it. Escape was now his only option. Continuing to fight Pollard on this mountain in his present condition was impossible. He needed to evade the hunter and somehow make his way to Geneva City, where he might get help with his wounds at least.

He found himself between two large boulders situated on either side of a narrow goat track. The track crossed beneath a massive face of granite to a slope of weathered rocks and head-sized boulders two hundred feet below; it moved out of sight to the left, around the granite face.

Slowly regaining his feet, he staggered down the goat track. He looked behind him and was shocked to see the trail of blood he left behind on the rocks. If there was no place to go ahead, he'd be trapped. Blood loss and the cold of the coming night would undoubtedly finish him off. He needed to get to a place where he could attend to his latest wound and stop the heavy bleeding.

Shaw stumbled along, trying to maintain his balance on the goat path that was sometimes no wider than a few inches. Then suddenly the track came to an end. To continue on would require him to emulate the goats that made this track over the millennia. Shaw knew it would have been difficult for a healthy man to make that climb. In his present condition, it was simply beyond his ability. He could barely walk. There was no place left to go. He looked back at the glaring trail his dripping blood had left and shook his head. A blind man could follow that. He was trapped.

"Sarah," he whispered, "I'm sorry." Then, putting his head against the rock face, he closed his eyes and tried to think of a way to survive.

* * * *

Two hours passed. Pollard looked at the sky and judged there was less than four hours of daylight left. He was certain his last shot had scored solidly. Even so, he didn't take any chances approaching the spot he'd last seen Shaw. He moved slowly, keeping low and never lifting his eyes off that position.

When he finally reached a point directly opposite, he peeked around the corner. Shaw wasn't there. Pollard shook his head. The man had disappeared again, but this time he'd left a great deal of blood on the rocks, and a well-defined trail of it leading off down the slope. Judging by the amount of blood, he knew he'd scored another solid hit on his opponent. He fully expected that Shaw was already dead, lying in the rocks somewhere below. Still, he hesitated. There was no reason for haste. He'd act as he always had, with patience and deliberation.

Half an hour of inching along the trail brought him to where Shaw had fallen. From his position, he could see a wide swathe of blood on a boulder and in the track of the blood he saw where Shaw slid down over the rock, apparently no longer in complete control of his body. Below, Pollard spotted the broken remains of Shaw's rifle, halved at the wrist of the stock, its telescopic sight bent and damaged beyond repair. He nodded to himself, satisfied that Shaw had to be beneath the boulder on the slope, either dead or incapable of resisting.

He circled the boulder slowly and was chagrined to see the blood trail continue off down the goat path. He shook his head in admiration. Like a wounded animal often did, this man refused to give up. Bringing his rifle to his shoulder, Pollard slowly started down the goat path, following the drops of blood; prepared to fire the instant he encountered his quarry.

"Don't move!"

Pollard stiffened as Shaw's voice came like a thunderclap from behind him. Pollard was physically stunned: it was impossible that Shaw had managed to remain hidden. Even so, he had no doubt that Shaw covered him. While Shaw's rifle was broken, he'd certainly have a sidearm. His surprise was total; he was astonished that he'd made such a mistake. Slowly, he turned to look at Shaw.

He was amazed that Shaw was even on his feet. He'd never seen so much blood on a man still conscious – or still breathing for that matter. But Shaw *was* conscious and breathing, and despite his left side being soaked in blood from the shoulder to the boot on his left leg, the gun in his hand was steady enough. He looked bad, however. His face was gray and his eyes feverish, sunken into their sockets. This was a man on the edge of death but, despite this, Pollard sensed no fear in him.

Shaw stood next to a boulder pushed back into a depression that had concealed him. His body tilted hard to the left, leaning on the rock for support. Shaw had tied a cloth around his left arm, binding it hard against his chest; a wad of cloth cut from his shirt served as a pad to staunch the blood-flow, yet even that cloth was soaked through and fresh drops dribbled from it.

"Put the rifle down."

Pollard complied, gently setting it against a rock and moving away.

"Why don't you shoot?" Pollard asked calmly. "You know I would."

"I know," Shaw rasped. "I know you would, and so might I, except I haven't found out who paid your fee."

Pollard smiled. "And you never will. I don't divulge a client's identity." He gestured at Shaw's wound. "You've done well, but you aren't going to make it, you know. You're losing too much blood. If I stand here another fifteen minutes, you'll be bled out. Let me help you."

Shaw shook his head and even managed a weak smile. "You've already helped me to this point. I'm not about to let you help me the rest of the way."

Pollard shook his head irritably. "Don't be a fool! There is no reason for us to fight any longer. We're both paid hands and I won. Let me help you so you can go home."

Shaw blinked a few times as if to clear his eyes. He seemed to be having difficulty keeping them in focus. "Maybe, but let's talk a bit more."

Pollard shrugged and gestured at the blood trail winding around the rock and out of sight on the goat path. "Your blood goes on down that trail. You fooled me well," he said with mild admiration.

"Blood going down a trail doesn't look any different than blood coming back up it," Shaw said.

Pollard smiled ruefully. "I wouldn't have thought of it. It's a good trick."

Shaw smiled weakly. "I almost didn't think of it. You see, to best accomplish it, you must first have a large quantity of blood. I'd have preferred a different ruse."

Pollard noticed movement down the slope and turned

his head. "It looks like that Roark woman doesn't listen any better than you, my friend." His satisfaction was complete.

* * * *

Shaw shook his head, his ears buzzing with a strange fluttering sound, like a moth flitting about his head. At first, he thought Pollard was trying to trick him. But something in the way the man looked impelled Shaw to blink his eyes to focus in the distance. When he did, he was aghast. At least two miles down the grade and crossing a mountain meadow, Sarah led the horses and headed back their way.

"Damn it all!" Shaw said hoarsely.

"Looks like she heard the shooting," Pollard said, admiration plain in his voice. "Or, maybe, she changed her mind about leaving. She isn't a timid girl."

"Who paid you?" Shaw asked again, with more force.

Pollard shook his head. "She's still half an hour away, maybe longer. You'll fall on your face long before she gets here. When you do, you'll be finished. There's still time. Let me stop that bleeding, and I'll be on my way. I don't want to kill you; I never have. I've proven I can win and that's all that matters to me. I always win. Let me help you and you can ride away with her. I'll give you one more chance if you'll just leave me alone."

Shaw thought about what Pollard offered. He actually believed Pollard would do exactly as he promised. In his own way, Pollard had a weird sense of honor. If he said something, offered quarter, he meant it. Shaw swayed a bit and reached out with his injured arm to steady himself against a rock. He winced at the sudden pain it caused, but Pollard didn't move or even give an indication that he'd noticed.

Shaw tried to clear his head but the buzzing was growing louder and he was having increasing difficulty focusing his eyes on Pollard's face. He knew that he had only a few minutes— if that —of consciousness left. It didn't matter anymore. He could let the man go. Maybe he should. But there was Stuart and Samuel — and then there was Sarah.

He looked into Pollard's eyes and, gathering his strength and concentration, he managed to whisper a name to the killer — and Pollard's eyes changed ever so slightly. Shaw finally felt certain he knew, at last, the identity of the client; and, if he was wrong, it didn't really matter all that much now.

Shaw smiled a brief, sad smile and felt his knees begin to buckle. Before he fell, he touched the trigger of his Colt and sent a bullet into Pollard's left eye socket that blew most of the man's brains out the back of his head. They both hit the ground at about the same instant and then Shaw felt himself sliding away.

* * * *

Shaw came awake in the darkness. He was propped up against a rock and Sarah was bathing his wounds with hot water from a pan resting on some glowing embers. Judging by the condition of the fire, it had burned for several hours. Every muscle in his body throbbed, as well as his head. A vast field of stars brilliantly lit the night sky. At the higher elevations, away from the dust and coal-smoke of Denver, the stars seemed nearly bright enough to read by. They provided enough light to easily allow Shaw to make out Sara's features. She looked worried.

She noticed he was awake and smiled. "Don't be mad at me."

He tried to find his voice but he didn't have the strength. The only thing he managed was a weak shake of his head before drifting off again.

Days passed. Shaw spent the first day drifting in and out of consciousness, never speaking. Every time he'd wake up, he'd see Sarah beside him. He was vaguely aware that she worked over him like a mother with a sick child. When he was awake, she made him drink tea and broth. She slept beside him to keep him warm. When pain caused him to moan, she put a warm cloth on his forehead and spoke soothingly. Just the sound of her voice reassured him.

Every few hours, he felt her bathe his wounds and change the dressings made from strips of cloth from their extra clothing. When she ran out of dressings, he heard her boiling the old ones to reuse.

Eventually, Shaw summoned the strength to speak. "There are some lichens you can boil that help fight infection. Look on the shady sides of the granite and any fallen cedar that's dried in the shade. Make a poultice and stuff it in the wounds. It's supposed to help."

"I'll find some." She gathered a pouch and knife and started off.

"Take a gun." Shaw said sternly. "Just because one devil is gone doesn't mean there isn't another one around."

For the first time since Shaw had been wounded, he saw her smile. "Oh, there's another one around all right, but he's too weak to cause much trouble." Then she was gone.

Shaw napped until he heard her return. He lay quietly watching her prepare the lichen into a poultice, saving some to put in his tea. Uncovering his chest wound, she started to gingerly poke a little into the hole by his left breast.

Shaw grunted. "Sarah, you're going to cause me a lot of discomfort anyway, so quit trying to be gentle. Just poke it in and be done. It'll go much faster."

"All right, Mister Stoic. You asked for it."

The next few seconds were agonizing. Once Sarah was done packing all three wounds, Shaw sweated heavily, while she spooned tea into his mouth. The fiery pain took a long time to subside into a continual throbbing.

"Now, in the morning, I want you to leave me some food and water, and go to Geneva City to hire a couple of men with a wagon so we can get off this mountain and back to Georgetown."

She started to protest, but Shaw stopped her. "There's likely to be a couple of miners who'll jump at a chance to make a few dollars in the fresh air. If not, there are supply wagons every day. Hire one and come back for me. It'll take you the better part of a day to get there and another to return, so you need to leave at first light."

"They're strangers, I'll—"

"The stable man has a wife and kids and they can see to your needs overnight. His wife also cooks meals for some of the miners when they're flush. They could use the money, so be generous."

Sarah left in the morning and on the second day, late in the afternoon, she returned. She rode up alone. Shaw was sitting up with his pistol in his hand. "Any luck?"

She climbed down and stretched tiredly. "I hired two miners. They'll be along first light. They have a wagon and will take us to Georgetown."

Shaw nodded. Then drifted off to sleep.

The miners arrived in the morning. The wagon was back along the road, so Shaw had to sit atop a horse for the two-hour journey to the mining road. Sarah sat behind him, holding tightly to prevent him from swaying with weakness and falling off.

Shaw had insisted they bring Pollard's rifle and pack. He said he didn't want to see such a fine weapon left behind to rust and decay. As Sarah had wished, they left Pollard's body and promised they'd never return to retrieve it or to bury it or tell anyone where it lay. Though they made the promise, Shaw could tell they were uncomfortable with the request.

"I'll tell the Law in Georgetown where he lies," Shaw

269

said. "They can take it from there." This seemed to satisfy the miners.

Once they arrived at the road, the men helped Shaw climb into the wagon and they headed back down the bumpy road to Georgetown. Once there, Sarah discharged them, each with a generous payment they'd probably not retain beyond the first saloon they came to.

The town's doctor tended to Shaw for the next week. Shaw fought fever and infections that nearly killed him. The local law was summoned and listened to the story about the killing of Samuel and Shaw's subsequent killing of Pollard. The marshal told Shaw he'd check the story with the county Sheriff in Soulard and, if it was confirmed, he'd be satisfied. Pollard was a known entity, not wanted by the law but known to them. A killer had been killed, and Shaw knew the man wouldn't be missed. Shaw also knew that had it gone the other way, they would have been equally satisfied. Lawmen wouldn't mourn the loss of a man like Shaw any more than it would a man like Pollard.

When he was strong enough to travel, he and Sarah made the train trip back to Denver where Sarah put him to bed. She informed Mrs. Bell that Shaw was badly injured and would require extra care. Once she'd seen to his care, Sarah broached the subject of returning to Georgetown to hire some men to help bring Samuel down out of the mountains.

"Before you leave," Shaw said, "I wonder if you'd get word to Duggan Hammer and let him know what transpired. We don't know if Pollard had any friends who might try to avenge his death. Duggan will know what to do."

"I'll send a message from the station," Sarah promised.

The next morning, she left Shaw alone in a large and quiet house, much like he'd always been. Duggan Hammer arrived that afternoon and remained for the next week while Shaw mended and gathered his strength. Of course

Shaw knew this also allowed Duggan the added benefit of dining on Mrs. Bell's fine cooking. During that time, Shaw told Duggan the entire story and sought his advice and opinions concerning how best to proceed. Together, they formulated a plan.

On the first day of the third week following his injury, Shaw was able to make his way from his room to the kitchen without help, but it tired him badly. Though his wounds were healing, the experience of barely cheating death had left him weaker than he'd ever been. What concerned him most was the uncertainty of how long it would take to recover his health.

The next day, Sarah returned. They sat together on a sofa in the living room that afternoon, quietly talking. The last three weeks were a blur and it was only the pain of his wounds and his weakness that reminded him that what happened hadn't been a dream. He'd been incredibly lucky. Had Sarah not disregarded his instructions, he'd surely have died on that mountainside, next to Pollard.

"I've had Samuel taken to a funeral parlor in preparation for the trip home," Sarah told him. "I've made arrangements for the transport of his body by train to Soulard. I'll have to hire a man with a team to get him back to the ranch. He'll lie next to Rebecca and Stuart."

Shaw noticed that while she was obviously sad, she didn't cry or show signs of needing any comfort beyond that of his company, so he remained mostly silent, letting her talk it out. He loved the sound of her voice.

"Summer is on us now and the ranch has been neglected for so long. I don't know what to do." She smiled wanly. "Do you have any advice?"

"What do you want to do?"

"I don't know. Part of me can't imagine leaving it, but the other part of me can't imagine life there any longer. My entire family is gone."

"I'll go there with you, if you want me to," he said. He

watched her face change, her eyes soften and she smiled.

"I know. You told me that once before."

"I meant it then. I mean it now. I can't imagine being without you, wherever it is; Eagle Town, Denver, or anywhere else for that matter."

Sarah reached out and held his hand. "I can't imagine it either. Let's take some time and think about it."

"I think you should put off your trip back to Eagle Town until I'm ready to travel. The business is not finished yet. There's still the matter of Pollard's employer, and I don't believe he acted entirely alone."

"Do you know who it is?

"I have a good idea. I mentioned the name to Pollard and, while he didn't verify my suspicions, he looked momentarily surprised. I might still be wrong. Another problem I have is I don't know who, if anyone, might be in it with him or why they hatched their plan in the first place. That means the danger to you is still real."

"We don't have to go back. I can sell the ranch and be done with it. There'd be no more danger."

"True. But I've learned something about you that tells me that there's still some unfinished business that you'd want to see concluded."

Sarah nodded. "Tell me everything, and together we'll decide."

* * * *

The end of the month found them in Eagle Town. He'd helped Sarah bring Samuel back to the ranch in a wagon they'd hired in Soulard. Shaw drove. They'd retrieved their horses from the Soulard stable and the horses followed behind the wagon, eager to take to the trail after their long stint in the stable yard. Once the chore of burying Samuel was finished, Sarah told Shaw she'd made a decision. "I'm going to have a single stone made that will include all three names."

Shaw nodded. "I think that's best." He knew Sarah's name would never be on that stone. She'd buried her past in this ground and he hoped her future would be tied to his.

"In the morning, I'm going to go to Eagle Town," Shaw said. "For the time being, I want to maintain a respectful distance. So for a few days, I'd feel better if you'd remain here."

Sarah listened quietly, without comment.

"I'll come back just as soon as I can."

She nodded and went about preparing a meal that they ate together in comfortable silence.

When Shaw rode back into town, no one seemed overly interested in his return. There was a surreal feeling that he'd never left, except for the pain in his left shoulder that constantly reminded him that he had. Tucker Frey seemed genuinely glad to see him, or maybe he was just glad to see Shaw's horse, which he'd grown attached to before. Frey had a hundred questions.

"Tucker, I'm still barely recovered. Right now, I'd like to get a room in town and catch up on some badly needed sleep."

Tucker nodded and Shaw could tell he was disappointed but seemed to understand.

"You get your strength back and don't worry none about your horse. He'll be fine right here."

Shaw thanked him and walked to the hotel where he took a room and paid in advance for a week.

He looked up from dinner that night to see Ross Bentley standing at his table. At Shaw's invitation, Bentley joined him and they shared a friendly meal while Shaw related the story of the fight with Pollard. Ordinarily, Shaw wouldn't speak of such things, but he knew Bentley was a fighting man and he'd appreciate it as only a fighting man could.

After dinner, Bentley proffered a cigar.

Shaw shook his head.

"Did you find out who hired the killing of Roark?" Bentley asked.

"I have an idea, but nothing firm."

Bentley drank some coffee. "Will it mean that you and I may have business later?"

Shaw wasn't sure how much he should tell this man. He liked him, but he knew he was the sort who worked for the brand. The general consensus was that Pollard had made a mistake when Stuart was killed. Shaw hadn't said anything to anyone other than Sarah and Hammer that would alter that belief in the townspeople's minds. Folks were satisfied with that and Shaw saw no reason to tip his hand. While he liked Bentley, he wasn't sure he could trust him just yet.

"I hope not," Shaw said. "To tell you the truth, I'm not completely sure yet. But between you and me, when I know for sure, I'll pass it on to you as a professional courtesy."

Bentley nodded. "That's good enough for me." He stood and shook Shaw's hand. "You did well, even if it cost you so much. I truly hope we don't have to fight each other."

"Those are my feelings exactly," Shaw agreed.

The next afternoon, Shaw paid a visit to Marshal Blake's office. Blake didn't appear either surprised or happy to see Shaw. It was plain the marshal was disappointed that the trouble Shaw represented hadn't yet gone away. He motioned for Shaw to take a seat and poured him a cup of coffee.

"Is it over?" Blake asked.

"What you really want to know is whether or not I found out who paid Pollard? Or maybe, you want to know if I ever told Samuel and Sarah about your involvement in finding a shooter for Hardy?" Shaw paused to let the marshal stew over his questions. Then added, "The answer is 'no' to both questions."

Blake nodded. "Don't forget Mason. He's a hard man. I

don't want him knowing I told you about Pollard either. If he didn't kill me outright, I'd still be finished in this community."

"Mason won't know, I promise you. I made a deal and I'll keep it," Shaw assured him. "Whether or not it's over depends on a few more things I have to find out."

"Like what?

"Well, Pollard never told me who hired him so, from everything we know, Mason still seems like the most likely suspect. Do you think there's enough evidence to arrest him?"

Blake shook his head. "It would be hard. Just because half the valley believes it doesn't mean a judge would order him held for trial or that a jury would convict him. Do you have anything else you can give me that I can take to Soulard?"

Shaw shook his head. "No. Not yet. But I have an idea where to look."

"Can I help?"

"Better you stay out of it for the time being. I may need your help later."

Blake nodded. "All right. But try and keep the law in mind. I don't want to have to arrest you."

Shaw smiled. "Marshal Blake, I will never give you a reason to arrest me. When I know for sure, you'll know for sure." He stood and headed for the door.

Blake stopped him with a last comment: "You look like you had a rough time."

Shaw nodded. "It was rough, but the hard part's over." He turned and left the office.

* * * *

Shaw let a couple days go by, both to regain lost strength and to give whomever the guilty party or parties were time to consider his return and what it might mean.

Perhaps they'd act on it and tip their hand. Since no one took a shot at him, he decided to retrieve his horse for a ride back to the ranch.

Tucker Frey greeted him warmly.

"You're looking better."

"I'm feeling better."

"Are you leaving again?" Tucker asked.

"For a few days. I have something I want to look over," Shaw said, and then he lowered his voice a bit. "There's something I want to check out; something I came across a while back that's always bothered me."

"Can you tell me what it is?"

Shaw shook his head. "Not yet, but soon."

Tucker looked disappointed, but smiled. "Oh, hell, Matt, after you left there wasn't much to talk about in town. Now that you're back, there's all sorts of gossip. People expect we're friends and I'm kind of a celebrity." He shook his head. "It's been a while since anyone paid any attention to this old stable hand. I was sort of hoping you'd tell me something everyone else didn't already think they knew."

Shaw understood and smiled. "We are friends, Tucker. How about this," Shaw offered with a conspiratorial wink. "What if what everybody else thought they knew was right had always been wrong?"

Tucker's eyes widened in complete surprise. A sudden, sly smile crossed his lips. "I knew it! You've solved it, by golly you have!" Then he frowned. "But you aren't going to tell me who, are you?"

"Not yet. I don't want to put you in danger. There are people who'd kill for that information. Keep it to yourself for now." Then, as an afterthought, Shaw asked: "After I left town last, did anyone else of note disappear for a few days?"

Tucker thought a moment, and then his eyes brightened. "Why, yes," he said. "Blake said he had business in Soulard. He was gone for several days."

276

"Who'd he leave in charge?"

"His brother Tom, same as always. It's not unusual for Blake to have to attend to some business here and there. He comes and goes from time to time. Tom's a miner and sometimes deputy."

Shaw pondered that and nodded. "Thanks, Tucker." He took the reins of his horse and turned it toward the door but thought of something and stopped. "Tucker, I found something down the mountain from the Roark place. It's where the killer held up while he waited for his chance at Roark. You keep this to yourself, but I'm going to go back down there and check it out in the morning, give it a good looking over. I wanted someone to know, in case it goes bad for me and I don't come back. If that happens, you get the information to Blake for me, will you?"

Tucker Frey nodded soberly. Shaw could tell Tucker was truly disappointed he hadn't shared more information with him. Shaw felt a little guilty using the man like that, but he also knew before long the news would get to the people he intended it to reach.

He rode out of town in the direction of Sarah's ranch.

* * * *

In the morning, Shaw sat on a stool in front of the miner's shack in the quiet valley, letting the early sun warm him while he watched the meadow dance with typical high-country life. Later in the day, hummingbirds would buzz around the wild flowers growing along the base of the hill behind the cabin but, for now, the valley was alive with dragonflies darting about the meadow and making occasional trips down to the stream below it to skim a drink. Shaw was enjoying the morning, his senses made more acute because of the events he'd set in motion, and the final confrontation he expected to take place before long.

The sound of three horses coming up the ravine from the direction of Eagle Town confirmed his plan had worked. When they rounded the corner and passed between two tall pines, Shaw saw who they were and he experienced a brief moment of satisfaction, but one also tinged with a strong sense of sadness.

Again, he was facing long odds and there were no guarantees that, once a fight started, the outcome would be in his favor. He had no doubt before this morning ended there'd be death and bloodshed.

Shaw waited for the riders to fan out, facing him where he sat. "I found your mine, Tucker," he said with a slight smile.

Tucker Frey nodded. "I figured as much. I knew the moment I mentioned it to you, I may have made a mistake. But, you're an easy man to talk to. When you started talking about the Kent spread and his mine, I figured I was safe. I just didn't see how you could put it all together."

Tucker Frey was in the center. On his left was the owner of the Royale, McGinnes. On his right, a miner Shaw hadn't seen before. All sat easy on their horses, trusting that the advantage they held would keep Shaw in line. No one had drawn a gun. Shaw decided to tease them with a little bit of information.

"Pollard let too much slip as well. Something he said made me finally realize the Roark boy had been the target all along. This just didn't make any sense if Pollard had been working for Mason. It had to be somebody else who needed Stuart Roark dead, but who and why? Passion, greed or revenge; it's always one of those three. In this case, the only thing that made sense was greed."

McGinnes chuckled. "There's a lot of greed in Eagle Town." Shaw noted the Irish brogue had disappeared.

Shaw looked at him easily. McGinnes suddenly seemed discomfited by Shaw's gaze. Being a good man with a gun himself, McGinnes probably hadn't been worried about

Shaw's reputation. But now, when faced with the man and knowing everything that had happened to him in the last month and still he'd survived, spoke volumes about his abilities.

"Yes, McGinnes," Shaw agreed evenly. "Greed is everywhere." Then he added, "Even I'm sometimes guilty of a little greed." He let that hang in the air.

Frey cocked his head at that. "Are you suggesting something — maybe you could be bought off?"

When Frey asked that, McGinnes looked at the hostler in surprise.

Shaw nodded. "There's been a lot of fighting and a lot of killing. I nearly met my match with Pollard. As you can see, I'm still not fully recovered. Maybe it's time I considered getting out of this line of work. Maybe settle down somewhere and watch mares drop their springtime foals."

"That's tempting," Frey said. "More killing would just bring more questions, and we'd have to satisfy that Roark woman, or deal with her."

"She's satisfied, Tucker," Shaw said. "As far as she's concerned, Pollard was the end of it." Shaw dug his boot heel in the dirt and got up. Taking off his hat, he set it on the stool behind him. The cool mountain air felt good on his brow. "Of course, we all know you'll have to clear it with Blake first," Shaw said.

Frey's eyes widened in surprise but he gave nothing else away. "I don't know what you're talking about," he denied. "Blake's not part of this."

"Oh, I'm afraid he is," Shaw said. "He arrived an hour before first light. I know because I was watching from that little cluster of rocks yonder. I saw him settle down with his rifle behind that stand of aspen. Then, I snuck back into the cabin to wait the dawn." Shaw wiped his forehead. Still a little weak, any exertion brought a light sheen of sweat to his face.

"I suppose had I been sitting in the open, he'd have shot me before y'all rode up but as you know, I'm a careful man. Call out and have him come on down and join the party," Shaw suggested. "Then you can ask him if he likes the idea."

Shaw could almost see the wheels turning in Tucker's head. He knew the man was considering the angles, wondering if Shaw might be bluffing. Finally, without turning his head, he let out a loud whistle. "Blake." Frey called. "Shaw knows you're there. Might as well come on down. Don't shoot him." Then he smiled. "Yet."

A moment later, Blake stood up, a rifle in his hands. Gathering his coat and hat, he started down the slope to the cabin. When he arrived, he was slightly out of breath.

"You're a difficult man, Shaw; a regular pain in the ass!" Blake observed when he walked up to the group. "And, you're way too calm. What's your ace in the hole?"

Tucker suddenly realized Blake was right, and he sat up straighter and looked at Shaw expectantly.

Shaw nodded. "Say there's this letter in the hands of a friend in Denver. Maybe this letter outlines everything I've learned and say it also includes information given to me from Pollard before he died." He let all of this sink in, their eyes darting, and then he continued, "Say this friend will take this letter to the magistrate in Denver if he doesn't hear from me in a couple days. Maybe that's my ace in the hole." Then, as an afterthought, he added, "Or, maybe I just expect we can come to an understanding, Blake. I've already made it clear to Frey and McGinnes that I'm ready to find a healthier climate to heal up and grow old in with a woman who is recently widowed." Shaw smiled. "I don't ask for much, except a stake and a promise that I'll be left alone to spend my money in peace."

Shaw watched as Blake thought this over, scratching the stubble on his chin for a few seconds. "And the letter?"

"After I'm gone, it shows up in your post and you can

do whatever you want with it. My friend has no idea what information it contains."

Blake chewed his lip. Shaw knew the lawman had a lot to consider. It was obvious that he wasn't happy with the way events were unfolding.

"In my office, you said Pollard didn't talk," Blake said.

"I lied. I apologize for the deception, but I needed you all together. Truth is, I suspected you and Tucker, but I didn't know about McGinnes and that other fellow over there." Shaw paused and smiled. "Do you think I have the time to write another letter?"

Blake and McGinnes exchanged glances, but Tucker Frey chuckled. "Well then, let me introduce that other fellow." Frey inclined his head toward the miner. "Meet Blake's brother, Tom."

Shaw nodded at the man. "Howdy, Tom."

Tom didn't reply.

"I admit it took me a while to figure it all out before my fight with Pollard, but a lot of things that I kept finding or hearing just didn't add up," Shaw said. "Take this cabin, for instance. When I got here, it was in too good a shape to have been an old abandoned miner's cabin. When I discovered the killer had spent much of the winter holed up here, I figured it must have been in good shape prior to his arrival. Either someone prepared it for him, or someone was using it periodically and keeping it up. But why? Then I thought back to what Tucker there had said about losing a mining claim."

Tucker shifted and looked a little embarrassed as the other men glanced at him. Shaw noticed his discomfort and grinned. "And then, when I was having a nice conversation with Pollard, he mentioned something about having watched Sarah through his telescope after he'd made the shot that killed Stuart Roark. Then I'd remembered Samuel mentioning that at the moment Stuart was killed, Samuel had been standing by a lit window. Pollard would've had to see him standing there. So it was obvious the target was the boy all along. I was just slow picking up on it."

Nobody spoke, so Shaw went on. "Then it all started to fall into place. Stuart rode the ranch, tending the stock and hunting; no doubt, he either found the cabin or had come close to finding the mine. Maybe he mentioned it to someone, or somebody observed him and it was generally decided he had to go and quickly. Killing Roark wouldn't be enough. Sarah would still own the ranch and she'd have Stuart to help her. Killing Stuart made more sense. It would keep him quiet and would probably send Roark around the bend or make him angry enough to fight."

The men shifted uneasily in their saddles, but nobody reached for a weapon. Yet. Blake's knuckles whitened on his rifle.

Shaw watched them carefully. "Roark already had trouble with Mason and this was well known in the valley. If Roark went looking to settle with Mason, Mason's men would finish him and Sarah would be forced to sell the ranch." Shaw shook his head and smiled ruefully at the simplicity of the plan.

No one spoke to confirm what he'd outlined.

"You fellers don't say much do you?" Shaw commented.

"You're doing the talking, Shaw," Blake said.

Shaw nodded. "Blake, I have to tell you I was some fooled. I do have to admit that for a while I thought your lack of effort investigating the murder was a matter of incompetence or professional laziness. But there was still that matter of you knowing Ballou, or rather Pollard as it turned out. Then you gave me the names of Hardy and Keyes and when I shared that information with Samuel, they turned up dead. I was positive Samuel had killed them out of revenge for their part in Stuart's killing. I even told Sarah of my suspicions.

"But as things progressed, that didn't add up either after

I'd had a chance to think about it and after Pollard offhandedly mentioned he hadn't heard from Keyes in quite some time. He also said that he didn't know Hardy, except to say he'd heard Hardy had been killed." Shaw smiled. "That made it clear that he didn't yet know Keyes was dead and that someone in Eagle Town was in direct contact with him."

"Why?" Blake asked.

"Think about it," Shaw said. "Hell, these kinds of things aren't safe to be sent via telegraph. Whoever was talking to Pollard was doing so face to face and arrived in Georgetown before my party even got there. Whoever that person was probably hopped a train to Dodge City before the Roarks and I even left Eagle Town. Then, he had to hang around until we'd spoken with Keyes so he could kill the lawyer and grab one of the trains for Denver. From there, it would be a simple thing to go on to Georgetown and warn Pollard we were coming. Since you weren't on the train with us to Denver, you had to wait a day and grab the next one. Either way, that's a busy schedule."

Blake looked amused. "But why would it have had to be me?"

"You knew Pollard and you knew who Keyes was. Heck, Pollard came to see you personally. That always bothered me, though you did a pretty good job of convincing me it was incidental based on your history with the man. Once you offered that Hardy was Mason's lawyer and the man looking for a long-shooter, you planted a pretty good seed of suspicion in Mason's direction."

Blake looked smug at that observation.

"Then there was the fact that you seemed comfortable with a sticker in your hands, at least you were the first day I walked into your office. After a while, it just seemed to fit," Shaw said. "It was a little tough on Hardy, though, don't you think, since his involvement was a complete fabrication?"

Blake didn't respond to that last comment. "If what you're saying is true, why wouldn't I have killed Keyes before Roark could talk to him?"

"I don't recall telling you that it was Roark who talked to Keyes," Shaw said with a smile, and Blake's face blanched when Shaw pointed out his error. Shaw went on as if he hadn't seen Blake's discomfort. "You couldn't kill Keyes in advance. You were smart enough to know that after Hardy turned up dead before I could talk to him, I'd be mighty suspicious of you if the same thing happened to Keyes before I could talk to *him*, seeing that it was you who provided both names. Besides," Shaw added, "you had to tell Keyes what to say when he was questioned, so we'd hop the next train to Denver and make our way to Georgetown."

"That still doesn't explain why I would've killed him," Blake said.

"Keyes had probably outlived his usefulness. And his death could always be laid at the feet of Roark, as could Hardy's. Since Pollard intended to kill Roark, it would all be tied up in a neat bow. No one outside the Roarks and me knew Pollard's name. Pollard would make sure no one ever would."

"It's a lot of guesswork wrapped around a couple inconsequential facts," Blake said. "You haven't established how you determined I was the one in contact with Pollard."

Shaw flashed another sly smile. "Hell, Blake, Tucker told me you left town after I headed back to the ranch. You had plenty of time to get to Dodge City before we did."

Blake looked at Frey, irritation evident in his expression, but he didn't speak.

Shaw smiled at the suspicion he saw building in Blake's eyes. "Don't blame Tucker, Blake. He was just hedging his bets. In truth, Pollard is the one who convinced me about you."

"How so?" Blake asked with a tight expression.

"Well, before I killed him, I happened to mention your name and his reaction all but told me I was right." Shaw smiled, slyly.

"Enough of this!" McGinnes said irritably. "You seem to have figured it out for the most part, I'll grant you that."

"Not everything," Shaw said. "I still don't know where you fit in."

McGinnes smiled. "I'm a mining engineer," he said proudly. "Frey and Blake have a mine that's potentially rich enough to need a mining engineer. Now does it make sense?"

"Aye, that it does, lad," Shaw replied in a mock Irish brogue.

McGinnes' eyes narrowed, but he continued: "Now, explain to me how all of this just goes away. There's been a bit of killing connected to this whole affair that the authorities would want to have answers to."

Shaw nodded. "We tell the truth, the whole truth and nothing but the truth. Well, maybe not the *whole* truth, but enough to weave a pretty good story. For instance, Stuart gets killed by an unidentified marksman in an apparently botched assassination attempt on Samuel Roark. When Roark goes hunting Stuart's killer, Hardy, Keyes and Ballou — also known as Pollard — are identified. Roark kills Hardy and Keyes and then Pollard kills Roark. Eventually, I kill Pollard after nearly losing my own life. Everyone is happy — except the dead men — including half the undertakers west of the Mississippi, I might add."

"There's still the question of who hired Pollard," Blake said. "The authorities wouldn't be satisfied without that."

"That's true," Shaw said, "but there's no more hard evidence now than there was before. It makes sense. Everyone thought it was Mason before this, and they still can think that. You said yourself that there wasn't enough evidence to convict him. So what? Let the world go on

285

thinking Mason was the one, no matter how much he denies it. The law can't touch him and I doubt he'll mind all that much having that mystery associated with his name. People will eventually forget, or simply quit caring."

"But there's the little matter of my secret gold strike," Frey said. "I need title to this ranch."

"Sarah will sell it. She's already talked about it. There are too many bad memories. She won't even ask top dollar."

Frey frowned. "You can guarantee that?"

"I can guarantee that," Shaw said.

"I don't like it," Blake groused. "I don't like knowing that Shaw can hold this over our heads the rest of our lives."

"How do you suggest we handle that, Blake?" McGinnes asked.

Blake looked at Shaw and shrugged. "He can only hold it over our heads the rest of *his* life."

Shaw watched as Blake's words seemed to sink in to the others. It was obvious they were prepared for a fight; had been from the minute they'd arrived. Shaw knew that buying him off offered an acceptable alternative to killing him, but killing him was certainly the safest bet.

Blake dropped the muzzle of his rifle and centered it on Shaw's chest. He put his thumb on the hammer of the rifle but, before he could cock it, Frey spoke out. "What about the letter, Blake?"

Blake glanced at Frey irritably. "If we put our heads together just a bit, don't you think we could come up with a way of having Shaw tell us who has the letter?"

Ross Bentley stepped out of the cabin with a gun already drawn on Blake. "Lower the rifle carefully, Blake," he commanded.

Shock was plain on the faces of the four conspirators. After a moment, Blake spoke up. "What's your concern here, Ross?"

"I'm just looking after my employer's interests," Bentley said. "And his reputation."

Blake looked sick; he lowered the barrel of his rifle, but didn't drop the weapon.

Shaw read the thoughts on Blake's face as clearly as if reading his mind. "Bentley, you don't have to worry about Blake," he said. "He's out of it."

Bentley cocked his head. "It doesn't look to me like he's out of it."

"He's out of it." Shaw said. Then he looked Blake in the eyes and with a genuine smile, continued, "Blake. There's just one more thing I need to tell you." He paused for several seconds before pointing the forefinger of his left hand at the center of Blake's chest. "I lied about the letter."

Blake was punched hard in the center of his chest as a heavy rifle boomed from the hillside behind the cabin. Blake took a hard step back, his rifle falling from his grasp. Shaw had seen the heavy bullet strike the marshal centered exactly in the breastbone where he'd been pointing. Shaw didn't bother waiting to see him fall, as the man was dead on his feet. Instead, he immediately turned toward Frey and drew his Colt.

Frey's horse jumped a bit at the shot and Frey was trying to drag his pistol out of his holster while maintaining his grip on the saddle horn. Shaw hammered a quick shot into his belly and then another that struck him a little higher in the middle of his chest. Frey lost his grip on his pistol and the pitching horse thrust him from the saddle like a limp sack of grain. Frey's boot hung up momentarily in the stirrup and the horse pitched about, tumbling the old man's body under the hoofs for a few seconds. When his leg finally slipped free, Frey lay unmoving.

Ignoring Frey, Shaw turned to the next man in line, McGinnes. The Irishman didn't stand a chance. In his panic to draw his weapon, his revolver's barrel hung up on the holster lip and he'd accidentally triggered a shot that glanced off his knee cap and burned the right flank of his horse. The animal reared wildly and Shaw stepped left while both he and Bentley fired into McGinnes from different sides at precisely the same instant. The stiffening of the Irishman's legs in the stirrups pushed him from his saddle and he fell hard on his back.

Bentley turned to face the last man, while Shaw stepped around the pitching horse and noticed McGinnes had finally managed to pull his gun from its holster. Another gun cracked from the direction of Tom the miner and a bullet whipped by Shaw's head but he ignored it, calmly firing his three remaining shots into McGinnes' body from only six feet away. The shots seemed to anchor him to the ground as if a huge stone had been placed on his chest. His arms flailed at his sides as he convulsed in the final act of dying.

Shaw heard Bentley's pistol bark three times in rapid succession and he didn't even look in that direction. He knew that Tom gamely tried to get into the fight and he also knew that Bentley was the better man. Shaw realized suddenly that Tom never uttered a word the whole time that morning and now he'd been silenced forever.

When the shooting was over, there were four men lying in meadow grass outside the miner's cabin. The horses had run off, two of them some distance away into the meadow where they stopped to look back. When their riders didn't come for them, they started grazing contentedly. The third horse, the one McGinnes' bullet burned, had galloped off down the trail with its empty stirrups flailing. It was probably still running for town.

Bentley opened his Schofield revolver and reloaded while surveying his handiwork.

Shaw trembled slightly. His head hurt and ears rang from the pounding gunfire. He was still weak from his injuries and the release of the emotions of the fight left him drained and near physical collapse.

"Better sit down," Bentley advised. "You're still weak."

Shaw nodded, but he remained standing. Soon, he started punching cartridge cases from his empty Colt in preparation for reloading.

"I am still weak," Shaw admitted. "I lost a lot of blood on a mountain a few weeks ago. It takes a long while to get it back."

"It does at that," Bentley agreed. "But you're a mite better off than these men."

Shaw looked at the dead men momentarily and turned his eyes to the gunman. "Thank you for agreeing to come," he said. "I didn't know how many I'd have to deal with. I was sure about Frey and Blake, but McGinnes and the miner were a surprise."

"Happy to help," Bentley said. "I admired a chance to side with you. It sure beat having to fight you. You don't seem to want to die easy." He looked at the dead men and shook his head. "The town's going to go crazy. I'll send a man to Soulard to alert the sheriff. With my witness statement, you shouldn't have any trouble."

Shaw nodded. "About Blake ..." Shaw hesitated a moment, then said, "I'd like it to go down that I killed him."

Bentley gazed at the hillside where the shot originated. Then he looked back at Shaw. "Sure," he said. "I saw you. You centered him with your first shot when he dropped the muzzle of his rifle on you. He should've had the hammer cocked, but he was a fool as well as a bad lawman." Bentley paused, and then smiled. "How're you going to explain a seven-shot Colt?"

Shaw shrugged. "I have a spare gun in my saddlebags. Besides, maybe no one will ever count the holes... Anyway, thanks Ross."

Bentley walked to the gully that ringed the meadow to the north, where he and Shaw had hidden their horses the night before. Bentley tightened the cinch straps on both mounts and led them back to the cabin, leaving Shaw's horse loosely tied to the rail of the shelter behind the cabin. Then he went to a ravine where Blake had tied his horse in the early hours before dawn. Gathering up that animal, he returned to the cabin. When he'd mounted, he looked back up the hill, then to Shaw.

"Tell whoever was up in those rocks that he made a mighty fine shot."

"I will," Shaw said.

Bentley nodded and turned his horse toward Eagle Town with Blake's horse in tow.

* * * *

Shaw stayed in the meadow for another hour, resting and letting his strength come back a bit. He tried not to look at the dead men or pay attention to the flies that had already found the blood. Once he felt strong enough, he mounted his horse and took the long way around to get back to the ranch. Had he been healthy, he'd have made the hike into and out of the valley on foot like he had the first time. As it was, he was almost done in before making it back to the cabin.

Sarah sat in the rocking chair on the porch where Shaw had been sitting the first time he'd seen her. Even though it had only been about two months, it seemed a lifetime had passed since he'd fallen in love with her. Pollard's rifle was propped against the wall. Shaw saw that it was freshly capped. She'd reloaded it after killing Blake. He smiled sadly, tiredly.

"You shouldn't cap it until you're ready to fire again," he said.

Sarah looked at the rifle briefly and then back at Shaw. "Is it over?"

He sat down on the porch and gazed across the ranch-yard, letting the air cool the sweat that had dampened his shirt. In his weakened state, even the slightest exertion caused him to perspire heavily. The summer breeze felt good. While he sat there, he gauged the amount of work necessary to get the ranch back into shape and operating. He glanced up the hill to the tree and the three graves laying in the shade of the tall pine.

"The hurting part is over, Sarah," Shaw said softly. "The healing part will take a bit longer."

She nodded and let her head rest against the back of the rocking chair. She closed her eyes for several minutes. "I wonder if I should stay." Her voice was wistful, almost a whisper. Shaw didn't answer immediately. Sarah opened her eyes to find him looking across the clearing toward the mountain pass he'd used to enter this little valley.

"There's time to decide that. With the mine, there are a lot of options for you to consider," he said. "Then of course, there's the question of us."

Sarah smiled. "No, Matt. There is no question about us, as far as I'm concerned. It's *only* us." She got out of her chair and came to sit beside him on the porch. She put her head on his shoulder and he took her hand, and they sat there for a long time together in comfortable silence.

"Will you miss it?" she asked softly.

"Miss what?

"The traveling, the adventure; whatever it was that kept you constantly on the move, kept you from finding someone and settling down?"

Shaw smiled a bit sadly at the thought of all the years he'd spent alone. "*You* kept me from settling down, Sarah. In my mind, you were always there. I had to keep looking until I found you."

Sarah smiled and shifted a little closer. A single tear fell down her cheek.

They sat like that together, without moving or speaking.

Then, after a while, when the time seemed right and the creeping shadows and gathering high-country chill offered a hint of the coming evening, Shaw stood up and took Sarah's hand and helped her to her feet.

He led her into the cabin and quietly shut the door.

About the author

Dan Chamberlain has been a police officer, a Chief of Police and a special Agent for the Air Force Office of Special Investigations. After retiring from the Air Force, Dan served as Director of Security for an international corporation and has also been a successful "feature" contributor to national circulation firearms magazines. Combining his love of the old west with his investigative skills, he's crafted a "murder" mystery that will satisfy the lovers of both the traditional western and the detective novel. Dan currently lives in Southern Illinois with his family where he's embarked on another career as a registered oncology nurse.

Acknowledgements

Many authors would like to have the reader believe that the final product being enjoyed is theirs alone. Nothing could be further from the truth. Perhaps there are writers who can craft a story from start to finish without making mistakes, but I doubt they are much fun to converse with at gatherings, even if their prose leaves one breathless.

A good editor improves a story and a good writer learns to become a better writer by accepting the editor's efforts on his or her behalf. It was my good fortune to have Duke Pennell assigned to edit my book. Certainly this story is much more effectively told now than before, but more importantly for me, the things I've learned through his mentoring me on this first effort, will serve me throughout my writing career, however long that may be.

Many thanks must also go out to Nik Morton for taking a

chance on a new author and working diligently to give the project every chance for success. The story is written, but much hard work remains to be done before one can declare success.

And finally, one must acknowledge the reader who keeps this genre alive. The "Western" is not the most popular genre to pursue as a writer. The readership is smaller and many publishing houses have decided to ignore them in favor of genres that are more commercial. Still, a dedicated readership deserves a dedicated cadre of writers who will craft new stories with new ideas and new characters, rather than rehash the tired old western clichés the detractors would have the reader believe is all that's left to them. So, thank you to all the readers who still look for a good "western" when the mood strikes. There are enough of you out there to make people like me keep typing away.

1359036R00159

Made in the USA
San Bernardino, CA
12 December 2012